650

Ola may

COMPASS OF THE HEART

A novel of discovery

PRISCILLA COGAN

Simon & Schuster

Simon & Schuster
Rockefeller Center
1230 Avenue of the Americas
New York, NY 10020

SIMON & SCHUSTER and colophon are registered trademarks
of Simon & Schuster Inc.

Designed by Karolina Harris

Manufactured in the United States of America

1 3 5 7 9 10 8 6 4 2

Library of Congress Cataloging-in-Publication Data
Cogan, Priscilla.
Compass of the heart : a novel of discovery /Priscilla Cogan.
p.   cm.
Includes bibliographical references.
1. Indians of North America—Fiction. I. Title.
PS3553.O4152C66   1998
813'.54—dc21   98-2411
CIP

ISBN 0-684-84764-7

"At a Concert of Music," from Collected Poems, second edition, by Conrad Aiken.
Copyright © 1953, 1970 by Conrad Aiken. Used by permission of Oxford University
Press, Inc.

"Coyote," from Coyote, by Bill Harley. Copyright © 1987 Round River Records. Used
by permission of Marian Reiner.

"Let's Do It" by Cole Porter. Copyright © 1928 (Renewed) Warner Bros. Inc. All rights
reserved. Used by permission. Warner Bros. Publications U.S. Inc., Miami, FL. 33014.

(continued on page 352)

ACKNOWLEDGMENTS

For the incredible generosity of their love, I want to thank:
  Duncan Sings-Alone—soul mate,
  Polly Parson—sister and survivor,
  Frances Cogan—mother and role model.

For their support in the writing life:
  Katie Rock, Lesley Shore, Helen Chen.

For their teachings and love of the Pipe:
  George Whitewolf and Larry Redshirt.

For her fine editorial insights:
  Laurie Chittenden.

For their love of dreams:
  Jacob Goering and Long Man.

For her visionary experiences:
  Laura McKelvey.

For their help in keeping me solvent:
  Barbara Henins, Michael Schwartz.

For their promotion of story and music:
  Jennifer Barker, The Magpies, The National Storytelling Association,
  FAB.

For sharing the last days of his life:
  Wilbur Holcomb.

And last, but not least, the circle of friends, family, and booksellers who
have spread the word about this book.

For my husband,
my best friend
C. W. Duncan
(Sings-Alone)
whose polymorphic character
is a living testament
to an Author
of incredible imagination,
heartfelt compassion,
and an outrageous sense of humor

PROLOGUE

THE STORY OF COYOTE'S QUARREL

WITH MOLE WOMAN

No one wanted Coyote's family next to his tipi in the winter encampment. Not only did Coyote make eyes at the women, but the trickster figure was lazy and full of himself. Poor Mole Woman, his wife, had to scratch for moss, grubs, herbs, and rose hips to feed the children, while Coyote dreamt his heroic dreams and sang his spirit-calling songs.

One day, the deer nation took pity and left a spotted fawn in her path. Grabbing onto the fawn, she yelled out to her oldest child to run and fetch his father. Coyote could kill the fawn and the family could feast on venison. "Tell him to hurry, because the fawn is strong, and I cannot hold it forever."

The boy sprinted to his father's lodge, where Coyote was snacking on Mole Woman's pitiful horde of food. Breathless, he reported to his father about the captured fawn.

"Tell your mother I will come quickly, just as soon as I ready my bow and arrows." But Coyote was ill-prepared to hunt, so caught up had he been in his songs and his dreams. First, he had to enter the woods and cut a sapling for a bow and two small berry branches for arrows. Borrowing rawhide lace from his moccasins, he fashioned himself a bowstring. Plucking plumage from his war bonnet, he feathered the arrows. All this took considerable time. Poor Mole Woman was weakening as the fawn struggled to free itself.

Coyote finally appeared, just as Mole Woman could hold on no longer. The fawn leapt out of her arms and into the air. Coyote shot his first arrow. It skidded under the fawn into the snow. The fawn stumbled. Coyote strung his second and last arrow and took aim. The arrow soared over the young animal. The fawn skedaddled into the woods.

At that moment it became all too clear to Mole Woman that Coyote had forgotten how to hunt. Storming back to the lodge, she discovered that Coyote had been raiding her meager supply of food for the children. Enough was enough. She could tolerate this abuse no longer. When he returned to the lodge, Coyote heard in detail what his woman truly thought of him. Wounded by words, he lashed back, jabbing her with his flint knife. She stumbled out of the lodge, dabbing herself red from a waist-pouch of dried sumac seed. He pursued her to where she lay crouched on the ground, immobilized. Thrusting again with his weapon, he stabbed at her. She shifted ever so slightly. The knife plunged into the earth, ripping her clothes. He returned to his lodge, satisfied he had killed her, so covered was she in the crimson color of blood.

Perhaps the first night alone with the children, he felt delivered from the nagging pressure of the relationship with Mole Woman. But, by the second night, Coyote grew hungry and pitiful, missing his woman. His children needed a mother to care for them. He dispatched the four oldest to their Uncle Kingfisher for rearing but kept his youngest and favorite child, a small baby.

Together, Coyote and his infant son wandered several months, hungry and in search of a home. Finally, out on a large prairie, they stumbled across a woman in red-painted buckskin who was digging up bitter root. The sight of her activity reminded the sorrowing Coyote of his faithful wife, Mole Woman. Leaving his young son snugly bound in a cradle-board hanging off a tree limb, Coyote approached the unfamiliar woman.

"Good woman, I am a stranger in these parts. Tell me the news."

She kept to her task of digging up the roots, her face hidden from his view. She did not acknowledge his presence.

Coming closer, Coyote spoke more forcefully, "Good woman, tell me a story. I have been traveling a long time."

Her back still turned to him, she growled, "Oh, I have such a wicked story to tell. Coyote abandoned his children and murdered his wife." She looked up at him and, instantaneously, he recognized her. It was Mole Woman. Concerned about the welfare of her son, she had been following them.

In the old days, it is said that Coyote impetuously grabbed his knife and attacked Mole Woman, meaning to kill her once again. Transforming herself into a real mole, she burrowed down into the dark sanctuary of Grandmother Earth.

But, in this new age, I like to think that Coyote, upon recognizing the journey of his own grief, reached out to Mole Woman for reconciliation. That Mole Woman, upon confessing the sting of her angry words, opened her heart to hope. And that neither of them forgot that love, in its infancy, needs to be cherished, protected, and cradled in the tender arms of the living tree.

. . . because no good thing can be done by any man alone, I will first make an offering and send a voice to the Spirit of the World, that it may help me to be true. See, I fill this sacred pipe with the bark of the red willow; but before we smoke it, you must see how it is made and what it means. These four ribbons hanging here on the stem are the four quarters of the universe. The black one is for the west, where the thunder beings live to send us rain; the white one for the north, whence comes the great white cleansing wind; the red one for the east, whence springs the light and where the morning star lives to give men wisdom; the yellow for the south, whence come the summer and the power to grow.

But these four spirits are only one Spirit after all, and this eagle feather here is for that One, which is like a father, and also it is for the thoughts of men that should rise high as eagles do. Is not the sky a father and the earth a mother, and are not all living things with feet or wings or roots their children? And this hide upon the mouthpiece here . . . is for the earth, from whence we came and at whose breast we suck as babies all our lives, along with all the animals and birds and trees and grasses. And because it means all this, and more than any man can understand, the pipe is holy.

—BLACK ELK

Black Elk Speaks

1

WAKAN TANKA

mystery

O N E

Coyote's Tracks

"Ah, do not mourn," he said,
"That we are tired, for other loves await us"

—William Butler Yeats
Ephemera

"Love is very tricky," cautioned the old Lakota medicine woman, "and Coyote's tracks are all over the territory." She rolled a couple of sage leaves under her tongue while staring out the window at the threatening sky. Over the past few months, she had come to respect the sudden, awesome power of Lake Michigan storms that swept over the Leelanau Peninsula, unfettered by the drag of land.

Hawk watched and listened attentively. Forty-one years he had known Winona, his mother's cousin. She was not one to waste words. As his teacher, she understood more about his love-tattered life than anyone. He pulled out a cigarette; it was going to be a long winter's afternoon.

"People blow a lot of smoke to cover up ignorance," she observed.

He lit the cigarette, slowly drew in blue tendrils of smoke, and exhaled deeply. She was right, of course.

Squat and of lumpy proportion, Winona eased back into the armchair, her moccasins barely brushing the floor. A brown flannel shirt of uncertain vintage with frayed cuffs topped a nondescript housedress. Although her wrinkled face attested to years of sun and hard work, her body was still strong and healthy, her eyes black and keen. Like shuttling spiders, her fingers worried over a ragged spot on the flannel shirt where the button had vanished and only a broken web of thread remained.

Shifting her gaze back to him, Winona added, "Men are blind when it comes to love. They look to the sky for high and mighty visions for themselves and the people. They forget what is important. Visions don't mean shit without grounding. If it weren't for Mole Woman, Coyote would never find his way home."

Hawk nodded, thinking back on the first of his two marriages. Young, wildly in love with his new wife, he had been unable to tolerate the truth of her restless eyes. Only six months into their marriage, another man claimed her heart, spiriting her away in a beat-up Chevy. He swore at that time never to trust a woman again.

But he soon learned never to say "never."

"Love is very tricky," Winona reiterated, "and we two-leggeds need all the help we can get. It seems to me that when a wind blows in one direction, it sucks the energy from the opposite direction. It creates a hole. Anything flows into a vacuum. Nature always seeks a balance. Don't you see?"

But what Hawk discerned was that Mole Woman was blind too.

"As soon as death shivers by, life begins to sprout. We are always wheeling round into our seasons, Hawk." Winona studied the sad, contemplative face of her cousin's son, a rugged handsome man. The mother in her wanted to reach out and soothe his troubling thoughts.

His eyes lost focus as memories of his second marriage, like uninvited guests, piled into his imagination:

A ferris wheel, spinning to the top of the world,
then plunging to the bottom of the universe.

Rising Smoke, *at the county fair*
her black liquid eyes, straight ebony hair,

white teeth in a dazzling, world-toppling smile.
Crazy, crazy in love with her.

Rising Smoke *racing the rodeo barrels,*
tamer of wild horses,
riding him crazy into the ground.

Rising Smoke, *pregnant and proud,*
belly hanging over the saddle knob,
spurring the rodeo audience wild.
> *Her horse slipping, falling*
> *Crowd hushed,*
> *Running, running to her*
> *Underneath,*
> *The baby crushed.*

Rising Smoke *drinking with him*
Rotgut whiskey days blurred into weeks,
Two lives wasting.

The carcass of a marriage:
> *furniture, photographs,*
> *empty bottles,*
> *ferris wheel memories.*

"No sooner does one think one has discovered love, then hate is set into motion," Winona said. "No sooner is one into the joy of living, then death begins its stalk upon that life. The Creation is always balancing itself. We human beings are the only ones who delude ourselves into thinking that love makes us permanent, that love is unchanging, that love is the endpoint." She waited for him to say something, but it was too painful.

"I get up each morning," she continued, "take my Pipe out, the Chanunpa Wakan, and offer it to Wakan Tanka. I thank the Creator for my life. I am grateful for what the Pipe has given me, for the teachings of the animal and plant nations, and the kindness shown to me by Wakan Tanka. It was through the Pipe that I married Davis. When he died, I felt my life was over too. I know he's there waiting for me to cross over and join him. Even when a person dies, the love keeps on living."

"Death is one thing. Divorce is another." Sourness saturated his voice. The unforgiving hardness of the wood chair pressed against his spine. His eyes shifted to the window. Stripped of leaves, the trees outside looked as if they were begging the sky for a winter's white robe.

"Listen, Hawk, you and I both know that love can bring great happiness and fullness," Winona interrupted, "and it can also pierce the heart with its deceptions and false expectations. The tracks of Coyote are everywhere. He's always looking for the careless pleasure of love. Just when you are about to give up hope, pay attention, Hawk! You may spot an entrance into a deep passage where the only way is down. And you must go, for there is no other way to the heart, and in discovering your heart, you may, perhaps, be lucky enough for Love to find you."

Of course, he thought, *Mole Woman lives underground.*

The short, stocky woman pulled out her lightning pipe and began to fill it with tobacco. Winona noticed that the zigzag beaded design held as steady as her words. Sometimes the tiny beads vibrated, and the lightning bolt would shiver on the leather, drawing her attention to the pipe.

Hawk patiently waited, no word having crossed his lips. The appearance of the pipe signaled that Winona had more to say. He settled back into the chair. She tamped down the tobacco with a sliver of deer bone, as if to poke each word into his soul.

"You'll have to find your own way now. It's time for me to go home. I've taught you what you need to know. It's time you take another teacher."

A shudder moved through him. He guessed at what was coming next.

Winona continued. "All my medicine articles I leave to your care, except for my two pipes. This lightning pipe, my social pipe," she stroked the long sumac stem, "was given to me by Davis as my 'learning pipe' in those days when I first started living with him. I prayed with this pipe every morning, asking for direction, asking for love. Long before I knew I was in love with Davis, I knew the pipe loved me." With her right hand Winona encouraged the smoke to travel up the stem; her left hand cradled the red bowl of catlinite stone.

"Every morning I'd pray to the Grandfather of the Yellow Face, Wiyohiyanpa, to tell me where I could make my home. It was this cha-nunpa that woke me up. Sometimes we two-leggeds can be so empty that we don't even recognize the door to love when it opens before us." She looked at him sharply.

The familiar sweet smell of tobacco permeated the living room. All was quiet. The grandchildren had not yet arrived from school. Winona's daughter, Lucy, and her husband, Larry, were still at work. It was the time of day, midafternoon, when Hawk was able to catch precious moments alone with the elder, his teacher.

"I want you to give this social pipe to Meggie O'Connor, the psychologist. I know that I am not the only one here with special feelings for her." She cast a knowing glance in his direction.

He started. *How much did Winona know?*

He parried, "But she's a white woman."

She brushed aside his comment as irrelevant. "She's a woman of good heart. You know, I've been teaching her, too, these past couple of months. Lucy sent me to Dr. O'Connor, hoping the psychologist would heal me of the notion that I'm going to die soon. So, I taught her a thing or two about healing." A mischievous grin lit up her face.

For a second, Hawk felt sorry for the hapless Meggie O'Connor. Over the past couple of months, as the part-time handyman at Meggie's place, he had witnessed the awesome magic of Winona's words upon the thirty-nine-year-old psychologist. "Meggie O'Connor was no match for your tricks," he laughed.

But Winona found no humor in his teasing. "No tricks, Hawk. All I did was teach her a thing or two about the web of the world. She needed to know that we human beings don't live *above* the Creation but *within* it. That the tree nations, the stone nations, the deer, the spider—they are all her sisters and brothers."

Winona shook her head, her voice serious. "I'm no conjurer, Hawk. My words knocked at her heart and jerked open her eyes. Meggie

O'Connor was hungry and didn't know it. I taught her that the world around her was alive. That the Grandfathers would pay attention to her prayers. That the Grandmother upon whom she walked would reach out, give her strength when she needed it. She didn't know these things. She wasn't walking in any balance."

Hawk regretted that he'd ever suggested that Winona's medicine was part sorcery, even if it was in jest.

"Magic is for people who, drawing from a well of emptiness, thirst for power," she continued. "Magic is for those who want to collect power into themselves. Medicine is for those who will use the power for the people so they can live as human beings. The only power I have is the one that flows through my Chanunpa Wakan. It's the same power, out of the Four Winds, that the Grandfathers send down to the Grandmother. It is the same power, She returns to Them, out of her Body. You know I'm talking of the Great Giveaway, don't you?"

He nodded, silently.

"So give Meggie O'Connor this lightning pipe, Hawk. It needs to go to another woman. It's a teaching pipe. Maybe, just maybe, she'll have the luck I did and meet a man worthy of her spirit." Once again, Winona leveled shrewd eyes upon her cousin's son.

He pretended not to notice.

"The Chanunpa Wakan, my Sacred Pipe, goes with me. When I cross over . . ."

Involuntarily, he shook his head. *I don't want to hear this.*

Her voice grew forceful, sharp, commanding. "Listen to me, Hawk. You're the only one I can count on to do what I ask. Tomorrow night, you will gather the family together here in the living room. I will give the children their Christmas presents a day early. I will talk to them about the power of the Sacred Pipe; they will see for themselves that power. They will never forget what is to happen. It is for the young people I do it this way."

"Do what?" He hated to ask.

She knew he was playing dumb. Yet, like a mother with a recalcitrant child, she explained what he already suspected. "With my Chanunpa Wakan, I am crossing over tomorrow night. My life's work is done. I'm tired. The Spirits are coming for me. The Pipe will take me across. Then you must bury me with my Sacred Pipe. Lucy will want a big casket. You must insist," she instructed him, "that I be buried in the flimsiest casket, so that I give away my body back to the Grand-mother. I will feed the grasses which have nourished the animals who have given me life all these years. I am to be laid down on my back in the casket, wrapped in a Chief Joseph blanket, with my Pipe in my hands. Bury me, Hawk, where no anthropologist can dig up my bones." She chuckled.

Hawk continued to look away. *But you're not sick. You're not suici-dal. You're not even depressed. Why leave us now? Who will be my teacher?* A storm of thoughts assailed him. Her words precise and pragmatic, like nails to a coffin, hammered in the certainty of her death.

"The money from Davis's estate is all taken care of in the will; it goes to Lucy and the grandchildren. Give Larry two of my eagle feath ers. The rest of the medicine is yours. If you decide to leave the Pipe road in the future, take my sacred articles and give them to a medi-cine person where they can be safe, respected."

He was about to protest that he would never leave the medicine path, when she waved him off.

"You don't know what will be asked of you in the future. Find your-self a teacher, because now, more than ever, you will need that guid-ance. You know just enough," she laughed, "to get yourself in a heap of trouble. The evil ones are not particularly interested in one who knows nothing. Go to Laughing Bear on Pine Ridge reservation. Maybe he will help you, for it was Davis who taught him. But, beware, Laughing Bear is just a two-legged too."

What does she mean by that? he pondered

"Bring the family together tomorrow evening," Winona continued. "Then, they will see the power of the Sacred Pipe. What will Lucy and all her modern science and nursing degrees make of that?" She shook her head at the thought.

Winona finished smoking the lightning pipe, circled it in respect to the Grandfathers, hoisted her stiff body off the chair, walked over to the outside door, opened it to the frigid air, and blew out the ash, say-ing, "*Mitakuye oyas'in,* All My Relations."

"Remember, Hawk," she added, "everything we do, we do in the name of All Our Relations."

Winona returned to the chair. "You will do these things for me, Hawk." It was less a question and more of a statement of fact.

Of course he would. He loved the old woman.

She sighed a pleasant sigh, one that spoke of anticipation. "Davis is waiting for me. My Pipe is ready. I am ready. The time is ripe for me to go home."

TWO

CHRISTMAS EVE'S HOMEGOING

A throe upon the features—
A hurry in the breath—
An ecstasy of parting
Denominated "Death"

An anguish at the mention
Which when to patience grown,
I've known permission given
To rejoin its own.

—EMILY DICKINSON
A Throe Upon the Features

Her neatly braided black hair slapping against her slender neck, six-year-old Eva shook her head and protested, "But, Grandma, Christmas doesn't come until tomorrow. We're not supposed to open our presents until then." A stickler for rules, she was proud of her ability to know right from wrong, especially about important matters.

Winona cupped the child's pouting chin in her old hands. "Indian time is not the same as white time. On Indian time, we do what we need to do when it is important, not when the clock or the calendar tells us. *Wi*, the sun, doesn't wear a watch and say, 'Oh, my clock tells me it's time I get out of bed and go shine on those good people in Peshawbestown. He simply knows when it's time. And I *know* it's time for gift-giving."

Eight-year-old Adam, chunky and all elbows, nudged his sister aside and handed his grandmother a shoe box wrapped in red paper. On the front was pasted a big paper heart, the word *GRANDMA* scrawled over it. The box was heavy; carefully, she peeled the tape off the edges.

Watching from the side, Lucy commented, "He worked long and hard on this gift, Mom."

Adam cast an appreciative look toward his mother.

Winona lifted up the shoe box lid and extracted seven Petoskey stones, polished to a high-glossed sheen; each fossilized cell in the rocks stood out clearly. "Oh, Adam," she marveled, "of all the things I have seen in this part of the Leelanau Peninsula, it is these beautiful stones found along Lake Michigan that I love the most. At home in South Dakota, I tell the young people that the stone nation, *Inyan,* is alive. The stones are the oldest voices on this continent; yet most human beings see them as dead and lifeless." She held one up to the lamp, "These stones show the very cells of life in them. From my heart, I thank you. *Pilamaya.*"

Eva was not about to be overshadowed by her gawky brother. "Here, Grandma." She thrust a small box into Winona's hand.

The old woman put on her eyeglasses and gingerly unwrapped the paper. From inside the small box she pulled out two red, beaded hoop earrings with a yellow lightning design. Immediately, she replaced the earrings she was wearing (a pair given to her by Lucy years ago), looped the silver wires through her ear holes, and gathered the lightweight Eva into her lap.

Looking at her two grandchildren, so different in size and grace, so alike in coloration, Winona pronounced, "You two make me happy. These gifts come from your heart and from your hands. They will go where I go."

Caught in a web of confusing emotions, Lucy couldn't help but notice her discarded earrings lying on the side table. Proud of her children, she was pleased that her mother loved them. Yet the hurt from years of neglect as a child hungering for Winona's approval puckered even the sweetest moments between them. "Here, Mom," Lucy said, offering a gift-wrapped book.

Balancing Eva with one hand, the old woman tore off the paper with the other. Adjusting her spectacles, she read aloud the title, *"Healing Plants."* Then, scrunching her eyes into a baffled expression, she peered over her glasses at her daughter.

A smile tightened into a grimace as Lucy compressed her prominent chin and dark eyebrows toward the beak of her nose. *I'm never good enough for her.* "It's a newly published book, Mom, on your area of expertise. I thought you'd enjoy reading it." Her voice sounded high, strangulated.

Winona asked, "Will the book talk to me, like the plants, and tell me what I need to know?"

Lucy discerned a mocking undertone to the question. Eva slipped off her grandmother's lap.

For Winona, the question was intended to teach.

For Lucy, the words pricked her at the site of old wounds. *You will never know me, Mom. I am here, right in front of you.*

Unseeing, Winona removed her glasses. She clapped her hands. "Let's have some of Dr. O'Connor's cookies." Larry, all too willing to interrupt his wife's momentary mood of self-pity, retreated to the kitchen to fetch the tin box of gingerbread figures. Winona passed them around, saving the biggest one for herself.

"You know," she said to the children, "I am reminded of a story about the first man and the first woman. They were told to make babies. So, they took the dough and shaped up babies just like these gingerbread people, with eyes and arms and legs.

"Carefully, they slid the first batch into their mud kiln, but since they hadn't done this before, they got too anxious and pulled out the first batch much too early. The babies emerged pale, white, underdone. Ugly.

"The next time, the man and woman grew careless and lazy. They let the batch of dough people sit in the oven far too long. Burned to a crisp, these babies came out all scorched and black.

"So, the man and woman decided that, maybe, the dough needed some extra colorful ingredients, such as dandelion blossoms. They cooked up this third batch, and all the babies turned out small and yellow.

"Finally, they understood that they had to return to the original recipe and pay attention to what they were doing. This time, because the man and the woman didn't let their minds wander, the batch of dough people turned out perfectly—a delicious reddish brown color.

"So, you see, children," she announced, munching enthusiastically on her gingerbread person, "that is how the four races—white, black, yellow, and red—came into being. And that is why it is important to always pay attention to what you are doing."

The two children stopped eating and started studying their gingerbread people. Eva delicately picked at the raisin eyes, while Adam smudged his finger around the whole of his cookie. Even Lucy settled back into her chair.

Her mother continued. "Children," she said, and all the adults listened, "tonight, there is going to be a powerful teaching. I want you to pay close attention. Be proud that you are of the red nation, that the blood of the real people flows through your veins. Tonight is the night before the birth of Jesus—a time when only our people walked this land. We know that Wakan Tanka has many ways of helping us, because we are truly pitiful two-leggeds. There is the Pipe road; there is the Jesus road. There are many roads which lead to Wakan Tanka, for He is the Great Mystery of this universe. You each have to choose that road which speaks the language of *your* heart. Tonight, children, it is the Pipe road I travel, for at midnight the Pipe will collect my spirit and take me home."

Lucy gasped involuntarily and clasped her husband's arm.

The children cocked their heads, not understanding what was being said, frightened as they saw fear rippling over their mother's face.

Larry studied his mother-in-law's expression and concluded she was serious. He wrapped his large arms protectively around his wife.

Hawk hunkered down in the corner chair, sinking into sadness.

"Children." Winona bent low in her chair, softly addressing the grandkids. "Death is nothing to fear. Remember that our ancestors have always said, 'Today is a good day to die.' Death is just part of life, that's all. It's not the end of the story."

But Adam and Eva didn't look the least bit reassured as they sat on the floor, their bodies pressed against their mother's legs.

Winona understood that she had to tell them why she was leaving them. "One night last summer I was praying with my Chanunpa Wakan. The Spirits came to me. They said I had worked hard for the people. They gave me the choice—to cross over in the dark of winter or to stay a little while longer. I told Them I was tired and ready to go. For a long time I have taught others what I know of the ancestors, mended bodies with the help of the plant nations, and helped lost people find their wandering souls.

"At first, I thought the Spirits would just come some night, grab up my spirit, and leave my body behind in the bed. But that would have been too easy. All my life, I've had to do things the hard way," Winona laughed, shaking her head.

"Besides," Winona continued, addressing the children, "it is for your benefit that They do it this way. Always the Chanunpa Wakan is teaching us. Pay attention. What you see tonight is something you'll never forget. When you talk about it with your school friends, most of them won't believe you. They'll say you're making it all up. All your life you'll hear people talking about our ways as if they're lifeless rituals of a dead people. Even your own people will speak like that." She cut her eyes at Lucy.

Looking back toward Adam and Eva, Winona said, "I want you to be proud of who you are. You come from two great nations—Oglala Sioux and Ojibway. Tonight, all the stories I have told you about our people and our way of life, the traditions and the teachings, will help you know the truth of what you see. So keep your eyes open."

Winona paused, scanning the faces of Lucy, Hawk, and Larry. Sucking on her front teeth for a second, she then chuckled. "The whites have a saying that you can't teach an old dog new tricks, but the Spirits know different. They want you grown-ups to know that the Pipe is not just some 'religious symbol.' The Chanunpa Wakan is alive. Sometimes, when you hold the bowl in your left hand, you can feel the heartbeat of the Grandmother. The Pipe breathes. In every breath, our prayers are spoken. And in every breath, our prayers are answered. We two-leggeds are given not what we want but what we need—to live as human beings.

"Now, Adam, I heard you telling your mother the other day that you would simply die if you didn't get a certain electronic game. There's a world of difference between *wants* and *needs*. It's a lesson that even old people like myself have to keep learning, over and over again. Well, I've got your Christmas gift, Adam. It's not any game, that's for sure. But it's something that will teach you about who you are. I've made you something." The old woman pushed herself stiffly off the chair, reached around in back, and pulled out a dance costume—a fox-pelt back, a fox-head skin for the crown and forehead, a staff wrapped in red cloth with dyed turkey feathers, topped with the head of a red-tailed hawk. Adam's dark eyes grew as large as walnuts. She extracted two moccasins, each beaded with the image of a fox head on the front, and handed them to the boy.

"For you, Eva, I have made a different outfit." From behind the chair, Winona dragged a shirt box. Eva eased open the lid and lifted out a small, brown, elk-skin dress—the front covered with shells sewn onto red cloth patches. Two soft moccasins, covered with intricate beadwork, matched the color of a pair of earrings. Delighted, Eva held the dress up to herself and began prancing around the room.

"Lucy," said Winona, "it was hard to know what to give you. You and I have always gone separate ways. Tonight, you will learn something about the ancient powers that all your science won't be able to explain. But, for your Christmas present, I decided I needed to give you something very modern." Deep into her pocket she reached, tugging out a small square package no bigger than her hand.

Lucy unwrapped the gift. Inside a plastic case was an untitled cassette tape. Perplexed, she looked up at her mother. *Always it had been like this; neither one of us understanding the other. Neither one of us quite trusting the other.*

"Later," Winona explained, with a dismissive gesture of her hand. "It is for later, when you are ready."

Winona donated Davis's old tools to her handsome son-in-law, Larry. The burnished red tool box brought a smile to his face.

Hawk then rose from his chair, saying, "If you stay until tomorrow, I will give you a more conventional gift. Otherwise," he said, "I'm going to be stuck with it." Out of his jeans pocket, he yanked a lumpy leather pouch. "If you're not going to stay, well then, maybe this gift will be useful to you where you're going."

Wide-eyed with delight, Winona eased open a pouch of blue corn seed.

Hawk explained, "The Hopi have grown this corn for centuries. It should grow anywhere. Take it as an offering from This Side. Let the Spirits know we haven't forgotten everything They've taught us." The last words caught in his throat.

Winona nodded. From behind her chair she reached for a hand

drum on which was painted the red-tailed hawk. She passed Hawk the drum and drumstick, the head of which was soft, stuffed deerskin. "Only men are to call the Powers by drumming, for the drum is the Grandmother. Bring your male energy to Her, and through you the people will hear Her heartbeat. But, remember, you must always begin by offering tobacco on the surface of the drum."

Lucy swept her short, coal-black hair off her face and checked the wall clock; already it was after eleven P.M. The children, still ogling their gifts in the other room, would have long since been sent to bed if their grandmother hadn't insisted that they be allowed to stay up.

Winona called to her grandchildren to come sit down before her on the floor, and from her armchair she proceeded to talk to adults and children alike, half-lecture, half-instructions. She spoke to them of her burial wishes and of the gifts of the lightning pipe to Dr. O'Connor, two eagle feathers to Larry, and assorted medicine articles to Hawk. Winona gave explicit directions about being laid on her back inside a fragile coffin, the Sacred Pipe cradled in her hands. "All that much easier to give back my body to the Grandmother, to feed the grasses and animals that have given life to me."

While her broad, flat Plains Indian face fought to maintain stoic control, Lucy's mind revolted. *No. No. No. This can't be for real.*

Winona turned toward the stricken face of her daughter. "Many times, I've given thanks to Wakan Tanka for looking after you, when I was not able to be a good mother to you. Here you are, mother of two wonderful children, married to a good man, and educated too. As a nurse, you will always have a way of supporting your family. You have stayed away from alcohol because you saw how it destroyed what should have been good times for us both. I am not proud that I drank away most of your childhood, and if it hadn't been for Davis . . ." Her words trailed.

"I know, Mom," Lucy said, reassuringly reaching out to touch her mother's hand. *But to know is not to forgive,* silently whispered the hurt in Lucy's heart.

Winona continued, "You and Davis were proof to me that, after a harsh and unforgiving winter, the spring always comes to renew the land. And although you never knew it, you were the reason, Lucy, I finally stopped the drinking. I could no longer look into your eyes.

Shame is like that—rotten meat on which the self tries to feed and purge all at the same time. So, little ones," she said, smiling at the two children, "be grateful for a mother who takes such good care of you."

Lucy winced and thought, *Too little. Too late.*

Winona admonished, "I can't make it up to you, Lucy. You will have to learn to love yourself, despite my absence. Know that I love you. Know that I have always loved you."

She turned her attention to Hawk, slumped in the corner chair. "It's time now for me to go home. Davis is waiting. I shall fill my Chanunpa Wakan." Hawk reluctantly pushed himself up from the chair, his lanky legs growing heavier by the moment. He lit a bowl of sage and smudged the room and its occupants. Like a shroud, a deathly quiet settled over the room. The children moved over to the couch and again nestled against the legs of their mother. They were a little bit scared, not knowing what to expect, but also curious.

The old woman awkwardly, arthritically knelt, unrolling her medicine bundle. Into a small smudge bowl she rolled a ball of sage and lit it, washing her arms and face in the smoke. Next, she extracted the long oak stem and the catlinite bowl of her Pipe. Facing west, she anchored the stem into the bowl and, wafting it through the smoke, she rocked and cleansed the Pipe of any negative influence. With tobacco pouch and tamper in hand, she began filling her Pipe:

"Wakan Tanka, Great Mystery, with this Pipe, I greet you and ask you to take my spirit across.

"Wiyohpeyatakiya, Grandfather of the West, with this Pipe, I give thanks for my life visions. I ask for your guidance in crossing over.

"Waziyata, Grandfather of the North, I am grateful for the gifts of healing. As I cross over, I ask your help in gathering unto me some of the lost souls trapped between the worlds.

"Wiyohiyanpata, Grandfather of the East, help my family accept my going. In their hearts, teach them about this journey.

"Itokagata, Grandfather of the South, help me with this mystery of passage from one life to another. Help those left behind to keep the Chanunpa Wakan with awe and respect, to understand that tonight they see but a little of its strength.

"Mahpiyata, Sky Beings, I ask that You light the way into the darkness for me.

"Makatakia, Grandmother, help me as I walk along the way. Ground me in my travels."

Winona sang the White Buffalo Calf Woman song. Adam hummed along, his grandmother having spent hours teaching him the sacred song. Holding the Pipe out before her, stem first, Winona moved stiffly to the chair and sat down. She scrutinized her family. "A week ago, the Spirits came to me and said, 'Okay, you can cross over whenever you want.' I asked Them to wait until tonight. I had all these presents to give. Over there, in the corner," she nodded toward the television set, "stands the warrior woman. She is here now, impatient with me."

All eyes riveted to that corner.

I can't see anything. Mom is hallucinating, Lucy thought.

The space looks empty to me. Larry saw only the television.

I see a faint glow of light, that's all, Hawk sighed to himself.

I love my new dress, Eva daydreamed.

Adam was struck with wonder. *Yes, I see Her standing there. She has a horse. Her face is smiling at my grandmother. Where did She come from?*

Winona sank back into her chair, holding out her Pipe, facing the corner. "Yes, I'm ready now." She closed her eyes.

Lucy was lost in her own thoughts. *This is utter madness.* She rose and moved to her mother's side, tears slipping down her face. She wrapped her fingers around the right wrist of her mother, reassured that her heartbeat was steady. *I will keep her alive.*

Fifteen, twenty minutes, Winona's heart kept to a steady rhythm. The clock bent toward midnight. *Ka-thump, ka-thump, ka-thump* . . . the heart counted the history of sunrise to sunset, the days from childhood to motherhood to old age, a sturdy beat of time across the generations. *Ka-thump, ka-thump, ka—*

The beat stopped.

Winona's life broke off.

A clap of thunder shook the air.

Lucy screamed. The children jumped. Larry grabbed the telephone and dialed 911. Hawk sprinkled a pinch of tobacco on Winona's stilled tongue.

/ / /

Later that night, the snow began to fall, coating the empty limbs of leafless trees and gradually obliterating the parallel tracks of the ambulance from the driveway. Larry stood stolidly by the kitchen window, holding a forlorn Lucy in his arms. " 'Dead on arrival,' the rescue squad said. But what did she die of, Lucy?"

Silence haunted the house and mocked the question, each person locked deep into their own thoughts.

I love my dress, Grandma. The little girl wept into her bedroom pillow.

I will follow your teachings. In the living room, Hawk buried his head, burdened now with new responsibilities.

Lucy seethed, age-old embers searing the heart. *Abandoned again. Why, Mother? Why?*

Not knowing what to do next, Adam perched inside the open doorway, looking west, waving goodbye in the direction of his grandmother's departing spirit. *Grandma, She was beautiful. I saw Her take your left hand and lift you up from the chair. I saw you slip from your body, like smoke from the pipe.*

Grandma, I saw you smile.

THREE

THE CRACK OF DAWN

Screaming the night away
With his great wing feathers
Swooping the darkness up;
I hear the Eagle bird
Pulling the blanket back
Off from the eastern sky.

—IROQUOIS INVITATION SONG

Hawk awoke, restless—haunted by the specter of Winona's death on Christmas Eve and pressed to make some decisions now about his own life. A confusion born of past and future meddling in the moment. Looking out his trailer window toward Lucy's house, he could see snow-covered, flat cedars, stately white birches, mottled gray maples, and brown-and-green tufted pines compress and crowd his range of view. So different from the miles upon miles of unobstructed vision on the Pine Ridge reservation back home in South Dakota. Back there, small groves of cottonwood trees dotted the sweeping grasslands, hardly slowing the prairie winds whipping about the occasional shabby, prefabricated house and singing through rusted automobile corpses in the side yard. Out on the plains, a man could look long distances and know what was coming. But here, in Northwest Michigan, storms raged in off the Lake with sudden, unexpected brutality, with winds that roared like freight trains.

His sole reason for leaving Pine Ridge to come to the tiny Ojibway and Ottawa reservation of Peshawbestown in upstate Michigan had been Winona, to glean from her knowledge of plants and traditional ceremonies. With her death, it was time to pack up his belongings and head home. He missed the *Paha Sapa,* the Black Hills, which his people called "The Heart of Everything That Is." He longed for the sight of *Maco Sica,* the Badlands, with its mysterious geological formations. But, on the Lakota reservation, what awaited him was unemployment and the temptation to drink away his boredom. Seven years of sobriety and still he had to be on guard.

Dropping his feet onto the floor of his small trailer, Hawk pushed himself out of bed, his hip twinging in pain from old rodeo injuries and a touch of arthritis. "Helluva way to greet the New Year," he muttered.

His razor blade was dull, and so was he. Only after several close scrapings of stubble and a couple of flesh offerings was he finally satisfied. He was letting his black hair grow long with the hope that eventually he could fashion two braids, but, for now, he had to be satisfied with a skimpy ponytail. He fastened a red headband across his forehead. Pulling on a clean pair of jeans and a Western shirt, he stood up to admire himself in the mirror of his tiny bathroom. *A fine-looking man,* he thought, sucking in his gut and puffing out his chest, *even if I am forty-one.*

Lifting his jacket off the hook, he tugged on his winter boots. Grabbing a pouch of tobacco, he opened his trailer door and squinted toward the east. Pink and golden hues in the sky told him sunrise was only a few minutes away. During the night, the snow had drifted down on the ground like large white, unlined sheets upon which the local wildlife had inscribed their distinctive signatures: the split ovals of the deer, the crisscross hatching of hungry birds, the cauliflower print of Adam's dog, and the deep, uneven punctuation of the jackrabbit tribe.

He crunched over to the clearing between his trailer and Lucy's house, stamping his feet to keep warm. From his mouth emanated cold streamers of air. Slowly, the great yellow ball of fire eased up over the frozen horizon. Arrows of the sun shot through the pines and the cedars, great shafts of light piercing the forces of darkness. In thanksgiving for the new day, Hawk sprinkled an offering of tobacco on the ground and sang a song of greeting.

The sun, *Wi,* rose higher and higher in triumphant ascension. Alive to the miracle of morning, Hawk listened to the birds answering his song with their own antiphonal chorus—the raven's *caw,* the demanding shriek of the blue jay, the melodic *phut phut* of the cardinal, the little chickadee's *dee-dee-dee.* Shading his eyes against the morning light, Hawk watched the birds streak and dive across the sun in their rites of celebration. His eye caught a distant flash of speckled wing, in rhythm with the morning's pace. With a predator's scream, a majestic eagle rose with the sun, toward the sun, into the sun, until Hawk lost it in the fierceness of Wi's face.

"Wanbli Gleska, Spotted Eagle, welcome," he cried out. *I live for these moments.*

The birds chattered back in response. Cold to the bone, Hawk strode back through the fresh snow to his compact home. Out of old habit, old cautions, he stooped to check the tracks all around the trailer, to see who had come in the night, sniffing for careless garbage. He spotted a set of tracks different from those of Adam's dog, lighter in tread. Coyote. The animal had apparently seated himself on the snow to the right of his door, maybe to scratch an ear or wait upon the presence of the man within the trailer.

"Happy New Year to you too," mumbled Hawk, before entering his trailer.

Barely had he stripped off his outer gear when a thumping on the door interrupted his breakfast ritual. In stocking feet, he padded to the door and opened it. There stood his cousin, Lucy Arbre, and from her mouth white dragonlike breath hissed forth. The cold Michigan air froze his manners.

"Well, aren't you going to let me in?" Lucy demanded with an insistent voice and shuttling feet, sticking out her chin. Lucy was not about to stand quietly in the cold. She didn't wait for him to answer but pushed on past him into the trailer.

Plunking herself down beside the tiny kitchen table, Lucy complained, "You'd have more room in this place if you cleaned it up some." Her eyes roamed over the indiscriminate scatter of his clothes draping what little furniture he had.

If the truth were known, he liked the softening effect his clothes had on the sharp angles of chairs and doors.

She pulled out two cigarettes from her pack, offered him one, lit hers, and handed him the lighter. For a moment, the two of them savored the familiar smell and dragged on their cigarettes in silence. Getting up from the table, Hawk microwaved two mugs of coffee, doused each with ample portions of creamer and sugar, and handed one to her. Over the past few months, he had come to know his cousin better, a fine, compactly built woman, blunt, full of opinions, and of a good heart. People always knew where they stood with Lucy. He liked that about her.

Her morning criticisms didn't faze him. In his exuberance for the new day, he was still flying into the sun with the eagle, pacing the circle around the trailer with the coyote, singing and gossiping about the dawn with the birds. He narrowed his eyes at Lucy, scrunched up his face, and replied, "Dee-dee-dee, dee-dee-dee." Even the grouch in her had to laugh at his imitation.

"You think I'm for the birds, don't you?" she said, puffing on her cigarette. She flipped her bangs back off her face.

"I had a visitor last night," he digressed.

"Who?" she asked with interest, "A woman?" Lucy suspected that there was something not quite right about a forty-one-year-old man footloose and free of marital responsibilities.

"Don't know if it was a woman or a man, but I suspect it was a male from the size of the prints. Your mother warned me he might head my way."

Lucy looked puzzled.

"Coyote," explained Hawk. He eased his long legs under the table.

"Can't be," she replied. "There are coyotes and wolves in the Upper Peninsula and some have been sighted down by Detroit. But nobody up here has seen any coyote."

He grinned at her. Winona had frequently complained to him how Lucy safeguarded her world with "can't-be" certainties. "People like Lucy wear blinders to truth," she had said, "so that they can dim the awesome power of Wakan Tanka."

Lucy turned philosophical on him, "You're thinking of her, aren't you? You know, Hawk, I keep getting the feeling that she's hanging around here somewhere, only I can't find her. I still can't understand how Mom died the way she did, gathering us all around, knowing the exact moment of her death. She always loved drama and she certainly grabbed center stage this time. And why did she choose the night before Christmas? Why couldn't she have waited until after Christmas?" The quarrelsome tone in her voice presaged tears.

"Perhaps," he began, "she was making a statement about the power of the Pipe, that for the people it comes before the Jesus road. Perhaps, she wanted to tell her grandchildren how death comes before life. How in the hell do I know?" He rubbed his chin, noting a place he had missed with his razor and thought, *Is this the way it is going to be, my always noting what I have missed when people come to me with questions? Who is going to help me now with my questions?*

Lucy's voice turned sad, "I really miss her."

Hawk nodded.

She drew deeply, hungrily on the cigarette, burning it down to a hot nub. "There were so many things unsaid between us. Old resentments in me, old guilt in her. I wanted so much for her to be proud of me, to love me as her daughter. Yet I couldn't forgive the past. Always a wall rose up before me, between us. Her eyes would turn away from me. Was it shame? I don't know. What I believed in my heart was that she didn't love me enough to include me in her vision. I was her 'modern daughter.' Why do I think she was always silently laughing at me, when she would call me that?"

Because she was *laughing at you.* He kept his thoughts to himself.

"To want your mother to love you, to not trust her offerings is a terrible thing, Hawk. She never really knew me, my hopes, my vision. I may not be a 'traditional,' but I love the people. I chose to be a nurse in Indian Health because I want the people to be strong and healthy. I hope my children will be proud of their heritage, both Oglala Sioux and Ojibway. When my son asks to dance in the pow-wows, I will help him. I want both my children to grow up full of possibility, not trapped into a reservation-style existence of drinking, unemployment, early pregnancy, and children with fetal alcohol syndrome."

Lucy's eyes grew fierce. "I'm teaching them to look to the future. Nothing can stop them from becoming what they want to be, except themselves. I suppose that's why I gave them the names of the first man and the first woman. I want more for them than was possible for me. They will have strong beginnings, before they're nudged from the nest. They won't have to flounder to fly, like I did. The future is theirs. I don't understand why my mother was so hung up on tradition." Lucy shook her head.

Hawk replied, "She would say that without a past there can be no wisdom for a future, that everything would have to be learned again." Then, as if tired of speaking for his dead teacher, Hawk got up to shave the lone stubble on his chin.

Lucy watched Hawk standing in front of the mirror, his body tall and strong, but not as muscular as her husband, Larry. While Larry's face was more angular, eastern, Hawk's face was rounder, flatter, with high cheekbones, deep-set black eyes, a definitive nose, and a strong, determined mouth. Both men had necks solidly rooted to strong bodies used to physical exertion. Lucy was glad of Hawk's presence. He would carry on Winona's teachings. When lonely, she might be able to reach into his words and find her mother there, echoing from afar. The cassette tape from her mother was safely stored in her dresser drawer, waiting for the day when she would be able to listen to it without tears or bitterness.

Smoothing his hands over his cheeks, peering into his own reflection, he asked her, "What is your vision for yourself, Lucy?"

She exhaled blue smoke toward him, obscuring the clarity of her image, her cigarette down to its last ash. She pondered the question. "First, it was to get away from Pine Ridge. Second, it was to find a man I could love. Third, it was to have children. Each step I've made, there was always the next step. My children are my life now. I have no vision for myself, apart from my vision for them."

He turned around toward her. "You have them for only a short time, Lucy. They'll soon grow up and leave you to build their own lives."

"I know. I know." She buried her anguish in scrounging around for another cigarette and lighting it, set a backfire to the burning emptiness within. At that moment, the daybreak sun cascaded through the trailer window, streaming through the white haze of cigarette smoke and frosting her black hair with streaks of natural gold.

FOUR

NEW YEAR'S DAY

A touch is enough to let us know
we're not alone in the universe . . .

—ADRIENNE RICH
XII. Sleeping, turning in turn like planets

The ascending sun roused Fritzie, Meggie O'Connor's wire-haired fox terrier, from his winter dream of chasing rabbits. An unruly mass of coarse and curly white hair, a large saddle-spot straddling his back, a boxy head and button eyes, short but powerful legs, and an upstanding tail endowed Fritzie with an undeserved air of dignity. Sniffing the atmosphere for rabbit, his nose detected instead the scent of his human being. His legs ceased twitching to a dream run; his eyes slowly opened to the outlines of the bedroom floor. It was time to awaken his two-legged from sleep, to ask her to let him out on his early morning jaunt, while he still had rabbit on his mind.

Rousing up into a leisurely stretch position, Fritzie dropped open his cavernous jaw and yawned, revealing two large upper canine teeth. He banked his front legs low and then extended them high, before sauntering over to the large nesting place of the woman. A cold nose into her draping hand did the trick.

She groaned, moaned, and then sighed herself awake. To show his urgency and catch her attention, he pirouetted several times in the air by the bedroom door, metal tags clacking under his collar. Her toes touched the floor. Her hands twisted the knob and eased open the exit. Her feet padded after him down the stairs to the porch. With a satisfying yank, that door yielded passage to the outside.

There, his nose told him, dwelt rabbit.

Meggie O'Connor addressed her own reflection in the large hallway mirror, a trick she had taught her clients who needed help in self-motivation. "Today is a special day," she announced to herself. "Today is the first day of the New Year. It is said that what you do on New Year's Day will predict what will happen the following twelve months, and the feelings you have on New Year's Day will haunt you throughout the year. So, today, Dr. O'Connor, choose your actions wisely and remember to be grateful for your existence."

Pronouncements done, Meggie continued her self-examination in the mirror. Her summer freckles had long since faded into the background as her peach complexion bloomed rosier in the winter frost. Little lines etched the edges of her blue-green eyes. With precise movements into her shoulder-length, wavy, fine brunette hair, she plucked out the few gray hairs visible to her. Yes, time was definitely making a march upon her skin and body. In just three weeks she would be marking the midpoint of her life: her fortieth birthday.

Over a breakfast of hot oatmeal and coffee, Meggie made a decision. She would welcome this new phase of life by holding a birthday party for herself at Chrysalis, the family estate she called home. High atop a hill, south of Suttons Bay, Chrysalis stretched for seventy-eight acres of plowed fields, wildflower meadows, cedar forests, ramblings of sumac, and apple orchards. The large white cedar-shaked house, built and decorated in the years preceding the Great Depression, stood as a testament to the vision of Meggie's maternal grandmother. French windows graced the first floor and green shuttered dormers the second floor. Before Meggie moved there two years earlier, the house had endured the long winters unoccupied, empty of family, except for an old ghost or two. Now the house and the land graciously accepted the yearlong presence of Meggie and Fritzie.

Meggie drew up a list of friends to invite to her birthday party: her colleague, Dr. Beverly Paterson; her neighbors, Katya and Paul Tubbs; her veterinarian, Sam Waters; and the elderly identical twins, Sasha and Savannah Todd, who lived down the road. Pausing a moment and absentmindedly chewing on the pencil, she impulsively added Hawk to the list. It was time for her friends to meet him. Meggie decided that she would ask each person to bring a gift of a love story, a lyrical poem, or a silly song something to share from the heart or the funny bone. Grinning with that thought, she barely noticed her hand appending another name to her list: Winona. "Time to get on with life," Meggie scolded herself and crossed out the name of the old woman.

The mind, however, held no such eraser. Thoughts of Winona commanded Meggie's attention. *What a puzzle you were, Winona. You took all I knew and held dear about symbols and psychology and challenged me to look at your world filled with signs and paranormal events. All of which, you told me, pointed directly "to the truth of things." What you knew scared me, Winona.*

Meggie shook her head to clear her thoughts and rose from the table.

Heading toward the door and the job of shoveling snow, Meggie stopped suddenly and twisted back around, catching sight of the crossed-out name. The power of a name, carelessly scrawled on a birthday list, called out to her, telling her there were more urgent concerns than clearing snow. Changing her direction, she turned toward a closet.

On an upper shelf, enclosed in a leather bag, rested the lightning pipe. After the memorial service, Hawk had surprised Meggie with the gift of Winona's pipe. "She wanted you to have this, so that you could learn from it." That was all he said, but his eyes and the reluctant tone of his voice spoke volumes about his anxiety surrounding the gift. Meggie wondered why it should worry him. After all, Winona had taught her the ways of respect.

The pipe had become familiar to her. In the therapy sessions with Winona, the old medicine woman had used both the lightning pipe and traditional stories to wrench Meggie from her scientific, agnostic worldview and guide her toward a sacred world—a world alive with Spirits, ancestors, and the medicine wheel of life. With the lightning pipe, Winona had taught Meggie how to pray real prayers. With the stories, the old woman had shown Meggie how to listen to her own heart. In the Lakota tradition, Winona was known as a healer of lost souls. At first, Meggie had gone along with the old woman's teachings, hoping to ease her into the conventions of psychotherapy. But it wasn't long before Meggie began to question who was healing whom.

Everything Winona taught pointed back to the Pipe. Even a crossed-out name on a list. From the closet shelf, she took down the tanned deerskin pipe bag. Cradling it in her arms, she headed outside to pray.

Laying an old rug on the open porch, Meggie unlaced the pipe bag, extracting the long dark sumac stem decorated with a beaded lightning design and fringe, the salmon-colored, chipped catlinite bowl in a nest of light gray dried sage leaves, a ziploc bag of dark brown sacred tobacco mix, and a tan braid of sweet grass.

To greet the New Year, Meggie found herself on her knees, making prayers of thanksgiving for her life up to that moment, for the present journey of Winona to the Other Side, and for guidance into the near future.

Fritzie danced around his human being in the cold morning air, thrusting a frozen tennis ball toward her hand. She paid no attention to him but busied herself with a leather bag. He could catch no scent of food, only the stale smell of old grasses. She sang in a high voice, never once mentioning his name or addressing him. After many words, a pungent smell of smoke plumed out of the stone and stick she held in her hand. And still she showed no interest in playing ball with him, no matter how much he feinted at her.

Disheartened, he dropped the ball by her feet and wandered off to survey the fading scent of night animals about the place. If she wasn't going to throw the ball, then he had important work to do. The early morning sun reflected into his pitch black eyes as he scouted to the east of the house, his human being having gone deep into silence.

"Winona," Meggie cried out in the silence, "was I one of those lost souls you were meant to heal?" The fingers of her right hand brushed alongside the stem, as if to guide the smoke through the lightning pipe. She did not expect an answer.

I wonder where you are now?

Death had come quickly when, at last, Winona had given her consent. In blinding speed, crashing through dimensions, through layer upon layers of filamentous light, Winona's arms had gathered shrieking ghosts, trapped aeons between the worlds. Hanging on tenaciously, she thrust them with her toward the concentrated, blinding brightness before her. Turning her head neither to the left nor to the right, she clung onto the back of the powerful horse of the warrior woman.

The last barrier to the Other Side assailed all her senses, threatening to topple her and the ghosts back into the void, but she pulled the haunted forms close to her and followed the lead of the Spirit guide. Over to the Other Side, she slid off the horse, exhausted, releasing the ghosts. They slithered off toward the Four Directions, fleeing in terror from the backward void which, for years, had sucked upon their energies.

The warrior woman deposited her at an intersection, saying, "This is as far as I go with you. My job is to return across the Great Divide and find the others willing to make the journey." She wheeled around her horse; they disappeared back along the torturous path they had just traveled.

Winona settled down on a soft spot, unable to find her bearings in the unfamiliar place. Nothing around her made any sense. It was as if cataracts had clouded her vision, permitting her to perceive only swirling movement, bands of sharp light, and shifting shadows. It was one of those rare occasions when Winona didn't have the slightest idea what to do next. If Space could offer her no clue, then maybe Time could . . .

Holding onto her Sacred Pipe, the Chanunpa Wakan, she decided to wait. Dazed and bewildered, it took a few moments for her to realize that her Pipe, filled right before her death, was now empty. Somehow, during the passage through time, space, and other dimensions, the Pipe had been smoked. She clung to it as her only source of certainty in the new world.

Every time a human being Back There called out her name or brought up her image, she felt the gentle tug of gossamerlike strands at her back, strings that dangled through the foggy boundaries between Back There and Here.

At first there were many tugs.

Winona faced the direction which her Pipe told her was west. She was content to wait a long time. For Davis or a guide. For a sign or a signal to tell her where to go and what to do next.

Even if it would take forever.

Meggie prayed hard for Winona's passage into the next life. Following the pipe ceremony, Meggie experienced a rush of energy. She busied herself with chores. She shoveled snow and hauled firewood to the east porch. Inside, she stoked up the woodstove, simmered a lentil-and-ham soup on the electric range, baked low-fat oatmeal muffins, and cleaned the dog dishes. She changed the sheets on the bed, washed three loads of laundry, checked in with her answering service to pick up client messages, and only then sank back exhausted onto the living room couch with a book, praising herself for the productive morning.

What she really wanted to do was to go to the telephone and call that enigmatic man, Hawk.

Cousin to Winona, Hawk had appeared in Suttons Bay soon after Meggie's first encounter with Winona in her therapy office. One day, he had arrived at Meggie's kitchen door, sent by the crippled caretaker of Chrysalis as a replacement handyman. By working part-time jobs in the area, Hawk found he could support himself, while spending valuable time with his medicine teacher, Winona.

Lanky and laconic, Hawk had introduced himself to Meggie as "Slade," his white name. Sparse on information about himself, Slade gradually revealed that he was a mixed breed: part Lakota, part

Cherokee and Apache with a dash of German, Irish, and Mexican thrown in for spice. Alongside each other, Slade and Meggie worked on the place, chainsawing trees and stacking wood. Not once did it occur to Meggie that Slade was kin to her client, Winona, or that he was, in fact, the mysterious "Hawk" whom Winona kept mentioning in her therapy sessions.

Disillusioned with marriage and men, Meggie initially kept a wary distance from Slade. Fritzie, however, unabashedly adored the new handyman who, under the table, secretly slipped oatmeal cookies to the terrier. But events conspired to bring Meggie and Slade closer and closer to each other, and underneath the modest exterior of the man, Meggie discovered a delightful, delicious sense of humor. During one vicious snowstorm, a birch bough had crashed down upon Meggie's head, and if Slade hadn't arrived in the nick of time to find and transport her to the hospital, Meggie might have died.

After that incident, Meggie began to suspect that there was a great deal more to Slade than what she had already learned. Right before Christmas, he gifted her with a colorful pair of quill earrings, made from a porcupine she had shot while they were out hunting. In gratitude and out of her growing affection for him, Meggie had placed her hands on his cheeks and kissed him full on the lips. And later, without thinking, Slade had answered her kiss with one of his own.

Meanwhile, in the therapy sessions, Winona continued to dangle Hawk's name in front of Meggie. She extolled his charm with women, his respect for the old ways, his keen intelligence, the difference between Hawk and other men, and his need for a strong woman to stand beside him. Meggie wondered if Winona was spinning a web, lacing the two of them together. But Meggie remained confused, mistaking Lucy's handsome husband, Larry, for the "Hawk" of Winona's focus. Only during the memorial prayer meeting after Winona's death did Meggie finally discover that all along her friend, Slade, was a pipe carrier and practitioner of the old medicine ways. And that his ceremonial Indian name was Hawk.

Meggie sighed. Now that Winona had died, there was probably nothing in Michigan to keep Hawk/Slade from returning home to South Dakota. Pushing the novel in front of her face, Meggie sternly reminded herself to get used to the idea of his departure.

Fritzie sensed that his human being was not happy. Leaping up onto the low divan by her sprawling legs and feet, he thrust his damp nose under her book, demanding an ear rub. She laughed at his antics and scratched behind his ears. Mission accomplished, Fritzie turned round three times on the soft divan, nestled his nose across one of her legs, and settled himself in for a winter's nap.

With the plow attached to the front, Hawk's truck rumbled up the mile-long driveway to Chrysalis. Hawk noted that while his pick-up was old and cranky, the old girl still had a lot of life left in her. She coughed in protest when he turned off the ignition. The afternoon sun sparkled off the wind drifts of snow. He noticed that the path to the kitchen door had been recently shoveled. Hawk knocked twice, wedged open the door, and shouted for Fritzie. The wire-haired fox terrier came flying out of the nether regions of the house like a white, hyperactive mop, skidding across the tiled kitchen floor, flinging himself with joy at the man. Meggie soon followed, book in hand.

With a grin, she motioned for him to come on in from the cold, but he gestured for her to come outside, inviting her to share in the dazzle of snow and sun.

"Okay, I'll get my jacket and boots on while you entertain Fritzie," she answered.

Already the dog had dashed around the house to the east porch, the last site of his beloved but tattered tennis ball. He returned with the ball safely ensconced in his jaws. He dared Hawk to grab it for a game of tug and shake. Each time Hawk was able to yank the ball out of his mouth, Fritzie threw his body skyward, teeth clacking together like a shark in a feeding frenzy. High up in the air, the yellow ball twirled round and around, caught in the blindness of the afternoon sun, only to fall gracefully back into the snowbanks. Fritzie, too, leapt high in pursuit, springing stiff-legged from the ground, eyes focused on the ball's eventual return.

A snowball clipped Hawk's left shoulder, rudely interrupting the dance between man, dog, and tennis ball. Hawk turned around just in time to see a second missile aiming for his chest and Meggie sporting a wicked smile. He abandoned the game with Fritzie to face his new predator.

Seeing that Hawk had revenge on his mind, Meggie bolted toward the kitchen door. An old rodeo hand, Hawk caught up to her long before she could reach the security of the house. With a low tackle, he brought her down into a big pile of soft snow. As if she weighed no more than a sack of potatoes, his arms turned her over and over as they rolled down the hill, legs and arms akimbo, to the sound of her shrieks and his laughter. And there, midpoint on the hill, red-cheeked and snow-encrusted, full of her humbling, Hawk planted a New Year kiss upon Meggie.

Standing up and brushing the snow off his body, he looked down at her triumphantly and said, "That will teach you white women not to attack us red men willy-nilly." Gallantly, he proffered Meggie a hand to help her up.

She posed as if ready to arise, all the while restoring her sense of balance, tensing her muscles, and smiling up at him. Meggie thrust out her hand toward him. Grabbing it, he pulled her upward, tilting his own body off balance. Catching that very moment of suspense, she yanked him forward. Out his feet slipped from under him, his whole body nose-diving forward, arms flailing—much like a dodo bird trying to attempt flight. "Ah-ha," she proclaimed, and with an exuberant push on his plunging bottom, she guided him in a tumble past her to the bottom of the hill. Only then did she stand up, hands on her hips, announcing, "Perhaps that will teach you red men not to underestimate us white women."

And that was when Meggie walked over to the sprawled form of her friend and bestowed upon him the second kiss of the New Year.

Thus, the New Year began with grief, a gift, a prayer, rabbit dreams, the beginnings of a new journey.

And two kisses.

FIVE

MID-JANUARY

All our knowledge brings us nearer to our ignorance....
—T. S. ELIOT
The Rock

"Two kisses and that's it?" exclaimed Bev Paterson in an incredulous voice. "That was two weeks ago, and you're still walking around in a cloud?" She shook her boyishly cropped hair in amusement at Meggie. They were sharing bagged sandwiches in the downtown Suttons Bay offices of their private practice, located in a blue-gray framed building overlooking the grizzled, wintry visage of Lake Michigan.

Meggie responded to her colleague's teasing. "I told you, he's not been around. He had to return to the reservation to find a new teacher. He'll be back in time for my birthday party." Lifting up her mug of herbal tea, Meggie tentatively sipped the hot liquid; it burnt her tongue. She had tried to steep her words in more confidence than was truly brewing inside.

"Sure, that's what men always say." Bev couldn't keep the sarcasm out of her voice. " 'I'll be back,' they promise and then they disappear on you." Silver and enameled earrings jiggled against her long neck, as if nodding in agreement.

It had been only two months since Bev's lover, Coulter, had left Traverse City with much provocation and little notice. As psychologists and as friends, Meggie and Bev had talked late into the nights, dissected love into meaningful anecdotes, and digested, day by day, Coulter's departure. Slowly, Bev's pain transmogrified from grief to bitterness, as if the hardness of that position would protect her from it ever happening again.

To cover the same ground would change nothing, so Meggie shifted the topic to that of her birthday party. "You know, it will be the first time Hawk will have a chance to meet you and my other friends. You can look him over and tell me everything you like about him."

"I take note of your careful choice of words," Bev scoffed. "You only want me to tell you the positive. God, Meggie, we women are so blind when it comes to romance. We place men on pedestals, overdramatize their achievements, and think them wonderful creatures for being sensitive when they pay the slightest attention to our feelings or listen ten minutes without interrupting. Why is it that what we consider *ordinary* communication between women to be so extraordinary for men? Do you realize how often we women go around praising our particular lovers by saying, 'He's not like most men,' as if only the exception to the general breed would do for us?" Bev chomped down on her turkey and alfalfa sprouts sandwich.

"I do have a certain amount of anxiety about your meeting him," confessed Meggie. "I wonder how you'll take to someone different. He isn't at all like other men I've known."

"See? What did I tell you? To be worthy in a woman's eye, the man has to be the exception." Bev gestured triumphantly in Meggie's direction and then, in a conciliatory mood, added, "But I promise to be good Saturday night and hold my tongue."

Meggie nodded in appreciation. The friendship between the two women had stretched and grown over the previous two years, bound together by experience, emotional honesty, and words that comforted. They could be real with each other, without pretensions, without masks, without a need to be careful around one another. They both recognized that their relationship, like a living mirror, nurtured and

reflected the face of their deeper selves, their shadows, their profiles—
and the passage of their lives through the defining prism of time.

"It's time to nourish our souls as well as our bodies," Bev insisted,
slamming shut the metal file drawer overflowing with painful life
stories and case histories. Both psychologists had finished their psychotherapy practice for the day.

Meggie looked up from the typewriter, having translated her last
client's stream-of-consciousness into an intelligible flow shaped by
themes and internal oppositions. While full of admiration for the dis-
ciplined energy of her slim, athletic colleague, Meggie had no desire
to plunge into any end-of-day aerobic activity. "Jogging in the dark
does not appeal to me," she sniffed.

"No, silly. I've already exercised today. Let's stop off at the Fire
House Deli for a light supper and take in the new exhibit at the Tamarack Craftsmen Gallery in Omena." Bev's enthusiasm was contagious.

It was a tempting suggestion. But . . .

Bev guessed at Meggie's hesitation. "For God's sake, you're worry-
ing needlessly about that dog of yours. You're afraid that he may be
sitting on one of your kitchen chairs, his long snout hungrily sniffing
out the breakfast crumbs, his front paws scratching the tabletop, his
hind legs tightly crossed so that he won't pee on himself."

Meggie began to laugh. "All right, I guess another couple of hours
won't make that much difference to him."

"Listen, you can get yourself a gyro and take half of it home to him.
Fritzie will love you forever." Bev threw open the door and, over her
shoulder, tossed off an observation, "It's very easy to please both men
and dogs, once you know what it is that they want."

The Tamarack Craftsmen Gallery's main room sported a great vari-
ety of art: blown-glass bowls of shimmering colors, birch log lamps,
stone necklaces, gigantic vases with deer vaulting out of the ceramic
skin, possums of dog hair and porcupines of toothpicks, life-sized
cloth dolls of elderly people captured in eccentric, charming poses,
and paintings in water, oils, acrylics, and mixed textures. Whimsy and
wit illuminated the artistic displays.

To the left, above the side gallery room, a sign announced the special exhibit: INTERIOR LANDSCAPES. Bev preceded Meggie, stepping down into the smaller side gallery, saying, "Thank God, nobody can see into *my* inner psyche!"

A large black-and-white photograph of a man's outline overlaid an image of a smaller female figure whose wispy boundaries encompassed a picture of a sleeping baby in which was centered a tiny red heart. Bev stepped back to view the piece, then wryly commented, "It's a sexist creation. Man thinks of woman. Woman thinks of baby. As if that is the be-all and end-all of a woman's existence." She sidled over to the next piece while Meggie stayed there studying the images.

Behind her, a gravelly female voice intruded: "Man keeps secret the inner woman. She is the one who can feed his heart. She is both adult and baby; he doesn't realize that she is always within him."

Meggie pivoted around to see an attractive woman with honey blond hair standing with her hands on her hips. She was wrapped up in a navy blue cape with bright purple swirls and wore fashionable knee-high boots and black leather gloves. Earrings of translucent pink stone globes hung suspended in gold from each lobe. Her glasses had steamed white during her passage from the cold winter night to the warm gallery lights. She slipped them off, erasing the condensation with an embroidered handkerchief.

"You're talking about a man's anima, the need for him to discover the feminine side of himself," Meggie said, but the woman looked confused by her terminology. By way of explanation, Meggie added, "I'm Meggie O'Connor, a psychologist in Suttons Bay."

The woman nodded but offered no name in return. She continued to examine the photograph, so Meggie moved on, following Bev to the next creation. In the middle of a brilliantly colored acrylic painting of the New York Stock Exchange, a large, white, dignified rabbit wearing a checkered vest and standing on two hind legs was consulting his fob watch. Bev whispered into Meggie's right ear, "Who was that woman?"

Meggie shrugged her shoulders. "But I know this character," she said, pointing to the rabbit in the painting. "He's late for a very important date."

"It's easy for artists to mock the world of finance as Wonderland.

They rarely ever get to participate in it," Bev whispered, lest the other gallery visitor was an artist.

Past metal sculptures of animals devouring each other, the two of them encountered a four-foot, light brown wooden brain with a convoluted surface constructed of small horizontally stacked drawers, sitting on a long blue "brain stem." An adjoining table with pen and paper strips invited gallery visitors to write a thought and place it in one of the brain's drawers. Bev pulled out one slot and extracted a piece of paper on which was typed:

Ambrose Bierce's definition of the brain is "an apparatus with which we think that we think." Cynic's Word Book, 1906.

"Ah, the artist thinks we need a bit of prompting." She replaced the quotation in the drawer, then scribbled on a piece of paper: *The brain is an electric grid; babies are made during the power outages.* Grinning, she showed it to Meggie before depositing it into the drawer.

On the far wall, a montage of sexual imagery excited Bev's curiosity. She left Meggie to contemplate the complexity of the mind.

Meggie slid open a different brain slot, and her motion caught the attentive eye of the other woman. A lone fragment of folded paper lay there. It read: *While the mind may outline the images, it is the heart which paints the world in color.*

Meggie looked up to see the woman disappearing into the main gallery room.

Meggie picked up a piece of blank paper from the adjoining table and wrote: *"A miracle—I am falling in love again."* She pulled open a drawer closest to the midsection and folded the secret into the brain's core.

꙼ ꙼ ꙼ ꙼

"My name is Andrea." The woman proffered a hand toward Meggie as she rose from the waiting room couch. A new client but a familiar face and voice. It took a moment for Meggie to place where they had met. The art gallery.

Thin, conservatively dressed in gray slacks and pullover sweater with a splash of cranberry color, Andrea exuded nervous energy. "I have never seen someone like you, a therapist, before," she explained as she entered Meggie's office, "but I liked what you said about a man needing to find his feminine side. Perhaps that is also true for some women?"

"Of course it is," Meggie answered. "Sit wherever you would like," she invited, sweeping her hand across several comfortable armchairs and a large white couch decorated with pillows embroidered with Celtic designs. The salmon pink adobe colors of her office evoked warmth and calm.

Andrea seated herself in an armchair and let herself peer round the room, studying the prints and etchings on the walls. "You've done a nice job with the interior decoration," she observed.

"I didn't catch your last name," Meggie said, pulling out a clipboard of insurance questions.

"That's because I didn't give it to you." The woman's eyes lit upon a large stuffed wolf dressed in sheep's clothing perched precariously on a bookshelf. She smiled in recognition.

Meggie waited. There was more to be said.

"No insurance, no last names. I want only to be known as Andrea. I will pay you in cash."

Meggie set aside the clipboard. It was as good a place to begin the therapy as any. "May I ask why?"

Andrea set down her pocketbook, which, until that moment, had been clutched in her lap. "Because I don't want anyone to know that I am seeing you. Not my husband, not my insurance agent, no one."

"Not even your husband?"

"Especially him. If I told him I had gone to see a psychologist, he would swaddle himself in the lashings of shame."

"Shame?" Meggie leaned forward, recognizing that the first minutes of therapy are sacred. It is during the first moments when the client learns whether her or his voice will be heard, whether it will be safe to speak of pain. Only by adhering closely to the words of the client could Meggie be sure not to interrupt the process.

"Yes, shame." Andrea hammered the word as she spoke it, leaving no doubt that it had been nailed on him by the both of them.

Meggie nodded to encourage more explanation.

"My husband assumes that everything I feel is a result of *his* actions or *his* neglect, as if somehow I don't exist apart from his guilt. Not that he doesn't have good reason to experience guilt though . . ."

"And when he assumes that everything you feel is due to him, what's that like for you?" Meggie chose to focus the questions back on her client.

"It's as if *I* don't really exist."

Meggie expected resentment to emerge, but therapy always has a way of twisting and turning through unexpected chambers of the human heart. She pushed, "And?"

"It's as if I don't *really* exist." Instead of anger, sadness and doubt fluttered through the sentence. No longer was her husband the author of the statement.

"And when you don't exist, what's that like for you?" Meggie knew she was moving quickly into the core area, but her client needed to know that someone was interested in how she experienced living.

"A black hole follows me everywhere I go. I have only to step back, and it will swallow me forever. So, I don't ever look back. Ever." She nodded toward a ceramic tableau on a side table in which a goofy dragon lurked behind a mustached knight in full armor, its large claws covering the knight's eyes.

Making the conscious choice to stay blind. Meggie wondered to herself how a person could maintain a sense of self without a history. "Does it ever change color?" she asked.

"What?"

"The hole. Does it ever take on another color than black?"

Andrea's face lit up. She laughed and said, "What a clever question. You don't even know that I'm an artist, a painter by trade."

"Then you come equipped with a palette of colors." Meggie appreciated Andrea's ability to flow from one level of conversation to another.

"I paint landscapes. That's why you found me at that exhibit. The room I use as a studio has a view of Lake Michigan, the Leland marina, and the Manitou Islands. Mostly I paint the water and the islands, the clouds and the gulls. Naturally, I work in a lot of blues."

"Are there people in your paintings?"

Andrea shook her head.

"And when you paint, what happens to the black hole?"

"It sits there right behind me, waiting. Sometimes, I visualize it as a grave, but there is no headstone. Nothing that will tell me what it contains. It is as empty as an echo and as deep as the mind can bury it."

"And when you turn around to look, do you see it there?" Meggie wondered how concrete this reality had become for her client.

"No, it's as I told you. The black hole is always *behind* me. It shifts as I turn." Her voice questioned Meggie's intelligence.

"What would happen if you were to put the black hole in one of your paintings?" Meggie rotated the woman's words and images like a carbonized diamond in the sun, seeking the flash of possibility and new light.

Andrea looked shocked.

Meggie knew immediately that she had committed a therapeutic blunder.

"Why then," replied Andrea, her voice deadly calm, "I would have to kill myself, wouldn't I?"

"And how close to killing yourself are you?" The question had to be asked.

Andrea smiled, as if the thought of suicide brought her secret pleasure. "Every day. Each and every day, I ask whether it is better to continue to live like this or to die. Each and every day," she paused, "I have to make a choice. That's how close I am to the edge of my life. To paint, however, is to create, to affirm life. I don't know what I would do if I could no longer paint. I think the hole might expand and swallow me whole. You see, Dr. O'Connor, I've never dared come to a therapist before, because I know most therapists will tell me to simply turn around and peer down into the stinking black pit. And I can't afford to do that. Instead, I paint."

Don't push her to confront her past, at least not for a long time, Meggie thought. "So, what brings you to therapy now, when you have been so afraid a therapist might push you in a direction you do not want to go?"

"Two days ago," Andrea answered, "I was walking along the beach off Northport State Park, not another soul in sight. But this particular day, I became aware that I wasn't alone. Over in the water, close to the beach, I noticed an eye staring at me. And as I walked down the beach, it followed me in the water, stopping whenever I stopped. Perhaps it wasn't an eye, perhaps it was simply a shimmer of tail—yet it was intelligently tracking my progress down the beach. I went to the edge of the water and looked out to where it was sandy and clear on the bottom and waited for my fellow traveler to catch up with me. I could recognize his progress by the ripples across the calm surface of Lake Michigan.

"He kept swimming closer and closer to me. And when he drew really near, I could see it wasn't simply one fish, it was a whole school of fat carp, following the leader, who was tracking me. I turned around and walked back toward them. I drew abreast of the fish, and they swam in circles, keeping me in sight. I retraced my footprints along the beach, and do you know what? They turned too and swam back along the way we had come."

Andrea's voice was reverential.

"So, you see, Dr. O'Connor, if a being such as a carp can acknowledge my existence, then certainly I should be able to do the same."

Then, Meggie knew the truth of it: It was hope, not pain, that had brought Andrea and her black hole into the warm office with the adobe colors.

S I X

A FORTIETH BIRTHDAY PARTY

Stories are medicine.

—CLARISSA PINKOLA ESTÉS
Women Who Run with the Wolves

The birthday guests devoured the potluck dinner with gusto. Meggie noted that everyone seemed to take to Hawk and his quiet sense of humor almost immediately. Paul Tubbs kept everyone laughing with his office jokes, while Sam Waters secretly smuggled scraps to Fritzie. Sasha and Savannah Todd regaled the group with stories of the old days in Suttons Bay when it was little more than a fishing village. Even Bev and Katya Tubbs, undeclared rivals for Meggie's friendship, traded town gossip with each other. Meggie was having a good time bringing her friends together for a night of celebration.

With nary a crumb left from the meal, the guests adjourned from the dinner table to the living room, where Hawk had built a fire. It was time for the evening's entertainment: time to tell stories, sing songs, and recite poetry to the backdrop of dancing flames, made all the more cozy by the gusty winter wind rattling at the windows.

After everyone had found a comfortable place to sit, Meggie stood up and thanked them for coming. "It's an honor for me to have each one of you here. I know it's a different kind of birthday party, but becoming forty is an unusual time in one's life. Forty signifies, without any question, the entry into the middle passage of life. Beyond family, what is more important than one's circle of friends? And what do we have to offer each other that is unique? Surely it isn't something we can go to the store and buy with money. That is why I have asked each of you to bring me the gift of something sweet or sad, something serious or funny to share in the celebration of our friendship."

Meggie sat down and then jumped up in remembrance, "Oh. Katya has asked me if she could go first."

"I suffer from stage fright," Katya explained, rising from her seat and nervously clearing her throat. She hummed to herself for a moment. Then, in a silvery soprano voice, she began singing a cappella:

> *Amazing grace! how sweet the sound,*
> *That saved a wretch like me!*
> *I once was lost, but now am found,*
> *Was blind, but now I see.*

Thin but steady, Katya's voice laced the lonely notes into a plaintive, poignant sound. Something about the lyrics piqued Meggie's interest. *What was it?*

> *'Twas grace that taught my heart to fear,*
> *And grace my fears relieved.*

Ah ha, Meggie realized. *That describes my situation—Winona working her magic on me.*

> *How precious did that grace appear,*
> *The hour I first believed!*

Katya continued singing the following three verses, but Meggie found herself lost in reflection, catching only a few hymnal words, here and there. *Winona gave me the gift of a lifetime, shifting the axis of my world. I am surrounded by life in all the directions. At the center stands the Pipe, the heart and soul of the people.*

'Tis grace hath brought me safe thus far,
And grace will lead me home.

Flooded with gratitude, Meggie's eyes swelled with tears. Katya smiled knowingly at her. Her voice shimmered and soared above the night wind, tapping its own wild rhythms on the windowpanes.

When we've been there ten thousand years,
Bright shining as the sun,
We've no less days to sing God's praise,
Than when we'd first begun.

Paul glowed as the listeners burst into applause for Katya's performance. He clapped the loudest of everyone.

"I didn't know that you could sing like that," Meggie exclaimed.

"Neither did I." Katya blushed and sat down. "Sometimes the right tune can coax a voice into being."

"It's never happened to me," commented Bev. "When I try to sing, all my household plants shiver up and die."

Meggie observed Sam Waters shoot Bev a sharp and quizzical expression. She had hoped that he might take an interest in her colleague. Instead, he pulled out and fondled an old briar pipe before filling it with tobacco. Meggie smiled. She did not notice Hawk watching her.

Sasha and Savannah started nudging each other into action. At seventy-eight years of age, the identical twins had weathered their lives differently. Savannah, the extrovert of the two, was more athletic and heavier in build, had never married, and was a great fisherwoman. Sasha was quieter, had worked as a real estate broker for a short period, and had been married for twenty years to a businessman—who, it was rumored, had run off with his secretary. After the divorce, Sasha rejoined her sister at the old family home in Suttons Bay. As Sasha once remarked, "It was like I had never left."

The sisters never seriously argued, although they did admit to spats, mere expressions of grouchiness in the adjustments people make in their daily routines. What the Todd twins liked, more than anything else, was to have a good time. Their basic attitude toward others was: If you're not having fun, then something must be wrong with you.

If more of my clients would adopt that outlook, I would have a hard time making a living as a psychologist, Meggie reflected.

Savannah announced that since she and her sister were identical twins, they had the right to tell their story of love in tandem. Both women flounced off the couch, giggling and whispering about who was going to tell which part. The extrovert started. Savannah turned to the others who were seated and addressed herself particularly to the men:

"As you may know, I was an extraordinarily *beautiful* young woman up here in Suttons Bay. Excuse me," she bowed toward her sister, "let me correct myself. We were *both* considered to be the belles of the town."

Sasha smiled, correction accepted.

Savannah continued, with coquettish inflection of voice, "During the summer season, Father complained about all the young men lolly-gagging around the house. We never suffered for dates to the town dances."

Sasha interrupted, "Remember those rich young things that came over from Leland?"

"You see," Savannah explained, "even back then, wealthy families traveled upstate from Chicago for the five-month summers to escape the city heat and play mahjong late into the evenings." She waved down her sister who was about to interrupt. "Don't worry," she said to Sasha, "I am about to get to the story."

Sasha was straining at the bit, for this was her story too.

Savannah dropped her voice lower to lend dramatic flair to her presentation. "One fine summer evening, when the honeysuckle hung heavy with perfume, I knew the time had come to meet with my true love, the boy upon whom, for years, I had fixed my eye. He had finally asked me if he could come formally courting; Father grew tired of my sad looks and relented. I was in seventh heaven.

"In those days, courting was a much more formal affair than what you young people do today. It was full of romance and anticipation. I spent the whole day choosing my outfit, pinching my cheeks to a rosy hue, and staying on Father's good side. I was prepared to fall madly in love. My date was a handsome fellow with slicked-back hair, parted down one side. Oh, I was going to be the envy of all the girls in the town. And what I wanted to do most of all was to hook my arm into his and stroll up and down the town sidewalks so that every eligible female in Suttons Bay would observe me with him."

Sasha could wait no longer, "Tell them his name."

"Don't interrupt," Savannah scolded.

Once again, Sasha ordered, "Tell them his name."

Savannah looked at everybody, paused, and then peevishly admitted, "I can't remember his name, Sasha."

Sasha harrumphed, "That's what I thought. His name was George Turner. What you don't know," Sasha took possession of the story, "was that George Turner loved Savannah's long golden hair, even though she had dyed it blond. He used to say that he wanted to spend his life running his fingers through her flaxen curls. But my dear sister aspired to be a modern woman. The day before George came calling, she cut off her beautiful hair into a short bob. It made her look like a boy. When she looked into the mirror and saw what she had done, she realized what a dreadful mistake she had committed. A total disaster.

"Mercy, mercy. You can imagine the distress she felt. For a long time she had been fantasizing about a romance with George Turner, and now when it might, indeed had, become a reality, her most striking feature had been shorn. I generously offered to dye my long hair blond and go out on the date for her. George wouldn't have realized that it was me, because the two of us looked so identical. Heck, we did that all the time, switching dates without the men ever knowing it."

Savannah could stand being quiet only so long. "Now Sasha, if I had let you go out with George and if he had fallen in love with you, where would that have left me? This was my big chance in life. George was the kind of man whom a woman could both love *and* marry. Mercy. *That* kind of man doesn't come along every day of your life."

Bev nodded vigorously in agreement.

Sasha shrugged her shoulders. "Savannah decided to purchase a wig of long, golden curls from Bahle's store. Luckily, George was so daft and fixated on her, he probably wouldn't have noticed that the color and length were not the same as the original. Still, it was a ridiculous solution."

"Never mind that," retorted Savannah. "I attired myself in a gorgeous white cotton dress with eye-lace at the neck. My lipstick glowed ruby red, my nails glistened with bright polish, and the wig looked pretty realistic. Mercy, mercy," she laughed, "I planned to catch the banker's son and keep him for life."

She paused for effect. "He arrived, soon after the sun had set, the moon was rising, and the summer twilight made the crickets thrum. My heart began beating as fast as a butterfly's wings when I heard him knocking on the front porch door." Moving her liver-spotted, delicately veined hands to her left breast, Savannah theatrically cupped the perch of an aching heart.

"Meanwhile," interjected Sasha, "I decided that the wig had to go. Savannah isn't the only one who can fly-cast when fishing," she explained. "So, with my best bass rod, I positioned myself by the second-floor window overlooking the entrance to the front porch so that I'd get a good view of George Turner. And I waited. Sure enough, my sister paraded herself down to the first floor, sashaying that white cotton dress about her. Poor George Turner, standing there with his tongue hanging half out in awe of her, didn't even know that the bait had been already cast, and that she was about to reel him in. So, you see," Sasha addressed the audience, "I also had George's future in mind too."

Savannah cast a baleful eye upon her sister and took over the story. "Standing there at the door, George couldn't keep his eyes off me. He begged me for a brief kiss, but I knew Father was about somewhere, and so I let him know that maybe, after walking downtown . . ."

"She did that with her beaux, always promising," interrupted Sasha. "Poor old George, transfixed as he was, he managed to help her put on her lace shawl, and they both stepped off the porch onto the patch of ground where I had sighted my best chance. Before George could even clasp her hand, I executed a perfect cast out the window, lure still attached, and hooked the back of her wig. As my dear sister moved off into the darkness with her true love, the wig came sailing up to me by the second-floor window. Why, George couldn't believe his eyes. The line and hook were invisible to him in the dim twilight. There she was, his beautiful long-tressed date with the golden curls, suddenly bobbed and shorn, and a hairpiece that seemed to be rising up to greet the new moon."

To the laughter of the group, Savannah commented, "And that was the last time George Turner ever darkened our doorstep. My one chance in life. But, I do have to admit," she added graciously, looking at her sister, "it was a spectacular cast."

Everybody applauded.

Katya, still lost in the potential romance of the story, inquired, "But what happened to George Turner?"

Sasha answered, "Oh, George died as a pilot in World War Two. My fantasy is that one night, while flying, he thought he saw the blond wig sail by—still on its trajectory to the moon—and that this time he decided to give chase."

The twins flounced back down on the living room couch, obviously pleased with their dual presentation. Meggie's eyes swept the room, checking to make sure her guests were having a good time. Hawk gave her a private wink and relaxed by stretching out his legs. Evidently he was not planning to tell his story soon. The sweet smell from Sam Waters's briar pipe transported Meggie back into childhood when her grandfather sat in the same room, smoking a pipe and telling her stories about her mother's summer parties at Chrysalis, when the Todd girls were young and in love with George Turner.

Time folding back upon itself, Meggie mused to herself.

Hawk watched a reverie glide over Meggie's face like a fast, thin cloud that intercepts the sun's rays and momentarily reflects them back to the source. Her gaze returned to the room and caught him studying her. He turned his eyes away. All fall, as the handyman at Chrysalis, he had secretly been studying this woman; his respect for her had grown with each encounter.

"I know that I am not the only one here with special feelings for her," Winona had said.

Although nudged by Winona in Meggie's direction and drawn by his own loneliness and hunger, Hawk had held himself in restraint by one incontrovertible fact—Meggie was white, and he was Indian. He had dedicated his life to helping his people. To love a white woman, he had reasoned, would be a betrayal of his life's vision.

But his heart and loins cared not a whit for his heady visions. When it came to Meggie, Hawk saw himself slipping fast into the role of the besotted George Turner.

Paul Tubbs anxiously arose from his chair. "I guess I could go next." He waited, as if hoping that Meggie or someone would relieve him from the task. Everyone sat back, letting him gather his thoughts. It was obvious that no one was going to let him off the hook. As if for good luck, he rubbed his balding pate.

Addressing Meggie, he began, "On this, your fortieth birthday, I thought I would recite a campfire poem I learned as a child. Over time, I have found it very useful," he said, a mischievous smile crinkling into the corners of his mouth, "in understanding the origin of the difficulties men and women often experience in their relationships with each other."

"Ah hau!" Hawk chorused in approval.

Bev leaned forward attentively.

Paul reached down as if to scoop up some dirt from the floor and, shaping the imaginary material in his hands, began his recitation:

>*The good Lord thought*
>>*He'd make him a man,*
>*So He took a little mud,*
>>*an' He took a little sand.*

His hands shuttled in the air, as he turned toward his wife, Katya:

>*Thought he'd make*
>>*a woman too,*
>*But didn't know exactly*
>>*what to do.*

So, He took a rib
> *from Adam's side*
And made Miss Eve
> *for to be his bride.*

Put 'em in
> *that garden fair*
An' said they could have
> *most anything there.*

Paul's voice powered into a tone of greatest authority:

"But to this tree
> *thou must not go.*
Leave them apples
> *For the crow!"*

Slithering his right arm through the air and slathering his voice with guile and seduction, Paul worked the audience:

Then that snake came
> *a windin' round the trunk*
And, at Miss Eve,
> *his eye, he wunk.*

Reaching up and grabbing invisible fruit from invisible limbs, Paul bent toward Bev:

First she took
> *just a little pull.*
Then she filled
> *her apron full.*

She gave Adam
> *a little slice.*
He smacked his lips
> *an' said, " 'Twas nice."*

Straightening up, he marched back and forth in front of the hearth:

Then the good Lord
            came walking 'round,
Spied them peelings
            on the ground.

Alternating his voice between divine, angry majesty and squirming humanity, Paul thundered:

"Adam, Adam!
            Where art thou?"
"Here, Mr. Lord.
            I'se comin' now."

"Been eating my apples
            I do believe!"
"No, Mr. Lord,
            I 'spect twas Eve."

"From this garden
            thou must git!
Earn thy living
            by thy sweat!"

Sinking back into his more typical, mild-mannered demeanor, Paul hunched his shoulders, splayed his feet, and held out his hands, palms up, in an apologetic manner. The accountant in him tallied up the score:

To this tale
            there ain't no more.
Eve got the apple,
            an' Adam got the core.

The men laughed the loudest, in full agreement. Paul bowed in their direction, while the women pretended to huff and puff in protest. "Cross my heart, it's the truth," he retorted. "Just read the Bible."

S E V E N

THE SPICE OF GENDER

God made Adam and then He rested.
But since Adam made Eve, nobody's rested!

—ANONYMOUS

After a round of coffee and trips to the bathroom, the group reassembled by the fire. In contrast to the warmth and conviviality of the gathering, the winter wind howled and circled round the house like a dark, forlorn beast.

Hawk resumed his slouched, long-legged position in the old grandfather chair. Sam relit his briar pipe. Bev and Meggie cast glances at each other. Bev pushed herself off the comfortable couch, where she had been sitting next to the Todd sisters. Meggie replaced her on the couch, her face shining in the glow of the fire's warm shadows. Bev began:

"I was going to tell you all a story from *my* life, but, thanks to Sasha and Savannah, I decided to tell you another story from another time, another place. Call it the historical face of love.

"During World War Two, this country was in a ferment, moving troops to the coasts to ship abroad. In Illinois, a young man by the name of Walter, all of eighteen years of age, received orders to join his company on the West Coast. Now, mind you, he had lived all his life in rural Illinois. He was both excited and terrified. His parents, rural folk, traced their heritage to the hard-working, dour Scots. Proud of their boy, but restrained in their expressions of affection, they drove him up to Chicago to meet the troop train, knowing that it might be the last time they would ever see him."

Bev reached down to the little side table and sipped from her coffee cup. Everyone was quiet. She straightened up and faced the audience once again. "Walter was very proud of his new uniform, and in front of all the other young men, he resisted crying as he said good-bye to his parents. From the train window, he watched his mother waving her arms as his train pulled out from the station. His father stood there, back stiff and unswerving, face stern and grim, his hand lightly touching his wife for comfort. It was as if the last remnants of Walter's childhood faded in the smoke and cinder of the departing train.

"It was a slow journey, days and nights of riding the train, stops for more troops, long patches of countryside that he had never seen before. The view from the window pulled on him. He appraised the landscapes with a farmer's eye, recognizing that the blacktop soil of his father's Illinois farm was probably the best in the country for crops. Each day brought new, intriguing vistas. He stored memories of the passing scenes to describe in long letters to his father. He didn't know then that he was trying to ground himself in North America before departing her shores, as if the images of the land would later serve as lifelines to pull him safely back home from across the sea."

Bev's eyes reflected the intensity of a homesick soldier. She continued. "While crossing the vast stretches of Montana, the troop train came to a halt at a station in the middle of a fierce snowstorm. Luckily, the train station was warm and well lit. The women of the town rallied to bring sandwiches, hot coffee, and doughnuts for the soldiers. Walter took one look at the townspeople who had come out on that stormy night to feed the soldiers and felt right at home, for although they were mainly ranchers, they, too, were country folk making their living off the land. He particularly took notice of a young woman who was serving at the canteen."

Bev flicked back her hair. "Her eyes settled on him, the strong, prominent chin, the proud young face. She offered him a cigarette. It didn't take them long to start talking and sharing their life stories. He found himself sinking into her deep brown eyes. In him, she saw the brave warrior going off to risk his life.

"Her name, Lily, conjured up for him the sweet earth smells of summer days by the fishing stream. His name, Walter, suggested to her a dignity that stretched beyond his eighteen years. They traded addresses so they could correspond—his temporary, hers with the permanence of Montana. They made promises to write."

Bev shook her head sadly, "The storm cleared. The troops re-boarded the train. Walter and Lily said good-bye but not before trading one passionate kiss after an evening of too much coffee, too many smokes, and too little time."

Her face sad, she added, "He didn't write, of course. His world soon became one of dark nights and bloody days in a strange land. Lily? She thought often of him, wondering if he was still alive, that intense young man from Illinois with whom she had shared one kiss. Many soldiers passed through the Montana town on the train line, but no one impressed her as much as Walter. She continued to serve at the canteen, almost expecting to see him step off each train, fresh and eager and not yet contaminated by the horrors of war.

"Born and bred in that Montana town, Lily didn't even think of leaving home. When the war ended, the trains reversed directions, ferrying the weary men back to their points of origin. A bit older, a bit wiser, Lily still welcomed them with hot coffee and ham sandwiches whenever they stopped at her town.

"One night, just when Lily thought that the last troops had disembarked and eaten and that she could clean up the mess, she became aware of a bearded man standing in the corner, staring at her. A second glance told her that it was Walter, come home from the war with Japan. His left arm was in a sling, and she could tell his hand was missing two fingers. But it wasn't sadness or fatigue that was written all over his face. It was joy. For Walter had come back to claim his memory of a stormy night in the middle of Montana where he had met a young woman named Lily.

"Of course, there is much more to this story. Love always has its dramatic beginnings, but I need not tell you anymore. Except to say that the man's full name was Walter Paterson—and that my mother had a name that conjured up the sweet earth smells of a clear Illinois stream."

A collective sigh greeted the end of Bev's story, and both the Todd sisters wiped tears from their faces with strongly perfumed handker-chiefs. Bev sat down, satisfied that she had told the story well and had honored the memory of her parents.

Meggie smiled at her friend. The previous stories Bev had re-counted about her parents carried harsher tones, the devastating ef-fects of alcoholism upon a marriage and an only child named Beverly.

Back to a time of sweet dreams and a lover's promise, Meggie thought.

Meggie stole a glance at Hawk, but he shook his head. He wasn't yet ready. Then Sam Waters stood up, ambled to the fireplace, and, on the inner brick, knocked out the ash from his pipe. He stationed the empty pipe up on the mantle, placed his hands behind his back, and began to stroll back and forth in the shadowlight of the fire. He stopped and turned to the group.

"What an entertaining evening we have had so far, with beautiful song, romantic stories, and astute, biblical wisdom. To which I would like to add my own contribution." He arched his eyebrows and, with a straight face, recited:

> *In the Garden of Eden lay Adam*
> *Complacently stroking his madam,*
> *And loud was his mirth,*
> *For he knew that on earth*
> *There were only two balls—and he had 'em.*

The room exploded in laughter. The Todd twins feigned shocked expressions, though truth to tell, it was known that they had often in-dulged in bawdy tales with their women friends. Sam smiled and wrinkled his eyebrows meaningfully at Bev.

Bev simply could not resist the challenge. She rose to face Sam and answered with a limerick of her own:

A wanton young lady of Wimley,
Reproached for not acting more primly,
Answered, "Heavens above!
I know sex isn't love,
But it's such an attractive facsimile."

"Touché!" Katya shouted, getting into the spirit of things. Sasha screeched, "I've got one! I've got one!"

In Summer, he said she was fair,
In Autumn, her charm was still there:
But he said to his wife
In the Winter of life,
"There's no Spring in your derriere."

"Oh, posh, it's not true and you know it!" Savannah protested. She had to add one of her own:

There was a mature lady of Exeter
So beautiful that men craned their nexeter.
One knave was so brave
As to take out and wave
The distinguishing mark of his sexeter.

Having lost total control of his performance to the enthusiasms of his audience, Sam wrapped it up succinctly:

The limerick packs laughs anatomical
Into space that is quite economical,
But the good ones we've seen
So seldom are clean
And the clean ones so seldom are comical.

Everyone clapped as Sam bowed and took his seat.

Hawk nodded at Meggie, indicating she should go next. It wasn't that he was feeling reticent, just that he didn't know what story to tell. Hawk always liked to let the moment dictate the story he was going to tell, and that moment had not yet arrived.

Meggie stood up. "Looking around this room, I am struck by how many different ethnic traditions we each have. Katya's family came from Poland, Bev's from Scotland, Sasha and Savannah from England, Sam from Wales, Paul from Switzerland, and Hawk from this continent. And, as you all know, if I haven't already told you, I'm Irish-American and proud of it." Meggie gave Hawk a meaningful glance.

"They say that we are the fairest of all people. We never speak well of anyone. Many of you are acquainted with the Irish Blessing which says something about the road rolling out before you. Well, I'm here to tell you that's all sweet frothing and blarney. The *real* Irish Blessing is quite different:

Fer those that lov' us,
May Gawd bless 'em!

Fer those that don't like us,
May Gawd turn their hearts.

Fer those whose hearts will not turn,
May Gawd turn their ankles,
So that we may know 'em by their limpin!"

Meggie smiled wickedly toward Hawk, her words a direct challenge. There were hidden snowballs waiting for him if he wasn't careful.

"Yes!" echoed Bev in this not-so-subtle contest between the sexes.

"That goes for the Polish women as well!" said Katya, nudging Paul on the couch.

Meggie strode over to Hawk and announced, "Your turn. I'll take your chair, if you don't mind." Her eyes danced flirtatiously in the firelight. She offered a hand to help him up off the cushion, the same hand she had used to push him down the hill.

"I can do it myself." He laughed, not trusting her for a moment.

/ / /

At first he had thought to perform a sweet story from the Cherokee tradition, but when Sam took the group's mood into a bawdy direction . . . presto! A story from the Blood Piegan tradition presented itself to him.

Standing before the group, Hawk announced, "I am going to tell you the true story of how men and women came together. It was not as easy as you might think." He snagged their interest.

"Long time ago," he began.

"A very long time ago, the Old Man had finished creating the world and everything was as it should have been, except for one minor detail. He had managed to put all the male human beings in one camp, four days away from the camp of the female human beings. So, while the rest of the world was quite happy making families, the nation of the two-leggeds had no babies.

"The Old Man could see what a terrible mistake he had made. He proposed to go about solving the problem himself. Descending into the camp of the men, he had himself made Chief. Then he said to the men, 'I think, some four days away, there are some very interesting creatures we should meet. I will send out a scout to their camp.'

"The scout traveled four days and four nights before coming across the camp of the female human beings, upon which he spied from a hilltop. What strange and wonderful people they were. The women had tipis made of tanned buffalo hide, beautiful jewelry of bone and quills in their ears and around their necks, and fine clothing. They were also interesting in other ways."

Hawk smiled appreciatively at Meggie, Bev, and Katya. "They had a different shape to them that was most intriguing. The male scout scurried back to the men's camp to report on everything he had seen.

"The female chief, however, picked up the scout's tracks and knew that no woman from her camp had created such large footprints. So, she sent her own scout to follow the tracks four days and four nights to the men's camp, where the scout hid and made her own observations. What unusual creatures. The male human beings had constructed crude shelters of brush and raw, stinking hides. Their outfits were plain and tough. But the men possessed fine weapons, bows and arrows, and a lot of meat drying in the sun.

"They were very interesting in other ways as well." Hawk flexed his biceps while mischievously arching his eyebrows. "Their bodies were strong and muscular, so different in shape from those of the women. The female scout hurried back to the women's camp to tell them what she saw.

"Meanwhile, the Old Man Chief stirred up the men, talking about the women's camp. Finally, they all agreed to go pay the women a visit. Three days out, the female scouts picked up their approach and warned the women, who immediately dressed in their best clothes and lined up to greet these new and fascinating creatures. Oh, what a disappointment. For out of the woods came the men, dirty, grimy, un-washed, with matted hair, and only scant rawhide over their loins.

" 'We don't want to have anything to do with these smelly two-leggeds,' cried out the Old Woman Chief. She picked up a rock and threw it, striking the head of the Old Man Chief. Soon, all the women were throwing rocks at the men, driving them back into the woods." Hawk raised his arm in mock fear and staggered backward.

Katya started giggling.

Hawk continued. "Sore and angry, the men retreated to their camp, vowing to have nothing to do with those hostile two-leggeds. The Old Man huffed, 'Now I know why I put their camp so far away. Females are mean and dangerous creatures. I should never have created them.'

"Meanwhile the Old Woman Chief entertained second thoughts about the matter. 'The men are ignorant,' she told the women, 'and we need to teach them. They just don't know any better. Perhaps, we should stop trying so hard to impress them.' "

Bev smiled.

Hawk shook his head. "The Old Man Chief knew if he didn't think of a solution, the race of human beings was doomed. So, he reluc-tantly suggested that they travel to the women's camp once more. But this time, he dragged all the men to the river first and showed them how to clean up, using sand to scrub their bodies. He instructed them each to pick the best and cleanest outfit to wear. The men headed once again toward the women's camp.

"The women scouts picked up their approach. This time, the women had just completed a buffalo jump, in which they had driven a herd over a large precipice. Now, the women were gutting and skinning the animals and were covered in blood from head to foot. The Old Woman Chief advised her women to receive the men as they were. 'They will appreciate our being dressed like them.'

"But when the men came out of the woods, they were appalled by the sight of the bloody, stinking women with matted hair." Hawk wrinkled his nose in exaggerated distaste.

" 'They are so ugly,' exclaimed the Old Man Chief. 'I am glad I put their camp so far away from ours.' The disgusted men shrank back into the woods.

"The Old Woman Chief snorted, 'It seems that we can't do anything to please them.' But she had to acknowledge that there was something about the men that they needed, and so she persuaded her women to try once again. She had them wash their hair and clean up, put on their best chokers, earrings, and doeskin outfits, and paint their cheeks with red paint. Thus attired, the beautiful women headed out toward the men's camp.

"The Old Man was cross and feeling out of sorts, as were all the other men. 'Why are the women so ugly and mean, coming at us with knives and stones? Why can't they be beautiful, sweet smelling, and good tempered?' "

Hawk grinned mischievously at Meggie.

"A male scout came running into camp and announced, 'The women are coming. Let us get our bows and arrows and drive them away, before they hurt us.'

"But the Old Man Chief ordered the men into the river to wash up and put on their best clothing. 'Paint your faces with the red paint. Put on your best fur outfits. Smudge yourself with cedar smoke and rub your chest and arms and legs with fat.'

"When the women arrived, they came singing." Hawk nodded toward Katya. "The men had never before seen such exquisitely beautiful creatures, and they all fell into a trance of appreciation. 'Let me do the talking,' said the Old Man.

"He approached the Old Woman Chief, appraising her with new eyes, delighted at what he saw. In turn, the women studied the men.

The men's bodies had a kind of raw strength to them that they found most pleasing.

"The Old Man said to the Woman Chief, 'Would you like to go into the woods to talk and try something that has never been done before?'

" 'I like to try new things,' she answered. They left the group.

" 'It would be easier to have this conversation lying down,' the Old Man Chief said. And so the two of them lay down upon the ground and began to talk, and one thing led to another.

" 'This is wonderful,' enthused the Old Man. 'I didn't know that it could be as pleasurable as this.'

" 'Oh,' the Old Woman Chief sighed with delight. 'Why, it's even better than buffalo tongue.' "

Bev and Meggie burst out laughing, Katya blushed, and the Todd twins looked puzzled.

Without a pause, Hawk continued, "And the two of them returned to the camp to tell the others about it, but you know what? All the men had already paired off with all the women and gone into the woods for their own special conversations. When they returned, their eyes were smiling. Their mouths were smiling. Their bodies were smiling.

"And before long, all the women moved into the men's camp. They quilled and decorated the men's clothing. They tanned the deerskin. The men hunted for the meat. There were many special conversations that happened. Then there was love. Then there was happiness. Then there were marriages. Then there were babies.

"Ah hau!"

Everyone applauded the story. Bev couldn't help commenting, "Sometimes men still do stink."

Sam chortled, knocking his pipe against the fireplace, "Sometimes, women still come after us with stones in their words and knives in their eyes."

"Ah hau!" chorused Hawk.

"Don't you dare say a word," Katya warned her husband with a baleful eye.

In laughter and good-natured joking the party began to break up. As the guests reluctantly departed, they thanked Meggie for an entertaining evening. Paul Tubbs especially commented how the stories and humor had soothed his spirit. Bev and Sam Waters departed together, deep in debate. The Todd twins laughed and joshed each other. Katya was anxious to go relieve the babysitter at home. Only Hawk remained behind to help clean up.

"There's another story I want to tell you," he said to Meggie, "before we wash the dishes." He sat down on the couch by the last embered light of the fireplace. "It kept intruding upon my consciousness this evening," he explained. "But I could not share it with the others. For some reason, I do not know why, it is important for me to tell this story to you on your fortieth birthday."

Meggie nestled at the other end of the couch, wrapping her arms around her knees, attentive to the serious expression on Hawk's face.

He began, "A man left his village to go hunting one day, for his people were hungry and starving. It was a time when even the plants did not give nourishment, for there had been a four-year drought. His only weapon was a long wooden lance with a sharp flint edge. There were plenty of tracks, but none of the animals would show themselves to him, because the people had forgotten how to treat their relations with respect. No longer would the animals give their lives to the two-leggeds, so that the two-leggeds might live, because the people had neglected to offer tobacco to the spirits of their kill.

"The man wandered all day. Toward dusk, a great storm blew up over the plains. Dark thunderclouds rolled in, dispelling the sun. Lightning flashed all around him, and the man fell into despair. The sky angrily shook, snaking great bolts of power down into Grandmother Earth, and terrified the hunter. He waited for rain to soften the Grandfather's fury, but no rain came. He flattened himself on the thirsty ground, arms over his head, humbled and afraid.

"The hidden animals laughed at the man's predicament. It served him right, they thought. 'Maybe that will teach the human beings to hunt in respect of the giveaway of the animal and plant nations.' One animal, however, took pity on the two-legged and decided to offer him another chance to fit into the Creation."

Hawk's gaze lifted from the fireplace toward the ceiling.

"When the lightning stopped, the man looked up and was startled by what he saw. Before him stood a giant buffalo, unlike any other buffalo he had ever seen. Attached to the buffalo's hair, a thousand prayer ties—pinches of tobacco tied in red cloth—fluttered in the wind. The buffalo stomped the ground with giant hooves and spoke to the man.

" 'Kill me,' the buffalo ordered.

"But the man refused. He understood that the enormous buffalo was Wakan, sacred. He would not destroy such a magnificent creature.

"Again the buffalo snorted, 'Kill me.'

"The man shook his head.

"The buffalo roared out a third time in frustration, 'Kill me.'

"Once again, the man shook his head, crying out, 'I cannot do this! Do not ask this of me.' The man jammed the shaft of his lance down into the ground, the flint point sticking up toward the sky.

"The buffalo reared high in the air, shaking his massive head, tobacco ties rippling along his sides. Thundering forward, the buffalo reared and impaled himself on the flint point. He fell to the Grandmother, his blood gushing out on the dry and dusty ground.

"With his last breath, the buffalo commanded, 'Take my heart to feed the people. Take my hide to clothe the people. Take my skull to make your altar. Put sage in my nose and eye sockets. Place your Pipes against my horns. Remember the buffalo who came to the people so that the people might live.' And then he closed his eyes forever.

"The man obeyed. He cut out the buffalo's heart. He took the hide. He scraped the skull. And just when he had done his work, the skies opened, and the rain returned to nourish the Grandmother.

"*Mitakuye oyas'in.*"

Meggie was stunned by Hawk's story, touched in places that only Winona had reached with her teachings. Hawk had kept his eyes on her while telling the story. Only once before had she seen him speak this way—when he had conducted the prayer ceremony for the spirit of the dead Winona.

Then she knew.

Hawk, a teller of sacred tales, would become her next medicine teacher. She smiled to herself, thinking, *a second gift from Winona.*

Sitting Over There, Winona grinned and nudged the thought even deeper into Meggie's mind. She complained out loud, "Why do I have to work so hard to get people to see what is right there in front of them?" *If that white psychologist could make the transition to Hawk, then she wouldn't need to pester me so much.* The old medicine woman could feel a slight shift, a loosening of one of the silken threads that had been pulling her backward. Able to relax, Winona sighed. She could wait a long time. To amuse herself and pass the time, she decided that she would continue to keep a close eye on what was happening in the lives of those she had left behind.

A little meddling from time to time wouldn't hurt a thing.

"Tell me, Hawk," said Meggie, hunched over the dishwasher, "was the buffalo story one of the old Lakota myths?" She didn't tell him how the tale continued to resonate deep within her.

He shook his head, paused, and answered, "The Spirits speak to one in many ways. This was a vision given to me, a strong vision, to guide me the rest of my life. This was the first time I have ever shared that vision with others."

"Why now?" she asked, curious.

"Because," he reckoned, "you were ready and you needed to hear it."

E I G H T

PARTY POSTMORTEM

Buffalo gals, won't you come out tonight,
And dance by the light of the moon?

—TRADITIONAL SONG

The clock read a quarter past midnight. The dishes had been cleared, the woodstove banked, and Fritzie let out for his last minute run. Working alongside Meggie in the kitchen, Hawk could feel the sexual tension rising between them, a brew of passion that had simmered all during the fall and boiled over into two New Year kisses. He could no longer deny the heat between them. *White or Indian, maybe it's not so important,* he thought, feeling his brain succumb to the fever of his body.

While avoiding his eyes, Meggie leaned toward him as they stacked bowls by the sink. Tenderly, Hawk reached out and with both hands he cupped the length of her face, noting the flush of her cheeks. Her face, like a baby's skin, spoke to him of the gentleness of an indoor life. With the back of his right hand, he stroked down her cheekbone. She looked up at him and smiled, not breaking the magic of touch with words. With sure movements, Hawk turned her away from him, encircling her from behind with his arms, pulling her back into full contact with his body. His lips found the sensuous curves of her neck and began to nibble.

Meggie felt her body bank into the reassurance of his touch, his arms cradling her, their bodies in sway with each other. She gave into the vulnerability and bent her neck toward his kisses, leaning her head back against his shoulder. She closed her eyes, narrowing her focus into the moment. Hawk's lips began to pull at the strands of her hair, and her breath started catching into little gasps. She reached her hands toward the outline of his waist, the warmth of his shirt.

Hawk whispered into her right ear, "Meggie, if you want me to go home tonight, then I should leave now, before this goes any further." He swallowed hard.

She can decide; it will be a sign for me, he thought, knowing he was rationalizing, not paying attention to the conflicts inside him. His teacher at Pine Ridge, Laughing Bear, had warned him, "You're too much of a mongrel as it is, Hawk, with your mix of Lakota, Cherokee, Apache blood. It's okay to have sex with a white woman, but what ever happens, don't fall in love with one. There's been too much bleaching of our people as it is. Whites and Indians don't belong together."

On the surface, he agreed with his teacher. The traditions, the ways of seeing and being in the world were so very different for the two races. A gap that would be hard to transcend, a difference difficult to translate. Yet, an undertow of fascination continued to pull him closer and closer to Meggie. Her self-confidence, playful competitive spirit, and ability to laugh at herself were qualities he had not encountered in other women he had known. He loved spending time with her— playing, working, teasing each other. She approached their cultural differences not with prejudice but with great curiosity. Her naivete both amused and charmed him.

She can decide for the both of us, he carelessly reckoned.

Meggie turned to face him, studying his eyes, the love in his face, the loneliness of a man far from home. The eyes, black and wide-set under arches of formidable eyebrows, his nostrils flat, the cheekbones high, the set of his jaw strong, his neck solid as his body. Definitely the face of another culture, a face of the Plains people. Across the gulf of two cultures, she felt pulled by web strands that transcended history. Without a word, she reached up and curled her fingers around his broad and dark face and kissed him long and deep, inviting him to stay the night in her embrace.

They were crossing a line in their relationship.

He knew it.

She knew it.

On the night of her fortieth birthday, after two years of postdivorce chastity, after four months of cutting wood, shoveling snow, and working alongside Hawk—Meggie took him to her bed, held him, and brought him homeward in the precultural language of man to woman, woman to man.

After making passionate, quick love, after making slow and lingering love, after making the kind of love that tenderly explores the body familiar, Hawk succumbed to sleep. Meggie kept the watch of the night, her hands stroking the curvature of his back, her fingers trailing his unbound black hair. In deep, abiding wonder, Meggie watched the keep of the night.

A full moon slowly hoisted itself into the black sky. Her bedroom window, facing west and fully twelve feet across, welcomed the still light flooding across the room. Meggie's eyes closed briefly as the moon climbed high and began to descend toward the horizon.

With a jolt, she awoke. From the comfort of the bed, snuggled against Hawk's sleeping body, she peered out into the night sky. There, framed by her window, five full moons arced in a half circle. Rubbing her eyes, trying to dispel the hallucination, she sat up straight and pinched her arm to make sure she was fully conscious. The solidity of the five moons did not waver. Puzzled, she turned toward Hawk whose face was lit by sleeping innocence; she didn't have the heart to rouse him.

Curling up behind his back and wondering at the magic, she let her eyes grow heavy, counting down the moons. She fell once again into a brief nap.

Abruptly, her eyes snapped open. The five moons had vanished. A swollen, full moon had replaced them—its bright, cold surface shimmering with streamers of light undulating on the bedroom floor. The wavy movement of amber light on the floor, doubling and redoubling back onto itself like an astral surf, seethed with lunar life force.

Meggie sat up once again to make sure that she was not trapped inside a dream. Bits of sparkle danced in the moon surf. Meggie remembered what Winona told her about Spirit lights. She reached out momentarily to awaken Hawk, but compassion once again won out over curiosity. He was dead to the world. She stopped her hand right above his shoulder, suspecting that the lunar display was meant for her eyes only.

All night long the moon continued to interrupt her sleep. Her eyes grew tired and heavy with fatigue.

In the morning's early light, Hawk awoke and stretched out to touch the softness of Meggie's cheek. She yawned and blinked at him with droopy eyes. He could see that she was preoccupied. Relaxed and cuddling up beside her, he waited.

Groggy, she spoke of the night's awakenings, of the five moons, of the swollen moon with tidal rivers of light, and of the one moon sinking down toward the western rim. She expected disbelief. She expected curiosity. Instead, he sat up in the bed and asked her to repeat her account of the night. As if made nervous by her descriptions, he reached for her pipe bag and held it out to her.

"I don't understand, Meggie," he began, "why They are doing these things with you, but you need to pay attention." He shook his head. "It must be this pipe that Winona left for you. You better start praying with it. I want you to bring it to the sweat lodge."

"Bring what to the sweat lodge?" she asked, wondering if he meant the pipe.

He seemed to understand her confusion. "Next Friday night, I will pour the waters for the inipi, and I want you to come and pray about what you have seen this night. That is, only if you are not in your moon." He smiled at the unintended pun.

She knew he meant that if she was menstruating she could not participate in the sweat lodge ceremonies, pray with her catlinite pipe, or handle any of the sacred medicine articles. Winona had instructed her in the moon customs in the Native American traditions, the meanings of which she did not yet fully understand but still respected.

"No, I won't be in my moon," Meggie assured him, while wondering what she would discover in the inipi.

Long after Hawk had departed that morning, strands of the night's magic kept weaving in and out of Meggie's thoughts. Honored by the appearance of Spirits, rattled by the paranormal events, intrigued by Hawk's strong response, Meggie didn't know what to make of her nightlong experiences. What would be asked of her during the inipi ceremony? What would be told to her? Was Hawk agreeing to be her teacher? Where was this path into Native American rites taking her? And, most important, where did she want to go?

Meggie laughed at the barrage of questions assaulting her from inside, demanding answers. In this journey, initiated by the meddlesome Winona, Meggie could not see beyond the next bend in the road. But, at least, she was no longer stuck in a rut, in a life empty of sexual passion. New adventures and sacred awe awaited her. She reckoned that the gift of the night was not so much the lovemaking but the visitation of another dimension, an invitation for her to see beyond the veils of current reality into deeper mysteries.

From far away, Winona smiled—knowing that Hawk had been able to come home into the body of his lover. But for Meggie, home was no longer so familiar or comfortable. She was being jarred, awakened by the Spirits. Although the white psychologist didn't know it then, They were teaching her. Although she was not in her moon, They were letting her know that as a woman, the moon was always in her.

It amused Winona to turn back and watch, especially these two people. She approved of their affair but wondered if they could work out their differences. She had to admit that she felt a bit miffed that neither one of them recognized her presence. Only her grandson, Adam, seemed to retain that ability. Yet she was also aware of her growing detachment from the dramas on the Other Side. It was as if the strong passions that had colored her previous life were beginning to fade, leaving behind pale curiosity and an increased impatience for her new life.

2

WIYOHPEYATAKIYA

visions

N I N E

DISCORDANCIES

Before I built a wall I'd ask to know
What I was walling in or walling out,
And to whom I was like to give offense.
Something there is that doesn't love a wall,
That wants it down. . . .

—ROBERT FROST
Mending Wall

With love blossoming in her heart, Meggie vowed to decorate her office with spring flowers. On Monday morning, she decided to drive to the nursery before work. She called Fritzie to come in from his morning rounds, but he didn't respond. "Okay, if you want to stay out in the cold all day, that's your choice," she yelled. Only silence answered. She would have to leave him out for the day.

En route to the nursery, Meggie drove past a large horse farm set back among the rolling hills. A black Arabian stallion cantering the length of the fence caught her eye. With his neck arched and tail flowing in sinuous movement, the horse charged the fence only to pull up at the last moment and gallop back the way he came. Meggie stopped her car by the side of the road. In concentrated bursts of speed, the stallion rushed the fence again.

Surely, he will jump now, she thought, but the horse balked, braked his front legs, pawed the ground in frustration, and took off back along the fence line. Shading her eyes against the winter sun, Meggie glimpsed a brown mare, ears pricked with interest, standing quietly by an open paddock door, watching the stallion.

So, that's what he's all steamed about. Meggie found herself urging him to take the fence. "Come on, you can do it!" she yelled. She knew he had it in him to jump the fence. *If only he knew of the possibility.*

Lunging at the wooden barrier, time and time again, the stallion brought himself up short. The fence had been too long his container.

"You did what?" Lucy asked Hawk.

He grinned sheepishly. "I invited Dr. O'Connor to come sweat with the community next Friday."

"Weren't you the one who told me that you didn't want a lot of white people hanging around the inipi ceremonies?" Lucy always had a blunt way of getting to the truth.

Hawk shrugged his shoulders. Lucy was, of course, correct.

She pulled out a pack of cigarettes and offered him one, but he shook his head. He was trying to quit. Meggie didn't smoke, and it was a dirty habit anyway. His nostrils, however, greedily inhaled the smoke exuding from the tip of Lucy's cigarette. Lucy exhaled a long blue stream, while Hawk consoled himself with another cup of hot coffee.

"A bundle of contradictions, aren't you these days?" Lucy wasn't going to drop the matter.

"One white person isn't going to make that much difference," he parried.

"Ha, that's probably what our ancestors said when they met their first French trapper." Lucy exploded with laughter. "That was before we knew that the whites bred like rabbits."

She abruptly changed the topic, "What did you find out at Pine Ridge? Did you go and visit Mom's people?"

"Well, I saw your uncle and told him the story of her death. But mainly I went there to find out what I should do now, whether to go home or to stay here. I spent some time with Laughing Bear."

"That old fart? How's he doing? What did he say?" Lucy asked, eagerly. Obviously she wanted him to get on with his story.

Hawk, however, liked to pick his words carefully. Words had a way of trapping the truth into molds that made the truth bend to fit the form. To speak less was often to say more. Silence tended to enlarge the possibilities. He could feel Lucy's impatience surging at him. He began, "I went to see Laughing Bear and asked him to be my teacher. He put up an inipi for me so that I could ask the Spirits what to do next."

"And?" Lucy sounded annoyed with his narrative pauses.

"They said I'm to live where I can be of most help to the people. At Pine Ridge, there are a lot of people who already know how to pour the waters for the inipi, who know about healing ceremonies, who know the herbs. Here, in Peshawbestown, there are very few who do the inipi ceremony. I'm to stay here and find a way where I can be the most help to the people." *Could Lucy understand about giving one's own life to the direction of the Spirits?* he wondered.

"The people here are Ojibway and Odawa, not Lakota. They have their own ways of doing things," Lucy chided him.

"Sure they do. I'm not going to force our traditions down their throats. But you know the story of White Buffalo Calf Woman. The Lakota people were given the Pipe by Her and told to take it to the other Indian nations. That's all I'm doing. Anyone around here, no matter their tribe, if they want to learn about the Pipe, then I'll teach them what I know."

"Does that include people from the white tribe, the blacks, and the Asians?" Lucy blew smoke in his direction.

Hawk didn't answer.

Lucy pushed, "What's the difference between you and a Christian missionary trying to convert the 'savages' to your own brand of faith?"

Hawk chuckled, "Amongst us 'savages,' I think there are more similarities than differences in the way we see the Creation, when compared to the Christians. Besides, my 'bros' from other tribal traditions will teach me as much as I teach them."

Lucy leaned forward, "You're not planning to do any of the northwoods shape-shifting stuff?" Her voice carried a warning, a caution. As much as it all seemed like magic and fantasy to her, a part of Lucy was still scared stiff by the practices of some of the Ojibway and Odawa traditionals.

"Now, who is a bundle of contradictions? I thought you didn't believe in any of this?" Hawk smiled.

Again, Lucy changed the topic to more pragmatic matters. "But how will you live and make money here? You know, it's not like the old days when the people would take care of their medicine man. You can't just sit around seeking visions and chanting the prayer songs." Both knew his part-time jobs as a handyman weren't enough to sustain him over a long period.

He shrugged his shoulders. "Somehow," he reassured her, "a way will be found."

Incredulous, Lucy shook her head. "You think the Spirits are going to take care of that for you? Sometimes, Hawk, I think you've got your head in the clouds. I can see that I need to do some exploring for you. Do you have a résumé?"

He shook his head.

"Never mind," she said, "I'll help you with that too."

Hawk had the distinct impression that his cousin was about to organize his life. She left his trailer, muttering, "Men. Sometimes they're so helpless . . ."

Hawk didn't tell Lucy of the disturbing conversation with Laughing Bear about his growing involvement with a white woman. Laughing Bear had sternly lectured him, "It's okay if you want to have fun with her, but don't go falling in love with her. It's hard enough to have a mixed marriage, but you, Hawk, are walking the Pipe road, the medicine path. You can't mix white and Indian. She is outside our traditions. It would be too hard for you. It would be too difficult for her. She will pull you off the path. When you try to stand in two canoes the river's currents will pull you apart."

"He did what?" exclaimed Bev, curious about the immediate aftermath of Saturday's party.

Meggie felt sheepish in repeating herself. "He stayed over for the night." She finished positioning the hothouse flowers in her office.

Clustered like a family of attentive children with big ears, the yellow daffodils on her windowsill mimicked Bev's posture of curiosity.

"In what capacity?" Bev inquired, hands upon her hips.

Guile had never been one of Meggie's strong points. She turned from the flowers to her friend, answering, "As a lover."

Over Bev's shoulder, a single red rose perched in a vase by the office couch, its blood red petals unfolding in sacrifice. By the window, the cluster of bright yellow daffodils stretched out their trumpets to proclaim the sun. Meggie had positioned the flowers at opposite ends of the room intentionally. One flower alone, the others in congregation.

Bev shook her head in concern, "Oh, Meggie, I hope you know what you are doing! I mean, it's wonderful that you have finally found a man worth loving, but . . ."

"But what?" answered Meggie, undaunted in her cheerfulness.

"He's so different from you. I mean, you're white, Irish-American. And he's not."

"So what?" Meggie asked.

"Well, racial differences are important. I know that's not the politically correct thing to say, but it's true, Meggie. How is your family going to react? What will his people say? The Lakota have their own language, their own way of looking at the world. Every culture has its own peculiar expectations for a man and a woman. How are you going to fit into his world or he into your world? You can't be color-blind to those differences between you."

"So, he's dark. I'm fair. Is that a problem?" Meggie looked amused. "I would hope that we could somehow adopt the best of both worlds."

"Meggie," Bev protested, "he's an introvert; you're an extrovert. He's the quiet type, stays in the background, doesn't say much. You, on the other hand, love to talk."

"Sounds to me like there's a good balance between us," Meggie grinned, pulling a perky daffodil out of the vase and donating it to Bev, a peace offering.

But Bev hadn't yet finished. If race and personality arguments were insufficient, there were the obvious class differences. The daffodil trembled in her right hand. "You have a Ph.D. and are full of intellectual interests. He has only a high school education. His interests are . . ." She had to think, not knowing him too well. ". . . his pick-up, animals, and hunting. And telling wild stories."

Meggie's mind protested *No, No, No,* but she kept her thoughts to herself. Bev only knew Hawk as he had presented himself at the party. She did not know him as a teacher with the people. She did not know the contentment that had wrapped around Meggie, like a warm blanket, after a night of Hawk's loving.

Bev shrugged. She recognized the signs of love sickness washing over her friend—the newly bought flowers decorating her office, the smile of secret passion, the satisfaction found in connection. It would do no good to warn her of the obvious right now. Having lost her last lover, Bev knew that the path of romantic intentions was full of careless hope and hidden snares. Meggie would have to discover the booby traps on her own.

All day long, clients marched into Meggie's office confused and disoriented by the mazes of love: a forty-eight-year-old woman with breast cancer and an uninterested husband; a thirteen-year-old girl who had sacrificed her virginity to feel special to someone; a six-year-old boy mourning the death of his father and the grief of his mother; a twenty-two-year-old college student failing his classes on account of his passion for marijuana. All day long, her clients sought to find the shortest route to their own hearts.

"I was enticed up here to the northern woods by my husband with the promise that we would live by the water," her new client, Andrea, began. "I grew up around the warmth of the Chesapeake Bay. This area can never become home to me. God Almighty, the poor people up here don't even know the meaning of springtime. Barely has the last snow melted before it's summer and tourists are clogging the streets."

Andrea looked wistfully out the window of the Suttons Bay office toward the lake, the water a steely gray topped by unfriendly, choppy waves. "I know you want to know more about my husband," she announced. "Everyone does."

Meggie folded her hands in her lap and answered, "You will tell me whatever you need to tell me."

"Everyone loves him. He's got charisma—a soft, gentle smile that draws people to him like flies to honey. There's a tender, vulnerable, boyish quality to his eyes, a timbre of compassion to his voice, and an ability to make you think at the moment that you are the most important person in the whole world. Everyone loves him."

"Do you?" Meggie couldn't discern whether her client was being admiring or cynical.

Andrea looked out the window, measuring the landscape with her eye, reducing it to a series of harsh lines and cold colors.

"I no longer know." Her face softened into the fine lines of sadness. "There was a time, when we were first married, I could paint with the whole spectrum of the rainbow. The sun glinted golden speckles on the water's surface; the dunes glowed with heat; the clouds at sunset washed pinks and oranges across a pastel sky; the Lake possessed mysterious gradations of blues and greens. But look out your window there, see how the blue has deadened to gray? The Lake has locked away its treasures for the winter." She momentarily closed her eyelids as she clenched her teeth, causing grim lines to spider around her mouth.

Her anger has compressed into mute depression, Meggie thought.

"Does he know what you are feeling?" she asked.

"Heavens no," Andrea answered, her eyes widening in alarm. "I won't give him the satisfaction." She paused and laughed bitterly, "It's an entirely civilized relationship."

No compassion for herself. Thus, no compassion for him, Meggie noted.

"And if you did share your feelings with him, what would happen?"

"He would love it. He would use my anger to dig a mound of manure in which to wallow. It would confirm his essential midwestern sense of guilt." She paused. "But I don't express the anger. I keep it safely locked up inside of me."

"What would happen if you unlocked that anger?" Meggie pushed her.

"Why, then, I guess I would wait until he was asleep, take a knife, plunge down through his heart, and yank it from its roots. I would set the quivering organ upon a piece of driftwood and push it way out into the Lake, so it could never find its way back home again. That's what I would do."

Meggie's mouth went dry as she took note of Andrea's murderous smile. "How close are you to killing him?"

Andrea understood her concern, "I've put you at a disadvantage, haven't I? You don't know my last name, Dr. O'Connor. You don't know where I live. I tell you I am equally likely to kill myself or kill my husband. I realize that is not fair of me. What do you need?"

"An agreement between us," Meggie answered.

"What kind of agreement?"

"That you won't kill yourself or him. Otherwise, I will have to contact authorities to hospitalize you. I also have a duty to warn him of any imminent danger."

"But you don't know who he is, do you? I want to keep it that way. If I were to let go of my options of exit, I would be condemning myself to a perpetual prison, walls so high that I'd never witness the light of day. I can't give up that choice of life or death. And if you put me in a hospital, I can put on a mask with the best of them, be cheery and gay. The doctors wouldn't hear a peep out of me about wanting to kill myself or him." A slight smile curled up on the side of the mouth. She blinked at Meggie as if to say "checkmate."

"Here's my dilemma," Meggie began, hunching forward in her chair, "If you are always on the verge of either suicide or homicide, then I must tiptoe, compromise myself around you in the therapy process, just as you do around your husband. Otherwise, I might say something that will set you off. I would like to be as open and honest with you as you are with me."

A disarming argument, only Meggie wasn't sure that her new client would buy it.

Andrea thought a moment and replied. "Okay, I will make you a promise. I will not kill myself or kill my husband as long as I am a client in therapy with you. Is that acceptable to you?"

She's giving me time. It's the best she can do. Meggie nodded her head, "Agreed." She reached out and shook on it, noting how cold her client's hand felt.

The image of the stallion charging the wooden fence and braking at the barrier galloped across Meggie's imagination as a metaphor for Andrea's emotional constraint and sense of desperation.

Arriving home after her afternoon sessions, Meggie anxiously called out for Fritzie, but her fox terrier did not respond. It was unlike him to be gone so long. After dinner, and several times during the evening, she opened the door and shouted into the black night. She could hear the ghostly hoot of the barred owl down by the apple orchard, deer snapping twigs as they glided through the woods, the raucous screeching of raccoons scrapping over a morsel, but not a sound from her old friend. She set the alarm clock for an early morning search. Images of his fur being caught on an old barbed-wire fence or worse—his being crippled—haunted her dreams.

She heard him yap, not so much with pain but with frustration. The barking grew insistent. Opening her eyes, she realized that the noise was not solely in her imagination. Jumping out of bed, Meggie tore down the stairs, and there, pawing grimy streaks on the kitchen door, like a dirty ragamuffin, was Fritzie, demanding to be let into the house. She opened both the door and her arms to the dog, despite the slimy smell and the dried, caked mud on his white coat.

"Fritzie," she scolded, picking him up, "where have you been?" Obviously spent, he responded to Meggie's chastisement by sloppily licking her nose and mouth. She hugged him tightly, happy her old companion had finally come home.

Exhausted from his amorous adventures, all Fritzie wanted was to drink a bowlful of water and topple into bed. On his earlier morning travels to mark the bushes, he had encountered a mud-caked black female dog on the hillside. She sat down on thin haunches and wiggled three steps toward him as he stiff-leggedly angled over toward her, thrusting his nose under her tail to make acquaintance. She rolled over onto her back. She nipped him on the ear. Ignoring the invitation to play, he positioned himself behind her and tried to mount her. But she simply tucked in her tail and squatted. Scrambling out from under Fritzie's weight, she wheeled and danced about him, snapping at his front legs, beckoning him to give chase.

Half-crazed by lust, half-driven by her exuberance, Fritzie pursued the little female deep into the woods. All day long, his futile efforts to mount the little black dog ended with her playful collapse and his humping the air in driven desperation. He chased her in circles around trees and bushes, up and down dunes, in and out of fields and woods. She enticed him beyond the familiar perimeters. He marked their passage until there was no more pee in his bladder, and still he hoisted his leg at every fourth tree. They trotted past farms of sleeping cows and cherry trees, brick and wooden churches, stubbled meadows and unpaved roads; and always the trees beckoned them into deeper shadows.

Perhaps it had been the sun slipping down, perhaps it had been hunger and time for supper, perhaps it was simply exhaustion when Fritzie stopped and would go no farther. The traveling dog turned around, ran back toward him, and nosed him to move forward on her journey into strange territory. But familiar places tugged at Fritzie's heart. He backed away from the nuzzling of the female dog, his eyes telling her that he had gone as far as he would go. She must travel on alone. He didn't know where she was headed. Perhaps there was a human being expecting her at the end of the trail. Perhaps not.

It was time for him to go home. His human being was waiting for him.

❖ ❖ ❖ ❖

The strands that bound Winona to her old home continued to slowly give way, sometimes with a definite snap, sometimes with an easing, as if a strand simply dissolved from both ends in the acidity of time. From her stationary place, she kept a watchful eye, expecting her deceased husband, Davis, or someone she knew to arrive and unhitch her completely from her past existence.

Back There, time moved ahead. Over in the new world, time seemed to flow in all directions.

And she waited . . .

T E N

THE INIPI

I am both sides now;
I offer the pipe but know beforehand
how few will take it.

—LOREN EISELEY
Men Have Chosen the Ice

On Tuesday night, Hawk arrived at Chrysalis to eat a late dinner with Meggie. He didn't go home. Neither he nor Meggie had anything scheduled for Wednesday morning. If it weren't for Fritzie, Hawk and Meggie might have slept late into the morning. But as Hawk lay drifting in and out of brief dreams in the double bed, it slowly dawned on him that a pair of dark eyes were staring at him, a pair of front paws were pressing down upon the mattress edge, and from two rows of canine teeth issued forth the foul breath of dead fish and dried kibbles.

Hawk blinked.

Fritzie flicked an ear and shoved a wet nose into Hawk's face.

They were reaching a mutual understanding: It was time to get up.

Hawk scrambled around in the kitchen, finding and spilling the coffee beans, grinding them, filling up Fritzie's food and water bowls, affixing the coffee filter and percolating the dark brew, and finally carrying two coffee mugs upstairs on a tray. Meggie was just beginning to open her eyes. She pulled up the sheet to cover her nakedness.

Seeing the mugs, she exclaimed, "Oh, God's gift to a woman."

"Meaning me or the coffee?" he asked. He handed her a mug before climbing back into the warm bed.

"Last night . . ." She wiped the grit from her eyelids.

"Yes?"

". . . was truly wonderful," she sighed.

He nodded in agreement.

"But," she added, "I feel kind of shy this morning. Delighted and a bit scared."

"Of what?" He had put down his coffee cup and was now playing with a lock of her hair.

"How well do we know each other, Hawk?" She twisted around in the bed to face him, securing the sheet to her body with her elbows.

"A lot better than we did five days ago," he grinned.

"Well, there is still a lot about you that I don't know, that I don't understand. I want to get to know you better, Hawk. In the daytime as well as in the night." Meggie tried to maintain a serious conversational tone.

Only Hawk was spider-walking his fingers down the sheet on her near shoulder, under her breast and over her belly. "I want to get to know you a whole lot better too, Meggie. All parts of you."

She set her mug down on the night table. Teasing, she pushed at his fingers only to find them wrapping around her hand. "I really mean what I say," she laughed.

"Of course you do." He pinned her wrists playfully to the bed and slowly eased his body onto hers.

They were reaching a mutual understanding: to table the serious conversation until later.

After breakfast, Hawk told her he was free to do her bidding that day, until she had to leave for her afternoon psychotherapy appointments. "I am at your service," he bowed.

"I could use your help. I want you to make a loaf of nut bread," she replied. "It's my great-grandmother's recipe."

Meggie pulled out an old three-by-five note card on which was pen-
ciled the ingredients:

3 cups flour
1 cup sugar
2 tsp baking powder
1 tsp salt
1 egg
1 cup milk
1 cup broken walnuts
Let rise 60 minutes in well-greased pan. Bake at 300 for 50–60 min-
utes. Slice, toast, and slather with butter.

"Here," Meggie said, pulling out the canisters, measuring cups and
spoons, mixing and chopping bowls, baking powder, walnuts, and a
loaf pan.

"What about you?" He looked skeptically at her.

"Oh, I'm going to make a vegetable soup, and you can help me
there too. That is, when you're done with the bread." Out of the corner
of her eye, while chopping vegetables, Meggie watched Hawk attempt
to make sense of the simple recipe.

"I just dump it all in the big mixing bowl, right?" he asked.

She nodded and sliced away at the long carrots.

Three times he scooped the measuring cup deep into the flour can-
ister, not bothering to level off the peaks. A white granular mist drifted
up, finely coating his face and front with flour after he dumped the
cuploads into the bowl.

Meggie offered no advice as she washed the celery stalks in the
sink.

Hawk added the remaining ingredients and stirred the concoction
with a wooden spoon. Meggie could hear him breathe hard as he
muscled the mixture round and round the bowl.

Retrieving some leftover chicken in herb garlic sauce from the refrigerator, Meggie cut it up and threw it all into the soup pot with the
cut carrots and sliced celery. She added a large can of chicken broth
and a bag of frozen vegetables.

With his hands Hawk broke up the walnuts and, without measur-

ing, he threw about a cup and a half of them into the dough. Hard as
he stirred, the dough began to seize up like concrete. He slapped at it
twice with the spoon. He looked suspiciously at Meggie who was
cracking up in the corner. "What's wrong with it?" he asked, putting
his hands on his hips.

"You didn't measure your dry ingredients correctly. Add more milk,
but do it slowly, until you get it to the right consistency."

He grabbed the carton of milk and drowned the rigid ball of dough
in the liquid. "There," he exclaimed, "that should soften it up some."
He began to slosh the milk, trying to work it into the dough. Tiny
sprinkles of milk splattered upon the mask of flour dust on his face.

Meggie couldn't refrain from commenting, "Even in baking bread,
one must pay attention."

Hawk cut his eyes at her, remembering the story of how the four
races came into being when the first man and the first woman did not
pay attention to the recipe. With a much larger batch of dough than
was originally intended, he maneuvered the gloppy mixture into a
bread pan to rise an hour before baking. "Is there anything else you'd
like me to do?"

She knew he was hoping that the next task would not be of a culi-
nary nature.

"Oh, yes," she replied. "I want you to chop up these three large
onions . . ."

Over a lunch of toasted nut bread and fresh vegetable soup, Meggie
and Hawk resumed their morning conversation.

"We have to give love the time and space to grow," Meggie cautioned. She didn't know whether her words were meant more for him
or for herself.

This time Hawk didn't try to distract her with his flirtations or humor. Nor did he point out the contradiction with her earlier words of
wanting to get to know him better.

"Okay," he said, "we'll take all the time we need to see if what happens is good for the both of us. I'll give you a break until Friday." Friday morning he would come and stack wood in the shed. Friday
evening he would conduct the sweat lodge ceremonies.

Meggie's head nodded, thinking, *Love is a garden that needs time to bloom.*

But Meggie's heart argued, *Life is too short to postpone love for even a minute.*

Heedful of Laughing Bear's warning, Hawk's head also argued with his heart. Having Meggie come to the inipi ceremony was a step in the wrong direction, according to everyone he knew in the Native American world. Except Winona—she'd probably approve that he was following his heart instead of his head. Love has its own logic, she would say. Yet Hawk was deeply aware of the years of strong prejudice of the native people against the whites, and with good reason. *It wasn't so long ago that, in the fancy name of assimilation and termination of the reservations, the whites practiced cultural genocide on my people,* he reflected.

It would be easier not to ask her.

But the Spirits were working on her, he knew. That night of the moons was no accident. And then there was Winona's lightning pipe, pulling the energies toward Meggie. She would have no idea that what was happening to her was probably due to the presence of that chanunpa in the house.

There were many things that Meggie did not know.

Hawk found himself feeling protective toward her. Sometimes the Spirits had their own agenda, and it could be pretty tough on the human being. If he couldn't help her in some way understand what all this meant, then what business did he have in becoming a medicine teacher?

So, it is a good thing, he rationalized, that he had invited her to come to the inipi ceremony. He would have the women keep the door for the men's sweat lodge ceremony. By eavesdropping on the men's inipi, Meggie could learn about the structure of the ceremony and not be so frightened when it was her turn to sweat.

Friday evening, an intertribal community of Native Americans living in the Traverse City area—Ojibway, Odawa, Menominee, Cree, and Sioux—began to gather around the fire pit and sweat lodge area set behind the Abres' house. Everyone turned as Meggie's red car pulled up into the driveway. From the trunk of her car, Meggie gathered her belongings, piling towels high atop a bag of groceries and juggling her cumbersome load into Lucy's house. Hawk's heart skipped a beat at seeing her; he wanted to go wrap his arms around her and welcome her, but he felt constrained among his Native American friends. She emerged from the house and greeted him with a hug. *She doesn't know any better,* he thought.

Why is he stiff and distant? she wondered. She handed him a pouch of tobacco. Winona had taught her that tobacco was the sacred plant which the two-leggeds could cultivate and give as a gift to the Spirits.

"Good," he said to her. *She knows more than I thought she did.*

Dusk started pleating the corners of the sky, gathering in the quilt of darkness. As others from the community arrived and moved about collecting wood and stones for the fire, Hawk taught Meggie about the Spirit path, the fire making, the way to handle the Sacred Pipes, and the general structure of the ceremony. She was attentive, curious.

As the sun died slowly and the time approached to light the fire, Hawk marveled at the transformation in himself. With the rising of the moon emerged the authoritarian role of teacher. It was not a premeditated change. As he opened himself to the world of the Four Grandfathers and the Spirits, the personal anchors of identity gave way. He no longer really mattered to himself. The teachings that flooded into him filled up the void created by the emptying of the self, and the truth made him uncharacteristically assertive.

Baffled by Hawk's formality, Meggie put her feelings on hold. She quickly made introductions with the other men and women, noting that she was the only white person there. They kept a cool distance. *Is it the color of my skin? Is it because I am new and they don't know me?*

Lucy, however, greeted Meggie warmly and offered her a cup of coffee. The two women had come to know each other from Winona's sessions with Meggie. Lucy didn't seem to hold it against Meggie that the therapy hadn't worked and that her mother had chosen to die. *Neither one of us,* Meggie reflected, *was successful in persuading Winona to stay.*

Meggie watched the affectionate interchanges between Lucy and Hawk, even though Lucy had refused to adopt the old ways of her mother and cousin. *I wonder if Lucy can forgive a religion that gave her mother choice about life and death.*

In her teachings to Meggie, Winona had compared the physical structure of the sweat lodge to a pregnant buffalo. The lodge was round and squat with wooden ribs poking spindly shapes through the hide of forty worn blankets and a weathered skin of tarpaulin. Hawk urged Meggie to peek inside the lodge. She saw an inverted nest of crisscrossed saplings rooted into the sandy earth, their tops interlaced to a perfect diamond in the center. Meggie, no geometrician, estimated the diameter of the lodge floor to be no larger than six feet and the ceiling no higher than four feet. Surrounding a small central pit for stones, irregular carpet pieces sparsely covered the ground.

Hawk pointed to the gray rocks being heaped up on a foundation of wood in the fire pit. "Those rocks," he explained, "will turn red hot in the fire. They will then enter into the sweat lodge and settle in the center. But don't think of Them as just rocks to warm us on a cold night. They are Inyan, the Stone People, and this is Their lodge. They are my teachers. They will be your teachers. They will sing to you. They will show you visions. They will give up Their lives for you. Pay attention to Them when you are in the inipi."

Perched atop a small hillock before the lodge, a buffalo skull stared eastward, sticks of frayed sage protruding from the empty eye sockets and nose bone. Meggie recalled the story of the dying buffalo from the night of her birthday party. Hawk told her the hillock was created from the dirt of the sweat lodge pit; the skull served as the altar for the Sacred Pipes. "See the line running from the skull to the fire? That line is the Spirit path. Don't cross over it. Walk around it in respect."

The young men, who had been building the fire, placed forty-eight large rocks on a foundation of small logs and surrounded the base with sticks and split wood. They indicated to Hawk that it was time to light the fire. Opening up a pouch, he grabbed a fistful of tobacco, held it high toward the sky, circled it with a gentle motion in the air, and sprinkled it onto the wood. "I ask you, Grandfathers and Grand-mother, to give us good inipi ceremonies. I pray that no one be hurt in the sweat lodge. *Mitakuye oyas'in.*"

He knelt down on the frozen ground. Holding a match high, he prayed, "I ask you, the Lightning Powers, to come and make this fire burn brightly, so that we can do this thing. We are just two-leggeds and need your help. Hau! *Mitakuye oyas'in.*"

Carefully he struck the match and placed it against a small pile of wood shavings at the western edge of the fire. A burst of yellow flame kindled the twigs. Like a supplicant, Hawk bowed his face to the ground, and with small pieces of bark he urged the flames to grow and spread around the base. From such pitiful beginnings the fire gathered onto itself and crackled its ascent along small logs. Hawk sat back. The young men sighed with relief; the fire was lit.

Pushing himself up off the ground, Hawk felt the stiffness in his knee joints. He knew the cold would aggravate the limp he had earned from an old injury; before the evening was over, his hip would be aching from sitting hours in the cramped sweat lodge. It was al-ways physically hard on him to pour the waters for two consecutive inipi ceremonies, but no one else in the community was at the stage of learning where they could replace him. He took a twig of sage and placed a leaf under his tongue to distract him from the pain.

He asked the women to show Meggie how to make prayer ties with squares of red cloth, tobacco, and string. Taking the empty coffee mug back to Lucy's well-lit house, Hawk sought the relief of aspirin and another warm cup of coffee. Although Lucy was willing to have the community use her house as a base for operations, she had chosen to abstain from the old ways of her mother. Instead, she tended to the stove in the house and found some moments of privacy from all the hubbub. Hawk cherished both the generosity and stubbornness in her spirit. *She is more like Winona than she suspects,* he mused.

Off to the side of the fire, old stumps and rusted mesh chairs served as the staging ground for the tobacco-tie lesson. Sweet-Grass Woman showed Meggie how to sprinkle the tobacco into red cloth squares and tie it off with four knots, creating a short line of sixteen ties. Instinctively, Meggie found herself liking the young Ojibway woman who was sure in the movement of her hands. It reminded her of elementary school days when she would create a cat's cradle out of twine and twiddling fingers.

When Hawk returned, the women were almost finished with their tobacco ties. The men set three dark, sturdy, army-issue blankets and a six-pointed-star quilt over the opening of the sweat lodge. Tobacco ties in hand, Meggie strolled over to where Hawk bent peering into the lodge. She remembered Winona disparaging white people for asking too many questions and not paying attention, but she found herself full of curiosity. "The colors of the star quilt are of the four directions, aren't they?"

Hawk shook his head, saying, "Don't call Them the four directions. That's the white way. They are the Grandfathers. Over there," he pointed westward, "over there is Wiyohpeyata. He, of the Black Face, is watching, and it is from Him the visions come. There is a Grandmother there too. She stands beside Him."

Hawk pivoted to the right and pointed north, lecturing, "There, Meggie, when you are sick in your body, or full of angry, destructive thoughts, or when wounded in your soul, you can call out to Waziya and ask for purification and healing. He, of the Red Face, will listen to your prayers." He wanted her to learn and share this part of his life with him.

"And look now," Hawk added, his finger angling to the east, "when you have family troubles and are needing to know of things through an inner wisdom, Wiyohiyanpa is there to help you. It is the Yellow-Faced One who speaks through the heart."

Hawk touched Meggie's arm to orient her to the south, "There, Meggie, ask Itokaga to help you see things with the eye of a child, to know the wonder and delight at the freshness of the world. Because it is from Him, with the White Face of the noonday sun, we begin our earth walk and it is to Him we return."

He paused in his teaching, "So don't call Them 'the four directions.' They are not compass points or places on a map. They are the Grand-fathers."

Meggie looked up into the dark sky devoid of stars and moon and felt her cheeks redden with embarrassment. She knew Hawk was not chastising her but rather teaching her, yet she found herself hungering for the softer notes of a lover. She retreated to the other side of the fire and thought, *How am I ever going to keep the lover and teacher apart in my mind?*

He felt her withdrawal from him. The lover in him wanted to cry out, *Stay close to me.* The teacher in him answered, *It is the ceremony that is important here.*

Out of the shadows, two silhouettes gathered substance; Larry, Lucy's husband, strode into the fire circle. His long black hair, un-bound, flared off powerful shoulders. Adam, his young son, cavorted around him, obviously happy to be near his father. Larry nodded to the men and to Meggie. The eyes of Sweet-Grass Woman glistened in the dancing firelight, as they tracked Larry's approach toward Hawk.

In the cold and unforgiving night air, surrounded by the black fingers of leafless trees grasping at the light of the crackling fire, Meggie felt the layers of civilization strip away. Preparing herself to ascend into the realm of the sacred, she instead found herself slipping down into reflections on the two strong, self-confident men, Larry and Hawk. *When it comes to muscles or wisdom, what does a woman want?*

Meggie shook her head. *Why am I having these thoughts now, when I'm getting ready for a mystical experience?*

As the fire banked into hot red coals, the shadows of stark winter trees stretched out to diminish the light. The mood grew quiet; the stones glowed an incandescent red. Kneeling on the cold ground and facing west, Hawk unwrapped his medicine bundle, lit a small ball of sage, and smudged the bundle, its contents, and himself with the smoke. He assembled the Pipe and began his prayer to the Grandfathers and the Grandmother. Into the pipe bowl he placed smidgens of tobacco, akin to the ritual of the tobacco ties. Everyone kept silent out of respect for the filling of the Chanunpa Wakan. In the glow of the hot fire, Meggie felt her heart melting toward Hawk, the force of his person harnessed by the reverence for the Pipe. *How strong he looks. He handles the Pipe with awe.*

Plugging his Pipe with sage, Hawk placed it against a horn of the buffalo altar, the bowl touching Grandmother Earth and leaning on a tamper stuck in the ground.

Piercing the cold night air, an eagle-bone whistle announced the men's inípi ceremony. Six times Hawk blew on it, summoning the Grandfathers. With his eagle-wing fan, Hawk swept the air before him into the lodge, praying again that the Grandfathers would give them a healing ceremony, that no one would get hurt in the process. Sweet-Grass Woman nudged Meggie and softly whispered, "It gets very hot in there, almost two hundred degrees."

Bending down and following Hawk's example, the shivering men, bare-chested and otherwise attired in towels, piled into the cold lodge exclaiming, *"Mitakuye oyas'in."* Hawk positioned himself to the right of the door and had Larry sit in the honor seat to the left of the door. Adam snuggled next to his father. The men draped their tobacco ties over the sapling rafters. Sweet-Grass Woman asked Meggie to help her keep the door, while the other women accompanied Lucy inside the house to prepare the feast.

Hawk barked out a command to Sweet-Grass Woman to pass in the deer antlers to handle the hot rocks, sweet grass to smudge the inside of the lodge, fragrant cedar to entice the Spirits, sage sprigs to drive out evil, and tobacco for an offering. Meggie noted that the Ojibway woman seemed to anticipate what Hawk needed.

Why do I feel jealous? Meggie wondered. Meggie didn't like being the outsider who knew almost nothing about the ceremonies. She chided herself for her impatience, remembering Winona's description of whites as a people who were always rushing to knowledge without having struggled with the questions. Over and over, Winona had cautioned her, "Pay attention."

What was she doing, standing out in the cold, trying to enter into another people's ceremonies? Meggie knew the answer to that question was greater than either Winona's words or Hawk's magnetism. Truth to tell, it was the Pipe that had brought her there, and she didn't know where the Chanunpa Wakan was leading her. *Pay attention,* she reminded herself. *There may come a time when you will stop and go no farther.*

Hawk busied himself in preparation for the heated stones. He checked with the young boy to make sure he was ready for the ceremony. He called out to the two women, telling them to sit on the ground, after they had lowered the door, and put their ears against the lodge to eavesdrop on the men's ceremony.

"*Inyan!*" he ordered. Sweet-Grass Woman took herself over to the fire pit, grabbed a pitchfork, shoved aside the charred wood, hefted a red hot rock onto the metal tines, and blew off the embers and debris. One by one, she carried the rocks over to the sweat lodge. Carefully, she lowered the pitchfork into the dark opening of the lodge, holding it still so that Hawk, deer antler in each hand, could position each stone into the center pit. Following the placement of the first seven foundation stones, the men broke the silence with expressions of appreciation for the heat of the Stone People. They all laughed nervously when one large rock threatened to roll off the pitchfork into the lap of one of the men.

As the heat of the fire scorched her, Sweet-Grass Woman's eyes began to water and her feet to dance. She shook her head when Meggie offered to relieve her. Finally, she lifted up the twenty-fourth stone, a huge glowing rock that strained every muscle on her slim frame to haul it to the lodge. That stone brought great exclamations from the men, part welcome, part awe. It was going to be a *very* hot sweat; in the chilly night air, Meggie could feel the heat emanate in waves from inside the lodge. Ribbons of air undulated at the door, where the extremes of temperatures clashed. Fragrances of sage, cedar, sweet grass, tobacco, and warming earth saturated the lodge.

Hawk threw out the antlers, a braid of sweet grass, the bag of cedar, and the pouch of tobacco. Sweet-Grass Woman gathered them up and stowed them by the buffalo altar, to be used again for the women's ceremony. She signaled Meggie to take the pitchfork and center the remaining twenty-four stones, to pile wood on them so that the fire would burn brightly.

"Mni!" ordered Hawk. The woman handed in a large metal bucket filled with cold water and a dipper. From her vantage point at the fire, Meggie could see both Larry and Hawk touching the bucket to the stones, before placing it in front of Hawk on a bed of sage leaves. Filling the dipper, Hawk played with the sound of the water falling onto water, as if to entice the men with the cool liquid before they were to be closed up into the intense womb of heat. He asked the men if they were ready; they grunted assent.

"Lower the door," he commanded. On opposite sides of the door frame, Sweet-Grass Woman and Meggie unpeeled the layers of blankets, dropping them, one by one, and tightly stamping them in at ground level. Someone cried out that there was a crack of light near Larry. The Ojibway woman rearranged the blankets near him until a muted voice called out, "That's good. No light now."

Meggie perched on a small remnant of blanket spilling over onto the frozen ground. Sweet-Grass Woman wandered over to the blazing fire and lit a cigarette. Meggie wanted to go over and thank her for her instructions around the doorkeeping, only she didn't want to miss any of the action in the men's sweat. It occurred to her that her survival in the upcoming women's ceremony might depend on acquiring as much information as possible.

Her spot on the ground was opposite Larry; she could feel the outline of his back as she shouldered her body into the warming layers of the lodge skin. Meggie remembered how infatuated she had felt when she first met Larry in the fall, erroneously thinking him to be single and Winona's cousin. The stirring of her attraction toward Larry had been dampened by the discovery that Lucy was his wife. Meggie had a rule for herself—she would never get involved with a married man. She could not tolerate the idea of betraying another woman. Leaning against each other, outside to inside, inside to outside, was now the closest she would allow herself to get to Larry. Burying her cold nose into the tarp, Meggie could barely make out Hawk's muffled words to the men.

The rocks radiated heat onto him, their color in the lodge shimmering from white to red, illuminating the feet of the men. Hawk felt excited, as he did at the beginning of each inipi. Entering into the womb of the Grandmother, the glowing heat, the popping sounds and the dank smells of the ground thawing under the weight of the hot Stone People, the restless shifting of the two-leggeds searching for balance, the old prayer songs became, at the deepest level, a coming home for Hawk.

A profound settling of energies flowed throughout his body. He asked Adam if he was ready, always mindful that a child might find the darkness of the lodge intimidating. Adam replied affirmatively, his face lost in the shadows. Hawk reminded the boy that if it grew too hot, to snuggle down behind his father onto the breast of Grandmother Earth.

He thanked the men for coming. Hawk asked Larry to sing a Lakota spirit-calling song, one which he had taught the Ojibway man. Larry's voice cut into the stillness, a strong voice accented with high nasal intonation, a strong song with a repetitive chant and haunting melody. The other men picked up the song and followed his lead, the end of each verse slurring downward, pierced by Larry's sharp commencement of the next verse.

Dipper in hand, Hawk began pouring water onto the stones, his prayers interwoven with the singing of the men. In deep appreciation of all who had given up their existence for the ceremony, he addressed the trees, the plant nations, the stone people, the lightning powers, and the water of life. Hawk called upon all the nations to bend down, to hear and see what the pitiful two-leggeds were doing to put themselves back into balance with the Creation.

With each ladle of water onto the Stone People, the heat wrapped around the men, prickling their faces and chests. Sweat coursed down their bodies, washing away that which was false and unclean. The men's singing picked up fierce speed as the heat assaulted them, nettling their skin.

Hawk's last prayer was for the old ones, seven generations back, who had kept the ceremonies alive, despite persecution by the white churches. "Driven into the hills, they constructed temporary sweat lodges, performed this ceremony, then had to erase any evidence that they had done this. For until the days of President Jimmy Carter, the inipi was illegal. It is the old people whom we must thank, because they kept the ceremonies for their children and grandchildren. They risked arrest so that you, I, and the seven generations that follow can do this thing we are doing tonight.

"It is to you," Hawk intoned, ladling more water onto the sizzling stones, "our grandfathers and grandmothers, we give thanks. It is you whom we honor, because if you had not kept the old ways, what could we pass on to our children and our children's children? Ah hau!"

"Hau!" the men chorused in return.

A little voice, a child's voice weakly cried out, *"Mitakuye oyas'in."* The men repeated Adam's call for the door to be opened. In response, Sweet-Grass Woman and Meggie yanked up the front blankets. Steam cascaded out the doorway, white clouds rolling and tumbling into the cold night air. The men collapsed, prostrate with heat, the boy hidden behind his father's form. Sweat glistened all over Hawk's face and chest as he drew in gulps of the night air.

Peering out the door, he noticed Meggie looking anxious. He gave her a smile to let her know that it was going to be okay. He checked on the boy, who sat up, quickly restored by the fresh air. With the dipper, Hawk handed each man a drink of water. When everyone had taken water, he then offered Sweet-Grass Woman and Meggie the dipper. "As doorkeeps, you are as much a part of this inipi as those of us on the inside." Only after everyone had a turn did he then allow himself to take a drink.

"Time for the next round," he cheerfully announced to the men. Those who had been stretched out on the ground inside the lodge groaned, sat up, and adjusted their towels. Hawk felt alive, his senses finely tuned, his mind clear, his body sweaty and relaxed, his heart strong. Down came the door, and a damp darkness wrapped around the men. The stones, no longer glowing red, were obviously still preg-nant with heat. The men hunkered into endurance, knowing that the second round would take longer than the first, and that the heat, while not as piercing, would curl around them and melt their resistance.

The second round of personal prayers began with long words from Hawk, centering the men and himself into the webwork of all the na-tions. After a succession of entreaties for the winged ones, the fins, the crawling things, the four-leggeds, he prayed for the two-leggeds. "Grandfather," he cried, "please help the two-leggeds of all colors. We are so pitiful. We have forgotten that which we knew, that which our brother and sister nations still know. We war against each other. We cut up the Grandmother and claim to own parts of Her. We pray that She will forgive our foolishness and help us cleanse our ways. We pray that we can learn not to poison Her veins with our chemicals or carve up Her skin with our carelessness."

Hawk paused for a second. His voice grew sad. "I especially want to pray for my people, the red people. So long we have had to fight the white two-leggeds who try to tell us whether we are Indian or not. But now, my prayers are for what my people are doing to each other. Some of my people say only full-bloods are real Indians. Some say that only those with a BIA card are Indian. They forget that the blood of our an-cestors runs through our veins, whether we are full-blood, half-blood, part-blood. Grandfather, I ask you to help us have compassion for one another. Help us to be simple red men and to stay out of these wars. Many words of hatred will flow before we can find peace among our-selves, and my heart is sad about this."

Silence followed, the men absorbing Hawk's words. What hatred? They had not heard him talk of these things before. Hawk poured more water onto the rocks, and the stones shrieked in response, spit-ting water out onto the men's legs.

"Grandfather," he began again, "we know the time of prophecy is coming. I ask that you help us, the Lakota people, to lead the way. There are good people; there are bad people; there are ignorant peo-ple in all the races. For those with a good heart, let them know the Chanunpa Wakan and its power. We do not need to be jealous of the truth."

"Grandfather, it was a woman who brought the Pipe to our nation.

Many of our men go out and perform inipi and Pipe ceremonies across this country, yet they do not respect the women. They take advantage of the women and talk to them of ceremonial sex, but what they are doing is using the women for their own pleasure and making up ceremonial excuses. Grandfather, it is not easy being a man and resisting the temptations, but for those of us who are Pipe carriers, for those of us who are walking the red road, help us always remember that it was a woman who gifted us with the Pipe. Help us to give to our women the respect they deserve. *Mitakuye oyas'in.*"

"Ah hau!" the men chorused.

Larry began the personal prayers. Going around in a circle, the men took turns praying aloud about their lives, jobs, worries, gratitude, sick friends, and families. Adam's first words were to his grandmother. "I miss you, Grandma," he said. After short entreaties for his parents, sister, and school friends, Adam prayed an especially long prayer about his old dog, a mongrel of undetermined years. Hawk kept the round intense with judicious placement of water on the steaming stones. The men grunted approval for particular sentiments. Larry chanted softly as the prayers intensified the heat.

Hawk's state of consciousness began to enter into a trance and undergo a transformation while the men were praying. Like a bud opening up to the warmth of the sun, his soul unfolded, petal by petal, to the forces radiating onto him and within him. An exquisite paradox, he understood, of closing off his personal identity while opening himself to the experience of the universe. It was as if his soul were encased in a house of many rooms and he could feel the inner doors wrenching open against the resistance of the ego. Only through such a process of transformation, could Hawk become receptive to the Spirit world.

Sunk into silence when the sweat lodge door opened at the end of the round, he passed a jug of water around to each of the men. They drank deeply, depleted and exhausted by the intensity of the heat and the open expression of their hearts. Hawk's movements were automatic, his mind and consciousness elsewhere. He didn't check on Meggie or pay attention to the men. They didn't appear to notice the change coming over him as he went deeper into a place between the two worlds.

During the third round, no one had any questions to ask the Spirits or healing that needed to be done. After the door was lowered, Hawk prayed long and lovingly about the Sacred Pipe. With the water, he brought the heat up to a sharp intensity.

Out of the void, a voice spoke into his left ear, "Tell that boy his prayers are strong prayers, that his grandmother would be proud of him. He should never be ashamed of his love for the four-leggeds. He is to be called Stands By Dog. He is to learn what that name means. Hau!"

Hawk recognized the authoritative voice of his Spirit teacher, Three Legs, an old *heyoka* man of powerful medicine from several centuries ago. He replied, "Okay. Anything else you want to tell me?" Hawk knew that no one else in the lodge could hear his teacher's instructions. Larry broke in with the pipe-filling song to help keep Hawk focused on the conversation with his teacher.

The Spirit teacher answered, "Yes. I want to pour the waters for the women's inipi."

Hawk was baffled; he didn't know what Three Legs intended. Never before had he made that request. "How would you do that?"

"Don't worry. I'll do it, but you have to let me take over," Three Legs replied.

Hawk understood that Three Legs was talking of voluntary possession, a process that could take place only if Hawk agreed to sit back in his consciousness and let Three Legs use his body. He needed time to think about it. "Maybe," he answered.

Three Legs added, "It's been a long time since I have poured the waters."

Hawk wondered if Three Legs grew lonely for the physical world. "Okay, the women's inipi then," Hawk agreed.

Addressing the boy, Adam, Hawk spoke, "Spirits say that it is a good thing for you to care about your dog, that you are never to be ashamed of your love for the four-leggeds. They want you to take the name Stands By Dog and come to know what that name means. They say your grandmother would be proud of your strong prayers. Hau!"

Larry echoed the "hau," pleased that his son had been recognized by the Spirits and honored with a name to guide him in the days to come. Adam sat up proudly in the community of men.

The door came up at the end of the prayers, and the water jug was passed around. After a brief respite, Hawk had the women lower the door, and the men entered into the fourth round, the time for Hawk to make his personal prayers.

"Tunkasila, Grandfather, I am grateful for the ways you keep teaching me. I know so little. I want to help my people. I give thanks for my teachers, for Three Legs, for Laughing Bear, for Winona, and Davis. I give thanks for my medicine. I ask you to watch over the old ones in my family. Keep them healthy until it is their time to cross over, then take them quickly. I ask you to help the young ones, the babies and the children, to stay strong and healthy, like Adam here, so that they can grow up and find their place in this Creation.

"Grandfather, these men in the lodge want to learn how to become human beings, to take care of the women, children, and the old ones. It is not easy these days for a man to know how to be a man. Week after week, we stagger in here, pitiful creatures, asking You to help us find our balance, guide us through our problems. For those of us without a good job, help us find work so that we can support our families. For those of us with love problems, help us keep a clear heart. When it comes to women, Grandfather, each one of us is weak and confused."

The men shouted "Hau!" in unison.

Hawk continued, "You know my dilemma, Tunkasila, as I try to walk this red road and work for the people. I get pulled on all sides. With the help of that Chanunpa Wakan out there on the altar, I have not touched a drop of liquor for over seven years. But I am lonely, Tunkasila, and I need a woman beside me, a woman who can walk this road with me. Help me with this thing. *Mitakuye oyas'in!*"

His words, heartfelt and muffled, touched Meggie's heart. She nodded and pressed her ear closer to the skin of the lodge.

His words, simple and to the point, brought a smile to Sweet-Grass Woman. She signaled to Meggie that the fourth round was about to end. The two women positioned themselves and pulled up the door on a signal from the men.

The last round had been a quick round. The men smoked and

passed around Hawk's Sacred Pipe. They groaned as they exited from the warm lodge into the freezing night air. While the men dressed, the women retreated to the house to change into towels.

Hawk refilled his Pipe for the women's ceremony. He was excited, curious about what Three Legs planned to do with the ceremony.

ELEVEN

THE WOMEN'S

SWEAT LODGE CEREMONY

*So long as religion is only faith and
outward form, and the religious function
is not experienced in our own souls,
nothing of any importance has happened.*

—CARL G. JUNG
Psychology and Alchemy

The women piled into the sweat lodge. Hawk assigned Sweet-Grass Woman to the honor seat. Meggie sat in the far back, among the other women, all of them wrapped modestly in large towels.

Larry handed in the antlers, braid of sweet grass, cedar, sage, and tobacco to Hawk. The women hung their tobacco ties overhead as they got ready for the beginning of the first round. In came the first batch of sixteen large red-hot stones, which Hawk stacked onto the still-warm rocks of the men's ceremony. He handed the cedar to Meggie, instructing her to sprinkle it on the first seven rocks and then on all the rocks, once they had entered into the lodge. The aroma of cedar and sage and sweet grass tantalized the nose and made the eyes water.

Once the rocks and the water bucket were in and all was cleansed in herbal smoke, Larry lowered the door. The women grew quiet in the darkness. Hawk instructed them to peer into the red faces of the

Stone People and to pay attention. It was the last word he uttered during that round.

"Move back," Three Legs commanded. Hawk wasn't quite sure what his Spirit teacher meant. Except to yield, to release himself, and to create a space within which Three Legs could teach. Sitting way back inside, he sighed and let go.

From a distance, Hawk listened to his own voice chant an unknown song, a mournful song that mimicked the falling tri-tone howl of wolves. Through Hawk's hands, Three Legs rhythmically anointed the stones with water; they hissed and sizzled in response. Pinpoints of white light danced across the darkness. Hawk was both flabbergasted and delighted.

"It is good that you come here," spoke Three Legs to the women. "Pay attention tonight. You may even learn something." Recklessly, or so it seemed to Hawk, Three Legs slapped more water to the talking stones. "I am calling the Grandfathers here with my song."

Three Legs prayed for everything that went into the making of the inipi ceremony. He reminded the women that this was the oldest religious ceremony on this continent. He told them that the dancing lights were Spirit lights. He called out to Meggie, saying, "You with the red towel. The Spirits show themselves this way to let us know they are pleased with the ceremony. Just sit with them; don't put your head to studying them or analyzing them."

She leaned back against the lodge ribs.

"You with the skinny legs," spoke Three Legs, addressing the slender woman next to Meggie, "this next dipper of water is for our ancestors who kept the ceremonies alive when the white people tried to slaughter our people, send our children away to boarding schools, outlaw our religion, snuff out our stories, and kill our culture. We give thanks for the old ones, for the things they taught us. You would do well to remember your ancestors and what they have taught you. Each one of them had dreams which they passed on to your parents' parents and on to you. Everything we do here is in the name of seven generations. *Mitakuye oyas'in!*"

The water hit the rocks, and the steam overwhelmed the senses of the women. Three Legs burst into wild song, ending with a strong *"Mitakuye oyas'in!"*

From the outside, Larry flung up the lodge door. "I've never heard you sing those songs before," he exclaimed, obviously assuming that Hawk was conducting the ceremony.

Three Legs laughed, "Lots of things you haven't heard. Pay attention."

Hawk listened from his submerged perspective.

Meggie drooped from the intense heat. The cold air, shuttling in the doorway, provided relief. She noticed that several of the women had collapsed on the ground, while Hawk and Sweet-Grass Woman sat upright during the intermission between rounds. *Who is this man I love?* Meggie studied the expressionless Hawk. The stern comments about the whites, the authoritarian ways, even the grammar veered from his typical style of speaking.

The second round seemed interminable. Sweet-Grass Woman concentrated her prayers on family matters. She cried piteously about the death of her marriage and the loss of her children to the ex-husband. Looking to center herself in the ways of her people, she asked to know more about the red road.

Three Legs grunted and warned, "Be careful of the prayers you make, for They may give you what you ask for. Then you spend the rest of your life having to live out that vision."

Others prayed about their children and the old ones.

The slender woman began her prayers with long, heaving sobs. Three Legs poured on the water and started to hum a quiet chant. "I am not worthy to be here, Grandfather," the slender woman cried. From Meggie's viewpoint, the woman's prayers underscored the humiliation of her existence.

At the end of the entreaties, Three Legs announced, "This woman here is a good woman. She has done a lot for the people. Her prayers are good prayers, but she needs to learn how to accept the love of the Grandfathers and the Grandmother. When she can do that, then she can love herself."

It was time for Meggie to ask for what she needed. She prayed for her parents, both elderly and in good health. The heat opened her to the heart. Babies, friends, her sister and family, Fritzie—all were covered. "I want to pray for the land, Chrysalis, for the cedar trees that stand tall in the winter, for the animals that use it as sanctuary, for the birds that build nests in the maples, for the ghost of my grandmother who surveys the poppies and grapevine she planted, for the trillium and ladyslippers that greet the spring. I want to thank the land for giving me a home. Grandfather, I had thought it would be enough, living in the old family place on the hill, but I am lonely. I thank you for the love you have sent my way. *Mitakuye oyas'in!*"

Down deep inside himself, Hawk glowed, while Three Legs brought the round to a close. After a brief infusion of cold air, he ordered Larry to bring in the remaining eight rocks. The cherry red stones entered the lodge. The door came down again, and the third round began.

Three Legs announced to the women that this was the Pipe round. "I will tell you now the story of White Buffalo Calf Woman and how the Pipe came to our people. Whenever someone is new to the inipi, we must tell this story." He ladled water onto the spitting stones. The steam chased away the cold night air.

"There was a time our people had forgotten the ways of respect. The animals deserted them, and the people were starving. Two young brothers went out onto the plains to hunt for the buffalo. Coming toward them they saw a beautiful woman, alone and with no one to protect her. One of the young men said he was going to go and take this woman, wrap her in his blanket, but the other one warned him, 'The woman is *lila wakan,* very sacred.' But, like many young men today, he didn't listen. Sacred or not, he knew what he wanted.

"He approached the woman. She was dressed in white buckskin, and her eyes shone black. She signaled the impulsive young man to come forward. It is said that when he touched her, a white mist enveloped them. When it lifted, all that was left of the man were his bones on the ground and snakes crawling through them.

"She now turned to the other man and gestured for him to come to her. He was scared. Wouldn't you be? But she was *wakan,* and so he obeyed. She told him to go back to the camp of Chief Standing Hollow Horn and announce that she was coming. They were to build a large council tipi and to send out runners to the other encampments.

"In four days, the *wakan* woman arrived, carrying a large bundle and a fan of sage. Unwrapping the bundle, she presented the Chanunpa to the people and taught them how to use it in sacred ceremony. Before that time, the people had practiced inipi and tobacco rituals, but the Ptesan-Wi, the White Buffalo Woman, gave them the Pipe. She told them to carry it to other tribes. She taught them how to pray and to sing pipe-filling songs: 'That which is sacred below and that which is sacred above flow through the Pipe.' Seven circles ringed the red bowl of the people, seven for the seven sacred ceremonies she gave the people and seven for the seven campfires of the Lakota people.

"She honored the women, letting them know that through their connection to Grandmother Earth, they were as important as the warriors. The men were instructed to carve the bowl and stem of the Pipes, the women to decorate the Pipes with quillwork. It would be the Pipe, she said, that would bring both men and women together in the circle of love. She spoke to the children, promising them that someday they, too, would smoke and pray with the Pipe.

"When she had finished her teaching, the people walked with her out onto the prairie. A white mist wrapped around her, and when it lifted, they saw a white buffalo calf rolling in the dust. That is why we call her White Buffalo Calf Woman. Hau!"

The women shifted position, convinced the story was finished. Three Legs, however, was not done. "You with the skinny legs," he addressed the woman next to Meggie, "this is not just a myth. The story is not over for our people. The White Buffalo Calf Woman will come again some day when the people need her. Meanwhile, her Pipe is in the hands of Arvol Looking Horse at the Cheyenne River Reservation. It is said that there is a man in the Lakota tribe who will be worthy one day to smoke that Pipe. Meanwhile, Arvol is the nineteenth generation to take care of that Pipe and keep it safe. All the Pipes carried by the people are the children of that Pipe given to us by Ptesan-Wi. *Mitakuye oyas'in.*"

Three Legs told Meggie to pray to the Grandfathers about her experiences the other night. Silence settled into the dark lodge as Meggie stumbled over words to report accurately what happened. "I was asleep, Grandfather, and I awoke," she began.

She described the five moons and the giant moon with a surface of undulating light. "I am concerned, Grandfather, that these visions come from my imagination, yet I believe them to be real. I ask you to tell me the meaning of what I saw."

Three Legs poured on the water. The hot stones threw up wave after wave of heat. Two of the women began to cough. He told them to keep quiet. All of the women retreated under the onslaught of heat by lowering their heads to the ground. Finally Three Legs grunted and spoke to Meggie. She sat up to listen.

"Spirits want you to know that the lightning pipe given to you by Winona Pathfinder is very powerful. Keep it with respect and when you are not in your moon, pray with it, for it is going to teach you many things. In five moons, you are to bring that pipe into the inipi and spend the night with it, praying.

"They want you to know that things are not always what they seem. There is great power in the universe. Moons can grow large, and they can grow many. They want you to know that."

He laughed at a private joke and added, "They say that science doesn't know that yet."

Meggie waited and asked, "Sometime in June, then, I am to take the pipe and stay in the sweat lodge all night?"

Three Legs answered, "June or July, five moons. You figure it out. *Mitakuye oyas'in.*"

The door opened.

Three Legs turned the ceremony back to Hawk during the fourth round. Resuming full ownership of his body, Hawk thanked Three Legs for his teachings. He prayed long and hard for his people and asked his teacher and medicine helpers to guide him in his work for the people. At the end, he spoke of Meggie anonymously, "I ask You to watch over the woman in my heart. Do not put more on her than she can stand. My heart is full of happiness where once it was lonely. *Mitakuye oyas'in."*

Hawk's words warmed Meggie's heart. The door opened. Cool air rushed in to mingle with the heat, the sweat, the love, and the prayers. Despite the soaked dampness of her towel, Meggie felt clean and renewed.

Reborn.

The words of Winona resounded in her head: *"It is only when I enter the inipi and experience its power, do I finally know that I've come home."*

T W E L V E

S A C R I F I C E

It's time to go
down on all fours and dig
deep in the frozen bed of the woods,

and let the heart rest
that ran so hard, that grew
too big for this world.

— JIM SIMMERMAN
Maddy's Woods

The little black dog was hungry, lost, and looking for her family. Driving southward from the Upper Peninsula in Michigan, her human beings had deposited her with friends downstate before taking a trip to St. Louis. After moping around the unfamiliar house, missing the children and her adults, she had slipped out the back door to track her way home. She knew only to go north. At Traverse City, she made a wrong turn. Instead of moving northeast toward Mackinaw City, she trotted northwest up the Leelanau peninsula, where she had met Fritzie. Soon after their brief encounter, she loped into Northport and ran out of land. The vast expanse of Lake Michigan rippled before her. Undecided as to her next move, she stayed there several days, studying the cold, forbidding waters. Finally, she retreated southward, past Suttons Bay, following the coastline. She snacked on dead fish and live field mice to keep up her strength.

As the sun edged down the horizon and the little night critters began scurrying in the twilight fields, the dog trotted along a high fence.
On the other side, a black Arabian stallion snorted and cantered toward her. But she didn't pay him any attention; her eyes fixed upon a
group of young boys and a girl heading toward their respective homes
for dinner. Her ears perked to the possibility that they might be family,
but upon nearer approach, she could smell that they were strangers.

"Hey, doggie, doggie," six-year-old June Tubbs cooed, kneeling
down on the ground, as the scruffy mongrel cautiously advanced,
shoulders down, keeping a wary eye on the boys. The dog could hear
the excited strain of mischief filtering through their high-pitched
voices. The boys studied the black stallion, prancing nervously at a
distance.

"I could ride him easy," boasted one young man, appraising the
horse with an arrogant eye.

June's fingers burrowed in the little dog's dusty coat, finding the exquisitely right places to scratch. Taking comfort in the human contact,
the mongrel shivered in delight and moaned lightly in pleasure.

"Anybody could," said another youngster, " 'cept a girl." He tipped
his head in June's direction, but she didn't take notice.

"My sister can too ride that horse," Robert blurted out, convinced,
at ten years of age, that the family honor was at stake.

"Yeah, sure," the guys laughed.

"No, really!" Now it was a matter that the fellows didn't believe his
word. Robert simmered hot with anger.

June could feel his heat emanate in her direction. The dog's muscles tensed under her fingers. She looked up at her older brother and
his friends.

"You know how to ride a horse, don'tcha?" Robert hooked his
thumbs in his belt loops as he questioned his sister.

June nodded, wondering what that had to do with anything.

"Well, the guys here say you can't ride that black horse in the
meadow. I say you can." Robert gave his sister his most earnest, ap-
pealing look, the kind of look he would give her when in a jam with
their parents and in need of her help. In short, he was asking her to
ride the big stallion.

Secretly, June believed she was capable of accomplishing anything a boy could, but she had to admit that the black horse was huge, and that her only experience in riding had been at a Lake Leelanau riding stable on an old, heavy, white mare called "Christmas."

The stallion arched his neck, tossed his head, and whinnied out of suspicion that the human beings were up to no good. It was also time to head toward the warm barn and a bucket of oats. He pawed the ground impatiently but stayed where he was out of curiosity.

June buried her head into the mongrel's fur, and the small dog licked her ear in appreciation. Up to now, all of June's experiences with animals had been gentle, loving ones. Surely, the black stallion would be no different. "If you can catch him, I'll ride him," she answered and was immediately rewarded by a big, brotherly smile. His approval, so sparse and hard to win, made her feel proud.

One of the boys, nicknamed "Porky," pulled out a bruised apple from his pocket and held it up for inspection. "I've got the bait."

Another boy produced a squashed roll of twine from his jacket. "I've got the halter!"

As Robert could see the plan springing into action, doubt seeded his heart and fear began to sprout inside him. "Maybe we shouldn't . . ." he murmured, but the boys were too preoccupied with strategy to listen to him.

"Who'll go under the fence to get the horse?" one of them asked.

Nobody volunteered.

"It's your apple," they told Porky.

"Okay," he said. "But I'm going to stand on the fence rail so that I can get his attention." It was a safe compromise.

The group agreed that once a twine loop had been secured around the stallion's neck, Robert would hoist his sister up onto the horse's back. Her hand still upon the dog's neck, June rose from her crouched position. The mongrel's tail slapped vigorously against the child's skinny legs.

Porky lumbered aboard the fence rails and whistled to the horse. The brown mare in the distant paddock neighed out a warning. The chunky boy held out his hand with the enticing apple. The ears of the black stallion perched forward.

Although long past apple season, the sweet taste, the satisfying crunch, the smell of apple had not deserted the stallion's memory. De-

spite the mare's caution, he stepped forward, first one step, then two
steps, powered by the sight of the round, red fruit sitting in the chubby
boy's hand. Not for one moment did he drop his vigilance, keeping his
eyes trained on the other children and the dog. But the dog showed no
inclination to chase at his heels. Besides, the Arabian had been
around little children before, and while little two-leggeds were
slightly annoying, they were also easy to ignore. The apple summoned
him.

"Quick!" whispered Porky. "Gimme the twine with a loop in it."

Drawn by the apple, the sheer temptation of it, the stallion stepped
skittishly toward the boy's outstretched hand, unaware of the twine
in the other. The boy began making clucking sounds, like a sick
duck.

Ah, the smell of it! The Arabian opened large jaws, extending out his
tongue and teeth to engulf the whole apple, but the boy clutched onto
it. The stallion compromised, chomped half of it in his mouth, savoring the sweet liquid slathering about on his tongue. Transported thus,
his eye on the remaining apple, the horse allowed the boy to rub behind his ears and slip a piece of unobtrusive twine over his nose and
neck. The boy then relaxed his grip and offered him the second half of
the apple.

The kids were making a lot of *Ssh, Ssh* sounds, urging each other to
stay quiet as they nudged June and Robert toward the fence. Someone
grabbed the dog who was wanting to follow. From June's perspective,
the horse loomed as a giant beast. Anxiously, she looked to her
brother who turned his eyes away. Instead, he took her hand and
whispered, "Don't do anything stupid. Just walk the animal up and
down the fence line."

Porky believed his thin twine loop held the animal in restraint. Inside the fence, careful of the stallion's hooves, Robert bent down to
cradle his hands into a step for June, to boost her up onto the horse's
back. The child leaned against her brother for support, took a breath,
then let herself be catapulted up the side of the stallion.

As he felt the light weight settle on his back, the Arabian began to
prance sideways. He was not used to being ridden without reins or
saddle, or legs that didn't reach beyond the belly. He sensed excitement shivering through the children.

Robert stepped away, telling his sister to hold onto the twine loop, but the knot slipped and the loop fell away. "Grip with your knees and grab the mane," he moaned in fear. His sister looked so pitifully small on the back of the majestic animal.

"But he's so big," June answered, trying to stay calm in the midst of rising panic. She braided her fingers into the horse's black hair, tinctured gold by the sun's final glow on the rim of the horizon.

"You can do it!" Robert urged her on. "Just walk him down the side of the fence and back."

The horse stood there, awaiting human direction, but none was forthcoming until one of the boys leaned over the side of the fence and swatted the animal on its rump. "Giddy-up!" he commanded.

"Whatcha doing?" Robert yelled, shooting him an ugly, belligerent look. "Are you crazy?"

The noise of the slap startled the stallion. He backed away from the group, bobbing his head up and down. The small weight clung to his back, then two small hands brushed along his neck. A soothing high-pitched voice spoke to him. "My name is June," she said, and the fragility of it calmed him momentarily. He danced farther away from the boys and the dog, now yipping under restraint. Into the center of the meadow he sidled, waiting for the small voice to tell him where to go.

But June had no idea how to tell a horse anything without reins or stirrups. Her words, however, seemed to flow over him, because his ears twitched to catch each one of them. "You're a pretty horse. What's your name?" But as he couldn't speak back, she answered for him, "I'll call you Midnight."

Robert whistled to catch her attention and signaled for her to bring Midnight back to the fence, but June didn't know how. The Arabian stood still, at attention, flicking his ears back and forth. She felt comfortable on the large back of her new friend. Almost safe.

From the other side of the far fence, the brown mare whinnied in curiosity. Midnight's ears perked to the sound, and he began walking toward the paddock area, away from the boys. "Is that your girlfriend?" June asked. "Poor Midnight, you want to go see her, don't you?" She clucked in sympathy and patted his neck.

He began to trot; June grabbed onto the thick mane, her words,

"Whoa, whoa!" bouncing into the air, her small butt jarring against his broad back. She could feel Midnight's muscles tense between her spindly legs; she instinctively knew what he desired.

"Come back, come back!" yelled Robert. The boast, the plan, her compliance—it was all turning horribly wrong. The horse was running in the opposite direction. The boy crawled under the fence and took off, pursuing his sister and the stallion. The dog yanked futilely against the arms of the young boy holding her back.

The mare, too, began to step lively along the fence line, urging the stallion to come her way. Aware that a loping canter is much kinder to the human body than a bone-jostling trot, June dug her tiny heels into the stallion's side. "Giddy-up, Midnight," she commanded, not realizing that the stallion might take the fence. Jumping had never been a part of her riding lessons.

For several months, the black stallion had run the fence line, only to back off at the last moment, the hurdle being too great for him. Despite his fascination with the brown mare, he hadn't possessed enough faith in his abilities to attempt the high jump. But now, a tiny voice, a fragile sound atop his back, the human being, urged him on, gave him confidence, and he knew that he could do it. It was as if all he had needed was permission to go beyond himself.

Gathering in his strength and lengthening his stride, he ran faster and faster, the weight on his back almost imperceptible. He shortened his gallop at the last moment, contracting all the muscles from forward to upward and lifting—the horse, the child soared off the ground into the air over the fence, until gravity snatched them back down into a leg-shocking, body-bruising jolt, compressing horse and human and muscle back into the unforgiving hardness of earth.

And the child, unable to hold onto the mane, plunged cartwheeling through the darkening air, not a sound or a cry, but legs and arms flapping to no avail. Her body bounced into the ground near the mare; her head struck against a water trough. The mare, screaming in terror at the human body flung into her paddock, reared back and stormed the ground with her hooves, sharp and deadly and near the child.

Breaking free of the boy's grasp, the black dog tore across the pasture, whizzed past a panting Robert, dove under the fence into the paddock, and charged snarling at the mare's legs, driving both horses into a frenzy, backing them away from the child's inert body. In the confusion, the stallion rushed at the mongrel to protect the mare. His hooves flashed out at the little dog.

Robert grabbed his sister and dragged her under the fence to relative safety. "Go get Mom, quick," he yelled at his gaping friends. In a pack, they sprinted homeward as he turned back toward the crumpled body of his sister. He burst out crying, "Please, please, June, don't die." Frantically, he tried to wipe away the blood gushing from her head wounds.

The little mongrel lay still near the water trough, unable to move, her body trampled and pierced by the hooves of the stallion. No longer could she see the human child, the one who reminded her of family. The wandering dog's long journey was over, far short of her goal. Yet, out of habit, out of yearning, she positioned her head so that her eyes faced north. As the spirit exited her body, her eyes refused to close, seeing, seeing, seeing.

Not seeing.

Home.

The gray fog swept in from the Lake, a spectral shroud stretching out fingers of wintry desolation. The warm sweat lodge disgorged the drenched women, who hurried through the dark mist to the lamp-lit house. The long table was set and aromatic food bubbled on the stove. Meggie couldn't believe the depth of her hunger and thirst after her first sweat lodge experience.

Lucy intercepted her on the way to the changing room. "You got a telephone call. A woman named Katya, very upset. Wants you to phone her immediately."

Surprised that Katya had tracked her down to Lucy's house, Meggie changed into dry clothes, found the telephone, and dialed the Tubbs's number.

Katya answered, hysterical. "Meggie, oh my God! The ambulance took baby June to Munson Hospital in Traverse City. She was attacked by savage horses. I don't know whether she's going to make it. So much blood. Paul went with the ambulance. I'm dropping Robert off with the Noonans. Please, please, can you meet me at the hospital?"

Meggie looked wistfully at the food laid out on the table and the people gathering to find their eating places. "Of course, Katya. I'll be there in thirty minutes."

3

WAZIYATA
healing

THIRTEEN

THE LONG NIGHT

I wake and feel the fell of dark, not day.
What hours, O what black hours we have spent
This night! what sights you, heart, saw; ways you went!
And more must, in yet longer light's delay.

—GERARD MANLEY HOPKINS
I Wake and Feel the Fell of Dark, Not Day

"I have to leave," whispered Meggie to Hawk. "Katya's daughter has had an accident involving horses. I'm going to meet them at the hospital."

He helped her with her jacket. "Meggie, let me come with you. Lucy can take care of the people here." He nodded toward the famished group already seated at the table.

Meggie thought about it for a moment, then shook her head. "I think it is going to be an unending night at the hospital. Knowing Katya, she'd rather I come alone. Still," she paused, "how about meeting me for breakfast?" She raised her eyebrows and slipped him an extra set of keys to her house.

"Who knows when you'll get home?" he asked, pocketing the keys.

"You will," she replied.

Katya hadn't yet arrived at the hospital. In the lobby of the emergency room, Meggie found Paul slumped on a wooden chair, his head sunk into his hands. His face wore an expression of pure anguish. His life had spun out of control. Seeing Meggie, he stood up and threw his arms around her, as if he were drowning and she was the only thing that could save him. Instinctively, she rubbed his back with her hands, as she would have done for any frightened child.

He stammered, "The doctors don't know if she's going to survive the night. The next twelve hours are critical. Oh, Meggie, what am I going to say to Katya?" He pulled back and looked into her eyes for an answer, his shoulders drooping with defeat.

"Tell Katya the truth," she answered, sounding much more solid than she felt.

"My poor baby," he continued, his eyes darting toward the surgical area, "They told me I can't see her while they're operating on her. I wonder if she even knows I'm here."

"She's asleep, Paul. Right now, June isn't experiencing any pain." As she tried to reassure him, Meggie wondered if it were true. *If June survives the night, there will not only be physical wounds to heal but also scars upon her psyche.*

Katya arrived, breathless and demanding information, "Is she going to be all right, Paul?"

While studying his wife's face for reaction, Paul summed up what the doctors had said—which was next to nothing. "All we can do is wait."

Katya collapsed against Paul's chest, burying herself into his shirt. Together, Meggie and Paul encircled her with their arms, while she hiccuped sobs of fear. Exhausted, the three of them slumped down onto the hospital chairs, helpless. They held hands, trying to bind the anxiety in their grip. On the far wall, a large unadorned clock marked the sluggish passage of time.

Well past midnight, a man in his thirties came striding through the entrance into the emergency room. In a rumpled shirt but handsome and eager in expression, he stopped at the admitting desk to ask questions. The nurse pointed in their direction. The man approached them. "Mr. and Mrs. Tubbs?"

Paul and Katya dumbly nodded their heads.

He held out his hand to Paul and introduced himself. "I'm Reverend Young. I heard about your little girl. How is she doing?"

The parents shook their heads. Paul answered, "It's touch and go."

"I wonder," continued the minister, "if you would like to pray with me for her recovery?"

Katya's eyes lit with hope, and she held out her hand to the stranger, bowing her head and shutting her eyes. Paul also bent his face toward the floor. He would do *anything,* if it would help his little girl. The Reverend Young intoned a moving prayer for the little one in the operating room, asking God to give the parents courage, patience, and wisdom to know God's will. Katya bobbed her head up and down, as if to punctuate the prayer with her assent.

As the minister recited the Twenty-third Psalm, "The Lord is my shepherd . . . ," Meggie's imagination transported her from hospital to hilltop. Eyes closed, Meggie envisioned herself offering the lightning pipe and crying out into the dark void, *"I ask you to make Katya's little girl strong, so that she can play again with her friends. With this pipe, Tunkasila, I send my prayer."*

Meggie took a deep breath. Like a soap bubble that bursts in the air, the vision broke, spitting her back into the sterile twilight of the emergency room.

". . . and I shall dwell in the house of the Lord forever. Amen," concluded the Reverend Young.

Katya thanked him profusely. The minister gave her hand a reassuring squeeze before heading off to the nurses' lounge, returning with three Styrofoam cups of undiluted coffee that had overstayed the burner, its bitter taste awakening even the faintest of souls. He handed a cup to each of them and sat down between Katya and Meggie, settling in for a long night of waiting. "It's in God's hands," he sighed.

Realizing that June's parents needed to be able to huddle together in privacy for a few minutes, Meggie introduced herself and diverted his attention. "What church do you serve?" she inquired.

"Actually, two congregations. One in Northport and another is in Leland. And you?" He smiled at her. "What is it that you do?"

Meggie found herself reluctant to admit that she was a psychologist. Too often that answer chilled strangers, who acted as if afraid of revealing too much of themselves. She compromised, "I have a private practice of psychotherapy in Suttons Bay."

He leaned forward. "Well then, our line of work is similar, isn't it? Only you use modern language and concepts, whereas I call upon the wisdom of the ages and the images of a desert people. Somehow, I think the metaphors of the desert are appropriate to this age, this time. People are lost and lonely, are they not?"

His frankness disarmed her. She liked people who ended statements in questions, who moved beyond soliloquy to full dialogue. She nodded.

The Reverend Young took her nod as encouragement to tell more. "I don't know why I ended up in Michigan. I was appointed on the strength of my sermons and my reputation for fiscal management. But an old English teacher in high school is responsible for my oratory, and my lack of imagination around money makes me look ethical. And you? With your job you don't have to put up with endless committee meetings and squabbling parishioners fighting for your time and energy." He shook his head in mock despair.

Meggie was surprised by the easy confession, charmed by his humility. "I'm afraid I would make a terrible minister. The congregation would easily recognize my boredom. I'm not a good liar."

"Ah, that's just the point," he said. "I'm not a good liar either. I'm a much better pastor than minister. It's only when I can help people, that I feel I am doing the work I was called to do. Even when they are strangers, like tonight, for instance . . ." He nodded toward the Tubbs.

"You've never met them before?" Meggie was surprised.

He shook his head and explained, "Sometimes I have trouble sleeping at night. Thoughts plague me, like little devils. I often give up on sleep, afraid I'll wake my wife, Annie, with my tossing and turning. So I head downstairs and turn on my police scanner for company. That's how I learned about the little girl being trampled by horses. Terrible, isn't it? I knew the parents would be having a hard time. So here I am, sleepless and trying to follow my vision of what it means to minister to others."

A bedraggled, tired physician emerged from the operating room, heading toward the Tubbs. Both Meggie and the Reverend Young leaned closer to catch his words, "She'll need a lot of facial reconstruction, but she's going to make it. You've got yourself a spunky little girl."

Katya burst into tears. Her daughter was going to live. She and Paul hugged each other, then Meggie, then the minister, sharing their relief. It didn't matter that their daughter would be scarred or would require a long healing; the child was going to live. The long night of waiting was over.

Katya decided to take the first shift in the recovery room while June slept off the anesthesia.

The clock read three-thirty in the morning. The blackness of night had not yet yielded to the candles of morning. Meggie was free to go home.

Reverend Young congratulated the Tubbs and told Katya that he would return in the afternoon to see how June was recuperating. Together, he and Meggie exited the hospital into the cold night air, refreshed by its briskness. The gray fog had temporarily lifted. He walked her over to her car, saying, "I really appreciated this chance to meet you, Dr. O'Connor."

"Oh, call me Meggie, won't you?" she said.

"I'd be delighted," he responded, "but only if you call me by my first name."

"What's that?" she asked.

"My name is Karl. Karl Young." He smiled. "I'm sure our paths will cross again."

On the drive home, Meggie's weary mind raced through all the events of the night: the sweat lodge ceremony, the call from Katya, the emergency room, Paul's panic and Katya's desperation, the appearance of the Reverend Young, his prayer and comfort in the early morning hours. And she thought about the pipe and her own silent prayer. She drove past dark, solitary farmhouses, which seemed to elongate the passage of time, until, at last, the familiar driveway to Chrysalis loomed in the darkness.

"Home," she sighed, speeding up the long driveway. Her weariness released into a rising tide of excitement as she spotted Hawk's old pick-up by the garage.

He had obviously decided to accept her invitation.

F O U R T E E N

NIGHT'S END

Birds do it, bees do it,
Even educated fleas do it.
— COLE PORTER
Let's Do It

While Meggie was at the hospital, Hawk had tried to go to sleep, but he had found himself stirred by her scent on the sheets and worried about her long drive home. What a night it had been.

Alternately thrilled and scared by Three Legs' first emergence into the sweat lodge ceremony, Hawk needed a teacher's counsel. Winona could have told him whether the Spirit possession was a typical phenomenon for a person on the medicine road, but she had never explored the subject with him, except to say, "You must never let the Spirits take charge of you, or they will run you to madness."

So what does it mean? Is Three Legs going to drive me crazy? Or am I being chosen as a channel for my Spirit teacher? Looking into Meggie's full-length mirror, Hawk reproached himself, " 'Chosen,' eh? You think you're something special? Spirits can have a good time with a person full of ego." Hawk thumbed his nose at himself.

He pivoted on his right foot to study his profile, then returned to face the mirror. "More than ever, boy," he pointed a finger at his image, "you need to do a *hanbleciya* to ask about these things. More than ever, you need the help of a teacher." Laughing Bear had already promised to come to Michigan from Pine Ridge in the early summer to put him up on the hill for a vision quest. *But was that soon enough?*

Tired, Hawk lost interest in the shadowboxing of words and reflections; he began to roam restlessly through the bedrooms. Fritzie paced the upper floor with him. When Hawk thought he heard the sound of Meggie's car driving up the hill and a car door slamming, he became excited, only to discover that it was a gust slapping against the shutters. *A wish has the power to shape a wind,* he thought.

The injured child came to his restless mind, nudging aside his need for Meggie. In the dark, he smoked the Pipe for the girl, asking the Spirits to strengthen her body and restore it to wholeness. The house sweetened to the fragrance of the tobacco. And still Meggie did not come home.

Finally, he pulled an armchair over to an open window in the bedroom to better hear her car on the driveway. The exhaustion from the two sweat lodge ceremonies took its toll and weighted his eyelids shut. Falling asleep, Hawk tumbled deeply into a dream:

A man with long, stringy hair and broad shoulders was talking to him. "My son," he began, "sit down beside me. I want to tell you something."

It is my father before the time of alcohol poison, he realized.

The man's eyes crinkled with love and sadness. Hawk plopped himself down, legs crossed, his limbs scrawny and childlike. He leaned forward, elbows on his knees, attending to his father's voice. He had not heard that voice for years.

"I have a stone here for you, which I have carried around my neck in a pouch since I was a little boy." His father bent his head and, from his neck slipped off a deerskin purse attached to a twisted leather string. With his fingers, he spread open the pouch and plucked out a gray stone the size of a quarter, perfectly round, a pinprick hole in its center. He held it up toward the sky. Shafts of sunlight squeezed through the tiny

aperture. With curiosity, Hawk reached out to touch the stone. His father placed it in the center of the boy's hand.

Hawk rotated it in his fingers, trying to catch the sun at different angles. The father spoke: "When I was young, I went on a vision quest to find out about my life. I found this stone in my altar. When I picked it up, it pulsed with my heartbeat, and I knew then it was a Stone Man. My teacher told me to wear him on my neck, protected by sage and leather, as the Stone Man would help me live my life. My teacher also told me that this Stone Man was to come live with you when I cross over into the next dimension. I have not forgotten the words of my teacher, even though it was a long time ago."

His father took the stone from Hawk's hand, much to the boy's disappointment.

"When will it be mine, Daddy?" Hawk asked. He would have liked to have a Stone Man around his neck. The other boys would be jealous of him.

"You will know the time," his father answered. "It will be when the Stone Man comes to you. Not when you come to him."

Hawk awoke with a jerk, his head having fallen to his chest. Caught between childhood, dream world, and adult reality, it took a moment for him to reorient in the dark. It was then he heard the true rattle of Meggie's car rumbling up the driveway. Fritzie leapt up from a sound sleep and rushed to the door.

Hawk grabbed hold of Fritzie's collar and wagging body, "Shh, old fellow, let's give her time to get inside and surprise her." He petted the frenzied terrier down to a calmer wiggling, allowing Meggie to enter into the lower level of the house and make her unimpeded way upstairs. She was obviously tiptoeing so as not to awaken those who slept. Only when she had crested the last step in the darkness did he release Fritzie.

"*Oof,*" she exhaled, as the dog threw himself at her. She fell back a few steps.

Hawk guessed that her eyes had not yet adjusted to the blackness and, to her surprise, Hawk folded her gently into his arms and buried her mouth in a kiss.

As Hawk's lips silently took possession of her mouth, Meggie relinquished the brutal night and the images of the hurt child into the heat of life.

He brushed the hair off her face and caressed her cheek. She closed her eyes and leaned into him. Tension released into tears of relief, spilling over the causeway of her lids. With his thumbs, he caught her tears and wiped them aside. She pressed her head onto his chest, like a lost puppy who had finally found comfort. Clasping her hand, he led her into the bedroom. Not a word had crossed the threshold.

Exhausted, she slumped down on the bed while he slipped off her sneakers and socks, unbuttoned her shirt, and unzipped her jeans. It was then she remembered how sticky her body was from the sweat lodge ceremony. Her jeans adhered to her thighs, no matter how hard he yanked on them. She began to giggle.

With feet freed of shoes and socks, she kicked off the jeans and rolled away from him. "I've got to take a shower," she protested. But his hands drew her down to him.

"You are beautiful just as you are." And that was all that was said, his lovemaking pulling her back from the images of flashing hooves and the fright of a little girl.

Fritzie couldn't understand all the thrashing and moving about on the bed above him. He was happy, though, to have the woman and the man together. Tomorrow, the woman would feed him; the man would play ball with him. And he, Fritzie, would guard them both from the dangers of the northern forest. Each one had a purpose in his kingdom.

FIFTEEN

THERAPEUTIC STORIES

Man is the only animal that blushes. Or needs to.
—MARK TWAIN
Pudd'nhead Wilson's New Calendar

Katya knocked on the door and entered her son's bedroom. "Your father and I want to talk with you. Downstairs."

He knew his parents expected an explanation about June's accident, and he was afraid. How would they ever forgive him? He shut his eyes, desperately wishing for something other than the truth.

"Now!" she commanded. It was unlike her to be so stern.

Robert averted his eyes from his mother's face. Preceding her down the stairs, a sense of doom weighted his every step. There was no escape.

His father sat at the table, hands folded precisely in front of him, his face lined with exhaustion from the hours spent by his daughter's hospital bed. All his life, Paul Tubbs had worshiped order, especially when it came to emotions. Accounting and computers had provided him with a secure reality and carefully circumscribed his world. The near-fatal accident of his daughter obscured his fatherly frame of reference, his certainty in his ability to provide for the family and in the predictability of events. That old safe world no longer existed, and rage boiled inside of him.

"Tell me what happened." He articulated the sentence slowly and meticulously as his son and his wife assumed their seats at the kitchen table.

"It was the dog's fault," the boy began.

"Tell me what happened," Paul snapped, his words clipped, distrustful, like handcuffs of steel trapping, wrapping around the boy.

"Paul, *please!* Let him speak," Katya fluttered.

"The truth. What I want to know is the truth. Is that too much to ask from him?" Sarcasm swirled from son to wife, then back to son.

Robert shrank in his chair, shoulders hunched toward the center of his small chest, his eyes fixated on his father's large, knotted hands. "We were coming home through the back fields, by the horse farm. Tommy Noonan saw the horse first an' said that June couldn't ride him . . ."

Robert stopped.

"Go on," Paul ordered.

"But June said she could too, an' Porky had an apple an' one of the others had some twine for a halter an' . . ."

"And you agreed to this asinine proposal?" Paul's question and tone of voice convicted Robert, syllable by syllable.

Robert swallowed hard, "Well, I thought she'd jus' ride him for a second . . ." Tears began to well up, but he fought them down. His throat began to throb.

"I can't believe this!" Paul roared. "I can't believe that my ten-year-old son would allow his little sister to get up on a stallion with nothing but a piece of twine."

"Paul," Katya cautioned him.

"The boy doesn't have the sense the good Lord gave him." He shook his head in agitation.

Before his very eyes, Robert witnessed all the trust and faith and respect and love his father once had for him crumble and dissolve in a flood of fury.

"I tried, Daddy," he pleaded. "I tried to bring her back, but the horse ran off. I tried but I couldn't stop him. I tried, Daddy. But the horse jumped. I called her back but the horse galloped away from me. I tried. I ran as fast as I could but she fell, Daddy, she fell and I couldn't catch her, she flew off that horse, and I couldn't catch her. I tried, Daddy." The words, unfenced, gushed out of him, tumbled out of him, running tears and falling words and sobbing breaths and still no redemption.

"An' she was all crumpled there, bloody. An' I thought she was dead, Daddy. I thought the horse had killed her, that I had killed her. Ohhh . . ." the boy moaned, lowered his head, and sobbed into his arms, crossed and resting on the table.

Katya leaned over the table and brushed the hair off his forehead.

"It was all my fault, Daddy." He lifted up his head, still hiccuping tears. "I'm so sorry." But his father's stern look did not soften.

"*Sorry* isn't good enough," Paul answered. "*Sorry* damn near killed your sister. *Sorry* doesn't bring her back from the hospital. *Sorry* doesn't heal the scars on her face." Each sentence, like a judge's gavel, hammered into Robert's heart.

"I hate myself!" the boy screamed in a frenzy. He flung himself off the chair and tore upstairs.

"I hate myself!" he yelled, slamming shut his bedroom door and then pounding the wall with his head, planning to mash his brains to a pulp because life was no longer tolerable. *It would be better if I was dead,* he thought.

But the door opened and his mother grabbed him and wrestled him away from the wall, wrapping him round and round with her strong arms and her warm body. "Hush now, it's going to be okay."

"Hush now," she whispered.

"Hush now," and slowly he collapsed into the kindness of her love.

It was several nights later when Meggie heard the sound of a vehicle graveling up the driveway. Ever vigilant, Fritzie sounded the alarm and barked at the kitchen door. She wasn't expecting anyone. To her surprise, it was her neighbor, Paul Tubbs.

"I'm sorry, Meggie," he apologized, arriving at the door, "but I needed to talk with someone."

"Come in, come in. I'll make us some hot tea. Would you like some homemade nut bread?" She motioned him through the door.

The face of the short, balding man was tormented, creased by worry. He was not the same person who had been at the birthday party. Paul slumped down and mutely accepted her offerings of food and ginger almond tea. He looked as if he hadn't slept for days.

"Is June okay?" Meggie wondered if the child had suddenly suffered a setback in her recovery.

"Oh yes. The doctors think she'll be able to come home next weekend. It's not that, Meggie." He sipped the hot tea Meggie placed before him.

"Katya?" Meggie was guessing, running through the family members.

Paul nodded. "I've never seen her like that. She blew up and burst on me, as if I was somehow responsible for what had happened. We threw words at each other, hateful words. I was so angry, Meggie, at my son for his stupidity. Can you believe it? The boy actually accepted a dare from his friends and placed June up on the back of that horse. What did he think was going to happen? A stallion, for God's sake! So, when I asked Robert to explain himself, what does the boy do but try to blame a stupid little dog that just happened to come upon the scene at the wrong time. He's not only a fool but a liar and a coward."

Strong adult terms to describe a scared young boy, Meggie thought.

"Katya thinks I'm too hard on my son. Can you imagine? She demanded that I apologize to Robert, tell him that I didn't mean it when I got so angry at him. But, Meggie, I meant every word I said. How is he going to learn if he doesn't face up to what he's done? It's not like I hit him or gave him a whipping."

Too often Meggie had witnessed young people amplify and internalize the angry voice of the parent. And then later make a habit of beating up on themselves every time they experienced failure.

Paul paused in his monologue, his voice shifting from righteousness to shame. "Katya has thrown me out of our bedroom. Each one of us walks around, tiptoeing like ghosts, in what had once been a happy house. I avoid my son, to keep my anger in check. He wisely keeps his distance from me. Katya won't speak but a few polite words to me. 'What do you want for breakfast? What time will you be home? When are you going to the hospital?' Meaningless conversation. It's driving me crazy. Why has one accident broken us all apart?" He looked to Meggie, his eyes pleading for answers.

He was tearing himself apart on the inside. His world had fallen into chaos. *He's hunting for his lost self, when the world had once seemed safe,* she thought.

She reached out and touched his arm. "What happens to you when you look into June's face?" she asked.

Paul shuddered. "I hate what's been done to her. No child should have to carry scars like that on her face. I want to reach out and, with my finger, erase each cut, each seam, and restore my daughter's face to wholeness. I want to take her into my arms and tell her that it will never happen again. But I can't do that, can I?" He frowned and wiped invisible sweat off his forehead.

"No, you can't," Meggie echoed.

"How can I protect her, Meggie? How can I be a father who stands between her and a world that can slash across her face and frighten her to the bone? Tell me how, Meggie. I need to know what to do."

"Imprison her. Lock her up in the house. Tell her she can't go outside until she is an adult. Tell her that friends and creatures will only hurt her," Meggie answered.

Paul looked at her, perplexed, wondering if Meggie was making fun of him. But her eyes were kind, full of concern.

Meggie leaned toward him, "Paul, I will tell you a story:

"A little boy, with his father, spied a flight of stairs and climbed onto the first step. 'Daddy,' he exclaimed, 'catch me.' The boy jumped and his father caught him in his arms." Meggie opened out her arms in a welcoming gesture.

"The little boy clambered up two steps and called out, 'Daddy, catch me.' He leapt and, once again, landed safely in his father's arms.

"Three steps, then four—each time, his father caught him. Finally, the boy reached the top of the stairs. This time when he jumped, his father stepped back, and the boy fell hard to the ground, scraping his knees and jarring his bones. He looked up at his father, crying, and with anger in his voice said, 'Daddy, why didn't you catch me?'

"His father answered, 'Because I wanted to teach you not to trust anyone, not even your own father.' "

Silence followed as Meggie let Paul draw his own conclusions.

"That's a horrible story," he protested. "What kind of father would do such a thing?" Repugnance scrunched across his face.

"Paul, how else is a child to learn to stand on his own two feet if the father is always there to rescue him?" Meggie raised her eyebrows.

"But to set him up for a fall and then step back . . ."

"And couldn't that have been a father who so loved his son that he did what was difficult, so that the boy might learn about himself?"

"But I want my children to know that the world is good and loving and safe." Paul had always been a staunch Catholic, faithfully going to church, following the commandments, because he believed in a moral order and a loving God.

Meggie knew that the questions she was asking him pushed him beyond the borders of good parenting. *His world has tumbled upside down into a crisis of faith in himself, in his worldview.*

She nudged along the process, "God so loved his Son that he let him die on the cross, didn't He? Was *that* a betrayal of a father's love?" If Paul didn't ask the hard questions, there would be no transformation for him, no learning, no understanding of the role suffering plays in the human experience.

"You have a daughter who needs, most of all, to know that you and Katya love her." Meggie looked into his eyes, knowing that only when one begins to ask the question, can one begin to understand the human limits.

"You have a wife who needs, most of all, to know that you love her and will help her in whatever way you can," Meggie spoke slowly.

"You have a son who needs, most of all, to know that you love him, that you trust he will learn from his mistakes, and that you will help him when he needs that help."

She got up from the table and poured them both a second cup of tea. "You can't stand at the bottom of the stairs forever, Paul. You can hold them, comfort them when they are hurt, and help them get back up on their feet. Being a parent has got to be one of the most humbling tasks for a human being. Go home, Paul. Katya and Robert both need you."

Paul finished up his mug of tea and rose from the table. His face was more settled, determined. He had a direction, something he could do in the face of his helplessness. "Thank you, Meggie," he said. "You know, even if I could never allow myself to go see a therapist, you're worth every bit of money that people pay you."

Meggie smiled. A backhanded compliment from her accountant friend was better than none at all. Even pro bono, psychotherapy had its compensations.

Whenever Andrea entered Meggie O'Connor's office, the sun seemed to disappear behind heavy clouds. Meggie didn't dare point that out, lest her client take it as proof of eternal damnation. The anger of this woman was ferocious but confined in a brittle container. Unlike with Paul, Meggie didn't have the slightest idea what caused this client's anger in the past or what sustained it in the present. This session, Andrea cracked open the door.

"He loves women, and they love him."

"Whom are we talking about?" Meggie asked.

"My husband," Andrea sighed. "Before we were married, our relationship was hot and passionate. He admired my creativity, the way I could take a mental snapshot of the world and expand it with color and line. He said that I had the ability to re-create my existence, to change and paint it to fit my own sense of beauty. Whereas he felt stuck in the rawness of reality."

"He didn't know of the black hole that follows you?"

Andrea shook her head. "You know, right before we got married, the hole shrank to an infinitesimal dot. I simply forgot about it. It was like one of those cartoon movies where the character simply paints over the hole, and it disappears from the landscape.

"But, on the honeymoon," she continued, "the hole burst open with wide and gaping jaws, and I could see that I would never be able to run away from it. I know you're thinking that I must have some terrible sexual problem with him, but that isn't it. The lovemaking on our honeymoon was wonderful, and I treasured waking up alongside this man who represented such goodness in my life."

"What made the hole reappear then?"

"I can remember exactly when it happened." Andrea grew animated, agitated. "It was when he turned to me and said, 'Now, you are my wife, and we are family together.' "

"Go on," Meggie encouraged her.

She paused, unsure. "His words were like a gust of arctic wind. It snuffed out the light in me. I wanted to tell him, 'No, I'm your true love, your soul mate, your friend—but, please, not *family*.' But he wouldn't have understood. And from that moment on, the hole was back."

Do I dare? Meggie wondered. *Do I dare ask her about family? About what happened so far back that it had to be dropped into a deep well of blackness?*

"Were your parents at your wedding?" It seemed like a safe way to ask about her past.

"No," Andrea snapped out her reply. "They're dead and out of my life." She glared at Meggie, warning her not to proceed further with that line of questioning.

Meggie looked up at the haunted face of her client. *Her parents are very much alive in her psyche, roaming about like predators. It is family that she is trying to corral and imprison, family that is the source of her rage, family she would like to kill.* Meggie backed away from the black hole.

The two of them sat quietly in the room, Andrea biding the time to see if the therapist would respect her wishes, Meggie waiting out the silence to discover where the client would proceed. A silent standoff.

Meggie shifted the focus from the edge of the hole to the brink of hope. "The carp know you exist. Does God?"

"I didn't think therapists ever mentioned God," Andrea parried.

Meggie smiled, thinking back to the previous evening with Paul. "There is a story I want to tell you:

"A man was climbing a mountain when he fell and rolled right over the edge of a large and terrible chasm. By a strange quirk of luck, he was able to grab onto a small tree growing out of the cliff, and it stopped his fall. The drop below would certainly kill him if he let go of the tree, but he was too far down the cliff face to climb back up to the top. In short, he was stuck.

"So, he called out, 'Hey, is there anybody up there?' No one answered. Desperate, he began to pray, 'God, I've not been a good Christian, but if you can help me get out of this predicament, then I promise I will go to church every Sunday. Please, God, can you help me?'

"A deep voice answered, 'Yes, you called?'

" 'God, is that you?' the man asked.

"The voice replied, 'Yes, this is God. Do you have faith in me? Will you do what I ask?'

" 'Oh yes, God,' the man said. 'I'll do anything you ask.'

" 'Then let go of the tree,' the voice commanded.

"The man clung to the branch for a few minutes, weighing his options. Then he yelled up, 'Is there anyone *else* out there?' "

The rigid faults in the landscape of Andrea's defiant, defensive face cracked along the lines of laughter. "Is that where I am—hanging onto the side of a cliff?"

"I think," Meggie answered, "that all of us human beings find ourselves, from time to time, trapped in situations where we can't see any exit, any resolution to our problems. At those times, we can either give in to despair, or . . ."

"Or what?" Andrea perched forward on the edge of her chair.

"Or find the humor in the moment," Meggie replied. "Whether it be laughter at the predicament or laughter at ourselves."

"Hmmm . . . that's an interesting suggestion," Andrea commented. "It wasn't what I expected you to say."

"And what did you think I was going to tell you?"

"Carpe diem," she answered.

Meggie laughed, knowing she had a clever client. Looking out the window, she couldn't help but notice the sun still hiding behind dark and threatening clouds.

SIXTEEN

SPRING IN THE BLOOD

For winter's rains and ruins are over,
And all the season of snows and sins;
The days dividing lover and lover,
The light that loses, the night that wins;
And time remembered is grief forgotten,
And frosts are slain and flowers begotten,
And in green underwood and cover
Blossom by blossom the spring begins.

—ALGERNON CHARLES SWINBURNE
Atalanta in Calydon

Even though spring had blossomed early in Meggie's heart, winter
continued to clutch onto the land's surface. The sun tried to rouse
frigid Lake Michigan, but icy fingers clawed the gray shore. And in
mid-April, a foot of snow blew into Suttons Bay, a last shiver of winter's breath. No sooner had the snow been shoveled than warm air finally melted the ice, and crocuses broke ground. Stir-crazy, the people
of Suttons Bay began turning up sod for planting, as if to signal Mother
Nature that enough was enough. Rain replaced snow.

At the sound of the first thunders, sweat lodge ceremonies began in
earnest. Hawk explained to the inipi community that it was time to
start preparing for the ritual of "crying for a vision" in June, his *hanbleciya.* "It's a time when I'll take my Pipe out on a hill, alone, without
food or water or shelter, to pray and ask the Creator for guidance."

His teacher, Laughing Bear, had agreed to come from the South

Dakota reservation to conduct him on his vision quest of three days and three nights. To increase his endurance, Hawk fasted one day a week during March and April, two days a week in May.

Meggie grew to love the inipi ceremonies at dusk—the smell of damp earth and hot stones, the mystery of the dark lodge, and the company of communal prayer. The transformation of Hawk around the ceremony fascinated her, as he switched from passionate lover to equally passionate teacher. Meggie wasn't quite sure which Hawk she loved the most.

As the lover, Hawk delighted not only in her body but in her mind, enjoying how she impregnated her Caucasian worldview with a personal causality and pragmatism. His world was more spiritual, animistic, full of mystery.

But as the teacher, there was always an aloofness to him, as if he belonged to no one, not even himself. She felt proud of Hawk's leadership in the community, yet missed the tender intimacies.

He confided in her, "I know nothing. Everything I've learned has come from my grandparents, my teachers, and the Spirits."

Risking sharp criticism from Laughing Bear, he asked her if she would bring the lightning pipe and spend the last night of his *hanble-ciya* in the sweat lodge. He needed the balance of the female energy, and he wanted Winona's pipe there to support him in his most difficult hours toward the end of the *hanbleciya*.

"I would be honored," she replied.

"The first warm spring day when we are both free of work," Meggie warned him, "I want to take you out golfing with me."

He laughed, "Hey, I know nothing of the game."

"Precisely," she grinned, adding, "And the winner gets to demand a free wish from the loser."

Hawk could see the competitive spirit rising up within her. He knew that this would be her opportunity to strut her athletic skills, at his expense. She didn't give him much time to prepare.

"I'll show you the moves," she offered. Meggie taught him the proper grip, how to swing the driver and follow through, how to bank into a chip shot, how to still himself for the putt. "Of course," she cautioned, "you won't have any chance to win, because you have never played the game. But," she added, "I'll try and be gentle with you."

Two weeks slid by before the weather and work schedules cooperated. "You can use my father's old clubs, but his shoes won't fit you."

"I'll wear my sneakers," he replied, hoisting up the dusty bag of driver and woods and heavy metal irons. Hawk noticed that Meggie's clubs appeared leaner, the driver and woods made of metal.

They drove to the Veronica Valley golf course in Lake Leelanau, as it was in the best shape of all the courses that had opened early in the spring. "Besides, it only has nine holes, not eighteen. I don't want you to get too discouraged. Golf is a test of personal character," Meggie cautioned. Her new golf shoes gleamed with unsullied spikes, to prevent her slipping on the grass.

"Now remember what I told you," she said, as they pulled their golf carts up to the first tee. "To even up my advantage, I'll shoot from the men's tee, to give you half a chance." Her smile was wicked, twinkling with mischief. She was setting him up for a grand defeat, and he knew it.

It was going to be a tough day. Hawk must have looked a little bit anxious, because Meggie added, "Oh, don't worry. You'll do just fine. We'll play by beginner's rules."

"What kind of rules are they?" He didn't totally trust Meggie. There was devilment brewing inside of her.

"The lower the score per hole, the better. But, as a beginner, you're probably going to rack up huge scores, so beginner's rules are that you can't make more than eight. Any more shots after eight per hole, we'll record as a circled eight. You can take as many mulligans, or free shots, as you need off each tee. I'll tell you the other rules as we go along."

"You go first." He winked at her.

"You want to get a feel for what you are up against." She grinned.

Meggie teed up her yellow ball, then drove it about one hundred-and-twenty yards into the rough. "Not great," she sighed, "But just you wait. I'll soon warm up to my game."

Hawk teed up his ball. So many things to remember—the proper stance, the right grip, keeping his head down, swinging back slowly, letting the power flow through his arms without pushing the club. His white ball looked tiny, perched on the little peg of wood. More was at stake than simply the game. Hawk wanted to demonstrate to Meggie that he could enter into her world, learn new skills, and, at least, go down fighting.

He swung hard. The ball popped up high then down into a water hazard. *Damn.* It was not an auspicious beginning.

"No matter. Take a mulligan," Meggie urged him, as she fished out his ball with a long scooper.

He set up his ball again, counseling himself to be calm, be easy, be cool. He brought the driver down smack onto the ball. It twirled up into the air then plopped right back down into the water. *Double damn,* he cursed under his breath.

"Take another mulligan," Meggie cheerfully shouted, running again over to the water hazard with her scooper. "It doesn't count."

For a moment he glared at her, before remembering that it was the ball that was his enemy.

Easy now. Easy. Hawk let his arms relax this time in the upswing, giving only a tiny push on the downswing. He topped the ball but it rolled a good distance. Almost as far as Meggie's ball.

"Great shot," Meggie enthused, patting him on his back.

Hawk knew better, but he'd be damned if he'd give Meggie the satisfaction of seeing his frustration. *It's just a game,* he reminded himself. His second shot wasn't bad, the third went straight down the fairway, and by the fourth he neared the green. Meanwhile, Meggie strayed farther and farther left, ricocheting her ball from tree to tree. She didn't get down to the green until her fifth shot.

"I must have been an arborist in a former life." She laughed, aware that he was leading her by one.

He chipped onto the green and two-putted into the hole. *Not bad,* he thought to himself.

Meggie was on the green by her sixth shot and two-putted into the hole. "My, my, my," Meggie exclaimed, "You beat me that time, your seven to my eight. I've got to stop wandering off into the trees and settle down to the game." She looked determined.

Hawk stood up a little bit taller. *Maybe this game was going to be fun, after all.* Having won the first hole, he addressed the ball first on the second tee. On the right, a windmill twirled to a slight breeze. On the left, a few trees. At least there were no water hazards to tempt his ball. *Should be easy,* he judged. He swung. The ball glanced off his driver and skipped over toward the women's tee.

"Oh, too bad," Meggie clucked. She stepped up to the tee, took a practice swing, and slammed her ball two hundred yards out to the far curve in the fairway. A beautiful drive.

Hawk's heart sunk. *It's just a game,* he reminded himself. He topped his second shot, then zinged other shots past a metal sculpture of a horse and driver, and laced his ball down the fairway from rough to rough. Only the circled eight rule saved him from total humiliation.

Meggie, on the other hand, drove the ball down the fairway, ending up directly behind two birch trees on her second shot. With her nine iron, she aimed right for the hole. Twice, the trees pitched the ball back at her. Finally, she reached the hole for a score of seven. "Trees again," she explained to Hawk. "I can't get enough of them."

She asked for his score and grinned, "Our scores are now even."

"The game has just begun," he cautioned her.

They hauled their golf carts over a bridge, a miniature replica of the great Mackinaw Bridge. Hawk couldn't help noticing the large iron flowers decorating the side of the third fairway, along which ran a stream. *Oh no, more water,* he groaned. At least the fairway was short, only one hundred and forty yards.

With a scrambler wood, Meggie hit high in the air, right into a sand trap. "Oh, no," she cried.

Hawk successfully avoided the water. They both racked up scores of four.

"Still even," he triumphantly proclaimed and pecked her on the cheek. *I can see why people like this game,* he mused.

But the fourth hole was long and arduous, decorated with a rock pile in the middle of the fairway. Despite the coolness of the spring air, Hawk began to sweat.

Meggie sliced to the right, ending up in the rough. "Of course," she groaned, "There are trees over there."

Hawk topped his ball and kept hooking his shots to the left, until he finally knocked the ball into the hole for a circled eight. "Thank heaven for beginner's rules," he sighed.

Meggie's luck wasn't much better. After ricocheting off a tree, Meggie slammed her ball successively down to the green, only to chip over it. Finally, she wedged the ball onto the green into the hole. But before she could shout hooray, the ball perversely bounced back out. "Sometimes, I really despise this game," she muttered. Her final score was eight.

"We're still even," he grinned, amazed and pleased at his good luck and her misfortune. Maybe he wasn't going to have to submit to her wishes after all.

The fifth tee was guarded by a twelve-foot carved wooden Indian warrior carrying a tiny spear. "He'd do better with a golf club." Meggie laughed. She sliced her ball into the trees. Hawk drove straight down the fairway.

"Not bad," Meggie admired. "Beginner's luck."

Hawk winked at her, punning, "I hit like a tiger, don't I?"

Both followed up with good second shots. For once, Meggie soared over the trees instead of into them. Then, filled with her praise and a fresh sense of competence, Hawk faltered, topping the ball twice, and stumbled down to the hole for another score of eight.

With her three wood, Meggie slammed the ball down onto the green and grinned at Hawk. On this hole, she was going to beat his butt, and there was nothing he could do about it. Meggie carefully calculated the angle and the curvature of the green. She confidently stroked the ball. It blew straight toward the hole, then wobbled as if changing its mind, and veered off to the left, rolling down an incline. No matter, Meggie would bag it on the second putt. But again the ball rolled left, and only on the third putt, was she able to sink it.

"Score?" Hawk asked.

"Six," she growled.

She now led him by two points.

Meggie stepped up to the sixth tee and drove one hundred and eighty yards up the fairway. "Let's see you do that," she boasted.

His ball dribbled impotently over to the women's tee, but on his second shot he caught up to her ball. "I couldn't stay away from you," he joshed, patting her fanny.

Meggie grinned. She planned to increase her lead and show him a thing or two about the game. Exuberantly, she brought her three wood down upon the ball. It glanced off to the left and perversely rolled in between two large sand traps. "Oh no." She hung her head. "I don't know why I ever play this stupid game."

Meanwhile, Hawk's next shot aimed straight and true, landing right before the green. He looked over at Meggie struggling to position herself between the sand traps. Meggie socked the ball high over the front trap, dropping her ball near his ball.

"You can't stay away from me, can you?" He laughed, then executed a fine chip shot and two-putted into the hole.

Meggie's jaw tightened. She angled her sand wedge and sighted on the hole, pulling back into a half swing, but her wedge hit the ground before it hit the ball. The ball bounced only two yards. Another chip and two putts put her score up to seven, in contrast to his six.

"How long have you played this game?" Hawk inquired. He was twitting her now.

"Don't ask," she answered. She had to admit that he was playing better than she had anticipated. Her game was terrible.

On their way to the seventh tee, they passed a huge carved wooden bear that roared at them. Hawk jumped. "Are all golf courses like this?" he asked.

"You mean part golf course, part art gallery? No," she laughed. They passed a kissing bower with a Porta-John behind it. On the left, meandered a stream. A peacock and duck, good friends, strolled together in the sun past the fish feeding area. A carved statue of the Virgin Mary watched over the golfers and birds alike. Hawk groaned upon seeing the seventh tee. It required a drive over water. The entire right side of the fairway was bordered by a small lake from which arose a humorous sculpture of two human legs and feet sticking up in the air.

"Perhaps you ought to make an offering to the water gods, first," Meggie counseled.

"And you to the tree spirits," he retorted.

But he didn't, and, true to form, his first ball soared into the air, heading for the middle of the lake. It hit, then skipped merrily across the water's surface, bouncing up onto the dry bank. "Will you look at that?" he exclaimed. "I'm walking on water these days."

Meggie made a more conventional shot to the fairway. Chipping and putting, both scored five on the hole.

"You're only leading me by one stroke," he reminded her.

"But we have two more holes to go," she shot back. Steely determination outlined the set of her jaw and the cast of her eyes.

Pulling their carts behind them, the two entered Woodchip Way, a path to the eighth tee through dark woods, in which were set groupings of ceramic dwarfs and Snow White, wood-cut rabbits, a bear carved into a log, a plastic frog that croaked at them. They crossed a covered bridge, out into the open area.

At the eighth tee, Meggie announced, "This is a very tough hole, so don't expect that you'll be able to do well." She pointed out the rough, the woods, the stream to the right, the trees and pond to the left. The green wasn't even visible from the tee. The fairway curved around to the right, toward a white bridge traversing the stream.

Meggie drove into the rough but managed to avoid the trees.

Once again, Hawk topped his first ball to the women's tee, but made it to the hole in six shots. Meggie's game paralleled his, down to the same score.

The path, through a grape arbor to the ninth and last tee, was guarded by a large carved totem pole: an eagle crushing a fish in its talons while standing on top of a bear who was ripping apart a fish in its mouth. Hawk sympathized with the fish. He was pleased to have been able to hold Meggie's lead down to one point, because he knew her plan had been to drag him off to the golf course, give him a good drubbing, and chew on him a bit about their different scores before spitting him out with gusto. He had to admit, though, that he liked the challenge of her competitive spirit.

The ninth tee boasted a water hazard right at the start. Meggie took a mulligan, then drove to the right of the green. To avoid the water, Hawk drove left about one hundred yards, then chipped his ball near to the hole. Oh, that felt so good. *What a great game is golf,* he enthused. Having to take two putts didn't dampen his sudden feelings of accomplishment.

Meggie hit the ground on her second shot and had to chip again. Three putts and her score reached six. "Your score?" she immediately inquired.

"Four," he proudly announced. "I think I won the game. By one point."

Meggie's face adopted a puzzled expression.

Beside the porch of the clubhouse perched a tall birdhouse in the form of a miniature mansion. As they pulled up their carts beneath it, Meggie observed, "The birdhouse looks straight out of the movie *Psycho,* doesn't it?"

Indeed, Hawk had to admit it did. "How about the two of us going home to take a shower together?" He arched his eyebrows mischievously at her. "Remember, as the loser, you must grant my wish."

As they headed back toward Chrysalis in the pick-up, Meggie sat quietly, refiguring their scores, adding up the numbers. Hawk twitted her. "Didn't you warn me earlier that I shouldn't get upset when you'd beat me at this game?"

"There's something I don't understand," she said, holding the pencil in her mouth.

"What?" Hawk asked.

"You said that you had never played golf before. Right?" She eyed him suspiciously.

"That's right. I've never taken out clubs and played a course." He gave her a sanctimonious look, pursing his lips in exaggerated style.

"Even though I played badly, how were you able to beat me?" She studied his face, knowing he was hiding something from her.

"Couldn't it be that I am a natural athlete? Your equal in all things?" He grinned, looking straight ahead at the road.

Meggie frowned and rechecked the scores.

"You want the truth?" he asked.

"Yes, I certainly do."

"I am your equal, Meggie." He smiled a coyote smile at her.

She waited.

"But," he confessed, "this past week, I took a couple of lessons from the golf pro at Matheson Greens in Northport."

"So, that's it," she replied.

"Given your high score, it might be a good idea for you to take a couple of lessons too." He cracked up laughing. He knew it would be a long time before he'd be able to beat her again in golf.

Still, Meggie had to admit she was impressed by his very first game of golf. She'd even let him take a shower with her.

As equals, of course.

Bev watched her colleague and friend slide into the joyful depths of love, lost to reason, full of fantasy and anticipation. The mood was contagious in the office. Clients remarked, in the middle of their own distress, how happy Dr. O'Connor seemed to be. Not that they were envious, but, rather, they wanted to share in a portion of it. For herself, Bev gave up moping for her ex, Coulter, and turned her attentions to a new flame. "I'm learning," she confided to Meggie, "how to be flirtatious again."

Lucy studied Sweet-Grass Woman trailing Larry around the sweat lodge area like a bitch in heat. It was in the sway of her hips, the coy looks she cast at both Hawk and Larry, the earnest expressions of helplessness around the two men. Lucy wasn't fooled for one minute. Sweet-Grass Woman needed to be put into her place. Lucy dragged on her cigarette, contemplating a course of action.

"I need your help in the kitchen," she told the younger woman. Sweet-Grass Woman gave Lucy a polite smile and followed her to the house.

"I'll wash the knives. You dry." Lucy handed her a towel.

"You have such a nice home," Sweet-Grass Woman complimented her.

"I have a good family, wonderful kids, a strong man. My husband is a good-looking man. Women are drawn to him. I feel sorry for them."

"Why?"

"Because, if any woman tries to steal my man, I will shoot off her kneecaps. She will never walk again." Lucy handed her a large kitchen knife, blade upward.

"Oh," Sweet-Grass Woman started. She had to twist her hand to grasp the knife without cutting herself.

Lucy finished up the dishes. *Good, she got the point.*

June Tubbs bounced back more rapidly from the encounter with the horses than did her mother. While playing catch with the child, Fritzie would occasionally lick her scarred face. Katya hovered about, fearful that every animal would now turn wild. Seeing this, Meggie found herself irritated with Katya's constant and controlling anxiety. "You have to give June freedom to be on her own," Meggie told her.

Reverend Karl Young continued his contact with the Tubbs, following June's progress. Katya switched to his church out of gratitude for his concern.

One day, Katya confessed to Meggie, "Paul has really changed since June's accident. I'm not sure I like the changes. He used to be sweet, predictable, someone I could count on. After June's accident he charged around like a bull in a china shop, uncontrollably angry, merciless toward Robert, uncommunicative and sarcastic toward me. I grew afraid that the marriage might not survive.

"One night, after a terrible argument, he stormed out of the house and didn't return until late. I don't know where he went, but he came back different somehow. He dashed up the stairs into Robert's room, grabbed his son, and held him, like a crazy man. The two of them talked and cried together, and since then there have been no more words of recrimination."

Katya shook her head, puzzled, "Paul's grown quieter, more introspective, philosophical about life. Mind you, I'm relieved that he no longer blames Robert for what happened, but it's just not the same between us. Changes scare me. Why can't life ever stay the same, Meggie?"

Often, Meggie found herself bereft of answers to life's challenges. Sometimes it seemed to her the older she got the less she knew. Her silence only seemed to encourage people to confide in her more.

Even the normally impassive Sam grew eloquent when he spoke to Meggie about the black mongrel. "If she hadn't backed off those horses, June wouldn't be here today. The dog gave up her life so that the child could live. Do we even have a word in the human language to describe that kind of love?" Right after the accident, Sam had buried the dog by the north fence and installed a fieldstone to mark the spot.

When the ground softened into spring, the two women brought June to the little dog's grave at the edge of the field. Together the three of them planted roses by the stone marker.

"Why a flower with thorns?" asked June, as they finished the planting.

Her mother answered, "The thorns tell of the sacrifice and the harshness in this little dog's life."

"But why red roses and not yellow roses?" June pressed, wanting answers for everything.

Meggie looked up at the little girl with her scarred face, smiled, and replied, "Red is the color of blood. Red is the color of healing."

At night, Adam Stands By Dog took himself out to the deserted sweat lodge area, where he sat himself down on a log. He liked the dark, the way the mist blew in from the Lake and blurred the boundaries, the way the trees sprouted auras of light, the spongy sink of the earth beneath his feet, the lumpy outline of the sweat lodge in front of him. He especially liked it when his grandmother came from the Other Side to sit beside him.

"Grandson, what's the matter? You look tired." Winona's voice was soothing.

"I miss you, Grandma. You're not here to tell me stories. Why can't I see you in the house or during the day?" Adam kicked at a twig on the ground.

"Too many lights. Too much noise," she answered.

"Why can't the others see you, Grandma?" This observation really puzzled him.

"They're too grown up. It takes a long time for them to develop the blindness." Winona reached out to grope the empty air, like a person with no eyesight.

"But Eva doesn't see you, and she's still a kid," the boy protested.

"Eva isn't interested. It's not simply a matter of my coming when you call. You have to have a real need for me and confidence that I will be there."

"I hear Hawk call out for you in the sweat lodge, but you don't come. I watch and wait, and you stay away." He peeled the bark from the log.

"Hawk is too distracted. He's forgotten what you know, how to strip away the barriers between the worlds. I can't do it for him. Now, Grandson, what is the matter with you?"

Adam thought a moment, afraid to tell her the whole truth. "I'm not doing that good in school," he answered. He patted the bark back into place, but it no longer stayed attached to its mooring.

Winona knew that someday he would tell her the whole story. "Ah, you'll do well when you are good and ready. I want you to know, Grandson, how proud I am of you, that you now have a strong Lakota name—Stands By Dog. It speaks of a good heart. It is a name to grow into."

"Grandmother, I love you," he answered.

"*Pilamaya*, Grandson."

Adam watched as his grandmother smiled and faded, growing paler and more translucent by the minute, until all that had been behind her resolved into sharp focus, and she was no longer there. The mist clung to the trees like gray Spanish moss, and the world around him condensed into definition, as if the Creator had taken a black pen and outlined the ground, the sweat lodge, the rock pile, the scattered logs on the ground, his house, Hawk's trailer in the distance, and the empty space left by his grandmother.

SEVENTEEN

CRISSCROSSED TRAILS

Coyote, he's a wise one.
His wits are his disguise.
He's honest when he can be,
But when he wants to,
He can lie.

Oh, Coyote,
When you going to change your tune?
When you going to stop running
Round all night,
Giving your song
To the moon?

—BILL HARLEY
Coyote

Accustomed to the harsh brown tones of the South Dakota badlands, Hawk was astonished by the delicate green beauty of the Michigan spring. White trillium speckled the cedar woods. Yellow
bellflowers hung from their spires of green. Wild purple violets
bloomed on the moist ground. Traverse City held its annual mush-
room festival in celebration of the tasty morels.

Dawn breached the horizon earlier and earlier. Each morning,
whether at Meggie's place or alone at his trailer, Hawk rose to greet
the sun, to sing a sunrise song, and to offer tobacco for the new day.
During Meggie's moon times, he retreated to his own place. Both of
them, heady in the days of discovery, found they needed time apart
from each other to gather back onto themselves. Putting on the best
face to each other, there was much left unsaid, still left unknown.

True to her word, Lucy found Hawk a job—as a Native American storyteller in schools, Boy Scout meetings, church gatherings, coffee houses, and story concerts. That he had never before held himself out to be a storyteller by profession didn't bother her in the least. She concocted an imaginative résumé of performances that adhered only to the slimmest thread of truth. When he pointed out to her the exaggerations on the flyer she had developed, she rebuked him, "For heaven's sake, Hawk, you know you're a damn good teller of stories. You've listened to the traditional stories all your life; they're in your blood. Just because I enhanced your informal experience a little doesn't mean I'm telling a lie. The truth is you've always been a storyteller. You just didn't know it."

Much to his surprise, he discovered he loved performing the old stories, especially to the children. Being of mixed blood, Hawk knew the stories from several tribal traditions. Iktomi, the Lakota trickster spider spirit was vain and foolish; early on he had traded his good mind for good looks. Coyote, the trickster spirit of the southwestern tribes, was more cunning but equally vain and lecherous. Culling out the earlier stories, he fascinated kids, detailing ancient trickster battles between the western Coyote and the southeastern Rabbit—each trying to outwit the other.

Invariably, the youngsters asked questions about Native Americans. "Do they still scalp people? What do Indians wear at night? Have you ever killed anyone? Do you live in a tipi?" The questions reflected the children's exposure to cowboy-and-Indian movies on television. Patiently, he responded, always hoping to bridge the chasm between the cultures.

During his stays at the trailer, Hawk continued checking out the signs around his home. As spring blossomed, Coyote's markings became clearer. Tracks upon tracks, the animal's trail circled around his abode, reminding him of Winona. "Love is very tricky," the old medicine woman had warned him.

Without needing the benefit of words, the eyes of Sweet-Grass Woman spoke clearly: "I'm available, if you're interested."

"Don't fall in love with a white woman." Laughing Bear's admonishment resounded in Hawk's head.

Looking at Meggie O'Connor by the inipi, Larry whispered, "She's attractive, but she'll never understand you."

"Do you honestly know what you are doing?" Lucy asked.

Even Three Legs, his Spirit guide, put in his two cents of advice: "You're going to have to choose one of these days—the Pipe road or the white way."

But in the exuberance of falling in love again, Hawk refused to heed any sign of caution. "That coyote is just a coyote," he reassured himself, while day after day, the trickster figure came alive in his stories to the children.

‧‧ ‧‧ ‧‧ ‧‧

"I've gotcha now!" said Coyote to Rabbit.

"Hush!" replied Rabbit, "Can't you see I'm baby-sitting?" Rabbit held his nose to a ground hole, a little stick in his paw.

"Whatcha baby-sitting?" asked Coyote, suspicious that Rabbit was planning to fool him again.

"Shh," answered Rabbit. "There is a whole nest of baby field mice in the hole, and their parents asked me to take care of them while they were away. If any of them wake up, I'm to push them back into the hole with this little stick."

"Now children," said Hawk, "Field mice to Coyote is like a candy bar to you. So . . ." Hawk gesticulated like a hungry animal and continued the tale:

"Let me baby-sit for a while," Coyote demanded.

"No, I'll do it."

"Please, let me. I'll take real good care of them," promised Coyote. And Rabbit finally agreed.

After Rabbit left, Coyote drooled with hunger. He wanted to taste some of those delicious field mice. First, he pounded on the ground, saying, "Wake up! Wake up little field mice." But not a one came out of the hole.

"They must be sound asleep," Coyote said to himself. "I will stir them awake with this stick." And with the stick he reached way into the hole until he could feel the stick go bump against something. He pushed and he poked.

"Do you know what was in that hole?"

The children shook their heads, their eyes wide with wonder.

"Ten thousand yellow jackets."

The children screamed in delight.

And every one of them swooped down on poor Coyote, stinging him. He bounded straight for the water, cursing that Rabbit all the way.

Hawk turned to the children, warning them, "So pay attention, because otherwise you'll find yourself getting badly stung one of these days."

Finishing up a long day of psychotherapy, Meggie restored her office to some sort of order, replacing play-therapy toys on the shelf, emptying the wastepaper basket of its daily quotient of tissues, and plumping the pillows on her couch. There was a heaviness to her movements that bespoke more than just fatigue. Bev poked her face into the doorway, saying, "Meggie, you look so sad. Where is the face of the woman in love with love?"

Meggie shook her head. "The twins called. Savannah Todd has been diagnosed with lung cancer. The doctors don't give much hope of recovery. At her advanced age, they're not going to put her through any rigorous chemotherapy."

"Oh my God, what is Sasha going to do without her sister?"

Typical that people always seem to worry most about the ones that are left behind. Meggie shrugged her shoulders. She was tired of people always having problems.

It would be so nice if, just once in a while, life could flow smoothly for its travelers, Meggie thought. "There's going to be a prayer service for Savannah at their home tomorrow night. Want to go with me?"

"Well, you know I'm not much of a believer. But, then again, Savannah doesn't have a religious bone in her body either." Bev seemed to waver back and forth, mulling over the idea. Finally she assented. "Sure, why not?"

The next night, friends gathered at the Todds' home. Sasha played host and served everyone tea, coffee, and cookies on lace doilies. Savannah smiled, trying to put on a face of cheer, but she looked wan and afraid. Meggie's heart saddened at the forced gaiety of the twins. Katya and Paul were there, circulating around the group, most of whom were over sixty years old. Meggie noticed that everybody avoided mentioning the word *cancer.*

In a warm and intimate gesture, Bev marched over to the seated Savannah, took her hand, and asked her directly, "How are you feeling, Savannah? I heard about your cancer."

"Oh, that!" the old woman replied defiantly. "I'm planning to live to the fullest until the end. I'm going fishing with my sister tomorrow. I'm going to have taffy-pulling parties. And," she announced loudly for everyone present, "I do not intend to stop smoking or drinking sherry as my doctors ordered."

"Hush, Savannah, you'll do no such thing," admonished her sister.

Savannah ignored Sasha, adding, "And as for a prayer meeting, that was never my idea. I don't believe in such things. It's Sasha's doing. It was only when I realized that it provided a good excuse for a party," she looked graciously around the room, "that I was willing for her to call a preacher, who, if he knows what's good for him, will keep the praying to a minimum."

In the middle of her statement, Savannah did not notice the arrival of the minister. He paused in the doorway, listening to her with a bemused smile lighting up his face. "I promise, Miss Todd," he addressed her formally, "that I will keep my prayers brief and to the point, provided you help me curtail the prayers of others."

Everyone relaxed; Savannah's breach of good manners had been overlooked. Sasha rushed to repair her sister's damage. "Everyone, I would like you to meet the Reverend Young."

What a nice young man. He reminds me of George what's-his-name, mused Savannah.

Not bad-looking for a clergyman, observed Bev.

Full of charm and long on charisma, Karl was true to his word; he kept the ceremony short.

She arrived, unannounced, at his trailer door, bearing a casserole and a pie. As soon as he opened the door, Hawk recognized trouble standing there in tight jeans, long black hair, doe eyes, and an inviting smile.

Sweet-Grass Woman.

"I brought you something," she said. "Aren't you going to ask me in?"

It would have been ungenerous of him to refuse the food.

She swept past him with her right hip grazing his front. She set up the small kitchen table and dolloped the casserole onto his dishes. "Come eat. It's delicious."

Sitting down opposite to him, she confessed, "This is the only way I could get your attention."

"The casserole is excellent," he mumbled, his mouth full of the noodles, melted cheese, and tuna fish.

She kicked off her shoes and, under the table, inched a set of warm toes up his pant leg.

He pulled back and shook his head. "This isn't right," he told her.

"Why not?" she asked, reaching out to stroke his arm with a finger.

"I'm involved with another woman. Besides, I'm your teacher. Too many medicine teachers are already out there putting the make on women who come to ceremony. They're easy prey. It's not right to take advantage of a woman that way." In the cool air of his trailer, Hawk found himself sweating.

"Apple pie?" she asked, not paying attention to his words. She ran her tongue around her lips.

He knew she would jump into his bed if he gave her the least bit of encouragement. "It's not right," he repeated, sounding hollow even to himself. *Not right for him. Not right for Sweet-Grass Woman. Not right for Meggie.*

He didn't want to shame Sweet-Grass Woman, nor could he afford to prolong the temptation. In short, he didn't trust himself, despite his budding love for Meggie. "You must go now," he said. "Thank you for the food. I also want you to understand something."

Sweet-Grass Woman looked at him with mournful eyes.

"There's much more to you than simply your body, which, I admit, is beautiful. There is your spirit and your heart which you must protect and cherish. You need a man to love all parts of you, and I cannot be that man. To sample one part and discard the others is to make a mockery of you as a human being. There are many men riding the circuit of medicine who will take your power as a woman to restore themselves, and they will leave you empty. This is not right."

But I can understand why the men do this, when the women offer themselves so freely, he thought as he watched her curvaceous form retreat across the yard.

And such beautiful women, he sighed.

EIGHTEEN

WHEN SMOKE GETS IN YOUR EYES

They said someday you'll find
All who love are blind
When your heart's on fire,
You must realize
Smoke gets in your eyes . . .

—JEROME KERN AND OTTO HARBACH
Smoke Gets in Your Eyes

"I have a confession to make." Andrea leaned intimately toward her therapist.

"Okay." Meggie was all ears, surprised that her new client began their fourth session in this manner.

"I have been painting the same painting over and over. I am obsessed with the problem of chiaroscuro, the study of light and dark, shade and shadow. Trying to find something new to break through on the canvas. Nothing, however, brings me the illumination I seek. The landscape remains flat, two dimensional. And scary."

"Scary?"

"The trees in my painting reach out with branches that are like claws. The water is always frothy, slapping at the shore, dark and drab in color. The gulls do not ride the air for pleasure but, rather, pierce the skin of the lake for fish. The birches look cold, and grapevine smothers and strangles the young saplings. It's not a friendly place."

"What about the landscape inside of you?" Meggie felt confident that Andrea would understand the nature of projection.

"There's a difference. Inside of me, there are slashes of red and purple and black and heat. Outside, I'm stuck with blues, greens, white, and frost. As if a large metal door, the kind they made for the *Titanic,* separates what I paint from what I feel." She split the air before her with her hand.

"What would you need to open that door?"

"First, I would need to trust my husband," Andrea bound her hands together in her lap, as if holding onto a life preserver.

"What kind of trust?"

Andrea sighed and let her hands go limp. "Everywhere he goes, women can sense his vulnerability, his sensitivity, his ability to make that person feel she is the most important person in the whole world to him. He's a curious combination of charming little boy and everyone's confessor. Women flock to him and offer themselves to him. And yet," she paused, "he's lonely. I sit behind my steel door where he can't touch me. But," she added, with a kind of smug satisfaction, "I've never cheated on him."

Meggie remained silent, letting her client continue.

"From almost the beginning of our relationship, not less than a year after the honeymoon, he began the first of many affairs. He was discreet about it, fearful that he might lose his job if others found out. At first, I'd confront him, and he'd cry and ask my forgiveness and plunge himself into guilt with an indulgence that drove me almost as crazy as the affairs. 'It won't ever happen again,' he would promise.

"Of course, it did, and after a while, he stopped making those promises to me. He truly believes that what I don't know won't hurt me, so he goes to great lengths to conceal his affairs." Her right hand spun out, as if to pull an unraveling thread from her scarf.

"It's almost become a game for me to find out who is next in his long list of seductions. At first, I was stupid. I blamed the women, not him. I would follow him to a motel where a tryst had been set. One time, I took my car keys and scratched the hell out of the woman's car when she was in the motel room with him. Another time, I punctured all four of the woman's tires. *Poosh*—the tires deflated. It gave me great satisfaction, for the moment.

"Eventually, I realized it wasn't their fault for falling in love with him, when I had been the first in a long line of females who made that same mistake. So, I put the blame where it belonged." Andrea sat back, finished for the moment.

"On the man yearning for his wife hidden behind the steel door," Meggie pushed.

Andrea blinked, grew angry. "I know what you're suggesting—that if I had been receptive to him, he wouldn't have strayed. You think I'm at fault, don't you?" Her voice became accusative, shrill.

"What I think," Meggie spoke in a soft voice, "is that you and your husband are both human, both lonely, both disconnected from each other. Yet, you don't divorce, and that tells me something."

"What?" The defiance sharpened her pronunciation.

"That there is still hope you each have, that something new can happen to revive the marriage."

"Ha! You're dead wrong," Andrea snorted. "He stays married to me because divorce is unthinkable for his precious reputation as a stable, married man in the community. If he loved me, he would keep his pants zipped."

"Then tell me, Andrea," Meggie said, "Why do you choose to remain with him?"

"Oh," her voice trembled, "it's simple. I've never stopped loving him." Andrea once again locked her hands in her lap, paused, and looked up at Meggie, despair etched in her eyes. "And the landscape never changes."

It was more than curiosity that continued to draw Meggie to the inipi ceremonies. The intimate silence in the lodge, the public nature of everyone's prayers, the deepening appreciation for Hawk's knowledge, the widening sense of community—all these became increasingly precious to her. But, most important, Meggie found that she could enter the sweat lodge all frazzled from a week of psychotherapy appointments, people's problems, and client demands. In the simple ceremony she could find her balance once again.

Inside the sweat lodge, it no longer seemed to matter to anyone that she was white. In the darkness, everyone's skin looked the same. There was no recitation from any holy book or scripture, no written words to be dissected or reviewed in sermon, no fancy Sunday clothes to wear. Inside the lodge, attired only with a towel for a covering, they sat on the Grandmother. With songs, they called the Grandfathers and the medicine Spirits to enter the inipi. From their hearts, each one gave voice to his or her own personal prayers. Before Wakan Tanka, they were all simply two-leggeds trying to find their place within the Creation.

Outside the sweat lodge, Meggie was beginning to feel more accepted by the Native American community. Proud of her own heritage, she felt no need to apologize for being white. But sometimes the differences—the fry bread and venison, the earthy humor, the physical modesty between the sexes, the stories told that mocked white people, the pervasive distrust of all governmental agencies, the politics and gossip in the Native American world—sharply produced within her a sense of estrangement. During these moments, it was a lonely feeling being on the outside looking in. As she genuinely liked most everyone in the community, it was also new and confusing to Meggie to experience such emotions. But she suspected that her occasional sense of alienation was one that must occur daily for blacks, Asians, and Native Americans living in a dominant white society. Out of respect for the cultural differences, Meggie restrained her opinions and questions, stayed on the periphery, looked for ways to pitch in and help around the ceremonies and, most of all, paid attention.

Meggie was growing more and more comfortable in the sweat lodge community when suddenly a new face appeared, unannounced. A dusty brown car with South Dakota license plates barreled up Lucy's driveway as the young men started the inipi fire and the sun slipped down the earth's western rim. Hawk was deep in conversation with one of the men when a woman jumped out of the car and hurried to Lucy's house. Slender, with long dark hair, and obviously Native American, she knocked at the door and entered.

A few moments later, Lucy walked out to the fire, where everyone was making tobacco ties. She signaled to Hawk. He made his way over to where she stood; she whispered in his ear, her head nodding back to the house. Meggie noted that he seemed startled, then puzzled. He glanced over at her. Putting the young men in charge of the fire, he strode off toward the house. Lucy stayed out by the fire, observing with satisfaction that Sweet-Grass Woman sat far away from Larry.

Thirty minutes passed, and neither Hawk nor the woman had emerged. Meggie could hardly withstand the curiosity. *Perhaps she's a relative,* she told herself. Finally, the door opened and the two of them appeared, talking rapidly to each other. On his face, Meggie could read both intense interest and delight. Hawk brought the woman over to the fire area.

She's beautiful was Meggie's first impression.

Hawk addressed the group, all curious and eager to meet her. "I'd like to introduce Rising Smoke from Pine Ridge. She's a Pipe carrier and knows how to run the women's inipi ceremony." The other women smiled, pleased by that information.

Raising her eyebrows, Lucy commented, "She also knows Hawk real well. She used to be his wife."

Rising Smoke laughed, "I'm not sure that's something he'd want to brag on."

Hawk glanced over toward Meggie.

It was then that Meggie noticed how the blackness of the woods was creeping toward the group by the fire. Night was gobbling up all particles of light as the sun abandoned them to the advancing darkness.

Long after everyone had departed that evening after the inipi ceremonies and the feast, Meggie helped Lucy clean up the last of the dishes, while Rising Smoke entertained Hawk and Larry with reservation stories and family gossip. Meggie finally gathered up her sodden towel dress and food container and announced that she was going home.

"I'll walk you out to your car." Hawk pushed himself away from the table.

By his choice of words, Meggie guessed that he wasn't planning to come spend the night with her. As they approached her car, she inquired, "When will I next see you?"

But what she really wanted to ask was: *What is Rising Smoke doing here? What are her plans? Why won't you come home with me tonight?*

"Soon." He gave her a peck on the cheek.

But the following nights, Hawk stayed absent from Meggie's bed. Daily, he kept in touch by phone.

She asked him why she hadn't seen more of him.

He was busy with his jobs, he answered.

He was catching up on old gossip with Rising Smoke, who, temporarily, was staying at Lucy's house. He would be by soon, he promised.

There was nothing for Meggie to do but wait, a position of passivity that gnawed at her insides. There had been no commitments that they had yet made to each other. Into what had been a sense of joy and fulfillment now trickled doubt and despair. Maybe she had mistaken the intensity of his feelings for her. Maybe Bev was right—maybe she had simply fallen in love with love. Maybe she was crazy for thinking she could bridge the gap between two cultures. Maybe she had been fooling herself . . . Anxiety kept surfacing its ugly head; her sleep was restless in the empty bed.

A dream haunted her:

She was walking down a hill. To her right stood a fair-haired man with arms opened toward her. To her surprise, she knew his identity. He was the Apostle Peter. To her left, across a stream, stood a chunky, dark-haired man, obviously Native American. In his arms, he held out a Sacred Pipe. They were both asking her to make a choice.

The next morning, she awoke, another dream pressing at the back of her mind:

She was wandering down to the docks by which rested a large ferry-boat. The waters were pitch black, the air gray, a world without sun.

Tied to the pier was a rowboat with an old man and a dog sitting in it. The ferry had apparently just arrived and was not going anywhere for a while, so she approached the old man. The dog, curiously, had three heads, but otherwise seemed perfectly friendly. "Will you take me across?" she asked the old man. "I want to find Winona."

He shook his head, "No, you can't go across. Go check the passengers coming off the ferry. Maybe you'll find her there."

Meggie scrambled over to where people were disembarking. Waiting, waiting, waiting as the boat emptied itself, Meggie realized Winona wasn't ever coming back.

Half awake, half asleep, Meggie knew the night dreams spoke their own truth in the new morning.

Over on the Other Side, Winona discovered she could stand up. The pain in her back was easing as fewer and fewer people called upon her name and memory. Strands that bonded her back to the old life shriveled, much like an umbilical cord that ties a child to its mother and then is cast away with the refuse of afterbirth. Winona found herself adrift without the weight of old connections, for new ones had yet to be formed. She wondered to herself whether this period of being alone was a necessary time, a time of purification and healing so that she could shrug off the old debris and prepare herself for the next phase.

Still, she could not completely let go of her concerns for Lucy, Hawk, the grandchildren, and Meggie O'Connor. No matter how hard she tried, she was unable to break through their blindness to her presence. They simply did not see or hear her.

After dawn had chased off the grief of her dreams, Meggie forced herself out of bed. Work had always served as a balm to her vexed spirit. Besides, she grumbled to herself, what was Saint Peter doing anyway, invading her sleep? If the Christian traditions had fed her soul, would she have ever gone seeking a home on the Pipe road? What could Peter offer her that the Pipe hadn't already given her?

Her first client of the day was Andrea. Meggie was not happy with their limited progress and sensed that time was working against them. If the landscape didn't soon change, hope would disappear. Then Andrea might lock herself behind the steel door forever.

Something nagged at her, something that Andrea had said during the last session. Meggie reviewed her session notes once, then twice, before she saw it:

Meggie had asked, *"What would you need to open that door?"*

Andrea had answered, *"First, I would need to trust my husband."*

Meggie had almost missed it. Wherever there is a *first,* there has to be a *second.*

Meggie waited to see where Andrea planned to take the session, but her client was unusually quiet and withdrawn. *She is sliding into despair.*

"If you were able to trust your husband, what else would you need to open that door?" Meggie asked.

At first, it seemed that Andrea didn't hear her or didn't want to acknowledge the question. A deep gloom of silence settled into the therapy room. Meggie kept quiet, letting the question percolate.

"A ladder," Andrea finally spoke.

"A rope and night goggles," she added.

"A headlamp, a map, and a pair of waders. Yes, that should about do it." Andrea sat back in the chair.

Meggie waited for an explanation, knowing that Andrea was taking her to the black hole.

"I would need a ladder to get in, a rope on my waist for extra security, night goggles to see what is down there, a headlamp to illuminate the map to know where I'm going and where I've been."

"And the waders?"

Andrea grimaced, "You and I both suspect that there's a lot of slimy shit in that hole. I don't want to get dirty if I have to wallow in it."

"Would you like me to go down there with you or would you prefer I stay on top and hold on to the rope?" Meggie needed to determine Andrea's expectations.

"This is all hypothetical, isn't it?" Andrea commented. "It's based on the assumption that my husband will become faithful and trustworthy, and that I can then confront my own issues. I tell you that's not going to happen."

"That's the dilemma," Meggie said. "Because of that black hole dogging your steps, you can't open yourself up to loving your husband. When you close off to him, he looks elsewhere to other women. When he is unfaithful, you triple-lock that door and say it isn't safe to turn around and look down that hole."

And she is right; it isn't safe for her.

"I'm stuck, aren't I?" The way Andrea said that was deadly.

Meggie flashed onto Winona and how the old medicine woman talked to her during their sessions together, teaching her through the use of stories. "Andrea," she said, "I have a story from Greece to share with you:

"Demeter, the ancient goddess of the harvest, had a beautiful daughter by the name of Persephone. One day while picking flowers in a field, Persephone caught the eye of Hades, the king of the underworld. Riding in his chariot, he swooped down and kidnapped the terrified young maiden and dove down through a cleft of the earth into the darkness. Oh, Persephone screamed, not wanting to be parted from her mother.

"But Hades was determined to make her his wife. Demeter was so angry and full of grief that she withheld her gifts of fertility, and the land began to dry up. The people exhorted Zeus, the ruler of the gods and goddesses, to do something, so that they would not starve. Zeus told Hades he would have to let go of the young woman.

"While down in the underworld, Persephone had refused to eat or partake of any pleasures. When Hades informed her that she was free to leave, she became aware of her hunger. He offered her pomegranate seeds to eat, and she ate four of them. In that manner she was agreeing to return to the underworld for four months of every year. Every time she returns, her mother mourns the loss and the land ceases to produce. That is why we have the seasons."

"I don't understand what that has to do with me," said Andrea.

"Before Hades kidnapped her, Persephone was the innocent maiden, a child in her consciousness. But upon her return from the underworld, she had become Queen of Hades, a woman of power and knowledge. Now, if you had asked her whether she would have chosen to be kidnapped and plunged into grief, I am sure Persephone would have said, 'Not on your life.' But pain has a way sometimes of transforming one from the sweetness of idealistic youth to the wisdom of maturity. Yet there's a catch to it."

"What?" Andrea sounded skeptical, unconvinced that anything could be worth the pain.

"You have to face the hole and consciously climb down into it. Persephone chose to eat those seeds. No one forced her." Meggie waited, not sure what Andrea would say.

"I'm surprised," answered Andrea, "that she didn't choke to death on them."

🐾 🐾 🐾 🐾

Hawk telephoned Meggie at home, knowing that she would still be at work. He didn't like making excuses. On her answering machine he left a message telling her that he missed her and wanted to see her soon. Bewildered by the sudden and unexpected arrival of Rising Smoke, Hawk was taken aback by his happiness at seeing her. He thought he had successfully expunged his former wife from his heart. *I should have known better,* he reminded himself. *The quirky side of bitterness is always the corking of love.*

Hawk and Rising Smoke had a lot of old stories to tell each other. She knew his people. He knew hers. Conversation was easy, familiar. They had a lot of new stories to add to their repertoire. Once a single strand had united their lives, and when it broke, both had braided themselves into the lives of others. But neither of them had remarried.

Rising Smoke had finally defeated the curse of alcohol. "It was eating me up on the inside," she acknowledged. While boozing, she had stayed away from ceremony and given over her Pipe and medicine bundle to her teacher for safekeeping. But she had missed the comfort of her Chanunpa Wakan. "I felt empty without it."

Her teacher on the reservation put her through a series of exhausting inipi ceremonies to dry her out. "It was a choice," she laughed. "Either I was going to get sober or those sweat lodge ceremonies were going to kill me."

Hawk found it curious that he was silent about Meggie, reluctant to let Rising Smoke know of his budding love for the white psychologist. He told himself he would tell Rising Smoke about it later. He temporarily kept his distance from Meggie because he didn't want his former wife to start asking intrusive questions.

In the shadowy regions of his mind, Hawk knew that Coyote's tracks were spreading out in all directions.

NINETEEN

THE SNAKE

. . . Several of Nature's People
I know, and they know me—
I feel for them a transport
Of cordiality—

But never met this Fellow
Attended, or alone
Without a tighter breathing
And Zero at the Bone—

—EMILY DICKINSON
A Narrow Fellow in the Grass

May burst uncertainly upon the scene, wavering from nights of near-freezing temperatures to windy days of summer heat. Hawk began to lose weight, fasting in preparation for his *hanbleciya*. More and more, he sought time to be alone, working with his Chanunpa Wakan. The community of sweat lodge people watched him draw inward, away from others, readying himself to go up on the hill. He lectured them, "Take care of the Pipe. Be respectful. In all your days, you will never grasp its full power. Even though you may neglect your Pipe, your Pipe will never be unfaithful to you."

Typically gaunt from marathon running, Bev began to gain weight in the warming days. "Too much eating out at gourmet restaurants."

She laughed, patting her rounded tummy. The added pounds softened and sensualized her athletic body.

"Too much loving." She arched her eyebrows mischievously at Meggie. Bev's face, however, looked tired, as if she wasn't getting enough sleep.

"Too many men in my life," Bev groaned.

They were taking an hour's lunch break between clients. Meggie traded Bev half of her low-fat turkey and swiss cheese sandwich for half of a greasy, warm Reuben, piled high with corned beef and mustard, from the Firehouse Deli. "I'm into denial and not doing well with it," Meggie declared.

"Boy, that's sure not my problem," Bev exclaimed, focusing on the food.

"Too much love?" probed Meggie.

Bev rolled her eyes, "God, Meggie, I haven't dated so much since I was a teenager. I think I could have every night scheduled, but you know, the old body needs a rest." She looked up to see if she was scandalizing her best friend.

Meggie, however, was only half listening. Just a month ago, she had been the one flitting about the office in the throes of new love. She didn't resent her friend's exuberance. It was simply that Meggie no longer knew where she stood with Hawk. She wanted to chalk up his absence at night to the preparations for the vision quest, but intuition suggested that other forces were at work.

Licking her fingers after demolishing the sandwich halves, Bev bit into a juicy apple. "Sam Waters is an adventurous soul. I've done more things with him, from hiking two miles of dunes before breakfast to ice fishing on Lake Leelanau and freezing my butt. He's a wonderful raconteur, and he keeps me laughing with all his bawdy limericks and animal stories. But in bed, he's a dud. He's been a bachelor too long."

"And then," she gave Meggie a cryptic smile, "there's a second man whom I've begun to see."

"Why are you being so mysterious?" inquired Meggie.

"Because I'm not going to tell you his name."

Meggie was puzzled. It was unusual for the two of them to withhold information from each other. "I don't understand . . ."

"Let's just say that I don't think you would approve. Also, it might compromise you in your professional work."

"Whom you're dating is going to compromise my work?" Meggie was baffled. "Is he a client of mine?"

"No." Bev grew uncomfortable having said even this much. "It's too complicated. Someday, I'll tell you about it."

It's probably not the only situation about which I'm uninformed, Meggie thought. She felt she had only herself to blame. *Didn't I tell Hawk, in so many words, that we needed to give our relationship time and space? Not to rush it.* His absence from her bed was probably his way of trying to respect her wishes.

What a fool, her heart scolded.

As the tempestuous spring temperature shifted between winter and summer, the sun encouraged the opening of leaf buds and flower blossoms. Bursting with dazzling white blooms, the cherry tree orchards stretched across the sandy hills, as if in a bridal procession. Tiny blue forget-me-nots dotted the sunny roadside; violets snuggled into the shadows of the woodland. Thundering storms impetuously swept off the Lake to feed the thirsty roots of the busy plant kingdom. Dank earth smells competed with sweet honeysuckle, perfuming the air. All sorts of animals moved about restlessly, establishing their territories, courting potential mates with song, dance, and masculine display, building nests, digging dens, making a home for new life.

Meggie counted on Hawk to continue coming over on Fridays to help her clear out dead brush and sticker bushes, to give the young saplings at Chrysalis a chance to grow.

He didn't disappoint her.

After a morning spent with the clippers, Meggie's back ached from bending over to cut close to the roots. Hawk, ahead of her with the chain saw, was tackling the bigger bushes. She looked longingly at his strong back as he worked. Upon arriving that morning, he had wrapped his arms around her and warmly kissed her, as if there had been no sudden interruptions to their nights together. She held back the questions in her heart. Fritzie broke their embrace, jumping up and down between them.

Shading her hand against the sun's brightness, she watched the dog cavort around Hawk, barking at the buzz of the chain saw. Fritzie was clearly irritated by the racket; ears lowered against the noise, he moved away from the human beings.

The sound of a giant mosquito grated on his floppy ears. No matter what he did, nothing seemed to divert the man's attention. Fritzie sank down on the ground, amidst the tiny purple flowers of pachysandra, angling his nose in a scent-filled direction. He spotted a fresh hole in the earth, a deep hole. Rising in curiosity, Fritzie ambled over to investigate. The hole's diameter was about the size of his long nose. With his front paws, he scrabbled at the dirt to widen the cavity and wedged his nose deep down into the dark sandy opening.

Something down there smelled of slime and soil. Something down there hissed. Before Fritzie could yank his nose out of danger's way, a small rattlesnake shot up the hole and struck him between his eyes, then slithered back down into the shadowy depths. Fritzie leapt back, barking at first in alarm and then, increasingly, in pain. Pawing furiously at the crazy throbbing in his head, he began to dance in circles.

Head hurt. Head hurt. Bad hurt.

Immediately his nose began swelling as the venom surged into the bloodstream. Dizzy, uncoordinated visions of the world swirled around him. He felt the man's arms pick him up and restrain his legs. His breathing grew more shallow. As he struggled for breath, his throat commenced a rattling sound. He fought furiously against the man in order to free his legs, but the man's strong arms held him down. The woman ran into the house. His vision grew fuzzy, diminished.

"I got Sam on the phone. It will take him twenty minutes to get here. Oh Fritzie, old boy. Please, you've got to stay alive." Meggie's voice edged on hysteria. She placed a bag of crushed ice on his swollen nose. The terrier burrowed his head into the ice.

Hawk took control. "Can you hold him down?" Fritzie had stopped struggling as he fought now to suck oxygen into a closing throat.

She nodded. Hawk took off running toward his truck, returning with his catlinite social pipe and sprigs of sage. Quickly, he lit the sage and smudged the three of them—man, woman, and suffering dog. He filled the pipe and kneeling west, he asked the Creator to look down upon the little terrier and spare his life.

Meanwhile, Meggie kept applying the ice compress to Fritzie's head, as the breathing ominously slowed. Her attention split between the words of Hawk and the death rattle in Fritzie's throat. Her eyes were wild and beseeching.

With his right hand, Hawk directed the smoke all over Fritzie's body. Roused from dim consciousness by the pungent smell, Fritzie opened and momentarily rolled an eye at the man's hand. The eye closed, and Fritzie sank back into the numbness of overwhelming pain.

No sooner had Hawk finished the prayer ceremony and told Meggie "He's going to be okay" than she heard Sam's car tearing up the steep part of the driveway.

"Thank God," she whispered.

Fritzie slept all evening after Sam injected him with an antidote to the snake poison; the trauma had exhausted him.

"Had to be a Massasauga rattlesnake, but it's rare to find one this far north," Sam had commented. "Close call for that old terrier. He'll be moving about pretty slow for a while."

"Do you think the venom might have caused any brain damage?" Meggie anxiously peered down at the sleeping dog. The snake, indeed, had zapped the dog right between the eyes.

Sam laughed, "Possibly. But with a fox terrier, how would you ever know?"

As the veterinarian took his leave, Meggie gratefully pressed fresh homemade bread upon him.

Hawk built a fire in the living room to ward off the chill of night. It pleased Meggie that he didn't head home to his trailer. "I'll take care of that snake tomorrow," he promised.

Supper soothed her jangled nerves. Hawk's arms encircled her body as they cuddled on the couch before the crackling flames. She felt drained, worn out by the day's events. Yet, she needed to ask him a question.

"Hawk?"

He nodded dreamily.

"I saw something when you were praying with the pipe."

"Oh?" His voice was soft, mellow, receptive.

Meggie continued, "I was scared, convinced that Fritzie wasn't going to make it. You were praying, and Sam hadn't got here yet and . . . ," she paused, "up in the northern sky, a huge Indian man stood in the clouds, smiling and peering down at me. I don't know why, but, suddenly, I felt there was some hope for Fritzie. Oh, this is crazy. Probably just a projection of my imagination." She shook her head as if to ward off the memory of the colossal man.

Tenderly, Hawk stroked the hair off the front of her face. "What you saw," he explained, "was Waziya, the Giant of the North."

"So, you saw Him too?" she said in amazement.

Hawk's only answer was to tighten his grip on Meggie, kiss the top of her head, and shield her snugly in his arms.

As the hapless Fritzie snored unconsciously throughout the evening, Meggie's Victorian ancestors, trapped in photographs and paintings above the fireplace mantle, looked askance upon the two humans embracing on the living room couch. The fire crackled and played shadows over them, and the old house creaked with familiar sounds.

I love this man with all my heart. On the bed, she curled up into Hawk's warm back, holding on to him for the rest of the night.

I think I really love this woman. He nestled into her arms, wrapped securely around him. He fell deeply asleep.

Winona momentarily flitted into his dreams. She was not happy with him and spoke to him sharply, but he couldn't make out what she was saying. Only one word stood out distinctly: She called him "lazy."

Before he could question her further, she dematerialized in the rarified, fragile air of dream-space.

TWENTY

CRYING FOR A VISION

At the Earth's center
I am standing and
As I stand, I am sending my voice.
To you, Thunder Beings
As I stand, I am sending my voice.

At the Earth's center
I am standing and
As I stand, I am sending my voice.
To you, Buffalo Nation.
As I stand, I am sending my voice.

At the Earth's center
I am standing and
As I stand, I am sending my voice.
To you, Elk Nation
As I stand, I am sending my voice.

At the Earth's center
I am standing and
As I stand, I am sending my voice.
To you, Animal Nation
As I stand, I am sending my voice.

—LAKOTA HANBLECIYA SONG

The days quickened toward the vision quest. His medicine teacher, Laughing Bear, was due to arrive soon. Hawk took out his Sacred Pipe, the Chanunpa Wakan, to greet the morning. During his initial vision quest, his medicine had come to him. In the second vision quest, his Spirit teacher, Three Legs, first spoke to him in his left ear. He did not know what to expect for his third *hanbleciya*.

Hawk held out his Pipe before him. "Is there anything else I need to do to prepare myself?" The early sunlight glinted off the eagle feathers dangling from the pipe stem.

Three Legs's voice answered, "For this *hanbleciya,* I think I'll stay back in the camp and let you do it alone. I don't have any particular need to suffer the mosquitoes, sunstroke, or thirst." Hawk could hear him chuckling.

"I need you there," Hawk replied. Although he had never seen Three Legs, the timbre of voice and sense of humor of his Spirit teacher was both familiar and comforting.

More silence followed.

"Too many women," growled Three Legs.

Hawk waited for further explication.

"Too many women on your mind. You'll have trouble concentrating on the hill," came the response.

Hawk thought of Meggie and smiled. Her fair image shimmered in his consciousness and then, as in a pond's reflection, it rippled with the disturbance of another image dropping fast onto the surface—Rising Smoke, her dark eyes and smoky beauty spreading out into a tableau before him. Hawk thought of her and smiled again.

Three Legs was right.

"Any suggestions?" Hawk asked, knowing full well he would have to pay the consequence of an answer.

"Have Laughing Bear sew eagle feathers to your wrist, so that when you think of women, the breeze will catch upon the feathers and pull at your skin. You'll not think of women then."

No sooner had the month of June begun, than Laughing Bear arrived with his wife and three children. Lucy and Larry opened up their house and hearts to the burly medicine man and his family. Now that Rising Smoke had found herself an apartment in Traverse City and a job as a waitress, space was more available.

Hawk handed over the bulk of his savings to Lucy for food. She agreed to cook up a traditional feast for when he came off the hill.

Eva and Adam were delighted with their new playmates, and soon the five children were exploring the countryside, the creeks, the swamps, and the deep woodland area. At nighttime, they gathered at the edge of the adult circle to listen to the stories of the people and to watch them make a large number of tobacco ties in the colors of the Four Grandfathers. Hawk delighted all of them by trotting out new and old tales of wily Coyote, vain Iktomi, greedy Raven, and jealous Rabbit. One by one, the children collapsed asleep on the rug, much like a bunch of puppies worn out from a day of tumble and play, while the adults gossiped into the night.

The morning finally came with clarity of sky and sun, a perfect day to start a vision quest. Looking up into the sky, Laughing Bear grumbled, "Why is it that when I go up on the hill, I never get a beautiful day like this?" He smiled at Hawk, obviously recognizing the younger man's anxious excitement. "Come, we've got a lot of work to do, cutting your poles and altar sticks."

During the morning, Hawk and Laughing Bear gathered leafy saplings, always offering tobacco to the trees for their gift of life. Lucy stayed home from work and cooked lunch and traditional foods. Meggie had postponed her afternoon clients to help with the preparations. In the early afternoon, more and more of the community assembled to set up a men's sweat lodge ceremony. Sweet-Grass Woman helped keep the children out of the way, while Rising Smoke gathered together the sage, cedar, tobacco, sweet grass, antlers, and rattles for Laughing Bear.

Hawk asked Rising Smoke, "Would you fill my Chanunpa Wakan for me? It is good to have a woman Pipe carrier do this, to bring balance to my energy."

"What about my staying the last night of your *hanbleciya* in the sweat lodge, praying for you? You are really going to need some help then." Rising Smoke knew that the last dark hours of the vision quest were often the busiest and hardest to endure.

"I've already arranged for that with someone else. But I could use your help tonight. Will you spend the night in the lodge adding your prayers to mine?"

She chuckled, "I thought you'd never ask."

Before the special sweat lodge ceremony for the *hanbleciya*, Lucy served everyone kidney soup, fried buffalo heart, and slivers of raw kidney and heart. Adam bravely swallowed the raw meat after only two chews, but Eva embarrassed him by gagging over the meat. "Yuck," she grimaced, much to the amusement of the adults. It was obvious that Laughing Bear's kids didn't savor the treat either, but they knew better than to voice their opinions.

"Yummy," exclaimed Laughing Bear, picking up pieces of uncooked heart and chewing them, much to Eva's horror and fascination.

Strengthened by the meal, Hawk announced he was ready. *Ready and scared*, he had to admit.

The two rounds in the inipi were fast and purifying. The men staggered out of the sweat lodge, steam rising from their bare backs. From that moment on, no one in the community was allowed to talk to Hawk. They understood that he had entered into a sacred communion with the Spirit world; nothing was to be done to distract him.

In a line, the community followed Laughing Bear who led the way up an isolated hill at Lucy's place, singing the old prayer songs. Clad only in a towel around his midriff and soft moccasins on his feet, Hawk walked behind the medicine man, holding out his Pipe to guide his steps. Excited and anxious, he didn't know what awaited him.

Atop the hill, Laughing Bear directed everyone in the construction of the altar area. The mood was somber. Hawk stared ahead, motionless. When the poles, tobacco ties, and center altar had been set in place, Hawk entered the altar area and placed his Chanunpa Wakan on the pipe stand. The last strand of black ties was secured. Over a sweet-grass bridge, Hawk moved out of his altar area and stood there while one by one the community filed by and gave him a handshake or a hug, wishing him well on his lonely journey. Laughing Bear cautioned them not to look back once they had left the altar area, "or you'll pull him off the hill."

Lucy handed Hawk a quart jar of sweet, cool water for his last drink. He quaffed it slowly, knowing that three long and thirsty days stretched out in front of him. Lucy hugged her cousin hard. "Hang in there," she whispered.

He squeezed her hand in response.

Eva let him kiss her on the head. Laughing Bear's children solemnly shook his hand. He stooped down to accept a hug from Stands By Dog.

Larry tapped him on the shoulder, "We'll be praying for you, bro."
Hawk nodded.

Others in the community said their good-byes.

Rising Smoke promised, "All night long, I'll be thinking of you," and
impetuously kissed him on the mouth.

Meggie's heart skipped a beat. Briefly, jealousy flared through her,
and quickly she stifled her feelings. *I must keep my mind on the hanbleciya.*

She was the last of the community to say good-bye. Giving Hawk a
long hug, Meggie couldn't prevent her eyes from watering. "Come
back to us safely," she murmured.

Hawk found himself holding onto Meggie, as if to store up the
memory of her arms. Finally, he released her and watched her back as
she retreated down the hill. He would need her prayers during the
long dark hours of the third night.

Alone with his teacher, he listened as Laughing Bear prayed to all
the Grandfathers and the Grandmother. When he had finished, the
medicine man carefully stitched the eagle feathers into the flesh of
Hawk's wrists, while Hawk winced with the pain. Laughing Bear
raised and lowered his eagle-wing fan, prayed another sentence or
two, turned to Hawk, gave him a brusque embrace, and said, "Have a
good time," and took off down the hill.

Entering into his altar, an awful loneliness immediately assailed
Hawk. It would be a long time before he would see another human
face. He distracted himself by setting up house, positioning his blankets, straightening the sage, and inspecting the boundaries of tobacco
ties. Patiently, his Chanunpa Wakan awaited him, propped up on a
small pipe stand of two V-shaped twigs and a crossbar.

For the next three days and nights, without food, water, or shelter,
Hawk knew he would sit and pray and sit some more—hours of observing, hours of waiting, kneading the soul to a receptivity. The old

ritual of dancing to the poles and praying slowly returned to him.

Day wheeled round toward night, time marked not by a clock but by the journey of the sun, the heralding of the moon in the owl's cry, the song of the birds. Above him, the world flitted with soaring birds and scudding clouds. Around him, the crickets thrummed and the insects buzzed. Below him, the ants scurried with their parcels of food and a mole deepened her burrow. The beauty of the natural world dazzled him, and only when he sank into his own ruminations did boredom ever make its flat appearance.

A fat doe wandered up the hill and stopped to study him, stamping her front hoof impatiently in hopes of driving him off the hill. He did not move. She flicked her ears to catch the sound of him, and when he spoke to her, she bolted in a flash of white tail.

The first night, rain drizzled on him during the dark hours. He stayed awake, praying and waiting. Dawn arrived gray and dreary. A small chickadee hung upside down above him, cracking a seed on a small branch. Briefly, he napped. Ripping through the morning sky and shaking the earth, the Thunder Beings jarred him awake. Lightning seared the air and struck a tree nearby, so close he could smell the ozone. He jumped and looked for a spot to hide, his heart pounding. There was no such place. He stood up in the altar, holding his Pipe, and began to sing a prayer song. He was afraid and ashamed of his fear.

The lightning moved on, but the rain dropped all day long. The temperature plummeted. By sunset, the chill had settled to the bone. The second night gave no relief. He was soaked to the skin, and the rain kept falling. The soggy blankets afforded no comfort. His teeth began to chatter, and he rocked to keep his body warm. It occurred to him that he might not make it for the full three days and nights. There would be no shame if he had to leave the altar early. Still, he prayed and danced to the poles, singing the old prayer songs.

He knew that Three Legs was around and that the Spirits were watching him. Yet, insidiously, doubt and despair began to fill his heart. Sinking down on his knees and crying out with the Pipe, Hawk pleaded, "With this Chanunpa Wakan, I ask you to help me, so that I can stay here and do this thing." He shivered uncontrollably. The cold rain pelted his face and chest. His wrists ached with the eagle feathers. He did not think of women.

Darkness settled in quickly. He could hear rustling sounds in the woods near his altar. His heartbeat quickened both in fear and curiosity. A large white dog stepped into the clearing. Wagging her tail, she jogged leisurely toward Hawk and, paying no mind to the tobacco-tie boundaries, she crossed into his altar area. She slathered her tongue all over his face.

He was confused and didn't know what to do. Surely, it wasn't right to have a dog in the altar area. With his sternest voice, he commanded, "Go home."

The white dog pumped her tail in response but did not move an inch. He gave her a gentle shove backward. She licked his face again and, dumbly, retraced her steps toward him.

"Shoo! Go home!" He waved his arms at her.

Shaking large drops of rain off her furry coat, she plopped herself down on the ground, right next to his wet blankets. It was obvious that she wasn't planning to go anywhere.

And then Hawk realized he had played the fool. Hadn't he just asked the Spirits for help? He wasn't paying attention to Their answer.

All night long, between rounds of prayer and song, Hawk hugged the large dog, warming himself with her body heat and comforting presence.

The second morning brought the sun's welcomed relief. The white dog awoke, stretched, nuzzled the tired man, and took her leave. She did not come again.

Exhausted, he spread out his damp blankets and catnapped during the early morning hours. The sun rose high and hot, baking the chill out of his body. All afternoon he prayed, taking note of everything he saw. A vision of Meggie came to him: She was standing in a meadow surrounded by four large female buffaloes, their backs to her. It was as if they had circled around her to protect her.

He immediately prayed with his Pipe for the Spirits to watch over her, worried that maybe there was some immediate threat to her. That night would be her first night sealed into the sweat lodge. She should be safe. Three Legs had nothing to say to him about the matter. A gentle summer breeze wafted across the wrist feathers and set them to twirling.

In fact, Three Legs had been silent the whole time. Hawk began to wonder if, indeed, his Spirit guide had decided to bypass this *hanble-ciya*. By late afternoon, the scorching sun drove Hawk to the ground. Dehydrated, he couldn't stand up to pray; there was no escaping the merciless rays, no tree shadows in his altar area. In the distance, he could hear the community sending him songs of strength, but he was unable to sing back. His tongue was thick and dry. Pushing himself off the ground, he stumbled and fell, face forward. Dry heaves shook his body and sapped his strength. Hawk knew the warning signs of sun-stroke. His head, feverishly hot, throbbed with pain. He gulped air in panic.

"Grandfathers!" he cried out, "Help me. I'm sick. I can't do this thing without your help. If you want to take my life now, then I offer it to you. Today is a good day to die. Otherwise, Tunkasila, help me live."

He tried again to lift himself off the ground. His knee dislodged a blanket, revealing cool ground underneath. *Dummy,* he slapped his head. Of course. His blankets had prevented patches of rain-soaked ground from drying in the sun. Depositing the Pipe on the rack, he gathered up his blankets, and, like a pig wallowing in mud, Hawk scootched all over the altar area, rubbing his body against the damp, uncovered earth. He cried out, *"Wopila,* Grandmother! Thank you for taking care of me." As the fierce sun slowly dipped below the western rim, the throbbing in his head diminished.

Hawk knew then he was going to survive the *hanbleciya*. In the dark of the third night, his body temperature returned to normal. Covered with a layer of dirt from head to toe, he stood up joyful. He sang out his prayers of thanksgiving, sun dance songs, pipe songs, songs from the times when his people roamed freely through the plains and woodlands, times when the buffalo were plenty. He danced to the four corners. He prayed for everyone he knew and those he didn't.

"I thank you for my life. I cannot live without you Sacred Beings taking care of me. I am but a two-legged and pitiful at that."

Then, and only then, as the quilt of night wrapped around him, did Three Legs announce, "I'm here."

Hawk jumped, startled. Holding out his Pipe, he spoke, "Grandfa-ther, I've been waiting. There are things I need to know."

"Ask," was the reply.

"Grandfather," Hawk laughed, embarrassed by his own request, "I want to see what you look like."

A bubble appeared out of nowhere in which was reflected the face of an old Indian man with stringy gray hair.

"I want to see all of you, not just the face," Hawk insisted.

The bubble burst, and a man in skins stood before him, the body strong but bent with age. Three Legs chuckled and danced around in a circle. "How's that?" he challenged Hawk.

Hawk reached out his hand and touched his Spirit teacher. "How . . . ?" he began to ask.

Three Legs interrupted him, obviously impatient with these trifling questions. "We come in a form so you can recognize us. Now, any more questions?" He sat down in the altar area, cross-legged, facing the astonished Hawk.

Dumbfounded, Hawk scrambled for immediate questions. "Yes. I need a woman to help me walk this red road. I've fallen in love with a white woman. My teacher, Laughing Bear, tells me not to get serious with her. My heart tells me otherwise. And then, to complicate things, the last woman I had ever loved this way has returned to my life. She's a Pipe carrier. She's Lakota and of the people. My head tells me that I should explore things with her to see if there is any love remaining between us. I'm just a man, confused by my need for a woman. Can you tell me what to do?"

Three Legs brushed him off, "That is not our concern. You figure it out."

Then he observed, "Women have always been a problem for men." Three Legs looked as if he knew what he was talking about.

Hawk offered his Pipe to his Spirit Teacher, who took and held it a while.

"Any more questions?" Three Legs touched the Pipe to his lips.

Hawk took a deep breath. "Yes, Grandfather. I want to know what I need to be doing for the people."

Three Legs smiled. "Now *that* is a worthy question. Come," he held out a firm hand, "there are things I have to show you."

Winona's curiosity had got the better of her. She couldn't help but turn around to check on Hawk. It pleased her to see him on the hill. Hawk's physical suffering was of no great concern, although she found herself at one point chiding him, "Pay attention, nephew."

He couldn't hear her; the distance was too great. When he discovered the damp earth under his blanket, she gave a throaty cheer. He didn't hear that either.

Finally, she couldn't stand it any longer. "Three Legs, you old buzzard," she hollered, "when are you going to help my nephew?" She might have just been shouting into the void, but only a brief moment passed before Three Legs announced to Hawk, "I'm here."

Meggie, during the first two days and nights of Hawk's *hanbleciya*, worried constantly about Hawk alone on the hill. The rain dampened her spirits, although Laughing Bear told her that Hawk was in no danger. Only in the latter part of the second day did the medicine man grow concerned. He called the people together, and in a Pipe ceremony they prayed for Hawk. "He's in trouble now," explained Laughing Bear, "but the Spirits instructed me to leave him alone."

By evening, Meggie felt like a nervous wreck. After the inipi ceremonies for the men and women, the community sealed her up in the sweat lodge for the third night. It was pitch black, and only her pipe tamper, stuck in the ground, oriented her to the west. The lodge remained oppressively hot with the stones still radiant from their heat during the ceremony. A mosquito, trapped in the lodge, kept her awake with judicious bites. Holding out her lightning pipe before her, she prayed first for Hawk and then for everyone else she knew. Several times her head began to slump forward with fatigue; during those times, the mosquito quit its temperate tactics and dive-bombed onto Meggie's flesh.

When she sang the Lakota prayer songs, she envisioned Hawk on the hill singing in unison with her. From his vantage point, she knew he could see the huge sky, the moon, and the brilliant traces of shooting stars. She imagined him dancing to the four poles and offering his Pipe to the heavens. In contrast, she was enclosed in the damp earthy darkness of the Grandmother's Womb, clutching onto Winona's pipe. The image of four buffaloes circled around her. Meggie wondered if she was suffering from an hallucination.

Deep into the middle of the night, when even the birds had gone to sleep, Meggie heard a noise rustling inside the sweat lodge. Remembering Hawk's instructions, she pointed her pipe into the direction of the sound. "If you're from Wakan Tanka, please come smoke with me," she said, her words sounding a lot braver than she felt.

She felt a gentle tug on the pipe stem. Her hands opened, and the pipe bowl slid slowly across both palms, until it rested at the very tip of her right hand, balanced and held by an unseen presence.

This can't be happening, she told herself. *No one came through the lodge door.* Yet, she also knew that the pipe, with its heavy bowl and long stem, could not hang unsupported in thin air.

A few minutes passed without a sound. Her hands remained frozen in the open position, until finally the pipe bowl and stem slowly retraced the journey back across her palms. Her hands closed around them. Her heart beat wildly as her eyes unsuccessfully searched for the other Being in the thick blackness.

A single voice spoke. She could not tell whether it was that of a woman or a man, so quickly did it speak, so startled was she by its words.

"Mitakuye oyas'in," the voice said.

"Mitakuye oyas'in," she echoed.

4

WIYOHIYANPATA
family

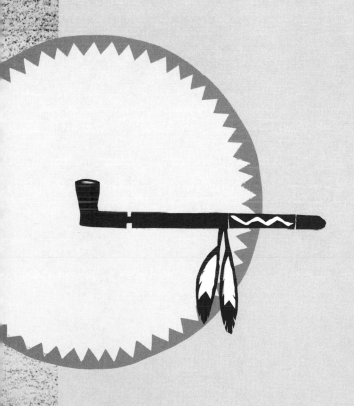

TWENTY-ONE

OLD VOICES

*Everything an Indian does is in a circle,
and that is because the power of the world
always works in circles, and everything tries
to be round.*

—BLACK ELK
Black Elk Speaks

A light flared in the dark as Lucy struck a match and touched the flame to her cigarette. Tiptoeing around her sleeping house, she groped into the back of a kitchen cupboard and found the freeze-dried coffee. Quietly, she warmed herself a mug of coffee and sat down at the kitchen table, drawing upon her cigarette. Five children slept in the center of the living room floor, their pillows forming an inner circle, their blanketed bodies spread out in all directions, like a wheel with leggy spokes. Everyone had grown exhausted during the *hanble-ciya,* even the children.

Thank heavens this is the last night, Lucy thought as she drank the last of the coffee. She didn't know why she had woken up in the middle of the night feeling charged with energy and purpose. In her bathrobe pocket, she felt the weight of the cassette tape she had taken out of her bureau drawer, the tape Winona had made for her.

Is that it? Am I supposed to listen to it now? Knowing this was the last thing her mother's fingers had touched before she died, Lucy pulled out the cartridge, running her fingers over the plastic, as if hoping her own fingertips would detect her mother's prints.

She retrieved a small tape recorder from above the bread box and inserted the cassette. Taking a deep breath, she wondered, *Am I really ready for this?* She pushed down the "Play" button. Nothing happened; nothing moved.

Is that a sign? Turning the recorder over, Lucy saw that the batteries had been removed. *The kids,* she chuckled to herself, suspecting that the children had taken the batteries to power their flashlights. Reaching over the bread box, Lucy found the recorder's electric cord and attached it to the machine.

"Okay, Mom, here's your chance," she said aloud. This time, the "Play" button started the tape rolling. Lucy pulled out another cigarette, sat back, and closed her eyes. She was ready to listen to her mother's voice.

"Okay," the voice said, then a microphone squawked as Winona tapped it for reassurance. "Okay, Lucy, this tape I make for you. You listen to it when you're ready. Okay?"

Okay, Mom. Blue smoke cut the darkness.

"Maybe I wasn't the best mother for you, but I always loved you. So, I make this tape for you. Just like when Davis died you made me a place in your home, your family. So, now, I make you a place in my family. You keep this tape and play it for the kids. It is for them, too, I make this tape."

Get to the point, Mom.

"We say that we must do everything in the name of seven generations—the seven generations before us, the seven generations that come after us. Whites take great pride in tracing back their family bloodlines, especially to the time when their ancestors came to this new land. The black people can't do that so easily because of slavery, the way their ancestors got sold off to other plantations. So, the black people in our country have a lot of trouble today because they don't really know what happened to their great-great-grandparents. Without that knowledge, how can they carry on the dreams of their ancestors?

"But our people don't have to count back to the time we arrived on this turtle continent, because we've always been here. In them history books they say we came over on an ice bridge from Asia. Don't you believe it. Our people have always been here. The land is in our blood. So, when we talk of doing everything in the name of seven generations, we're not talking just about your great-great-great-great-great-grandparents, we're also talking about the village, the band, the *tiyospaye*, the people.

"That is why we always remember the massacre of Wounded Knee in 1890, when Chief Big Foot's Minniconjou band was bringing in the people under a white flag, and the white soldiers got anxious and slaughtered them—men, women, and children. We tell the story of our encounters with the whites, the way treaties were made, smoked on, and then broken. The way the Lakota people were given the Black Hills in the Fort Laramie Treaty, until gold was found and the whites invaded our mountains like a horde of mice chewing up everything in sight. The government in Washington said nothing could be done about it. They offered us money for the land, but we have said, 'No. Money is nothing to us. The Paha Sapa is sacred. We cannot sell that which is sacred to us.'

"You must tell the children these things. Larry must speak to them about the history of his Ojibway people and what happened to them. We trusted the white government, but every treaty they have made with the red people on this continent has been broken. We fought the white people, but they were too many for us. They are a hungry people; they eat the land and spit it out. They forget that She is their Grandmother too. She feeds and clothes us. She takes care of us. They throw paper and trash on Her skin. They poison Her veins with chemicals. They think only of themselves, not the seven generations. So, tell the children, Lucy, that whatever they do, it must be in the name of seven generations. Tell them to be proud of who they are.

"If I were to tell you of the blood that runs in your veins, I'd have to admit you have some Crow in you. It was not unusual for our people to steal Crow women. And whenever the Crow had the chance, they would capture Lakota women.

"The first white man our band saw was a French trapper in the mountains, looking for beaver pelts. He had little hair on top and a bushy beard, when our people did not know about baldness or hairy faces. One of the old women in our village said that his face looked like a bird's egg trying to send roots into the ground.

"It didn't take long before more and more whites started crossing our hunting grounds. At first, when it was a trickle, we let them go by, but when it came to be a flood of people, we had no choice but to let them know they had to respect us as warriors. On one of those raids by our young people, a white woman was captured and brought back to our village. The women were, at first, curious about her, but when they discovered that she didn't know how to dress out a deer, make bone chokers, or put up a tipi, they soon lost interest. Besides, her pasty white skin was ugly to them; they called her Farting Woman and were unkind to her.

"But she was given to an old crippled man who had lost his wife in childbirth. At first, it is said, that she cried all the time, until her tears bleached the moon. She ran away once, but got lost in the woods, and her husband had to ride out to find her. He was gentle to her and taught her what she needed to know.

"It is said that she gave him three healthy babies in a row before the chiefs ordered the woman to be given back to the whites, in exchange for a gift of horses. But, by this time, Farting Woman didn't want to leave the village or her children. The white men came and had to drag her away, and we do not know what became of her. Her only daughter was your great-great-grandmother.

"So, you have white blood in you too. I don't know which is worse—Crow blood or white blood—but whenever I did something bad in my life, I knew it was one or the other. There will always be human beings who are the exception: good Crows, good whites, bad Lakota. Still, I'm glad to be of *my* people.

"It's not enough, Lucy, to tell the children the history of our people. It's even more important to tell them the stories that go all the way back to the beginning of time and the creation of this world. These stories teach our children how to live in balance with the Creation, how to respect the nations of fins, winged ones, plants, stones, crawling things, four leggeds, the Spirits. Don't dismiss them as just 'myths' and bedtime tales. Remember it was Star Woman who came down to earth as White Buffalo Calf Woman. It is these stories which tell the children who they are. So, tonight, I will go further back than even seven generations.

"Long, long time ago, when the animals could talk and Wakan Tanka looked down upon His Creation . . ."

As night spun across the sky into morning, Winona's voice wove the traditional tales into her daughter's identity, into the personal life fabric, strands created out of myth, history, and a people's heritage of meaning. Lucy understood that her mother's gift to her was the stories, passed down from generation to generation, lives strung together in the network of the telling. Tears crisscrossed her cheeks.

Out of the stories, she is braiding a bridge for me, reflected Lucy.

A passage to my people.

An arch to my ancestors.

A cord to my children.

A connection to my mother.

"*Wopila,*" Lucy whispered into the healing night.

Out of the darkness, morning crested the horizon. Laughing Bear roused Meggie, pulling back the flap of the lodge door and letting the sunlight creep inside. She blinked against the sudden burst of light. He crawled into the cold sweat lodge, sat down on the damp ground, picked up her lightning pipe, and listened to her story of the night. Shaking his head, he had her repeat three times her description of the pipe being taken from her hands. Before lighting the pipe, he said, "After the feast, Hawk will tell the people what happened to him on the hill. Then you share what happened to you. This Pipe was smoked by the Spirits. It must never again be used for anything but prayer. The Spirits have blessed it; it is now a Sacred Pipe."

Meggie noted that Laughing Bear kept shaking his head while telling her this, as if it made him uncomfortable, off balance.

Is it because I am white? she wondered.

What does it mean that Winona's pipe has now become a Sacred Pipe?

What will Hawk think?

Am I supposed to do anything different now?

Where am I going with all this?

Too many unanswered questions crowded into Meggie's brain, leaving her curious, confused, and afraid.

Hawk, still in his altar area, was relieved to see Laughing Bear striding up the hill to collect him. *It's over. It's over.* He could smell the smoke of the sweat lodge fire as he walked stiffly down the hill, holding his Pipe out before him. His heart cheered to see the community lined up, studiously avoiding his eyes. *Laughing Bear's instructions.*

No one spoke to him. He was still in a holy state. Quickly, he crawled after Laughing Bear into the inipi; the hot rocks followed, warming his cold toes. He began to relax into the heat. Soon, the sweat lodge door came down. Not allowed to listen, the community moved back from the lodge, lest there be something meant only for Hawk's ears.

The two men called in the Spirits through song and prayer. Then Hawk recounted his three lonely days and nights on the hill. He spoke to Laughing Bear and to the Spirits of his vision of Meggie surrounded by the four female buffaloes. He cried as he told of the suffering and calling out for help when chilled by the rain and burnt by the sun. He told of the white dog that came to sleep beside him and keep him warm, of Grandmother who cooled him with damp earth. Finally, he mentioned how Three Legs appeared and took his hand:

"We descended through a deep hole in the earth until we arrived at a cave. There, Three Legs introduced me to a council of seven elders seated around a strange fire made of eight sticks and flashes of lightning flame. I was not allowed to approach the men or enter into their circle.

"They talked about me, 'He doesn't listen good. He is still too young.'

"They talked to me, 'We are the teachers. If you travel this road again, you need to be ready. There are things we will ask you to do. You will put your life in our hands. Until then, understand this: If you feed everybody, you will die. If you feed no one, you will starve. The Pipe will tell you who is truly hungry. If you ask the Pipe for power, do it for the people. If you ask it for yourself, the power will destroy everything around you.'

"The old men nodded their heads in agreement. They did not look at me. They said, 'Go now. We will talk to you only through Three Legs. It is enough that you know we are here.'

"The next thing I knew I was back on the hill, on my knees, holding my Pipe. There was no hole in the earth to be seen. My teacher, Three Legs, had disappeared. Then dawn forced a crack between the dark of night and the edge of morning."

"Ah, hau!" exclaimed Laughing Bear, "It was a good vision."

The second round of the inipi ceremony was brutally hot as Laughing Bear poured on the water. The stones sizzled and sang as the Spirits talked to Laughing Bear. Hawk slapped his bare skin to distract himself from the nettling steam and croaked the songs he had been singing for three days.

Finally, Laughing Bear announced, "Hau!" signaling Hawk to pay special attention. "Spirits say they were pleased you didn't run off the hill, that it was a hard time for you."

Hawk could feel tears gathering at the corner of his lids.

"They say it is good that you called upon Them for help, that you will get what you need when you hold out the Pipe. You have your medicine. You have your teacher, Three Legs. And now you are starting to know about the other teachers. It was pretty clear what They were saying about the Pipe; They didn't add to that. Spirits want you to know that if you do a four-day, four-night *hanbleciya* next year or later, it will mean real changes in your life. They may give you an altar. They will ask a lot from you. It is up to you."

"Do I really have a choice?" asked Hawk.

"Yes," answered Laughing Bear sharply. "And don't make commitments to Them you can't keep."

"Hau!" *A year is a long time away.*

Laughing Bear continued, "Spirits like that white woman. Even more, They like that lightning Pipe of hers. It is a powerful Pipe. Last night when she was in the lodge praying for you, They came and smoked that Pipe."

Hawk sucked in his breath. *How could that be? What did it mean?*

"Spirits say that she may have white skin, but your vision showed you that, in her heart, she is a buffalo woman. They blessed that Pipe. Whatever you do with that woman, you must treat her with respect. Ah hau! Any more questions?"

Hawk couldn't think of anything left unsaid. "No."

Laughing Bear finished up the round, sent the Spirits home, and shouted, *"Mitakuye oyas'in."* As the door lifted, the steam billowed out in great waves. The two men smoked their Pipes.

Rising Smoke brought Hawk a quart jar of cool water and handed a few strawberries into the lodge to break the fast of the long and arduous *hanbleciya.*

Sitting in the lodge, Laughing Bear commented, "That was a powerful vision quest."

Hawk nodded, fatigued and relieved to be back among the two-leggeds.

The medicine man gave a wry chortle. "Myself, I still don't approve of a white person having a Sacred Pipe. But, then again, the Spirits never consulted me for my advice about the matter."

"It was a social pipe that belonged to my cousin, Winona Pathfinder."

"Ahh," the older man reflected, *"that* explains a lot. I thought that pipe was familiar. So that was Winona's lightning pipe." He shook his head in amazement and thought:

Pipes, too, have a way of moving in circles.

TWENTY-TWO

BLOOD AND GUILT

Without guilt
What is a man? An animal, isn't he?
A wolf forgiven at his meat,
A beetle innocent in his copulation.

—ARCHIBALD MACLEISH
J.B.

Overwhelmed with relief and exhaustion, Meggie was also dimly aware that her night's adventure gave her new status in the Native American community, a greater acceptance among the people. After the feast, Hawk told the group of his experiences on the hill, and Meggie recounted her night in the sweat lodge. Everyone listened, applying the experiences to their own lives. Even the children, hushed and wide-eyed with wonder, leaned forward, elbows on their knees.

Looking about the room stacked with people, Meggie noted that Lucy seemed unusually mellow, playful, and peaceful, with no hard edges to her. Off in the other direction sat Rising Smoke, wary and self-contained, her eyes continuously tracking the whereabouts of Meggie and Hawk, her hands fiddling with a pack of cigarettes, and her left foot tapping impatiently on the bare floor.

Hawk belonged to the community the rest of the day, visiting and chatting with them. At one point, Adam Stands By Dog came up to him and touched his arm.

"Did you see Grandma?" the boy asked, expectantly.

"When?" As soon as he responded, Hawk knew what the boy had meant.

"Up there on the hill. You didn't see her?"

Hawk shook his head.

Adam turned and walked away, his face expressing a curious mixture of disappointment and puzzlement.

"I saw you up there." Hawk nodded in the direction of the hill while momentarily seizing a moment of privacy with Meggie. The others were cleaning up the feast or chatting in Lucy's living room.

"You did? Did I flick a little black tail at you?" Meggie teased. Laughing Bear had warned Hawk of the black tail doe that occasionally came to a man on his *hanbleciya* to lure him out of the altar and lose him in the woods.

"No," he laughed. "You were surrounded by four buffaloes."

"I saw them, too, in the sweat lodge."

"I was afraid that you might be in danger."

"Danger? From whom?" A mystified expression wrinkled across Meggie's face.

Hawk shrugged his shoulders. "I must have been wrong."

"The vision of the four buffaloes was probably a touch of heat stroke," she grinned, and then added, "for both of us."

He shook his head. "Someday, Meggie, you will know more about those buffaloes and what they have to do with you. We both know what we saw. I just don't know what it means, that's all. Sometimes a person is given a vision about another human being."

"Why would the Spirits show you something about me? Why did They give *me* that same vision?" Meggie was really curious.

"Good question. You can be sure of one thing."

"What's that?"

"It wasn't accidental that the Spirits did it that way." Before Hawk could elaborate any further, the others in the living room were demanding that he come back and join them.

Passing a full-length mirror, Meggie caught a glimpse of herself. *Buffaloes?* Maybe she did need to lose some weight after all . . .

While Sweet-Grass Woman seemed to keep her distance from Hawk, Rising Smoke hung over him during much of the afternoon, bringing him extra glasses of apple cider, second helpings of dessert. After everyone had time to digest the feast and after the recitation of events, Hawk gathered the community outside for a giveaway ceremony. It was his way of giving thanks for the support of each community member for his *hanbleciya.*

First of all, he presented his teacher and guide, Laughing Bear, with a buffalo robe and made a speech of thanksgiving "for coming this long way from South Dakota to conduct me on my *hanbleciya.*" He slipped him an envelope of money to help with the journey home.

To Rising Smoke, he gave two eagle feathers for her to tie onto her Chanunpa Wakan.

To Lucy, he handed a large, stainless steel soup pot and a brand new tape recorder with batteries. Lucy threw her arms around him.

For Sweet-Grass Woman and the other women, he had created tobacco tie bags, replete with red cloth, string, and tobacco. To the men, he gave small catlinite smudge bowls in which to burn sage. Each child received a braid of sweet grass.

To Larry, he donated two axes and one maul.

Finally, for Meggie, Hawk unwrapped a large Hudson Bay blanket and put it over her shoulders. "That will keep you warm at night," he whispered.

"I can think of other ways to keep warm," she softly replied.

Everyone, children and adults, dove into the laundry basket of goodies—small shampoos, candy, gum, pens, and pencils. Hawk stood back, satisfaction and completion smiling on his face. He was also aware of a heavy fatigue spreading from his shoulders on down. All those nights of praying with but a few hours of sleep were taking its toll on him.

The women washed up the dishes and dried them, gathered up their sweat lodge paraphernalia, and collected the children. The men belched from eating too much and drinking too much cider and lemonade. They chided the women to hurry up, that there were things they needed to do at home. And so, as the sun began its slow drift down the horizon, the group began to break up and leave, ready to turn away from the sacred to the mundane.

Rising Smoke was one of the last to depart. Out in the driveway, she said her good-byes to Laughing Bear and his family, who were taking off, getting a head start on their long journey to South Dakota. In the next few weeks, he would conduct other men on their *hanbleciyas,* out on Bear Butte.

"A good time was had by all," Laughing Bear roared out the window as his pick-up bounced out the rutted driveway.

Smiling, Hawk watched his teacher's truck disappear around the corner.

Rising Smoke commented, "You know Lucy's got to be glad it's all over. She can get her house back to herself now."

"I'm glad it's over," he replied. "Although when is one's vision quest *ever* over?"

Rising Smoke didn't have any good answer to that question. Climbing into her car, she asked, "When will I next see you?"

"Soon." Hawk was frankly too tired to make any future plans.

Throwing him an enigmatic look, Rising Smoke asked, "Soon. As in Indian time or white time?" She reached down onto the passenger seat for a pack, pulled out two cigarettes, lit them both, and handed him one. Without waiting for an answer, she keyed the ignition and backed out and around.

"Soon," she echoed out the car window as she drove off.

Meggie hung up the last drying towel, thanked Lucy for all the food and use of her house, retrieved her new blanket, and stepped out into the yard just in time to see Rising Smoke's car pull away. Hawk threw a cigarette down on the ground and stomped on it. He looked up to see her standing there.

"You going home?" he asked.

She nodded.

"You want some company?" A bashful, almost boyish look crossed his face.

"Tonight?" Meggie enjoyed prolonging the moment, savoring the tease.

"I don't want to rush you or anything. You know, separate time and space and all that." Hawk was grinning as he danced her words back at her. "But, it might help us to get to know each other better, if you know what I mean. Besides . . ."

"Besides what?"

"I missed you while I was up there," he said, nodding toward the hill.

"I thought the eagle feathers sewn into your wrists were supposed to take care of that." Meggie opened her car door and threw in the blanket.

"Oh, the eagle feathers took care of the lust and all that. But, not the heart, Meggie. I was lonesome for you. I missed you." He tapped the left side of his chest, unable to say more.

She could feel herself melting, standing there looking at him—sunburnt, older than his years, worn out from the days on the hill, his face so open, genuine. "Hawk." She touched his cheek, still hot from the sun. She ran her fingers over his chapped lips, like a blind person trying to read the truth in his words. "Come home with me."

The strength in his hand wrapped around her hand. He climbed into the passenger side of her car.

"Don't you need to get a change of clothing?" she asked him.

"I'm too tired. I'll come back here tomorrow." He briefly closed his eyes, yawned, and let his head slump back on the headrest as Meggie took the back roads toward Chrysalis.

Just when she'd concluded that he had fallen asleep, he opened one eye and murmured, "I don't have any eagle feathers sewn on my wrists now."

"Meaning?"

He opened both eyes and glanced over at her. "A person can get too spiritual," he said.

"Oh?" She knew he was setting up the next line.

"And that's not good, because you've got to live in this world. What a man needs most at a time like this is . . ."

Meggie waited. She had a sense of what was coming.

"Grounding."

"Grounding?" That wasn't quite what she had expected him to say.

"There is nothing like a woman to ground a man in her own special way. Bring him back to earth when he has been flying high." He wobbled a flat hand in the air, mimicking a hawk riding the currents in search of live prey.

"And in what kind of special way does a woman ground a man?" Meggie cast a skeptical eye toward him.

He flew his hand, lightly feathering his fingers across her breasts, fluttering his hand up past her eyes, then into a dive, until his hand glided onto her right thigh. A perfect landing.

Meggie's foot pressed down upon the accelerator.

"I'm covered with three days of grit and grime," he groused. Hawk took a long, long shower after Meggie had taken hers. He groaned in the pleasure of the hot water falling upon his body.

Meanwhile, Meggie pulled out a silky emerald green outfit that she had been saving for such an occasion: a chemise that showed a smidgen of cleavage, with thin straps and matching underwear. Not garish but definitely suggestive, definitely seductive. She lightly dabbed a touch of scented oil under her earlobes, between her breasts, and right below her belly button. She could hear him in the bathroom, turning off the water and grabbing a towel off the rack. Meggie eased onto the bed, but not under the covers.

"Oooh," Hawk moaned in the next room, drying himself off. "It feels so good," he exclaimed.

Meggie waited.

"Oooh," he repeated himself, still in the bathroom. "I can't remember when a shower ever felt so wonderful."

She heard the rattle of the towel rack as Hawk threw the towel over it. She tried to arrange her body on the bed in such a way that she looked both alluring and yet casual, first bending one leg then putting a hand on a knee, switching the pose, holding it, then switching it again.

The sound of gargling next arose from the bathroom sink area. Hawk was probably rinsing his mouth with toothpaste.

Meggie moved to the side of the bed closest to the bedroom door. "Are you coming?" It seemed like a silly question to ask, but she was beginning to doubt that he would ever round the corner.

"Not yet," he answered, stepping into the bedroom, buck naked. A towel line demarcated the scorch of the sun on his chest, arms, and face—while his nether parts were of a much paler appearance. His eyes widened on seeing her in the emerald chemise, and his fingers reached out to stroke the soft, silky texture. He sat down on the bed, angling his body next to hers.

She moved to make more room for him.

"I love the soft curves in you, Meggie." Hawk's hand slowly traced the outline of her body, like a sculptor seeking the shape that reveals itself only when approached with delicate appreciation. He traced the indentation of her ribs down into the soft mound of her belly, the lower side valleys rising toward the jutting hardness of the hipbones, her body a panorama of natural beauty.

A tiny, delicious shiver rippled across her skin.

Hawk slid both hands under the emerald fabric, tenting it out, raising it up, exposing her belly and her breasts, but leaving the fabric to rest on her face, shading her eyes, her arms half in and half out, as if to tease her, keep her in suspense, so she couldn't see what he would do next. Both hands glided over her silky skin, fingers swirling, brushing over her body as if he were the artist casting her form into his memory—the outline of muscle, the sharp definition of bone, the satiny texture of skin, the forest of hair. On the tableau of her body his hands rose from the plateau of her midriff to cup the mountains of her breasts.

She could feel the softness of a tongue circling each nipple. The rigidity of his penis nudged her left hipbone.

Then his hands plunged and dragged at the edge of her panties, pulling them down.

And Meggie kicked them off, still unable to see what Hawk was doing. But she could feel him elongate his body next to her, and she gave herself into the emerald blindness, letting her skin see for her.

"Oooh," he groaned, as he touched her breasts with his mouth, his nose, his chin, his cheek. He burrowed his head into that space above the belly, between the breasts. He splayed his arms up toward her shoulders on both sides of her, brushing the fabric off her face.

"Oooh," he sighed, breathing deeply.

Once, twice, three times, he sighed a deep, deep breath.

"Umm . . ." he murmured, his voice slurring off into a downward slide, his mouth resting against her right breast.

All movement ceased.

His head grew heavy. His breath became regular. His unrequited penis slowly shrank against her left thigh. And then Meggie knew that three days and three nights of sun, loneliness, prayer, and little sleep had finally claimed their due.

"Oooh," she softly groaned, before the laughter percolated up from her belly, jiggling his head lightly upon her breast.

Even that motion did not bring him back to consciousness. He was dead to the world.

Andrea gazed at her father's pistol a long time before picking it up and inserting one bullet into its chambers. She was amazed at the heft of it, the sturdiness of such a weapon. She spun the barrel and thought of the morbid game of Russian roulette, how time and time again people have taken such a weapon and twirled the wheel of destiny.

"To live or not to live, that is the question." She put down the gun and picked up a paintbrush of short bristles and a palette dabbed with oils of many colors. She approached the easel and canvas with confidence. The time had finally come. Andrea knew exactly how she was going to change her landscape.

After a few moments, she stepped back from her painting and surveyed it with a newfound sense of satisfaction. From a nearby table, Andrea retrieved a short letter and tacked it to the top left of the canvas. In that position, over North Manitou Island, the note appeared like a large white cloud interrupted by sentences of flying geese:

> *I would love to meet you after work.*
> *Our time together is precious, even if*
> *we have to see each other in secret.*
> *Your love has restored my faith in men.*
> *Hugs and kisses until then,*
> *B*

"To B or not to B." Andrea inked in the rest of the name with "*itch.*" Somehow, it didn't really matter anymore to her that she didn't have the slightest idea who in the hell was B.

Andrea picked up the gun, aligned the bullet in the chamber, and wrapped a newspaper around it. It was an easy walk on the summer morning, through the busy traffic in Leland, up River Street to the church, where she found the minister, Karl Young, on his knees planting a weeping willow tree in a spongy patch of earth.

On seeing who was striding purposefully toward him, Karl stood up, trowel in left hand, uncertainty in his face. He extended his right hand toward her, both warmth and sorrow embedded in his voice. "Annie," was all he said.

The newspaper slipped off the gun. "I found the letter," she said. "You left it in your Sunday suit pocket." The sun glinted off the pistol.

He started to say, "What letter?" and knew it was a futile gesture.

"Damn you!" she yelled, squeezing the trigger.

As if in slow motion, Karl witnessed the puff of smoke, the retort of sound, before feeling the shards of pain. From metal to flesh, the bullet grooved its bloody mark.

* * *

The next morning, Bev paced back and forth, back and forth in Meggie's office.

"You're like a caged animal," Meggie told her. Meggie, too, felt off balance, returning to the world of work from the world of sacred ceremonies and paranormal events. In her hands the *Traverse City Record Eagle* sketched the few known details on the shooting of Reverend Karl Young.

"I have a confession to make."

"Huh?" Meggie raised her eyebrows. It was unlike Bev to be so unstrung.

"That mystery man I've been seeing on the side? Well, that man is married."

"Oh, Bev," sighed Meggie. *Married men are always trouble.*

"That's not the worst of it, Meggie." Rubbing her forehead with her hand, she continued, "The mystery lover is the minister, Karl Young, the one who got shot yesterday."

Meggie dropped the newspaper. "Is that why you didn't tell me his identity, because he's married?" Meggie remembered how secretive Bev had been about her new lover.

Bev shook her head. "I told you it was more complicated than that. Oh jeez, I can't believe the mess I've made." Bev paced around the room.

"Sit down, your anxiety is driving me crazy." Meggie pointed to an empty chair. "Now, tell me . . ."

On the chair at last, Bev bent over her knees, as if about to vomit. "Oh jeez, I hope I didn't have anything to do with the shooting. You see, I left him a note, a love letter. What if his wife, Andrea, found out about us?"

"You mean his wife, Annie?" A sick feeling began to stir in Meggie's gut.

"Her given name is Andrea, Meggie." Bev's face looked tortured.

"What did Karl tell the police?" Meggie had read in the paper that the police had interviewed the wounded minister from his hospital bed. Karl's upper thighbone had been shattered by the bullet; he would be in traction for several weeks before being released from the hospital.

Bev cradled her head with both hands, staring at the floor. "He told the police that the identity of the assailant was confidential information and that he would never reveal the name. He said . . ." her voice trembled, "something to the effect of his having gotten his just reward."

"So, the police don't really know who did it, do they?"

Bev shook her head and moaned, misery underlining her every word, "It's all my fault . . ."

Meggie called Karl's house. The answering machine clicked on: "Hello, this is Andrea saying good-bye. Have a good life." Meggie recognized the voice as that of her client. Nothing about Karl. A terrible thought assailed her: Andrea might have killed herself.

Meggie canceled her afternoon appointments and crossed the Leelanau Peninsula, driving over the hilly back roads. In Leland, she found a clerk at the bookstore who gave her directions to the church rectory and to Andrea's studio. The rectory was locked up, and nobody answered the doorbell.

Jumping back into her car with foreboding burrowing into her heart, Meggie drove past the marina, along the hilly back roads to Andrea's studio. It was a small one-room structure, rented to her by landowners who lived in the house next door. She banged on the studio door, but it was securely locked. She walked over to the house and was relieved to discover a woman outside, planting her annual flower beds.

"No, Mrs. Young hasn't been around since yesterday. I told all that to the police. They wanted to question her. I hear they can't find her." The woman stood up and brushed the dirt off her hands.

"Could you let me into her studio, please? I'm concerned about her safety," Meggie pleaded.

"Sure. Wait right here. I'll fetch the keys." The woman soon returned and unlocked the door to the studio. "Call me when you're finished."

Meggie pushed open the door. Immediately, she could see why her client had rented the space. Sun poured into the room from every direction. The wall that faced Lake Michigan was mainly window, encompassing a beautiful panorama of sand, water, boats, and the Manitou islands.

In the center of the room loomed the canvas with its singular landscape painting. With its fierce clouds and gray water, gritty dunes and grasping trees, Meggie recognized it immediately as the landscape that never changed. She read the note attached to the top left of the canvas.

Upon closer inspection, she realized that something new had been added to the scene—a freshly painted section with a human figure. Meggie peered closer. On the beach, a small man in a black suit was stepping backward. A Bible was clutched under his left arm, and a gold cross dangled from his white clerical collar, glinting in the sun and commanding notice. Some gulls were diving into the waters for fish; others were swooping over the man's head. Speckles of white dots on his black suit attested to the accuracy of bird droppings.

Curious, Meggie squinted even closer. The man appeared to be stepping back onto a black patch on the sand. His right arm was raised, as if waving good-bye to somebody off the canvas. Any moment now, if he continued to back up, he would . . .

Fall into the black hole.

At first, Meggie didn't understand, and then, like the sun that peeks out of heavy clouds and winks at the earthbound observer, the insight flashed upon her.

The black hole was Andrea's parting gift to her husband.

TWENTY-THREE

THE CIRCLE OF LIFE

A generation goes, and a generation comes,
  but the earth remains forever.
The sun rises and the sun goes down,
  and hurries to the place where it rises.
The wind blows to the south,
  and goes round to the north;
round and round goes the wind,
  and on its circuits the wind returns.

—ECCLESIASTES 1:4–7, NRSV

Thus, summer in Suttons Bay began with a bang. The townspeople gossiped as to the suspected identity of the assailant, the possible motivations for the attack, and the disappearance of the minister's wife. Karl Young was both admired and criticized as being too human for the job as minister. Summer also brought the "fudgies," vacationers from Chicago, Texas, and Indiana who, every year, trekked up to the Leelanau Peninsula and perched alongside Lake Michigan in homage to the sun, the water, and the peaceful rhythms of a slower life, blissfully unaware of strong currents under the placid Lake surface.

Meggie's elderly parents arrived, as did her sister and her family. Meggie had swept the house clean of Hawk's presence out of respect to her parents' age and sensibilities. Slowly, she would try and find a way to introduce him to her parents as someone other than simply the handyman of Chrysalis.

Meggie's great-grandmother had bought the land back in the early 1890s. Meggie's grandmother had designed and built the house on the hill. Meggie's father and mother had courted and married there, sixty long summers ago. In honor of their approaching wedding anniversary, Meggie and her sister arranged a homemade celebration of the event. Having invited all the original guests at the wedding, they repeatedly received envelopes returned "Address Unknown" or notes explaining that the person had died or was currently in a nursing home.

"Most of my friends are long gone," sighed Meggie's mother, still active in her mid-eighties.

"Most of my colleagues are dead and my students retired," commented Meggie's father, as he worked on his seventh medical textbook, sorting through pathology photographs.

For Meggie, surrounded by the debris of dissolving relationships, violent emotions, and marriages that could not withstand the stress between modern life and ancient vows, the night of her parents' sixtieth wedding anniversary took on special meaning. The highlight of the party was an old, scratchy movie of her parents' nuptials: the young bride gliding through a bower of flowers, her dress and her short-cropped hair the style of another era; the groom with a full head of black Irish hair, smiling confidently at his intended; the grandmother, proud owner and creator of Chrysalis, a woman known to Meggie only by her interior designs, grapevine hedges, and flowers sprouting everywhere on the land.

In black and white, the grainy film recorded the two young lovers joining hands for a lifetime. In living color, Meggie watched her father's bony fingers reach out and firmly grasp the hand of his ancient bride.

Summer also returned Hawk to the family circle. A message from Pine Ridge, South Dakota, to Peshawbestown, Michigan, informed him that his long-lost father lay dying in a hospital in mid-Ohio. Hawk obeyed the implicit summons, hoping to reestablish connection with the father he had not seen since he was a boy.

Expecting somehow to see a man still in his prime, Hawk was shocked by his father's wizened appearance, wasted by years of rotgut alcohol and hard living. His father had suffered a heart attack so severe that he couldn't sit up in bed; the damaged heart muscle could not withstand the postural shift. He lay on his back, his lips curled to compensate for a missing bridge of false teeth, confiscated by the nurses. He was happy to see his son.

Hawk scraped a chair closer to the bed, dislodging a cardboard box of his father's only possessions. It was mostly junk: an old watch, rusty fishing lures, some faded photographs, a tattered Bible, odds and ends dumped helter-skelter in the box. *The remains of a shabby life,* judged Hawk.

"I keep telling the nurses that I have a bad case of indigestion." The old man grinned at his son.

Hawk looked at him. *Should I tell him the truth? The doctors say he's going to die today or tomorrow.*

"I wish they would let me sit up. My back hurts. I've got gas. I tell them I need to take a dump, and what do they do? They put a pad under me, like I'm a baby. No decent man is going to crap in his own bed. The constipation is killing me," the old man complained.

"It isn't indigestion. You had a heart attack, a bad one." Hawk felt he deserved at least that much truth. *I'll tell him a little bit at a time.*

"Whatcha saying, son?"

Hawk winced at the word "son." *Why can't I call him "Dad"? Why am I still angry at this man?*

Before Hawk could answer, his father started asking him questions about his life, marriages, family, and friends. He repeatedly interrupted Hawk's account with his own remembrances. "I recall Lucy—a knock-kneed little girl when I last saw her. Her mother, Winona, *that* was a scary woman. She knew too damn much. I kept out of her way . . ."

Occasionally, his father snaked a finger out through the bars of the hospital bed, shakily reaching for a son's touch. Hawk gripped the old man's hand, much like his father used to do with him when he was a little boy. When the old man fell into a restless sleep, Hawk catnapped on the chair, not willing to let his father die alone in a sterile hospital room. When the old man moaned in discomfort, Hawk placed cool compresses on his forehead and stroked the white, wispy hair.

On and on, into the night, the next day, and the day after, the old man defied the doctors' predictions of imminent death. Hour after hour, Hawk witnessed his father's body shutting down, the outer portions—fingers, toes, calves, and lower arms—turning blue, while the old man's mind defiantly held on, explaining, describing, accruing to himself, story by story, an active presence in Hawk's memory. Until every anecdote, every joke had been told, and there was no more. Together, they laughed at the absurdity of life. Together, they cried at the finality of death. Moment by moment, they acknowledged their connection with each other.

"Lift me up," he commanded his son. "Let me have the dignity of crapping on the toilet." The old man was cramping again with gas pains.

"I can't. The move will kill you," answered his son.

"Then bring me a gun, so I can end it here and now. This is no way to die." His eyes took on a wild, trapped expression.

"I can't. The hospital wouldn't allow it. Too messy," Hawk replied, trying to bring a smile back to his father's face.

"Goddamn it! You're gutless!" the old man barked, his jaw set furiously. "Then help me stand up. I'll jump out the goddamn window myself!"

Hawk heard anger surge into his own voice, "You ask the impossible of me. After years of wanting to see you, you finally burst back into my life. And now you want me to help you kill yourself. I won't do it. I can't."

The storm between them subsided as quickly as it had begun. The father studied his son's face, thrust out a blue hand through the metal bars, a peace offering, his eyes pleading for understanding. "Son, help me. I see the little people standing around . . ." He waved his arm about the room. The desperation did not leave his face.

Today is a good day to die. The old Lakota refrain hovered there between them. The man was ready. The Spirits were ready.

"Okay," Hawk sighed, his voice heavy with sorrow. He left his father's room and found the nurse in the hallway. "My father needs something for his pain."

"You know the medication will kill him, don't you?" The nurse studied his face.

Hawk nodded.

"I'll get the doctor's permission to give him an injection." She telephoned the attending physician.

He returned to his father's room and taking the old man's hand into his, he began singing a sun dance song:

Eca Wanbli Gleska Wan
u tka kehapi k'un . . .

A Spotted Eagle
you said, was coming . . .

The old man tried to join in, their voices ill-matched by age and experience.

As the nurse entered with the needle on a tray, Hawk's father smiled appreciatively, his eyes glancing with fearful fascination at the needle and then back to his son. The nurse dabbed alcohol on the old man's withered arm and inserted the needle, pushing the plunger down on the clear liquid. Without missing a note, Hawk continued to chant the ancient prayer song, determined to sing his father across the passage:

A Spotted Eagle
you said, was coming.
He is coming now. He is coming now.

The old man's eyes began to flutter, but his handgrip remained firm.

"I love you, Dad," Hawk said, tears running shamelessly out of his eyes.

The breathing slowed to a stillness. The eyes ceased their restless searching. The blue hand released into the living hand. Hawk's voice continued singing his dance toward the sun, as the old man's spirit slipped free of the body.

The sun's warm, July radiance lit even the far corners of Meggie's office. A gentle breeze wafted through the windows, echoing with the sounds of children laughing by the water's edge. Meggie sat at her desk, opening her correspondence. The postmark of one envelope read "Denver, Colorado." The handwriting was finely shaped, like calligraphy—a writer who obviously appreciated aesthetic shapes.

Meggie extracted the letter. It read:

Dear Dr. O'Connor,

I kept my promise to you. I neither killed myself nor Karl. Even on that last day, his life was never in peril. I counted on it being harder for him to live with his wounds than to die from them.

In our therapy sessions, it became clear to me that I could not afford to heal my own sickness while living with him. So I did what I had to do. You and I were talking about closed doors and black holes. So, I finally flung open the door, pitched the hole to my husband, and ran away as fast as I could. Karl will wallow in it for a while, to be sure. He is good at that sort of thing.

As for me? I am finally unstuck, on a journey, destination unknown. The landscape changes daily. One by one, the warmer colors are returning to my brush. I have developed a new stroke to capture the playfulness of the wind circling the mountains. The shafts of green light in the lower forests beckon with mystery. The shadows are soft and inviting.

In the manner of stories, paintings also heal. As an artist, I can create my own fictions.

Many times since I've left, I have thought of you and our conversations. Once I even went into a grocery store and bought a pomegranate. I sliced it open with a knife and plucked out several seeds, but that was as far as I could go. I did not swallow any. I guess I'm just not hungry enough.

Yours truly,
Andrea

Meggie read and reread the letter, aware how carefully her former client worded her sentences to avoid any incriminating language. No confession to her act of violence.

The letter was full of hope and possibility. Emotionally, Meggie found herself caught up in Andrea's enthusiasm and newfound energy. Intellectually, Meggie questioned whether Andrea had truly changed anything but external locale.

TWENTY-FOUR

COMPLICATIONS

Words and eggs must be handled with care.
Once broken they are impossible
Things to repair.

—ANNE SEXTON
Words

Back home after his father's death, Hawk was relieved that the storm had temporarily washed out Coyote's tracks. He was anxious to spend more time with Meggie. The surprise appearance of his ex-wife, the arduous preparations for the vision quest, the arrival of Meggie's parents, and the death of his father had interrupted their relationship. It was time to rekindle romance. To his surprise, Meggie wanted to keep their relationship temporarily a secret from her parents.

"Are you embarrassed to be seen with me?" he asked.

She shook her head. "Hawk, they're from a different generation. They know I'm seeing someone. But until you and I are ready to make commitments, I don't want to answer their questions or have to respond to their opinions."

"Are you ashamed of my being Indian?" He was more blunt this time.

"No."

"Then what's the problem?"

Meggie blushed. *How do I tell him it's not race but class that would be the issue?* "My father is a doctor. My mother is a doctor. I have a Ph.D., Hawk. They're going to want to know why a well-educated woman falls in love with a man with a high-school education. When the time is right, I will tell them about you. In the meantime, I will protect myself from their good intentions."

He turned his face away from hers, surprised by the bite of her words and the wound to his sense of self-worth. *What matters is not the grade of education but the level of wisdom a man possesses,* he reflected. But words of protest, words of defense only gave honor to the fear of her parents. They were old. Maybe Meggie was right to take her time.

Hawk knew Meggie's words were not meant to humiliate him.

But the bite festered into the poison of shame.

Rising Smoke began appearing more and more frequently around the Arbre place, using her friendship with Lucy as a wedge into Hawk's company. Lonely for Meggie and disturbed by her words, Hawk found himself increasingly drawn back into the web of his ex-wife's lithe, strong beauty. Rising Smoke had a way of turning her liquid brown eyes on a man and making him go soft in the middle. He began looking forward to her brief visits that, week by week, grew longer and longer.

It wasn't in words but rather in gesture, in the lowering of the eyelids, the hint at the edge of the mouth, the glance at the periphery that told him Rising Smoke wanted to make love. At first, he tried to ignore her signals. But the young man in him remembered the hot passion between them, the taste of her sweet flesh, the sensation of her body wrapped around his.

Unlike the white world where words carry power, little was said about the escalating sexual energy beginning to spark between them. Late one evening, when heat quivered through every crevice in the trailer and the Arbre household had yielded to sleep, Hawk and Rising Smoke took a blanket outside and placed it on the ground. There, beneath the full moon and naked stars, past and present touched in their embrace, each caress retracing an old memory.

Lying there on the blanket, with Rising Smoke's head cradled into his shoulder, Hawk's thoughts drifted to Meggie. *I must be crazy. I'm in love with two women.*

"What?" asked Rising Smoke, aware that Hawk was deep in thought.

He didn't answer. *It's not right. It's not fair to either one of them. What am I doing? Who am I kidding?* A headache formed at the edge of his consciousness.

Rising Smoke's hand slid down to his groin. His member rose in anticipation, indifferent to his thoughts. She laughed, "You're thinking of me."

A pang of guilt tweaked his heart. *Oh Meggie, I truly do love you.*

The fingers of his ex-wife slid over his body smoothly, expertly, sure of their strokes.

Ah, Rising Smoke, I love the touch of your hand. He could feel himself drowning, engulfed by night, stars, and moonlight. A flash flood of passion swamped the feelings of guilt.

She doesn't need to know. He reached toward Rising Smoke and pulled her onto his body and into his heart.

❧ ❧ ❧ ❧

The moon hung in the night sky, clear and brilliant, illuminating the path to the south knoll at Chrysalis. Meggie kept a few steps ahead of her mother to make sure that there weren't any hidden stumps to trip the elderly woman. The scraggly arms of sumac bushes snatched at their clothes, like peasants begging for an audience. Frequently they stopped as the old woman stooped to inspect the flowers silvered by the moon.

It had been a lunatic whim of her mother to trace her childhood path to the clearing, where she had long ago hidden from her parents and brothers. Where, up in the large apple trees, she had found a private space to read the adventure novels of Robert Louis Stevenson and Rudyard Kipling.

"Now, at night? Be sensible, hon. Come to bed," Meggie's father had protested. His was the reasonable mind, anchored in patterns of comfort and stability.

But Meggie's mother didn't waver. Angling her arm toward the diamond stars and the sterling moon, she exclaimed, "The air is thick with enchantment. Don't you see it? Come, Meggie." It was an order, a conspiracy of women against the foolish logic of men.

Meggie knew better than to resist the commands of her mother, off on a moonlit adventure. The idea of the elderly woman caught in a tangle of sticker bushes or snagged by a grasping root impelled Meggie to play guide along the path. Moonlight dappled the forest floor and outlined the giant maples and oaks. Night animals scurried ahead of them. At a distance, the great horned owl's haunting call echoed across the field and through the woods. Meggie clasped her mother's hand. Together, they stumbled to the clearing on the knoll.

Exhausted from the walk, the old woman sank down onto a bed of night grass. She inhaled a long and deep breath, saying, "I love the smell of the sweet cedar and the wild flowers." She plucked a blade of grass, placed the broad stem between opposing thumbs, and blew a shrieking reply to the owl.

An owl from across the field answered, "Who . . . who?"

Lying on her back, Meggie peered up at the Milky Way, which looked like a trail of sugar crystals spilt across the night vault. "I remember as a child I thought the night sky was a large black tablecloth. That the light from the stars was where the fabric had been punctured. And behind the black covering of night hid the brightness of day."

"When I was a little girl," reminisced her mother, "I wanted the house built on this high point. That way, I could be close to the apple orchard and the woods. I could see all the way to Lake Michigan. Your grandmother, however, decided to build the house where she could plant her poppies, tulips, and grapevine hedges. She was always trying to tame the land, cultivate it, make it civilized. She used to despair that I would never grow out of my wildness and settle down into a young lady of society."

Meggie looked around her. It would have been a fine place for a house, surrounded by the woods. *All my life I have thought of Chrysalis as the place of my grandmother, but it is my mother who knows of the wildness.*

"Your grandfather, Meggie, gave me a choice—college or a debutante party in Chicago. He should have known better," she chuckled.

After college in the 1920s came a year of archeological exploration in Greece, followed by four years of medical school. Meggie knew her mother's history well. "And the wildness, Mom, did it ever get tamed? Did having us kids settle you down?"

Her mother blew hard on the limp grass stem; it fluttered soundlessly. She tossed it away. "I forgot about the south knoll. Diapers, PTA, and work—always too much to do. It seems to me that we spend so much of our youth dreaming the future and so much of our mid-adult life forgetting the past. Until you get to my advanced age, when you can't remember all the things you want to remember. I'd like to be closer to that young woman of reckless adventure." She started to struggle to her feet.

"Wait, Mom." Meggie put her hand on her mother's arm. "Let's not go yet. I want to tell you about the wildness in *my* heart."

Her mother looked at her expectantly.

"About a man I love who . . ."

"Yes?"

"Is from a different culture and race . . ." Meggie spoke haltingly.

"Go on," encouraged her mother.

"A wonderful man," explained Meggie, "with lots of life experience who is wise and genuine and . . ."

"Yes?" Her mother seemed curious.

"With a high-school education."

"Oh," remarked her mother.

"Oh" says it all, doesn't it? Meggie waited with baited breath for further comments.

"Help me up, dear."

Meggie scrambled to her feet and gently lent balance to her mother as she struggled to straighten out her arthritic limbs.

The old woman brushed off her pants. "I used to come up here alone during the courtship with your father. It was a good place for dreaming. If you love this man, Meggie, and he is kind and quick of mind, then what does it matter whether he has degrees or not? Still," she cautioned her daughter, "it probably would be wise not to let your father know at this time. He can be so *sensible*." Her voice fell off the last word, as if it were indecent.

Just then, two does and a buck leapt out of the woods into the clearing, heading to the field of corn below the hill. Meggie and her mother froze, awed by their delicate beauty. The deer glided through the grass, their large ears shifting to trap night sounds, their white tails flickering in the moonlight. Their noses sniffed the air, caught the human scent. Standing at rigid attention, they studied the human beings with great curiosity. Then, vaulting across the open space, they melted back into the woods, the sounds of their passage reverberating after them.

"Oh," cried Meggie. *Is love like that—beautiful, abrupt, and so quickly gone?*

"Ah," exclaimed her mother, "The buck has two does. Did you know that when I first met your father, he was engaged to another woman?"

Meggie looked at her mother, astounded. She thought she had known all the old stories. She shook her head.

"When I saw him, brown eyes, black curly hair, and with an Irish wit—I knew I had finally found the man of my dreams. It didn't take me long to fall in love with him."

"But what about the other woman?" Meggie could hardly stand the suspense.

"She was rich and beautiful, but I had something that she did not, something which dazzled your father and bewitched him. He broke off the engagement and came courting after me." Her mother smiled triumphantly.

"What was it, Mom?"

Her mother scanned her surroundings. Her hand swept in an arc about her. "Why, Meggie, all I did was bring him to Chrysalis—the place where the deer come and greet us and the owls sing and the apples fall."

"Was this *before* he became so rational?"

"Oh, Meggie, that's simply old age. He was a young man once, full of passion and dreams and Irish poetry. It's still there, but as you get older, you sleep more. You become less sensual, more sensible. Which reminds me that it's time for bed. I grow so easily tired these days. I must be getting old too."

"No, Mom," answered Meggie, "the wildness has *always* resided in your heart."

"Perhaps you are right, my dear." Meggie's mother smiled. Returning to the house, she led the way back.

Her mother hadn't asked and Meggie didn't tell.

Hawk is an Indian.

Successive days of unusually humid summer heat oppressed Meggie. Due to her parents' presence, she didn't have as much time or opportunity to be with Hawk, except when he came to make repairs on the place or when she was able to slip away to his place. *I miss him.*

At nighttime, she found herself dreaming about him. In her dreams she would always be working up on the south knoll, and he would glide out of the woods into the clearing, moving in stately fashion toward her. He would study her with great curiosity, say something to her, but she couldn't comprehend his words. He was either too far away or was speaking in a language she couldn't fathom. And then he would turn around, leaving her behind, dissolving into the shadows of the forest. Several times Meggie awoke in the middle of the night, listening in the silence for his message.

Although Meggie occasionally met Hawk at his cramped trailer, there was not the freedom of Chrysalis in which to relax and spend time in their loving with each other. She thought—*he's different somehow.* She reassured herself that autumn would come soon, and her parents would leave for a warmer climate. Her mother observed, "It must be hard for you to have us here."

Meggie lied and spoke the truth, "No, Mom. I love having you and Dad around."

Mornings turned rough in the summer's heat, especially when Meggie caught an intestinal bug that fluttered waves of nausea through her stomach. Three weeks into August, her stomach continued to complain, until it dawned on Meggie that even the flu doesn't linger that long.

A quick, confidential trip to her gynecologist confirmed both her best and worst suspicions at one and the same time. Meggie protested, "Pregnant? I can't be pregnant after all these years. I'm forty years old."

The physician philosophized, "Miracles do happen."

Meggie mused to herself, *Hawk is in a family way and doesn't even know it.*

5

ITOKAGATA
death/life

TWENTY-FIVE

THE TELLING

We dance round in a ring and suppose,
But the Secret sits in the middle and knows.

—ROBERT FROST
The Secret Sits

Meggie helped her parents pack for the long drive back East. She
was sorry to see them go, but their departure also meant that she
could enjoy the freedom of Chrysalis and Hawk's return. "Come Saturday night," she whispered into the telephone. "I'll make you dinner."

On Friday, she concocted a farewell feast for her parents: smoked
chub, baked potatoes, spinach salad, and cherry pie. "What can I do to
help you?" her mother asked.

Meggie handed her the flatware and napkins. "The table needs to
be set."

Her father poked his nose into the kitchen, "Smells awfully good."
Without being asked, he cut wedges of Stilton cheese, retrieved a box
of crackers, placed them on a plate, and poured three glasses of Leelanau White.

They sat out on the porch facing west toward the setting sun. "I hate to leave." Her mother looked wistful.

She wonders if she'll ever make it back up here. It was her place long before it was mine. Meggie watched her father reach over and kiss her mother's hand.

"Got to go back to work," was all he said, a phrase he had repeated at the end of every summer in Chrysalis. He stroked the back of her hand.

Maybe I should tell him about Hawk, Meggie thought.

But she didn't dare. Her father had no use for spiritual people of any kind, much less Native American and with only a high-school education to boot.

"I don't know why you won't let me introduce you to some of my younger medical colleagues up in this area," he groused. "I hate to leave my little girl all alone in this big house."

"I'll be fine, Dad," Meggie answered. "Remember your 'little girl' has been both married and divorced."

"That jerk!" He had never approved of Tom Lockheed in the first place, and later, after the divorce, when he learned that Meggie's husband occasionally had been violent with her, well, it was enough to set his teeth on edge. "You saw what happened when you did the choosing of a husband all by yourself."

It was an old argument not worth revisiting, and Meggie complimented herself on restraining from further comment.

The next morning, as their car headed down the driveway, her mother fluttering farewell from the front seat and her father driving, Meggie waved good-bye. Her hand kept stirring invisible currents of air—long after they had disappeared from sight.

She walked toward the house. In the distance, she could hear their car pull out onto the main road.

I guess we all have secrets worth guarding.

Night could come none too soon. Meggie cleaned house, set new sheets upon the bed, planned the meal, and crafted her baby announcement speech to Hawk. All kinds of scenarios crossed her imagination.

Over a romantic candlelit dinner, he'd look into her eyes and she would say, "Hawk, there is something I have to tell you." She visualized him responding with joy: "I've always wanted to have a child!" and hugging her in their newly cemented love.

Or, he'd say, "Meggie, will you marry me?" *And what then? Would I accept, when I swore to myself that I would never marry again?*

On the fringes of her consciousness, she was dimly aware of the possibility of his reaction being: "Meggie, we can't have a child now. It just complicates everything." *Surely, he wouldn't suggest an abortion?*

Meggie frowned. Maybe this relationship with him meant more to her than it ever would to him. It was a thought she kicked out of consciousness almost as soon as it registered. It simply didn't fit her euphoric mood.

This baby would be her gift to him. Whether or not they eventually married, the baby would always tie them together in love's perfect knot.

All day long Meggie sang romantic songs as she prepared to welcome her lover home to her entangled heart. She laughed and danced throughout the whole house, happily anticipating Hawk's arrival.

Grimly, Hawk noticed the return of Coyote's tracks, doubling and redoubling about his trailer. Tonight he'd confess to Meggie the truth about Rising Smoke. Afraid to lose Meggie, he also knew he could not continue to deceive her. She deserved better than that.

I'll tell her that I love two women. Maybe she'll understand how confusing that is for me.

He sighed, dreading the impending conversation.

In the kitchen of his trailer, Lucy inquired, "What are you going to do?"

"Tell the truth," Hawk answered. He didn't really want to rehash the issue with Lucy.

"Well, I know you probably don't want any advice, but . . ."

I really don't. He turned his back to Lucy while washing coffee cups in his sink.

Lucy disregarded his body language. "What I see is that you need a woman to help you on the Pipe road. Rising Smoke knows how to pour the waters for the women's sweat lodge ceremonies. You told me she's got powerful medicine."

"Rattlesnake medicine," interrupted Hawk.

"Well, she could do the medicine work alongside you."

"What are you telling me, Lucy?" He felt irritated; his cousin was trying to narrow his choices.

Lucy flashed back at his irritation, "Don't be in such a hurry. I haven't even finished what I was going to say." She sat back, arms folded, picking her words carefully.

"Rising Smoke is my friend, and I like her. But when it comes to marriage, she's like a viper. She'll flick out her tongue and sting you. You forget, Hawk, you were the one to leave her that first time. Underneath her skin there's a heap of bitterness stored up inside her. Right now, you're so taken with her beauty that when she shakes her tail at you, you think it's a welcome instead of a warning. She's a strong woman, but some of her strength is in the wrong places. She loves the old you; she'll make mincemeat out of the new you."

"You worry too much," Hawk said, dismissively.

"You're heading for trouble, Hawk."

"No," he replied, gathering up his clothes. "I'm heading to Meggie's place." He patted his cousin's arm on the way out the trailer door.

⁂

I will tell him the truth, thought Meggie, as she saw Hawk striding toward the kitchen door. Unwrapping her apron, she moved out onto the back screened porch to greet him. He swept her up into his arms, their embrace full of a summer's longing. His kisses were ravenous and many; it appeared to Meggie that he was reluctant to let her go. But the pot boiled over on the top of the stove, and Meggie had to push him away.

I will tell him the truth over dinner, she resolved, so happy to see her lover in the full privacy of her home. As she drained the steaming zucchini, he kept touching her on the face, the shoulders, the hip. She told him of her parents' departure. He spoke of Lucy and her family. Together, in the network of community and familial gossip, they located themselves.

Hungry, he began nibbling at her neck. She found herself wanting to set aside the meal on the back burners and head straight to the bedroom, but she had something important to tell him first, over dinner.

The dining room flickered in the warm glow of candlelight. Over the food, Meggie and Hawk exchanged longing expressions, eyes hungry and beseeching. He took her left hand and planted kisses on the back of it. For a second, his gaze became distant, preoccupied. A brief frown clouded his face, then vanished into a sunny grin. Meggie waited for him to say something, but he placed her hand over his mouth and squeezed it tightly.

At the end of the dinner, Meggie put one hand over her womb and reached out to Hawk with the other.

I will tell him now about the baby, she glowed.

"We need to talk about something . . ." she began.

His body clenched, as if warding off some terrible pain. Forcing himself to look at her, he said, "Oh Meggie, how did you know that there is something I have to tell you . . ."

⁛ ⁙ ⁙ ⁛

The anxiety inside him broke like a gushing torrent. Studying Meggie's face, he knew he loved her. *I want to wrap her in my arms and protect her from the hurt I'm going to inflict on her. I'm sure she must see the guilt on my face. How to tell her about Rising Smoke?*

He had procrastinated too long in confessing to Meggie, hoping to find in the act of making love with her forgiveness for his confusion. *How do I reveal to a woman I love that I also love another?*

"Meggie, I don't know how to say this," he pushed forward, "except to say it outright. I don't have any fancy words to sugarcoat it. I love you, Meggie."

She nodded her head, encouraging him to say more, touching him on the elbow. Her eyes were bright with excitement.

The words stuck in his throat. *This is so hard to do.*

"I'm confused, Meggie, because I find myself also loving another woman. I don't want to hurt you. I don't want to put distance between us. I love you and . . ." He couldn't complete the awful sentence.

She stopped breathing, freezing every muscle in her body. Only her eyes moved wildly, as if searching for a focus.

"I know you must be angry at me, Meggie."

Her eyes are driving me crazy with grief, he thought.

After what seemed like minutes, her diaphragm lifted, and she exhaled a long, piteous sigh. "Who?" was all she asked, her voice restrained and exhausted. She pulled back the outstretched hand, locking the fingers of both hands and resting them on her belly. "Sweet-Grass Woman?"

"No. Rising Smoke."

For the longest time she simply stared at him. A stream of emotions flitted across her face. Love, anger, confusion, panic, emptiness, but, most of all, raw pain. She struggled for emotional control. Her cheek muscles clamped tightly.

"I don't understand . . ." she began, then dropped the thought, as if not knowing where to take it.

"I have hurt you," he acknowledged, feeling a chasm open up and crumble the ground between them, minute by minute. *Please don't turn away from me, Meggie,* his eyes pleaded. He desperately wanted to reach out and hold her, to contain the pain sprouting inside of him.

She nodded her head. Her face drew up; she began to gag. Pushing herself from the table, she looked at him, eyes again frantic, and announced, "I'm going to be sick." She ran up the stairs to the bathroom, gesturing for him to stay down in the dining room.

He could hear her vomiting. The remains of their gourmet dinner sat on the table, an accusation of his insensitivity and evidence of her loving preparation. Feeling helpless with regard to Meggie, Hawk gathered the dishes and set about cleaning up. Upstairs, the shower water began to run. *Good, a shower will help her feel better,* he comforted himself.

His ears picked up the echoes of sobbing in the shower stall, at first just a light cry, then racking heaves of grief breaking loose. Over the kitchen sink, he gripped his head in his hands. When he heard the shower turn off, he busied himself with the dishes. *I will not burden her with my guilt.*

She came down the stairs dressed in an old ratty bathrobe. "I'm going to bed now," she announced, her voice drained and dead.

"Don't you want me to stay?" he asked.

"No," she answered, her shoulders sagging.

"Yes," she added, with tears starting up again.

"Hawk, I can't . . ." she amended. She turned her back to him, arms crossed, holding onto herself tightly.

She walked away.

I will tell him the truth about the baby now, Meggie had thought over dinner. But the truth had shattered into tiny slivers as Hawk announced his love for Rising Smoke. Each shard of truth cut deep into her, jagged rips into all her fantasies, hopes, and anticipations. Dinner rose up inside her, mocking her dreams, demanding that she purge herself to harsh reality.

The baby doesn't deserve this kind of truth, she angrily reflected.

But no matter how hard she retched, the truth weighted in on her like a stone in her gut that would not be forced out. Her stomach ached. Her heart swelled with pain. Her mind flailed about, searching for relief, something to sustain hope.

The baby. Our baby. My baby, she kept repeating to herself, as if in that tiny seed of life growing in her womb she would find her anchor and direction.

"What are you going to do now?" asked Bev, taking Meggie's hands into her own. She had come as soon as her friend had summoned her.

Meggie shrugged, trying to gather her thoughts into a coherent plan of action. Her emotions kept shifting the ground under her reason. Trying to reassure herself, she patted Bev's hand. "I'll think of something."

"Will you tell him about the baby?"

"I don't know." Meggie was confused. "If I tell him, it will force him to choose. He loves me, I know that. He loves her too. She came into his life long before he knew me. If I truly love him, then I think I must wait for him to decide. I can't have him marry me because I'm pregnant. What kind of marriage would that be?"

"What about your love for the baby?" Bev looked her straight in the eye.

"What are you asking me?" Meggie averted her eyes.

"Meggie, a baby needs a father as well as a mother. Although I can't imagine why you'd want to stay with such a creep. Maybe he's into some esoteric Native American practice of polygamy. Still, Hawk has a right to the truth. It's his baby as well. Let him make his decision with all the facts." Bev was both caustic and pragmatic.

Meggie shook her head vehemently. "Someday, yes. But not now."

"You know what I think?" said Bev. "You're furious with him for falling in love with another woman. You're going to withhold the knowledge of his baby from him. Right now, you're hurt and mad, and you're probably saying to yourself—it's *my* baby."

Despite the tears trickling down her face, Meggie couldn't help smiling in recognition of Bev's insight. *Yes, I am hurt. Yes, I am angry. Damn angry.* Already the outrage was making her feel stronger, infusing her with a sense of determination and independence.

The baby and I can make it by ourselves.

"But," intruded Bev, "it's not the truth."

What a mess. Winona, irritated with waiting, had turned her attentions back to the ones she had left behind. *So, Hawk has got himself two women, one baby, and a heap of trouble.* She wondered how he was going to work it out.

What he needs is a good kick in the butt.

As for Meggie, Winona couldn't understand why she was so damn passive. "Didn't he tell you that he loved you? Go fight for your man," the old woman hissed. She never could understand white people with all their confusion about what was important.

"*Wopila,* Wakan Tanka, for not making me one of them." Unfortunately, Meggie was deaf to Winona's words.

"Open your ears," shouted Winona—to no avail.

Lucy and Bev, however, seemed more malleable, receptive. Winona nudged them with her thoughts, encouraged their words. She couldn't be absolutely sure that it made any difference, but she liked what they had to say. It was difficult to traverse the barriers between Here and There. Winona snorted, *I'd like to think I have a little bit of influence left.*

Winona shifted her position and stretched her limbs. "Truth is, I'm getting impatient. When is the next life going to begin? Why hasn't someone come to show me the way? Where in the hell is Davis when I need him?"

She was bored with meddling in Hawk's affairs. Her cousin's son didn't seem to have the good sense the Creator gave him. Like so many men before him, swollen by either lust or power, he was playing himself right into the trickster's realm. She leaned down and whispered into his left ear at night while he was sleeping alone in the trailer, "You're taking that love between you and Meggie and stabbing it to death with your *honesty* and your *confusion.* Take that Chanumpa Wakan. Go ask Wiyohiyanpa what you should do."

But Hawk kept right on sleeping.

Exasperation chafed at Winona. *Why hasn't Davis or someone else arrived to cut the last strands of my connection to the people Back There? They don't even pay attention anymore to what I have to say.*

She grew raw with the waiting.

☙ ❧ ❧ ❧

Fritzie, too, felt impatient. Slowly, the summer heat cooled, and the days grew shorter. The yappy summer dogs departed for winter homes downstate, leaving the northern woods to deer, rabbits, foxes, raccoons, skunks, and porcupines. And Fritzie. Despite his earlier encounter with the rattlesnake, Fritzie was anxious to go hunting again. He was the protector of Chrysalis and of the woman.

But things were not right with the woman. She did not play with him as she had before. She moved slowly and seemed to prefer the dark spaces in the house.

Outside the house he discovered a rabbit warren with three entrances. The smell of their warm bodies, nestled into the earth den, excited the terrier instinct. Into the largest hole he squeezed his body, leading with his long nose, his front paws burrowing furiously into the underground passageway. He could hear the rabbits scream a warning as the tunnel grew smaller and smaller, the ceiling dirt falling into his eyes and onto his nose. With a powerful push from his hindquarters, he broke into a central room.

A rabbit startled, jumped in the wrong direction. Fritzie's teeth flashed; his jaw clamped down on soft fur to flesh. He shook the rabbit to and fro; the constriction of the tunnel did not allow his head much leverage. The rabbit's hindquarters kicked desperately. Surprised and rebuffed, Fritzie dropped his prey. Broken and bleeding from both sides with multiple puncture wounds, the rabbit dove deeply into the shafts, deeply down, toward the dark womb and grave of Grandmother Earth.

❖ ❖ ❖ ❖

As before, Meggie hauled the unrepentant Fritzie to the veterinarian. Sam Waters irrigated the dog's dust-clogged eyes. "Where have you been, old buddy?" He fondly scratched Fritzie behind his ears.

"In trouble, as usual," groaned Meggie.

Sam looked up at Meggie. Her face exhibited lines of fatigue and bags under the eyes. "Where have you been, Meggie? It seems to me that you've been keeping yourself out of sight lately." His voice was kind, a friend if she wanted one.

The memory of Fritzie's muffled barking from deep within the rabbit hole came to mind. Meggie had guided him back to the surface, coaxing and calling him first with terms of endearment, then orders, and finally threats of disembowelment. Apparently trapped in the rabbit warren, the terrier had been unable to move forward; his retreat was clumsy and backward, toward the pull of Meggie's voice. Upon emerging from the underground den, Fritzie began pawing at his irritated eyes.

"You're going to be okay, old boy. But I'm not so sure about your mistress." Sam rubbed Fritzie's belly. The dog moaned with pleasure.

Meggie shrugged her shoulders, not wanting to confide the site of her wounds to Sam but needing to convey the truth. "Like all animals," she answered, nodding toward her terrier, "even we human beings burrow underground at times."

TWENTY-SIX

SCARS

He jests at scars that never felt a wound.
—WILLIAM SHAKESPEARE
Romeo and Juliet

"I'm worried about June," Katya confided to Meggie. "School is about to start. Kids can be so cruel. Already a couple of boys have called her Scarface. Yesterday, she came home sobbing, telling me that nobody will be her friend. It just tore my heart out. Maybe I should home-school her this year, until the facial reconstruction is done. What do you think?"

I'd worry more about the mark the horses have left on her psyche. Meggie carefully choose her words: "The face she presents to others has been damaged, but that can be repaired. It is the face she presents to herself that will stay with her all her life. Keeping her at home for protection will convince her that the scars inside can never heal."

Katya sighed in frustration. "If you only knew what it was like to be a mother, Meggie, you would understand how helpless I feel when someone hurts my child."

But I do. Meggie nodded in sympathy.

※ ※ ※ ※

"I'm terribly concerned about Sasha," croaked Savannah from her bed. The effort of speaking to Meggie set off a racking spasm of coughing. The cancer was eating away at her strength and vitality. The old woman reached for the oxygen nosepiece.

With her right hand Meggie stroked one of Savannah's hands, noting the ridges of blue veins. Savannah responded with a squeeze. With her left hand, Meggie touched her own belly, as if to connect in the delicate moment the passage of life from beginning to end. If only she could impart to her dying friend the gift of new energy; if only she could take for her baby the gift of wisdom from a life rich in experience.

The ravages of the disease had rapidly wasted Savannah's figure to an uncharacteristic fragility, wherein the bones protruded and the muscles had receded. But her mind seemed sharper, honed by necessity to compensate for a failing body.

Not so for Sasha.

Upon greeting Sasha at the front door of the Todds' home, Meggie read despair in Sasha's face, the recognition that soon the life of twinhood would end. There was no spark of hope in her eyes, no dalliance in daily chores, no details of Savannah's care, no pleasantries exchanged. "She's up there in the second bedroom," Sasha said, her voice full of unspoken suffering as she shuffled off to her own room. Sasha had aged twenty years in twenty days.

Up in the sickroom, Savannah gulped the pure oxygen after having cleared her lungs, which were drowning in their own fluid. Turning heavily lidded eyes toward Meggie, Savannah said, "My sister, Sasha . . ." Sleep, however, severed the words, setting down the subject and cutting it off from the energy of its intent.

It was the last time Meggie ever saw Savannah Todd.

※ ※ ※ ※

A large package from Seattle, Washington, arrived at Meggie's office. In it was a letter. Meggie recognized the handwriting.

Dear Dr. O'Connor,

I want you to know that I am painting up a storm and am happier than I have a right to expect.

I chose not to visit Karl after his unfortunate accident. I couldn't bear to look upon his face, as I didn't know whether I would laugh (at my release) or cry (at his imprisonment). But would you tell him, the next time you see him, that I once truly loved him.

I will send him the divorce papers soon. Painful as it may be, death can make room for what is to be born.

But the main reason I am writing this letter is to tell you that I purchased a pomegranate this morning. I pried it open to the blood-red core and ate one seed. Not up to Persephone's standards, I realize, but (with regard to life) I figure I best take it one month at a time.

The next step for me is to find a therapist in Seattle. Perhaps you can give me the name of a colleague—someone who can help me find a ladder, rope, night goggles, headlamp, and waders?

I think I am ready now.

Andrea

P.S. In appreciation for all your help, I wanted you to have this painting.

Meggie tore open the rest of the package. Immediately she recognized it as a western landscape with what looked like a snow-capped Mount Rainier in the background. In the foreground, in a small suburban yard, flourished an unusual thorny shrub, dangling apple-sized red fruit. Right away Meggie guessed it was a pomegranate tree.

On the back of the canvas, in Andrea's beautiful scroll, was inscribed the painting's title:

Better Than a Black Hole

Meggie laughed.

She knew just the right person in Seattle for Andrea to see, someone who would let Persephone be the guide, someone who would protect Andrea from a free-fall descent.

The multiple fractures in Karl's leg did not come close to matching the break in his spirit. Concerned by his fragile state of mind, the psychiatric staff of the hospital restricted visitors to family members, guarding him against the unnecessary intrusions of concerned parishioners. Leaning on her professional contacts, Meggie finally gained permission to see him. The ward nurse took Meggie aside. "Reverend Young's leg is healing nicely," she said, "but he is becoming more and more depressed every day. We're all worried about him. He hardly ever talks, eats little, sleeps sparingly. He refuses to take the antidepressant medication prescribed for him. Maybe you can help?"

The two of them entered Karl's room. His shattered leg angled up from the bed, cradled in a sling. His face was turned toward the window, away from the door. The nurse announced cheerfully, "You've got a visitor, Reverend Young." She went to the bed and plumped up his pillows, adjusting his position so that he would have to interact with his guest. "There now, you two have a good chat, and if you need anything, the buzzer is by the bed." Turning her back on him, the nurse rolled her eyes at Meggie. Passing the psychologist on the way out, she mumbled, "Good luck."

Meggie sank down on a blue vinyl chair, indented with the impressions of former occupants. She smiled up at Karl, noting his stony, impassive gaze. If silence was what he wanted, then silence was what she would give him. They sat there for a long time as twilight began to edge its half light into the room. He glanced at her, then looked away, trapped by his leg harness.

He seemed to be waiting for his silence to freeze her out. She remained, anticipating an opening, an invitation.

I can be as stubborn as you. I can play this game too. Meggie grinned at him.

Finally, he couldn't stand it anymore. "You're not going to retreat, are you?" he grouched.

She shook her head.

"Even if I ask you to leave me in peace?"

Again, she shook her head.

"Why?" he demanded in an exasperated voice.

An insight struck her. Karl had made a mess of his life. His love affairs had contributed to his wife's violent departure. His career was in shambles. His body, temporarily, was in shackles, and his mind could not carry the burden of his guilt. By shutting off all communication with others, Karl was announcing to the world his unworthiness.

"Why won't you go?" he insisted, focusing a belligerent stare at Meggie.

Inspired, she answered, "I have come here because I need your help."

Baffled, his facial expression switched from anger to interest.

"Karl, I need to talk with someone who knows how to listen." Meggie could sense all the feelings of the past couple weeks rush in on her: the disastrous dinner with Hawk, Bev's rebuke, the brittleness of Savannah and Sasha Todd, the baby with no father, Rising Smoke. Tears gathered at the corners of her eyes; words choked in her throat.

Karl pulled himself upright in the bed, his voice strong and caring. "Well, go on. Tell me what's the problem. Maybe I can help."

The colors of the dying sun flooded the room with soft golden hues as Meggie quietly spoke her grief.

Adam looked out from the kitchen window as the last light dimmed in the west and the stars slowly began to emerge. His schoolbooks were sprawled all over the kitchen table.

Coming up behind him, his mother affectionately hugged him, tousled his hair, and peered out at the onrush of night. "I love this time of day too," she said, her voice wistful and dreamy.

"Mom," he said, "Do you think Grandma can always hear us from where she's at?"

Lucy touched her son's smooth cheek. "I don't know. I hope so. She'd be awfully proud of you and Eva. Why do you ask?"

"Because," he blushed, "I've a secret to tell her."

"Can you share it with me?" Lucy looked at her son.

He shyly glanced away and shook his head.

"Well, then," instructed Lucy, reaching up to a shelf and pulling down a pouch of tobacco. "Take this tobacco and go outside and offer it to the spirit of your grandmother. Then tell her the secret."

He nodded. In his small hand, he grasped the packet and headed for the door. Walking past Hawk's trailer, he could hear the laughter of Rising Smoke and his cousin. Away from the light of house and trailer, the boy headed to the sweat lodge area. Lifting up his hand, tobacco enfolded, he offered it to all the directions, just as Winona had taught him. "Grandmother," he called out into the dark, "I have a secret to tell you."

Winona appeared beside him, more faded than before, but still recognizable to her grandson.

His voice was high and thin, as yet unmarked by the distortions of adolescence. "Grandmother, I have a girlfriend at school. Her name is June Tubbs, and she is beautiful."

TWENTY-SEVEN

IN TRUTH

The truth is rarely pure and never simple.
— OSCAR WILDE
The Importance of Being Earnest

After his vision quest in June, Hawk had taken a vacation from his Sacred Pipe and spiritual discipline. Following the heady days of the *hanbleciya*, he had needed to return to ordinary life. When Hawk summoned him, Three Legs came and answered questions for the community but did not take over the sweat lodge ceremony. Safe but infrequently handled during the summer months, the Chanunpa Wakan languished in the medicine bundle. In truth, Hawk felt spiritually uninspired.

To be in love with two women at the same time was intoxicating, confusing, and, most of all, time-consuming. There were no eagle feathers tied to his wrist to pull him back onto the Pipe road. There was no elderly father to give him advice. Laughing Bear had warned him against involvement with Meggie; Lucy had predicted dire consequences to a renewed affair with Rising Smoke. His heart tilted him toward Meggie; his head counseled him to stick with his own people and Rising Smoke; his loins found both women to be incredibly exciting.

And through it all, he knew Coyote was laughing at him.

"I would love to make another baby with you." Rising Smoke peered up at him, her deep brown eyes inviting a response.

"What?" Hawk couldn't believe his ears.

"You heard me," she countered.

That's all I need right now to complicate my life even further. If I had a baby with Rising Smoke, I might as well kiss Meggie good-bye. And that's not something I am willing to do. Hawk chose not to share these thoughts with his volatile ex-wife. *No use stirring up a hornet's nest unnecessarily.*

"There was a time you would have jumped at the invitation," she chided him. "A time when you wanted nothing more than to father a whole brood of babies with me."

Hawk nodded in remembrance. They had done that once before: They had made a baby; they had lost the baby; and then, they had destroyed the life between them. In all their reconnecting discussions with each other, not once had the miscarriage been mentioned. They both knew it had not been a freak of Mother Nature but, rather, a consequence of their own negligence. Rising Smoke had had no business working in the rodeo when heavy with child. He shook his head to ward off the downward spiral of his thoughts.

Laughing at Hawk's apparent confusion, Rising Smoke got up from the kitchen table in the trailer and peered out the window. In the dark, she could barely make out the figure of Adam moving toward the sweat lodge area. "That's a strange kid."

"Who?" Hawk was unaware of the boy passing in the night.

"Lucy's son. He's too serious for an eight-year-old. Besides," she added, "the boy doesn't really like me."

Hawk chuckled. Rising Smoke always had acute radar for anyone who didn't approve of her.

"He's just a kid, hon."

Rising Smoke pulled out two cigarettes, lighting first one and then the other. Without asking him, she put one cigarette in his mouth. She exhaled authoritatively, "Some kids are not kids. They're born all grown up, just like him." She nodded toward the window.

"He's Winona's grandson," explained Hawk.

"Yeah, and she didn't much like me either."

Hawk smiled at her, remembering that, indeed, Winona had found Rising Smoke to be too self-preoccupied.

"She can't pass by a mirror without checking her own reflection" had been one of Winona's kinder descriptions.

Rising Smoke had always been beautiful. Men were drawn irrevocably toward her. He remembered his pride in being seen with her—the striking face, dark eyes, long black hair, well-proportioned body, and an amazing ability to work with horses.

The alcohol, the divorce, the passage of time—none of these had really dented the power of her sexual presence. But she was a puzzle to him. Hawk could not decipher her intentions. To make a baby with her would mean an enormous commitment between them; yet there had been no demands made, no promises given. They were still feeling their way into their own hearts.

"To tell the truth, I didn't take to Winona," continued Rising Smoke. "She never said much around me, but her squinty eyes dogged my every step in her house. I think she was afraid I was going to steal something. Her husband, Davis—now he was just as nice as could be. I never could understand what he saw in her." She stubbed out the dying remains of her cigarette.

Hawk dragged on his cigarette, annoyed at himself for resuming the habit. The weed tasted bittersweet. "They had gifts for each other," he explained. "Davis had brought Winona to the Pipe, to self-respect and a sense of her own power. She had brought him to an understanding of the Grandmother. Their marriage was like the river from which they drank; it did not drown who they were as separate human beings. It helped them walk in balance."

"Are you saying that we weren't able to do that?" Rising Smoke tensed her body, then relaxed and addressed her own question. "It seems to me," she smiled at him, her eyes seductive and beguiling, "that you and I could find our balance together." Ambling over to where he was sitting, she lowered herself onto his lap, her legs straddling his legs, her mouth sweetening for a kiss.

It didn't matter that Hawk could hear the manipulation inside her words, could see the calculation behind her moves, could guess what lay before them. History was repeating itself. And, despite such cautionary misgivings, he could feel himself yielding to the hope that lies within all disappointed memory—that the story might be relived to a different ending.

It didn't matter, in that moment, that he knew he loved Meggie, that his actions could abort the sweet future between them. The temptation to reawaken the past, to erase the pain, and to remember the joy proved too strong to resist.

Automatically, Hawk's arms wrapped around her hips as he pulled her into him, his hands cupping her rump. He could feel her breath surround him, her lips soft and inviting, her serpentine body swaying into the rhythms of the dulcet summer night.

There was no hint of the old sickness between them.

As the boy reached out for her, Winona began to slip away.

"It's time for me to say good-bye, Grandson. I can't be coming to visit you whenever you call me." Even at the edges, Winona was curling into the air, becoming more transparent, misty. Where once there had been substance, now shadow-dark trees usurped her space.

"Why, Grandma? I need to talk to you. You said I was the *only* one who could see you." Adam's eyes searched the darkness. His voice echoed with anxiety.

"You will always be able to talk to me, Grandson, and I will always listen."

He looked straight at her, but no longer was she visible. The trees stood stolidly, the black arms of their branches stretching out to grasp the evening vapors. Only in his peripheral vision could he make out the unnatural stirring of air, a gauzy film, the lightest of curtains between the realities—which told him that Winona was still present.

"But why are you leaving me when I need you?" A plaintive question.

"Because I must, and you are strong, Stands By Dog."

I'm not, Grandma. I'm not. I'm still a kid, and I don't want you to go.

But he did not say the words that would bind her to him. He knew better than to continue questioning his grandmother, for often she had answered his questions either by story or by telling him that he would grow into the answers when he had a little more experience and age on him.

He felt a slight breeze ruffle his hair and pass a gentle touch over his cheek, and then she was gone. There, then not there.

The woods closed in around him, the only light being that which dimly glowed from Hawk's trailer and his parents' house. Adam crouched down on the ground by the sweat lodge. With a sharp stick he stabbed the dirt and gouged a hole, a grave for both a young boy's anger and a young man's sorrow.

TWENTY-EIGHT

SETTLING OF ACCOUNTS

*Life is a gamble at terrible odds—if
it was a bet, you wouldn't take it.*

—TOM STOPPARD
Rosencrantz and Guildenstern Are Dead

News traveled fast in Suttons Bay.

"You heard about the Todd twins?" Katya anxiously greeted her husband. He had arrived home from a day of settling small accounts.

Paul nodded. By morning, everyone in town had learned of their deliberate overdose of sleeping pills. "Perhaps, it's for the best."

"What am I going to tell the kids? Robert and June especially liked them. Now, they're dead. Life is crazy! It seems to me just when you get old enough to acquire some wisdom, Death comes along, knocks at the door, and claims payment for all that experience. You spend all your time trying to figure out what life means, and then, boom, it's suddenly over." Katya shook her head.

Paul's arms enveloped his wife. "We can never know, Katya, what will knock at our door. We're just lucky to have the chance to pass the time together, however briefly."

Katya studied her husband's face. He had changed during the past year in fundamental ways. Work no longer defined his existence. Family and friends now took precedence over equalizing columns of numbers.

No longer could he prepare for every contingency of life. No longer could he be confident in his ability to protect his children from harm. The savage accident with his baby girl had shredded all illusions of safety. Aware of the fragility of human existence, he had learned to count each day as special, to cherish the moments of intimacy with his family. He held his wife tightly.

"Our baby," whispered Paul into Katya's ear, "June's going to be all right." They were lying side by side in their king-sized bed, ready to fall asleep.

Katya wrapped her arms around her husband, placing her head upon his shoulder. Together, the two of them banked solidly into the embrace, familiar lovers with each other. The mystery of the night encircled them and separated them from the distractions of the day. Katya burrowed her head deeper into the strength of her husband's body.

"Our baby," she softly whispered into the darkness, "is no longer a baby. She's even got a boyfriend. Our little girl is growing up, Paul."

Her voice was full of wonder.

.⁘ ⁘ ⁘ ⁘

Hawk awoke to harsh pounding on the door of his trailer. Squinting at the clock, he could see it was after midnight. Rising Smoke had left the trailer hours ago. *Maybe she left something important behind,* he thought.

He rolled out of bed and threw on a pair of jeans. The banging on the door continued, unabated and insistent. "Okay, okay, I'll be right there," he grumbled, switching on the light.

He stumbled sleepy-eyed toward the door and unlatched it. To his surprise, it wasn't a forgetful Rising Smoke; it wasn't a beleaguered Meggie nor a reproachful Lucy. Standing there before him, eerily illuminated by night shadows and trailer light, was Meggie's friend,

Bev—her fists upon her hips and her chin jutting out. "I've got something to say to you." Her tone of voice was sharp.

He woke up immediately. Something was wrong. "Come in." Brusquely, she brushed past him, checked around for a place to sit, and then claimed a kitchen chair. He could tell she was ill at ease. She made him uncomfortable by staring straight at his face. He sat down on the other kitchen chair, the small table serving as a buffer between them. He didn't know what to expect.

"I apologize for it being so late," she stammered. "I got lost finding this place, and I still don't know if I am doing the right thing coming here. Meggie may never forgive me for this. But sometimes a person needs a friend to tell the truth."

"Is she all right?" Hawk feared that Meggie was hurt. *I've hurt her*, convulsed through his mind.

Bev shook her head. "She's not all right, and that's why I'm here."

Hawk held his breath, *I can't bear to lose Meggie.* He panicked inside.

"There's something I have to tell you," Bev continued. "There's something you don't know. Some time ago Meggie confided in me that the two of you had become lovers. Well, obviously, one of those times, you didn't take any precautions." Her voice accused him.

What? What? Filled with dreadful images of Meggie being sick or wounded, his mind couldn't comprehend what this white woman was saying. "I don't understand," he said, jarred and confused by Bev's words.

"Meggie's going to have your baby."

Oh thank God, she's okay! He exhaled with relief, catching Bev's meaning on the rebound. "A baby?" he asked. His body jerked to a different kind of attention.

"*Your* baby," pronounced Bev.

"My baby?" With awe and reverence, he rolled the word *baby* on his tongue.

"Yes."

"My *baby*," he repeated, affirming the meaning of Bev's statement, shaking his head in astonishment.

A fourth time he spoke, this time savoring the truth of Meggie's pregnancy, "*My* baby."

6

MAHPIYATA

power

TWENTY-NINE

KNOWING

*. . . the highest point a man can attain is not
Knowledge, or Virtue, or Goodness, or Victory,
but something even greater, more heroic, and
more despairing: Sacred Awe!*

—NIKOS KAZANTZAKIS
Zorba the Greek

Meggie awoke, startled. She checked the clock; it was still the middle
of the night. Turning over in bed, she shut her eyelids, only to have
them rebound open. She buried her head into the pillow. The sound of
silence pressed in on her ears. Back and forth, her body shifted, until
in utter rebellion the lower sheet popped off the corners and shriveled
into the center, balling up under her legs. Meggie gave up and turned
on the light. Fritzie groaned and rolled over on his back, his four feet
stretched out stiff-legged in the air.

With sleepy reluctance and doggy devotion, Fritzie left his warm
bed and accompanied her downstairs. Meggie poured herself a glass
of milk, while he rooted through the kibbles in his food bowl, pushing
out two bits for every one he ate. Meggie had to sidestep around his
dish to avoid piercing her bare feet with the scatterings of his meal.

The night air was summer warm, despite the advance of autumn.

Finishing the milk, Meggie headed for the medicine closet to collect the lightning Pipe. She pushed open the porch door, giving firm instructions to Fritzie to stay away from prowling night creatures. They ventured outside.

Orienting herself to the west, Meggie knelt down on the damp night grass and unwrapped her medicine bundle. The moon, full and bright, cast a gold, ephemeral net over the trees and onto the ground. Meggie smudged herself with the sage, an act of cleansing before handling the Sacred Pipe. Curious about the sweet burning smell, Fritzie moved up behind her, sniffing the air. For good measure, she smudged him too, wafting the smoke in circles around him.

She gripped the bowl of the Pipe in her left hand, the stem in her right. She remembered Winona's words of instruction: "They are just stone and wood when apart from each other, but when joined together, know that you are holding the whole universe in your hands."

Inserting the base of the long stem into the bowl, Meggie felt the power of the ancient union of male and female energies, the extraordinary, lifegiving exchange between Grandfather Sky and Grandmother Earth. Slowly, she began the centuries-old ritual of filling the Pipe with tobacco, each move made with reverence and prayer:

"Wakan Tanka, Great Mystery, I give thanks for my life and ask your help to live as a human being. I ask you to recognize this Pipe and hear my prayers.

"Wiyohpeyatakiya, Grandfather of the Black Face, help me come to know what my life is about and to have the integrity to follow that vision. I am white. I have a Sacred Pipe. I carry a baby of two peoples in my womb. Teach me the ways of respect.

"Waziyata, Grandfather of the Red Face, help make my body strong enough to bring this baby to a good birth. More than anything, I want a healthy baby, a laughing baby.

"Wiyohiyanpata, Grandfather of the Yellow Face, to you I bring my broken heart. With this Pipe, I ask you to see the father of this baby and touch his heart. If it be good for him, for the baby, and for myself, I ask you to find a way that we can come together as a family around the Pipe. If it not be good for any one of us, then Grandfather, I ask you to help me find a way to release him from my dreams.

"Itogagata, Grandfather of the White Face, I ask you to watch over the old ones in my family. Keep them healthy until it is their time to cross over, then take them quickly. I give thanks for the passage of this baby into the time of his or her earth-walk. Help me to see each day with the eyes of a child, to fill my heart and head with wonder, and to take each step in the knowledge of those seven generations before me and the seven generations to follow.

"Mahpiyata, Sky Beings, thank you for teaching me that no matter how dark the night, there is always light, as long as we two-leggeds don't cloud our own visions. Hanhepi wi, Grandmother Moon, I thank you for your gift of life to me as a woman, so that for a short time the baby and I can exist as one. Star Nation, Lightning Powers, Thunder Beings—I know that this Pipe understands Your power much more than I ever will, and that it carries some of Your incredible energy. I ask that this Chanunpa Wakan help me become a healing pipeline for some of that energy.

"Unci Maka, Grandmother Earth, through my feet, I draw strength from You. As your granddaughter, I ask Your help in these months to come, as the child grows within me. I thank You for the way You nurture us and shelter us. We two-leggeds have not treated You with respect, and yet, Grandmother, season after season, You feed us and clothe us. Again and again, I come to You. I put my feet upon Your soft earth, Your skin. I feel Your heartbeat. I ask You to teach me about love. I ask You to teach me about forgiveness.

"Wanbli Gleska, Spotted Eagle, I ask you to take these prayers through the Pipe to the Grandfathers and Grandmother. *Mitakuye oyas'in.*"

Meggie rose from her cramped kneeling position. With the lightning Pipe held out before her, she stood in silence, facing west. The night was as clear as could be. The cold, diamond lights of burning stars shone as glowing sentinels across the great black universe. The moon radiated a deep full yellow, tinged with red. Fireflies pricked the dark with rhythmic flashes. As Meggie began to sing the Four Directions Song, Spirit lights flickered and danced in the night air, moving as a circle, closer and closer to the Chanunpa Wakan.

Her lightning Pipe reached out as a conduit between self and Sacred. Her eyes witnessed what her mind found difficult to believe. Her words spoke what her heart needed to hear. Her prayers had been simple and true. Her actions recalled Winona's advice:

"Follow man prayer with woman prayer. Stand up before the

Creator and ask for what you need to live as a human being. Then, go into the silence. Empty your mind, your self, and pay attention."

Holding the Pipe out before her, Meggie noticed minute shifts in the beaded lightning design, as if the Pipe was charging itself in the flow of sacred energy. Her head dismissed the perception, but her eyes kept watch all around her, as she cleared the receptive space within. A horned owl hooted in the distance. Fritzie snuffled in the bushes, catching the scent of night trails. Her own breathing sounded loud and intrusive.

A disembodied voice startled her: *"When you pray with this Pipe, you will get what you need. Remember Mole Woman who followed her husband from a distance, because she needed to protect the child. She told Coyote the truth that he needed to hear."*

It sounded suspiciously like Winona's voice. Meggie looked around, but nobody was there.

Mole Woman? What does that mean? She was puzzled. Belatedly, she remembered to offer her Pipe to the one who spoke. "If you are from Wakan Tanka, I ask you to come smoke this Chanunpa Wakan with me."

No one took her up on the offer. Nor were any more words of wisdom given.

In the ensuing silence, night wrapped its velvety arms around her, illuminated by twinkling white stars, an engorged yellow moon, pulsating fire bugs, and the circle of dancing Spirit lights. Meggie fired up the lightning Pipe in the darkness, so that it, too, added to the glow of life around her.

"You did what?" Meggie's voice was full of incredulity as she questioned Bev in the cloudy light of the next morning. She couldn't believe her friend would have interfered with her life in such a dramatic way.

"I went to Hawk's place last night and told him about the baby," Bev confessed, her hands fidgeting.

Meggie's voice grew hard, angry. "You had no right to do that. *I* choose what to do with *my* life. Not you. *I* choose how to address *my* problems. Not you. I never gave you permission to go to him. You were one of only two people I trusted enough to tell. How could you do this to me?"

Bev visibly shrank before Meggie. She defended her action: "Meggie, I was only trying to help. You love this man, and he is making a mess out of both of your lives. I had hoped that the news of your pregnancy would bring him to his senses."

"What kind of sense is that?" Meggie retorted, hands perched on her hips. "Now, if he comes back to me, will I know it's of his own free choosing? Or will it be out of guilt? Maybe, he'll return out of a sense of responsibility? Guilt and duty are not the same as love and commitment."

"But he has a right to know about the baby," Bev persisted.

Meggie fired back, "When you messed up so badly with Coulter last year, did I prance right in and set him right? No. Instead, I went to you and told you what a ninny you were being to go cold on the only man who had truly offered love to you because he had confessed a past that didn't agree with your fantasy of the ideal man. He left you because he couldn't tolerate your ambivalence. What's happened since? You've gone from one man to another. So, don't tell me that you've got it all together and have the right to interfere with my life."

Bev winced. Meggie could be strong and cruel with her words. In contrast, Bev's words sounded weak and defensive, "I simply wanted to help, Meggie."

"I asked for your support. I needed understanding and compassion. I didn't invite you to settle my problems. The obvious and immediate solution to a problem can short-circuit what really needs to happen. You took charge with *your* solution to *my* problem with the result that, now, I won't be able to trust Hawk's intent, no matter what he tells me. You've created a whole new mess for me."

"Oh, Meggie," Bev reached out and grabbed her friend's hand, "I'm so sorry."

Meggie shrugged her shoulders. "You don't understand, Bev. Winona's Pipe has changed my life. I'm learning to wait and to watch. I don't have to rush to action. If I take my Pipe out to pray, the power of the Pipe and the prayers set things into motion. I'm not alone in this universe. Hawk is touched by these same energies. But unless he finds his own way to me, our love will always be tainted by suspicion of manipulation. I didn't pray that the Grandfathers return him to me no matter what. I ask that we come together only if it is good for all three of us. Who am I to know what will happen in the future?"

"Would you have told him about the baby?" Bev asked, cautious about igniting another angry tirade.

Meggie answered, "Probably not in words. In the next few months my belly will communicate loud and clear to everyone that I'm going to have a baby. He has eyes. He'd have known."

"She did what?" Over morning coffee, Lucy interrogated Hawk about his late-night visitor. She could see dark thunderhead clouds, framed by the window, massing in the west.

Hawk rubbed the sleepy dust from his eyes. "Meggie's friend told me I'm going to be a father." He grinned sheepishly at her.

Lucy shook her head and scolded him, "Boy, you sure know how to make a mess of things, don't you? What are you going to do now? Set up household with both women?"

Ouch, winced Hawk.

Lucy didn't wait for him to answer. "You're in big trouble, Hawk. If you go to Meggie, then you're going to have to deal with Rising Smoke. She's not going to be sympathetic to your predicament. And she's one woman I wouldn't want to have angry at me. No way. If you stay with Rising Smoke, then you've got to figure out what you are going to do as the father to that baby. So, what *are* you going to do?"

"I don't know." He shrugged his shoulders. "Got any good advice to give me?"

"Oh, now you're willing to listen to my opinion?" Lucy couldn't resist saying.

"Well, you are a woman and . . . ," but Hawk knew no more where to take that thought than what to do next.

"You'd better take a good look at whom you love the most," Lucy counseled.

"But what if I love them both, Lucy?"

"Equally?" she asked.

"Differently," he answered.

"Then you'd best figure out what that difference is." Lucy paused. "You know what my mother, the traditionalist, would say, don't you?"

He shook his head, curious.

"She would tell you that when standing neck-high in shit, you'd best grab onto your Pipe before you drown."

Midmorning, the gray skies opened; raindrops lashed at the ground. Soon saturated, the soil could no longer absorb the water. Every footstep, pawprint, and hoof mark impressed its signature deep into the soft earth. The downpour blocked the sun, and the day grew chilly and dark.

In twilight's gloomy illumination, Meggie waded through puddles in the hospital parking lot. She had become a frequent visitor to Karl's room, their friendship having been forged out of deep distress and healing insights. The hospital staff encouraged her visits, as single-handedly, Meggie had lifted Karl out of a severe depression. It was obvious to everyone, including Meggie, that he looked forward to their conversations.

Not so obvious was how much the meetings meant to Meggie. *I've been able to tell him everything—about Hawk, about the baby, about Bev's interference. He sits there and listens to me as I cry or get angry. He never criticizes me. Only a couple of times has he offered me any advice: "Remember—Hawk loves you and Bev loves you and I love you. Be patient. The Creator hasn't finished with you yet." Not really an answer to my problems, but it helps. I don't know why, but it does.*

On seeing Meggie, Karl announced, "Hey, I'm going to be released from the hospital soon, on crutches and with no job." He was grinning.

"What about your two churches?"

"My bishop decided that it was in 'the best interests of all' to relieve me of my congregations. He recommended, strongly, that I undergo 'spiritual rehabilitation' before returning to the ministry. Do you think, Meggie, that forty days and forty nights in the desert will do?"

She laughed at his jest. *He's trying to fashion his next phase of life, and he doesn't have much time to do it.*

While Meggie was shaking out her sodden raincoat and draping it over the window vent, Karl became more serious. "I've been thinking that I may join a monastic order."

"You're kidding." Meggie couldn't believe her ears.

"No, I'm serious."

Meggie protested, "But won't you have to swear to chastity and poverty and all that?"

He nodded his head affirmatively.

"But, you've always loved women, Karl." Meggie couldn't imagine him deprived of the opposite sex. He was too much an enthusiast of life and love.

Karl again nodded, "Yes. That's been a problem for me. I've hurt a lot of people. It's easy to do that in the ministry. Women end up falling in love with their priest or minister as a shortcut to the Divine—only it ends up being a short circuit for them instead. That's why Bev was different from the others."

"Oh?"

Karl chuckled. "She didn't give a damn about God. It wasn't Karl the minister who interested her but, rather, Karl the man. I found that intensely satisfying to my male ego."

"We all have a need to be recognized and accepted for who we really imagine ourselves to be," Meggie said, stating the obvious.

"You must think I'm a scoundrel, Meggie," Karl frowned.

"Why do you say that?"

"The marriage vows say 'through sickness and health,' and I didn't try hard enough with my wife, Meggie. As you well know, Annie is a brilliant, creative, *and* tortured human being. Although she would never tell me what happened, I had my suspicions. She was delightfully loving when we were courting, but she changed almost immediately after the wedding—when I became *family* to her. A few years later, her sister confided in me that their father had sexually abused them from the time when they were little girls."

"Ah," Meggie nodded her head. *The black hole of traumatic memories.*

"Becoming her husband made me immediately suspect in her eyes, and she . . . we stopped making love. I tried to understand that it was important for her to be able to say no to sex, because she hadn't been able to say that when she was a child. I tried to love her into health but . . ." He lifted up his palms in the universal gesture of helplessness. "I failed. I didn't try hard enough, Meggie." Guilt wrote lines of despair across his face.

Meggie knew it was important not to interrupt Karl, that he had to tell the truth of himself in order to unburden his soul.

"I first turned all my energies to the ministry. But when you fly close to God and get swollen up with religious ecstasy, it's easy to slip and slide right off the heavenly clouds into the enticing arms of a woman. Passion adopts many forms. When you call out to the Sacred, it's frequently your own voice that answers. And you topple over into your own needs and rationalizations. I'm a fool, Meggie. Maybe God's fool, but also a human one." His hands fell to his lap.

Meggie cradled his hands in her own. "I have a story to tell you, Karl. About Coyote and his wife, Mole Woman . . ."

The rain began to let up as Meggie wove the tale of dreams, love, and loss between the trickster figure and his hard-working wife.

"What a fool Coyote was," exclaimed Karl, "to drive Mole Woman underground. Don't ever let go of the one you love, Meggie, if that person is your soul mate."

Soul mate. Is that why I can't pluck Hawk out of my heart? Meggie wondered.

"Coyote was lazy, that's true," commented Meggie, "but Mole Woman pushed him away with her words of anger. And, although she persisted in trying to track their relationship, when the time came for healing, her words were shaming ones. She didn't know how to forgive him. He needed a story of reconciliation and, out of pride, she spat hate at him."

"Or covered him with bird droppings?" Karl had seen the landscape painting and was trying Coyote on for size.

"I guess both Coyote and Mole Woman would have changed their behavior if they could have seen that the outcome of the story would be that the infant was left hanging alone, vulnerable, in the cradle board."

"Oh, I don't know, Meggie. Maybe we human beings have to play out our scenarios over time, long enough to distill wisdom from our painful experiences." Karl patted Meggie's hand. "Perhaps our 'if onlys' will goad us to greater efforts if love comes our way again."

"If you were so irresistibly drawn to women, Karl, why didn't you ever make a pass at me?" Meggie joshed.

Karl shook his head and paused. "I'm trying to think of a diplomatic response."

Meggie enjoyed teasing him, "It better be a good explanation."

"Meggie, you've got a sharp intellect, a good education, and professional status. You know your own mind, and you're very clear in your communications. Plus, you have an estate which you manage very well on your own. There is very little you need from a man. In short, you're headstrong, opinionated, overly self-confident, and you would step all over me. I need to be needed, not dominated."

"Are you telling me that I would make someone a good husband?" Meggie pushed him, knowing that Karl was pretty accurate in his description of her.

"Meggie, someday you'll marry again. But it has to be to a man with a strong sense of his own power who won't depend on you to define him. Someone who will love your strength and not be threatened by it."

Hawk, she thought.

Karl flexed his fingers and stretched his arms. "So, I'm off to the monastery to review my transgressions and radically change my life. Continuously patching up old wrongs is like putting a finger into a leaky dike; then one day the whole structure of your existence comes crashing down. And all your grievous faults swamp you and everyone else in a flood of your own making. In my pursuit of love, I've hurt a lot of people: Annie, Bev, my parishioners.

"In my quest for God," he continued, "I forgot my soul. Good deeds and adoring women did not feed the emptiness that grew inside of me. My soul has become like a neglected infant—ill fed, scrawny, and screaming me awake at night. I must now give it proper shelter."

"But a monastery?" she repeated incredulously. "Do you really think you'll be able to sustain a vow of chastity?"

"Meggie, I don't know," he answered. "I'll just have to trust in God, won't I?"

"Or," she enigmatically added, "the mother of your soul."

THIRTY

STORMY NIGHT

As pines
  keep the shape of the wind
  even when the wind has fled and is no
    longer there,
  so words
guard the shape of man
even when the man has fled and is no longer
    there.

—GEORGE SEFERIS
On Stage

Hawk unlocked the back door to Chrysalis and entered the kitchen. He had stood in the downpour knocking at the door, but only Fritzie made an appearance to welcome him. He shook the rain off his denim jacket and let the terrier out. The house was eerily quiet without Meggie. Out of hunger for her presence, he opened up the refrigerator door. He poured himself a glass of milk and sat down at the kitchen table to await her arrival. The dark, cloudy day dissipated into night, to the sound of rain steadily pattering on metal gutters and to the sight of shadows edging into the kitchen.

Fritzie demanded to be let back in from his twilight run. Hawk retrieved an old towel from the adjoining laundry room and rubbed him dry. The dog groaned in pleasure at the man's gentle hands. "So where's Meggie, old boy?"

Mistaking the meaning of the remark, Fritzie ran to his empty supper bowl.

Hawk laughed. "Yes, I'm hungry too." He knew where Meggie kept the dog food. Fritzie jumped about on the kitchen floor, excited over the prospect of dinner. Having filled the bowl and temporarily taken care of Fritzie's needs, Hawk strolled through the first floor of the silent house, restless.

What am I going to say to her? I don't trust words. Hawk paced the floor. He didn't know what to anticipate from himself or from her. He had no plan of action, except to take her into his arms and to tell her how much he loved her.

She will think it's only due to the baby. She won't understand how the pregnancy makes me want to protect her. She won't believe me now, when I tell her how much I love her. She'll tell me that the only reason I came tonight was because of what Bev revealed to me. And I'll answer that's not the only truth. Despite all our cautions, hers around time and space, mine around our racial differences, the love between us has been like a strong sapling growing up and branching out in many different directions and rooted deep. She'll say I should have thought of that, when I lay down with another, that a forest of saplings can choke out love, even when there are buds on the new tree. He sighed, trying to anticipate a woman's logic and knowing that he would probably fail at the task.

It's my child, too. He mentally rehearsed to himself, imagining a show of anger at her secrecy. But he discarded that scenario. Meggie would respond in kind. He dreaded open conflict with her. It was not what he wanted.

"So, what do you want?" he finally asked himself, confronting his image in the hallway mirror.

The silent reflection stared back at him, the look of a fool trapped in his own confusion.

Meggie was surprised to see Hawk's truck by the garage. *Of course, he would come now. Bev has seen to that.* Grim, cynical, and unprepared for this encounter, she didn't know what to expect from him—or herself. Her jaw muscles clenched.

A maternal urge rose up in her, fiercely. "Whatever happens, I will take care of you," she affirmed, patting her belly protectively while opening the car door. She could see Hawk exiting the back door, Fritzie leading the way. The dog bounded down to the car, barking excitedly. She noted that Hawk's face exhibited love, and uncertainty.

Oh, Hawk.

Her chest tightened, then heaved a sigh.

His hand reached out to help her from the car. His strong, familiar arms pulled her into his standing presence. She could smell the clean aroma of his body, and, for a comforting moment, she laid her head against his neck. He lifted her chin in his hand; their lips found solace in the other. She closed her eyes to all doubts, allowing herself the fantasy that Hawk had finally come home to her.

Oh, Hawk.

She absorbed his presence into her, like a parched sponge. Intense yearning flooded her, drowning all caution.

With reluctance, they broke from embrace, and hand-in-hand, their connection unsullied by words, the two moved toward the house. In loud yips and yaps of excitement, Fritzie shouted, "Hooray! Hooray!" and pirouetted in the air.

Meggie's pocketbook slid from her shoulder in the kitchen. Her raincoat dropped onto a dining room chair. Her shoes stopped at the stairway; his boots rested at the top. Together, their clothes formed a telltale trail to the bedroom, her bra tangled with his T-shirt on the wooden floor, her stockings buried under his socks on the rug. Neither one of them trusting to words of hurt and confusion, words of history and future, words of division and suspicion, their speech was of the body—the caresses, kisses, touch, and fierce hunger.

On the bed, she wrapped her naked legs tightly around him, opening herself up to the core, her arched back and hips begging him to become one with her. Mindless, in a frenzy full of desire, he plunged into her soft flesh, their two bodies exploding into consummation.

Oh, Hawk.

So quick, so passionate is the language of love.

So soon over.

For a brief hour, the rain stopped and night broke temporarily clear; clouds scudded by under a quarter moon, scurrying before the onset of another lakefront storm. The white-capped waves of Lake Michigan sopped restlessly at the clay bluffs in Leland, as the storm gusted from the west. Lightning could be seen shuddering over the Manitou islands, and thunder rumbled ominously in the distance.

Freed from the drag of land in Wisconsin, the wind gathered force over Lake Michigan, whipping itself up into a screaming frenzy by the time it reached the western perimeter of Michigan. Sounding like a freight train, the storm roared up the bluffs of Leland. Small trees bent over in obeisance to the wind's power. The blow swept debris before it, clearing the way for the angry jag of white lightning, the sky-rip of blue thunder, and the harsh drumbeat of black rain.

Decapitated, pierced by lightning, once-proud trees toppled to the humus-rich ground. Little animals crawled safely into the far reaches of their dens. The night owls postponed their hunt for the storm's passing. Capricious wind shifts set the branches of maples and oaks, birches and beeches into a wild orgiastic dance, testing the flexibility of their reach.

The wind battered at the house windows and shook the rafters. Electric lines, the cords of connection to civilization, broke and night darkened even deeper.

Winona felt alive and charged with new energy. Rapidly now, the remnant bands on her back were snapping off, stinging her with the sharp imprints of memory. She now understood that her task of waiting had been to address the memories, to make peace with her previous life. She had ruthlessly combed her earth experiences, worked through and cut out the snarls in which she had entangled her life, and braided that which remained—the essence of her existence. In the destruction of all sentimental attachment, Winona was releasing herself to a new beginning.

The wind rattled at the windows as Hawk and Meggie lay exhausted on the bed. The storm was not yet over.

"Are you going back to her? Are you staying with me?" Simple questions that deserved simple answers.

"I came because I love you."

"Or was it the baby that brought you here?"

"That too. Can't we simply be together right now?" Irritation crept into his voice.

"Yes, I know you don't trust words. But I don't trust your actions. You came tonight and made love to me, and I don't know what that means to you." The wind moaned deeply outside the window.

"Meggie, don't . . ." He put up his hand to her lips, to stanch her words.

"Don't shut me up." She brushed his hand aside. "You want to pretend in the moment that everything is fine. Just because I made love to you, it doesn't change anything. Just because I am pregnant, it doesn't change anything. When I say 'I love you,' my words mean something. Love is not simply a groan of pleasure upon the bed or a sweet note to the ear. Love is fierce and demanding, for without its fire, its strength, its commitment—how can it sustain us in the warp of time? Either you love me or you don't. Do you honestly think our love will continue to grow when you're off courting another woman—making comparisons, keeping secrets, and never fully giving yourself over to either one of us? For God's sake, be a man, Hawk, and not a sniveling, confused idiot!" Controlled fury emanated from her eyes.

Hawk's voice, too, gathered in anger: "I love you. That is the truth. I love her. That is another truth. I love that baby in you. That is the third truth. Your words are like rope, Meggie, used to bind the truth."

"What do you expect from me? Understanding? Compassion? I'm your lover, Hawk—not your therapist. I won't hold your hand and sympathize with your predicament."

Meggie fought to stem the tide of tears. "It would be so much easier, if I could shut off, dam up all my feelings for you—the love, the dream of us together, the longing for you in the bone, the hurt that eats away at me, the rage that is dissecting my heart. It would be so much easier to feel nothing, wouldn't it? Or, maybe you think I should be willing to share you with another woman, that Rising Smoke and I

can become the best of friends?" The tone of her voice turned harsh
and sarcastic. A tree limb slapped the side of the house.

"Meggie, I love you." He said it fiercely.

He said it softly.

He said it again and again as her anger grew.

Fritzie picked up the change of tone in the two-leggeds. From cries
of pleasure emitted atop the bed, to sighs of physical exhaustion, to
cautious words, to the storm building outside, to an edging sharpness
in the woman's voice—Fritzie's ears perked to a sense of approaching
danger. He loved the man, but the woman belonged to him. He was
part of her pack, and, therefore, her protector. He would let no harm
come to her without a fight.

The man's feet touched the floor. Fritzie rose from his bed and positioned himself in the center of the room. The woman's voice, formerly
soft and loving, turned hard with questions. The man said little, but
Fritzie could smell the sour odors of his unhappiness and her anger.

The woman sat up in the bed, pointed her finger, and spat out
words of anger as she would often do when he was a puppy and had
shamefully soiled on the rug.

The man hung his head and retrieved his clothes from the floor. As
her words grew louder, biting into the air, Fritzie barked in excitement and distraction. He did not like the two humans being in conflict
with each other. The man said something soft, cajoling. The woman
yelled at Fritzie to keep quiet—that much he understood. Chastened,
Fritzie hushed but thrust his body between the man and the bed to
block any threatening movement between the two-leggeds. The
woman grew quiet.

The man shrugged his shoulders, turned, and stalked out the bedroom. Fritzie accompanied him downstairs to the outside door. There,
the man, steeped in the smells of sadness, leaned down and rubbed
Fritzie's ears. Fritzie wagged his tail to show there were no hard feelings between them. The man opened the door to the raging storm outside and, lashed by the stinging rain, hightailed it to his truck.

Fritzie returned to the bedroom to check on the woman. He found her on the floor, curled into a bed pillow, sobbing as if the storm would never end. The wind wailed on the outside, as her cries of grief howled on the inside. Fritzie maneuvered his body past the buffering pillow, and while Meggie rocked her body, his tongue licked the salt of her tears.

THIRTY-ONE

GOOD SPELLS

Be still, while the music rises about us; the deep enchantment
Towers, like a forest of singing leaves and birds,
Built, for an instant, by the heart's troubled beating,
Beyond all power of words.

—CONRAD AIKEN
At a Concert of Music

Morning broke out of night clear and clean. Golden orbs of sunlight reflected off puddles, spiderwebs, and leaf dew. The world, having been purified in the storm, glistened and sparkled from crevice to corner. The birds celebrated in song; the trees gave over to the making of fall colors.

Adam and Eva dressed in excitement over the new day. Hawk was coming to their school for a storytelling performance. Adam conjured up bravura descriptions of the night's storm to tell June, while Eva chattered to her mother about costumes for Halloween.

Hawk awoke, tired in his heart. Forcing himself out of bed, he opened the trailer door to the new day. The bright sun rays, bouncing off watery surfaces, assailed his eyes; he blinked into the glory of morning. His heart lifted with the beauty before him. Taking tobacco in hand, he padded barefoot out to the sweat lodge area and offered it to the Spirits in thanksgiving for his life. An eagle circled high up in the western sky, catching a spiral of air current that lifted it up toward the heavens. *"Wanbli,"* whispered Hawk in reverence.

Later in the morning, the children gathered in the assembly room of the elementary school and dutifully recited their versions of the Pledge of Allegiance. The short wooden chairs were lined up row after row as the children stood, their hands over their hearts, their eyes to the American flag. "Now children, we have a special treat today," announced the principal, introducing Hawk who was bedecked in a buckskin fringed outfit.

Hawk nodded to the children and then asked them to move their chairs into a circle around him, while noticing an older teacher grimace at the disorderly scrape of chairs on the floor. The kids formed a large circumference around him. Behind them sat the teachers. "Hau. That's good," said Hawk approvingly. "We all live in the circle of life. We are all connected one to the other and should not have our backs facing our neighbors." The kids grinned at each other. Across the circle, Adam shyly waved at June.

Before telling his stories, Hawk brought out a few items to show the curious children. His wooden war club, carved with an eagle's claw clutching Grandmother Earth on one end and a deer hoof on the other, fascinated them. They oohed and aahed over the drum given to him by Winona, the handmade bow and arrows, the Stone-Age axe head found in a plowed field. Last but not least, they demanded to know what was in the deerskin sheath on a chair behind him. He pretended to be ambivalent about showing it to them. The dramatic hesitation had the intended effect: to intensify the children's curiosity. From the leather encasement, he pulled out a long wooden tube, the end of which was carved and painted into a mallard's head. "Do any of you know what this is?" he queried.

Eva raised her hand and pronounced, "It's a flute."

"That's right," said Hawk. "It's a love flute, but I dare not play it here. That might be too dangerous."

Several children blurted out, "Why?"

Hawk explained, "You see, when an Indian boy really takes a liking to a girl, then he takes this magical flute and goes outside her tipi and plays a love tune. The sound is enchanting, and it touches her heart;

she can't resist coming out of the tipi to find him. Now, if I were to play it here, I couldn't be responsible for the effect it might have on your teachers."

The children shrieked, "Play it! Play it!" They shifted around in their seats to gleefully eye their teachers. Hawk chuckled, noting that one disapproving teacher had crossed her arms in a defensive stance.

"Well, okay, if you insist," replied Hawk, lifting the instrument to his lips. A haunting *ooo*-and-*wooo* melody floated out of the flute. He winked at one young teacher, who, on cue, rose up from her chair and sidled toward him and the spell-binding music. The kids burst into laughter, watching her pulled forward by the haunting sounds. Just before she reached where he was standing, Hawk put down the flute, saying to the children, "I told you so. You should only play this flute for the one you truly love."

Adam cast a meaningful glance toward June.

Hawk placed the instrument safely back in its sheath. The teacher retraced her steps, her part completed. "Now," he announced, "I have some wonderful Coyote stories to tell you. In the Native American world, Coyote is a trickster figure who was given the job by the Creator to help put the Creation—and especially the human beings—back into balance. You should never trust him, but he will always teach you by his tricks. Sometimes, he even manages to teach himself by his own mistakes. The first story I will tell is how Coyote came to quarrel with his wife, Mole . . ."

The children hunkered down in their seats, mesmerized by Hawk's recitation of Coyote's travels and travails, the many byways that Coyote is forced to take when his strategies backfire. They laughed with the lessons: that to be lazy is to be hungry, that to be self-important is to be alone, and that to be disrespectful is to be shunned.

I want to be responsible, like Mole Woman, Eva vowed.

I am proud to be Indian, Adam glowed.

Coyote lives, Hawk winced.

Rising Smoke made tracks around Hawk's trailer. "Where is he?" she snorted. Carelessly, she threw a cigarette stub down on the ground and stormed off to Lucy's house. Hawk hadn't contacted her for two days, and she had a sixth sense for trouble. Lucy's face when she greeted her at the door only confirmed her suspicions.

"Where is he?" Her question to Lucy was brusque and hostile.

"At the kids' school." Lucy was uncharacteristically brief.

"What's going on? Something's going on. I can tell," Rising Smoke insisted.

Lucy turned her face away. Rising Smoke followed her into the house uninvited.

"Coffee?" Lucy asked.

Rising Smoke shook her head. She would take all the time needed to squeeze the information out of Lucy. It was one of her talents.

The two women sat down at the kitchen table opposite each other, Lucy with coffee mug in hand, Rising Smoke with a pack of cigarettes. Fiddling with her smokes, Rising Smoke ventured, "I know you as a friend and a sister."

Lucy countered, "I'm Hawk's cousin." She sipped from the mug.

The two women, familiar and estranged in their mutual suspicions, circled around each other like two dogs sniffing out their territorial boundaries. Neither snarled nor lifted her lip at the other, but, stiff-legged and formal, they kept their distance. For once, Lucy kept to her promise not to interfere.

Hawk would have to extricate himself from his own mess.

🐾 🐾 🐾 🐾

Hawk arrived to find Rising Smoke squatting on his trailer stoop. *Oh-oh*, his insides growled at him. He took his time gathering his thoughts and his storytelling items from the back of his truck. *What am I going to tell her?*

Rising Smoke gave him no time to form an answer. "Where have you been?" she demanded, hands on her hips.

"Telling stories at . . ."

"I know that," she interrupted, "Why haven't you called?" Her voice was harsh and insistent.

He moved past her, opening the trailer door with a free elbow, while juggling in his arms the war club, axe head, drum, flute, bow, and arrows. She did not offer to help. Carefully, he deposited the items on the unmade bed. She followed him into the bedroom.

"Look, Hawk. I know you better than anyone, certainly better than that tight-lipped cousin of yours."

Surely, she can't be talking about Lucy? Hawk wondered.

Planting her body between the bed and the door, Rising Smoke continued, "We started getting back together again. Then, suddenly, I hear nothing from you. You weren't here last night when I drove by. Where were you?"

The sharp edge to her voice honed his response.

"I was at Meggie's place."

"At that white woman's house? Doing what?" Her eyes were dark and piercing.

Hawk pulled off the heavy buckskin shirt. He stood there bare-chested before his angry ex-wife, determined to tell her the truth. "I went there last night to talk with her. She's pregnant. I'm responsible for that."

Rising Smoke sucked in her breath.

Hawk hadn't finished. *I will tell her all of it.* "We made love. We argued. She got angry at me. I left." He donned a Western shirt. Turning his back on Rising Smoke, he peeled off the buckskin pants, replacing them with his familiar jeans. He knew words couldn't speak what he was feeling.

Rising Smoke waited. There was more.

He faced her, looking directly at her. He answered her unspoken question. "It's not finished between Meggie and me."

"What do you want to be doing with that white woman, Hawk?" she hissed at him. "She'll never understand you like I do. Just because she's having a baby . . ."

Hawk interrupted the tirade, "It's more than that. Meggie needs me."

Rising Smoke swelled with anger. "If she hadn't gotten pregnant, you'd have stayed with me. That's a fact. What would happen if she lost the baby?"

Hawk's eyes turned stone hard. "Don't even talk that way." He detected a smirk forming at the corners of her mouth.

"So, what about us, Hawk? Are you planning to leave me again, like you did before?"

I can only tell her the truth as I know it. Hawk answered, "I haven't finished with Meggie."

Rising Smoke looked at him a long time, obviously disbelieving that what had been so sweet between them was curdling so quickly. She moved toward him. He stood stock-still, not knowing what to expect. She reached out with her fingers and traced a line down his chest, as if doodling absentmindedly on his body. When he relaxed to her touch, she slapped him hard across the face.

His cheek reddened with the blow. His fists clenched. She stood her ground, as if waiting for him to retaliate. He moved past her to the kitchen and yanked open the door.

Rising Smoke grabbed up her things and strode past him, her head held proudly. "Son of a bitch!" she swore at him, as she elbowed her way out the door.

"Yes," he acknowledged.

As soon as Rising Smoke's car had spun out of the driveway, Lucy bustled over to her cousin's trailer. "Oh, my God," she exclaimed, touching the tender splotch of bruised skin on the left side of his face.

Ever the mother hen, Lucy raided the icebox for some ice to put on Hawk's cheek. "She walloped you good, didn't she?" Lucy added in an admiring kind of way.

Hawk replied, "I think I just simplified my life."

Lucy bobbed her head in agreement, "I could tell by the way she slammed her car door that she's not happy. Remember, I warned you about her anger. So, what are you going to do now?"

He studied the developing bruise in the mirror, touching it gingerly with the ice. "Rising Smoke would like to kill me. Meggie doesn't want to have anything to do with me. And I don't have any more storytelling performances scheduled. So, I'm going home, Lucy."

"Back to South Dakota?"

He nodded.

"Why?" she asked. Her cousin was becoming totally unpredictable.

"I pour the waters in the inipi. I tell the people that when you're out of balance, go to your teachers, ceremony, purify yourself, ask your Chanunpa Wakan to guide you, put yourself back into balance with the Creation. It's time I listen to my own words, Lucy." He started pulling out shirts from his closet and laying them on the bed to pack.

"When are you taking off?"

"Tonight, after I take care of one last chore."

Lucy was dumbfounded. "You *are* returning, aren't you? The sweat lodge community needs you. You've got a pregnant girlfriend. You're not planning to run away forever and take off wandering?" Hawk had become family to her, a link to her mother's people. She would miss him.

"I've discovered that nothing is certain," was his cryptic answer.

Disheartened and discouraged, Meggie could hardly wait for the new day to be over so that she could plunge herself into dreams and sleep. The bright sunlight of the morning had offended her mood, which was as dark as the previous night's storm. Gusts of grief and whorls of anger battered the stoic, calm facade she presented to her therapy clients. At times, during the hourly sessions, her mind would wander, grow distracted by the reverberations of the harsh words of the night before—words that churned inside into a meringue of heat and hurt, words that hung undigested in the air, words that had neither soothed her anger nor brought them together. She was relieved to see the last client leave her office.

Nighttime offered solace and isolation. She crawled into bed early and fell soundly asleep. She did not hear a truck park down by the road. She did not awaken to the sound of muted footsteps tracking through the woods of Chrysalis. What roused her from the depths of sleep and sat her straight up in bed was a haunting melody, an *ooo* sound, a *wooo* sound, filtering through the softness of fir trees, a song of love lost and heart's yearning.

Surrounding her, the notes wove a spell of enchantment. From the bedroom window she peered out into the dark night, unable to make out anything but the outlines of tall, whispering trees, a respectful audience to the mysterious music. *Ooo* and *wooo* and downy under, the mallard flute intoned the simple complexity of love to her.

To the last fading note, to the silence that echoed in the deep woods, to the cough of a distant truck cranking up for a long journey, Meggie sat by the window, bewitched by the music and befuddled by her response.

I must be dreaming, she reasoned.

THIRTY-TWO

BAD SPELLS

*Evil needs to be pondered just as much as good,
for good and evil are ultimately nothing but ideal
extensions and abstractions of doing, and both
belong to the chiaroscuro of life. In the last
resort there is no good that cannot produce evil
and no evil that cannot produce good.*

—CARL G. JUNG
Psychology and Alchemy

Possessed of fury, a woman scorned, Rising Smoke picked up her Sacred Pipe. Hawk had stayed out of her way when she had gathered together her remaining possessions. What he hadn't seen, what he hadn't noticed, was that she had meticulously lifted a single strand of brown hair from the shirt he had worn to Meggie's house. She took that hair and carefully hid it in her pocket before storming out of his trailer.

Not out of love for Hawk, not out of any conscious plan for reunion with him, she set out to wreak havoc for one reason: Rising Smoke couldn't tolerate the idea of being denied what she wanted. She wasn't even sure whether she'd accept Hawk if he chose to crawl back to her. She would be damned first, before she would let herself ever again experience the loss of power.

She picked up the Sacred Pipe knowingly. With song and exhortation, she called upon the Spirits, good and evil, to come listen to her entreaties. She did not ask them to help her live her life for the people. She did not plead for guidance in her time of betrayal. She did not take her pain and open herself to love.

Rising Smoke picked up the Pipe and called upon her rattlesnake medicine. With the piece of Meggie's brown hair, she asked the Spirits to kill the baby in Meggie's womb.

"There are all kinds of Spirits in this world," cautioned Laughing Bear to Hawk. "Sounds to me like you've gotten hooked up with a Trickster Spirit."

Hawk was exhausted after the long drive to Pine Ridge reservation. He had come straight to his teacher's place. Winona had been right. Now, more than ever, he needed a teacher to set him straight.

Laughing Bear questioned him, "Have you been working with your Pipe?"

Hawk shook his head, "Women sort of interfere with all that, if you know what I mean." He grinned, knowing that Laughing Bear had once had a reputation for being a womanizer. Looking around the ramshackle house, Hawk suddenly noticed how empty it looked, devoid of female presence.

The medicine man explained his wife's absence, "She left, taking the kids with her. Said she couldn't tolerate all the people coming here for teaching and healing and a free place to stay. I told her that wasn't going to change, that my life is for the people. That's what medicine work is about. She said that the people are going to kill me with their demands." He lifted his heavy frame from the chair and laughed. "She's probably right about that too."

Hawk saw the fatigue in his teacher; dark circles under his eyes testified to poor kidney function. Winona had warned him that the people wear out their medicine teachers and no longer take adequate care of them, as they once did in the old days. He felt compassion for Laughing Bear. He felt ashamed that here he was, another confused soul, coming to ask for guidance and ceremony from his teacher.

Originally intending to stay only a couple of days, time enough to ask his questions in an inipi ceremony, Hawk vowed to stay longer at Laughing Bear's home. He would clean up the place, cut wood for the winter, cook his teacher some healthy meals, and nurture the man's lonely spirit with humor and conversation. Only when Laughing Bear seemed stronger would Hawk ask him for the help he needed. In the meantime, he knew Laughing Bear would relish the opportunity to teach him more about the Pipe and the red road.

"You have to be aware," began the medicine man, "that there are Good Spirits, Evil Spirits, and Trickster Spirits. You have to know how to test Them, to be sure who is working with you. The Trickster Spirits will spin and spit you out into a mess. The Good Spirits will humble you with Their power. The Evil Spirits will promise you power and then suck out your soul."

"Wicked. I am so *very* wicked," exclaimed Bev, bouncing into Meggie's office.

Meggie looked up at her, exhausted from lack of sleep, worry over Hawk's sudden absence, and the drain of pregnancy on her body's energy.

"I went to see Karl. I told the hospital staff that I was his second cousin and had traveled miles to see him. Was he ever surprised. You know what he said to me?" Bev didn't wait for an answer.

"He plans to enter a monastery. Can you imagine that? He's going to take a vow of chastity and poverty. You know, Meggie, sometimes men are totally indecipherable. They go to extremes of action because they don't know how to work out their feelings in a normal, healthy way."

"Unlike the other half of the population?" Meggie could only get in a brief sentence.

"Right. Why can't men be more sensible like women? But his mind is made up, so what could I do?"

Meggie knew that Bev only feigned helplessness. "So what *did* you do?"

She grinned, "Promise you won't tell anyone?"

Meggie nodded, knowing that her friend would confess anyway.

"I said to Karl that I really admired his resolutions but that he needed to know what he was giving up. Only in that way would the sacrifice have real meaning."

"Bev, you didn't . . ."

"We did. We had a stimulating, arousing, prechastity conference right there in the hospital bed. I don't think it was a consultation that he will soon forget. He had to admit it was pretty divine."

"Women are always trying to put it on you around ceremony," Laughing Bear commented. "It's hard when you're young and trying to walk that red road. The young medicine fellows traveling the circuit begin playing mind games with the women. They can't get away with it so much here, on the reservation, under the watchful eyes of the old women."

"Uncle," Hawk spoke the term of respect, "what did you do about it when you were younger?"

"At first I was straighter than an arrow, but that arrow boomeranged around and shot back at me, trickster-style. I slept with a lot of women, but they'd get weepy on me, want something more. Hell, I don't never claim to understand them. It helped when I got married. A medicine man needs a woman for balance. But women, they don't like to share their man with the whole community." He pointed around the empty house.

Laughing Bear was not gentle with Hawk. "You've gotten lazy with your Pipe. What have you done since your *hanbleciya?* What are you doing for the people back there? What kind of listening have you done to your Spirit teacher? Take your Pipe and work with it. Don't let all this women stuff take your mind off what is really important. Work with the Chanunpa Wakan."

In between the flocks of people who periodically descended upon Laughing Bear's place to ask questions and seek healing, Hawk and Laughing Bear began a series of inipi ceremonies. At times, the teacher had the student pour the waters, so he could pray about his missing wife and children. Other times, Laughing Bear took charge and instructed Hawk to ask questions in the Pipe round of the sweat lodge ceremony. Daily, Hawk grew stronger with his Pipe. There was no woman to distract him from the Sacred.

Hawk told Laughing Bear about the time Three Legs had taken over his body and conducted the inipi ceremony. "Winona never told me about possession."

"Be careful, Nephew," his teacher warned. "Remember, even the Good Spirits have Their own agendas. If you let Them, They could ride you to the ground. Pay attention. Always test out what They tell you by what you know to be true. When it's all over, it's not Them but *you* who has to be responsible for what you've done with your life."

Hawk taped plastic over the windows to insulate the house for winter. He drove miles to cut wood for the inipi ceremony and the woodstove. He cut back on the high fat in Laughing Bear's meals and bought vitamins for his teacher. He put the man's house in order. And, in so doing, Hawk began the process of putting his own house in order. His low-key humor worked like a salve to his mentor's wounded soul. The older man obviously enjoyed having him there, a son respectful to his teachings.

Three Legs began to reappear in Hawk's sweats. "Where have you been?" inquired the Spirit teacher.

"Around," answered Hawk.

"You mean you've been going in circles," observed Three Legs.

At night when he lay down, after hours and hours of conversation with the younger man, Laughing Bear would hear the mournful sound of the love flute drifting from the sweat lodge area. The notes were not the sweet sounds of seduction but rather the sad, low notes of a man whose heart was aching for the woman he loved. The mallard flute called out to the lonely inhabitants of the night, asking them, beseeching them to pass along the message of the man's desire. Laughing Bear's heart beat with the same yearning.

The blizzards descended upon the plains of South Dakota long before they hit the dunes of coastal Michigan. By early November, there had already been one good-sized prairie snowstorm. Soon, it would be too difficult to continue the inipi ceremonies. Daylight and Hawk's supply of money were growing shorter and more sparse. In one of the last sweat lodge ceremonies, the Spirits spoke to Hawk through Laughing Bear: "A man becomes a man through his father and grand-fathers and great-grandfathers. You have something that belonged to your father."

"I have only a box of his junk," Hawk replied.

Again They said, "You have something that belonged to your father. He wanted you to have it, to help you be a man. Find it, put it in a leather pouch, and keep it on you for protection."

Laughing Bear snorted with laughter and shouted, "Hau!" Later, he informed Hawk that the Spirits had caustically added that it seemed most modern men treat their fathers' contributions as "junk."

"You have been like a father to me," Hawk added, bringing pleasure to Laughing Bear's heart.

Meggie hadn't yet told her mother or father about the pregnancy, even though she was beginning to put on some weight around the hips. She desperately wanted her situation with Hawk resolved, to protect herself from the well-meaning advice of relatives. A couple of her clients made some passing reference to the extra weight, but none of them seemed to suspect the true cause.

Having passed the three-month mark with its bouts of morning sickness, Meggie was growing more relaxed in her pregnancy. She called Lucy and discovered that Hawk had disappeared to Pine Ridge Reservation.

"When does he plan to come back?" Meggie tried to bleach the anxiety out of her voice.

"I wish I knew but Laughing Bear doesn't have a phone." Lucy's voice was full of compassion. "How are you doing?"

Meggie gave a noncommittal reply that didn't answer the real question. The emptiness Meggie felt in her heart was balanced only by the fullness in her womb.

Even Karl had left the area to enter into a monastic retreat. He had warned her that there might be an initial probationary period in which he would not be allowed any contact with the outside world.

She had heard nothing from him. She missed her friend, but she ached for her soul mate.

As the weather grew colder, both Fritzie and Meggie took afternoon naps whenever possible. The fireplace crackled and blazed with the heat of birch logs. Just as Fritzie had settled into a comfortable deep sleep, he awoke, hearing Meggie cry out, "Oh! Oh no, it can't be!"

The dog jumped up and ran to the couch where Meggie had been sleeping. A book fell from her lap onto the floor. The strong smell of blood assailed his nose. The scent was coming from her. Again, she called out, "No. It can't be!"

He recognized the fear in her voice. She rose and stumbled to the telephone, dripping a red trail across the room's rug and up the wooden stairway.

Something was very wrong.

The woman began to scream in pain.

7

MAKATAKIA
grounding

THIRTY-THREE

HOME

*Humour is, in fact, a prelude to faith; and
laughter is the beginning of prayer.*

—REINHOLD NIEBUHR
Discerning the Signs of the Times

"It's time for you to go home." In the Pipe round of the inipi ceremony, the Spirits spoke bluntly to Hawk. They added, "Laughing Bear
is ready to get on with his life."

"Grandfathers," inquired Hawk, "where is home for me?" *All these
weeks, I have been waiting to ask this question.*

The Spirits lectured him: "Ask your mind to clear the way. Let your
heart speak wisely. Open yourself to the truth. Then, and only then,
will you be ready to work with the Pipe. If you have trust, the Pipe will
lead you. When you bring questions to the Pipe, take responsibility for
the answers given to you. Wherever you are, the Pipe will make a
home for you."

"Hau!" Hawk answered.

Laughing Bear began to chuckle, "Spirits want to know if you have
any more questions for Them."

This would be the last inipi with Laughing Bear for some time. *It is now or never.*

"Yes," Hawk answered, "Grandfathers, I want to marry the white woman, Meggie O'Connor. I am lonely for her. She is a strong and good woman, and she carries my baby. I want my teacher, Laughing Bear, to marry us. I have great love for this man. He has offered me his home, his knowledge, and his time so that I could come here and heal. He is a *wicasa wakan,* a holy man. He gives his life to help the people. Grandfathers, my teacher does not believe in marriage between the red people and those of other races. He warns me that marriage to a white woman would pull me off the Pipe road. I ask you now to look into this woman's heart, to look into my heart, and to tell me what to do."

"Sing the Pipe song," commanded Laughing Bear. The medicine man poured ladle upon ladle of water onto the sizzling stones. The heat rolled in great waves over their bare backs; Hawk's voice soared with the old prayer song. Catching his breath between verses, Hawk could hear his teacher grunt and groan while questioning the Spirits. Dancing Spirit lights sparkled throughout the dark sweat lodge.

The prickly steam nettled Hawk's face and throat; sweat poured out of his body. It was getting harder and harder to inhale. Hawk croaked out the last of the song while diving to the Grandmother for comfort. Always in the prayers, in the lodge, in the outside world, it was to Grandmother Earth the homeward-bound Hawk returned.

Laughing Bear began to cough with the heat. "Spirits say you are to go to this woman and ask her what she wants. The Pipe road is hard, but she has a good heart. If you marry her, you must marry her by the Pipe. That means you will be married to her forever, not just in this life. There can be no more marriages for you. No more women. You will have to teach her more about the Pipe and the traditions. It will not be easy for her. We have told Laughing Bear that if she agrees to this, he is to bring the two of you together in the blanket ceremony. Ah hau!"

Their answer made Hawk's heart sing with joy.

Their answer stunned Laughing Bear and left him choking on his own convictions.

Coming out of anesthesia made Meggie's insides ache. After she lost the baby, the obstetrician had performed a D & C and had tried to console her: "Mother Nature knows best." But Meggie blamed her forty-year-old body for being unable to nurture the baby girl. She felt defeated. After years of infertility, it had been a miracle to get pregnant, an affirmation of the future and of herself as a woman. To have the baby slip out of her before it could survive the outside world brought home to Meggie the slash of death and the sink of despair. No philosophical aphorisms, medical explanations, or words of sympathy could erase the harsh reality of an emptied womb.

Lying in the recovery room, which was filled with other patients, Meggie ruthlessly combed through the events of the past year for some shred of meaning, some vision to sustain her through the doubt and self-questioning.

Over a year ago she had met Winona, and the old woman had shaken up Meggie's life with her teachings. She had shown her a path, a way to find balance in herself and ultimately to love. *What would Winona say to her now about the miscarriage?*

"Oh," Meggie moaned.

A nurse came over. "Are you all right, dearie?"

Meggie lied, "Yes." Tears gathered at the edges of her eyes.

The nurse turned to her other charges and left her alone to her thoughts. A parade of the dead traipsed through Meggie's mind: Winona, Sasha, Savannah, the little baby. She envisioned her parents as next in line, generational row by row of people, taking their turn, marching stolidly through their brief lives. "What's the use of spending all our time to learn things, when it's wasted at the end?" Her voice slurred from the anesthesia. She began to sob.

"Now, now, dearie." The nurse affected a soothing voice, "You're going to be all right. You're just feeling the aftereffects of having been asleep. As soon as the anesthesia wears off, why then you'll feel much better."

Sourness rolled up green from Meggie's stomach. She caught it in her throat and forced it back down. She couldn't stand to vomit and cry at the same time.

Distracted by a door opening into the recovery room, the nurse looked up. "I'm sorry," she informed the visitor, "you'll have to leave. Only medical personnel are allowed here."

A familiar voice answered, "That's all right. I'm Dr. Paterson."

"This is highly irregular," protested the nurse.

"I take full responsibility."

Bev. That liar, passing herself off as a medical doctor. Meggie was relieved.

Bev made her way past the nurse to the bed. Fishing into the pocket of a white medical jacket, replete with stethoscope, she retrieved a tissue and handed it to Meggie. The nurse croaked, "Harrumph," and shifted her attentions to the other patients. Bev put her finger to her lips, signaling Meggie not to expose the ruse.

"Where did you get the doctor's jacket?" Meggie giggled.

"I borrowed it for a short time from the doctors' lounge," Bev whispered.

The nurse cast suspicious glances at the two.

The fuzziness in Meggie's head began to clear. "I think I'm going to be okay."

"Yah," grinned Bev. "I brought you today's mail: lots of bills, insurance payments, and one letter from Bar Harbor, Maine."

"Oh?" Meggie raised her head from the bed with interest, "Read it to me."

Bev tore open the envelope and fished out the brief letter:

> *Dear Meggie,*
>
> *God is making His peace with me.*
> *The silence helps.*
> *(Writing to you is forbidden.)*
> *Your loving friend,*
> *P.S. You're right—chastity is unbearable.*

As Bev looked at the unsigned letter, Meggie burst out in laughter. "Is this from Karl?" Bev asked.

"Sounds like he is needing another one of your professional consultations, doesn't it? I wonder how he spirited the letter out of the monastery?" Meggie shook her head in delight.

Bev grinned and gave her a big hug. "Do you mind if I keep the letter?"

Finally, the physician gave Meggie permission to leave the hospital. As Bev left to retrieve the car from the parking lot, the nurse wheeled Meggie out the front lobby door, positioning her next to three other wheelchair occupants—all mothers holding new babies, waiting for husbands to convey them safely home.

THIRTY-FOUR

INTERRUPTIONS

Who can sail without the wind?
Without oars, who can row?
Who can leave a friend behind
Without the tears that flow?

—TRADITIONAL SWEDISH SONG

With very little sleep, Hawk drove eastward in the dark pitch of night, having crossed the wide-open spaces of the Great Plains of South Dakota, south and eastward past the agricultural fields of corn stubble and river valleys of Iowa and into Illinois. Turning north around Chicago, he headed up the Michigan peninsula with Meggie and the baby on his mind. He reflected on how he would declare his unequivocal love to Meggie as the late-rising sun shimmered on the highway.

Upon reaching the Leelanau Peninsula, Hawk decided to stop first at his trailer to clean up, shave, and change his clothes before surprising Meggie with his early-morning arrival.

Lucy, who had been up at the crack of dawn, was delighted to see him. She wandered out of her house to his trailer with a cup of strong coffee. "Am I glad you're back. The community has been badgering me about your return. I also got a call from Meggie." She raised her eyebrows at him.

He responded with curiosity, "Yes?"

"It was a couple of weeks ago. She wanted to know where you were and when you were coming back."

"What did you tell her?" he asked, grimacing as he cut himself with a new razor blade. The trailer was cold and dusty. He had been away too long.

Lucy surveyed the trailer with disgust. "You really need a woman in your life, Hawk." She brushed off a chair with a dish towel and sat down. "I told her that I didn't know if you were ever going to come back."

She'll think I've abandoned her. Hawk dabbed at the bloody cut on his cheek. He confessed, "She deserved better treatment from me."

"Yes, she did. So did Rising Smoke," Lucy commented with typical bluntness. "What are your plans?"

"As soon as I shower and find clean clothes, I'm driving over to Chrysalis to talk with Meggie. I'll ask her to marry me, and I'm going to take care of her and the baby."

"What makes you think she still wants you? Besides, I don't think that white woman needs a man to take care of her. She's pretty capable of taking care of herself." Lucy smugly folded her arms in front of her and leaned back in the chair, grinning at his discomfort.

"What do you suggest? You're a woman," Hawk threw it back at her, but he also valued her advice.

"If I were you, I'd tell her in great detail *why* you want to share the rest of your life with her. It's not enough to tell a woman that you love her. You've already insulted her with your *love* for Rising Smoke."

Lucy suddenly looked distracted. "Oh, I forgot. Rising Smoke came by yesterday and dropped off a package for you." She rose from the chair and left the trailer muttering, "I'll go get it." The door banged noisily after her.

Meanwhile, Hawk stepped into his small shower unit and washed off the grit and grime accumulated after many miles of travel. A clean pair of jeans, a warm brown corduroy shirt, a rolled bandanna headband, and a bright beaded bolo tie spiffed up his appearance, despite the developing bags under his eyes.

Lucy returned with a large, soft parcel in brown wrapping, which she handed over to Hawk. He carefully untied the string. Slipping off the brown paper, Hawk uncovered Rising Smoke's medicine bundle—

the blanket wrapped around her Sacred Pipe, her rattles, sage, sweet grass, smudge bowl, tobacco, and rattlesnake medicine. Alarmed, Hawk questioned his cousin, "What did Rising Smoke say to you about this?"

"She told me that it would be safer with you, that she could no longer carry the Pipe. She seemed very upset but wouldn't stay and talk to me."

"Damn," Hawk hit the kitchen table with his fist.

Lucy looked startled. "What's the problem?"

Hawk felt enormously frustrated, caught between his own personal needs and his responsibilities, as a person of medicine, to his community. Everything in him called out to go to Meggie and tell her how much he loved her. Yet the significance of Rising Smoke's action meant he had to turn his attentions back to his ex-wife. Quickly he threw on a heavy sweater to ward off the cold air. As he exited the trailer, he explained to Lucy, "Rising Smoke left me her bundle because she plans to drink herself to death. Otherwise, she would never have let go of her Pipe. I've got to find her and get her help, before it's too late."

"But what about Meggie and your proposal?" Lucy knew what was important to the heart.

Hawk looked at her with tormented eyes. "When someone brings the Chanunpa Wakan to me and asks for help, I have to help them. That's what it means to be a Pipe carrier. You don't say, 'No thanks,' or maybe, 'I'll come by tomorrow.' What else can I do?"

He slammed the trailer door behind him.

*   *   *   *

Later that morning, Bev sailed into Meggie's office. "Did I tell you that I've decided to try chastity for a while too? It can't hurt, can it? I mean, you were abstinent a long time after your separation and divorce from Tom. And you looked okay—well, maybe a little jagged around the edges."

"From two men to none. You're losing your touch," Meggie teased.

"Well, I've got to do something different with my life. I can't think straight anymore. By mistake, I pushed the erase button on our answering machine. Luckily, there was only one message."

Meggie looked up from the computer where she had been making client entries. "Yes?"

Bev playfully whispered, "It was a man's voice. He didn't say whether the message was for you or me. I didn't recognize the voice."

Meggie rolled her eyes at her colleague. She would have preferred there be no distractions from her work.

Bev continued, "Simply put, the message was 'I love you.' I waited for the hot orgasmic breath or the erotic follow-up, but the person hung up the phone. Do you have any current male patients undergoing passionate transference toward you?"

Meggie shook her head, "Probably a prank call." She dismissed it from her mind and returned her concentration to the screen. The infallible logic of the computer was a welcome antidote to the intense emotions of the heart.

Hawk sped to Rising Smoke's apartment, but she wasn't there. At the restaurant where she worked, they informed him that she had handed in her resignation on the previous day. He drove around Traverse City checking the bars, but no one had seen her. Midmorning, he stopped and impulsively called Meggie's office to tell her he was back. Unfortunately, only the answering machine talked back to him. He left a cryptic message.

About to return to Suttons Bay on M22, he discovered Rising Smoke's car parked on a side street. His eye next spotted the familiar but forlorn figure resting against the chain-link fence that surrounded the small Traverse City zoo. There she stood peering through the wire mesh at a shaggy buffalo in a small enclosure; the buffalo, in turn, studied her. Hawk pulled over his car, got out, and gingerly approached his ex-wife. From the smell, from the unsteady sway of her body, Hawk could discern she was drunk.

Tears streaked down her eyes. She had not yet noticed him coming up behind her. He heard her clucking to the buffalo, "*Tatanka.* We've come so low, you and I, you in your cage, me in mine." Pouring a small libation on the ground, she lifted a bagged bottle to her lips as Hawk's hand closed over hers.

"That's enough." His voice carried a soothing quality to it. He dislodged the bottle from her hand and dropped it in a receptacle, while balancing her with the other arm.

"Heh," she protested, "Thaz's my bottle." She waved her arm futilely after it and fell against the fence.

He gripped her with a firmer hand and pulled her over to her car, setting her down in the front seat. Passersby stared at her with disgust, a public spectacle. Hawk paid them no mind.

"I'm gonna be sick," she announced and promptly began to vomit into the gutter. Whipping off the bandanna from around his forehead, he mopped the sweat off her brow. His own stomach soured as her body worked to purge itself of the alcohol. She groaned, holding her belly, but refused to go to the hospital.

"Go 'way. Leave me 'lone," she growled and flailed at him feebly with her arms. "You don' know what I've done."

"Hush," he chided, as a parent would do to a recalcitrant child.

When the retching was done, he shut the passenger-side door, slid into the driver's seat, and rolled down the window. The smell of alcohol, vomit, and self-hatred issued in waves from her slumped form. From the glove compartment, he retrieved her keys and drove straight to her apartment. He could feel his energy flag as he maneuvered her up the stairs to the front door—too many hours spent on the road without sufficient sleep. Unresisting, she stumbled with him into her shabby bedroom. He lowered her gently down on the bed, took off her shoes, washed her face with a damp cloth, and drew a sheet up to her shoulders. She tried to talk, muttering, "My medicine . . . that white woman," but her words were incoherent; she quickly fell asleep.

After splashing cold water onto his own face, he took inventory of her one-bedroom flat, hiding her pocketbook and car keys. Under the sink, in the cupboards, on the kitchen countertop, he carried out a bleary-eyed search mission to empty any remaining bottles of alcohol. When satisfied there were none to be found, he grabbed a pillow and a blanket from the bedroom and made a bed on the living room floor. He couldn't stay awake a minute longer.

Hours later, into the early morning of the next day, Hawk woke to the touch of a female hand exploring his pockets. His eyes opened to a face of cunning determination.

"Where are my keys? Where's my money?" Rising Smoke demanded, quickly extracting her hand.

"I hid them. You were in no condition to drive, and I wasn't about to let you go out and buy more booze." He rubbed his eyes, checked his watch, and found it difficult to believe he had slept for over twelve hours. The floor seemed incredibly unforgiving as he stretched his aching muscles.

"Get out of my apartment," Rising Smoke ordered, hands on her hips, her face reflecting the sickness in her system.

Pulling himself up into a standing position, Hawk ignored her. Instead, he ambled into the kitchen and rummaged around for the freeze-dried coffee and a pan of water for the stove.

Rising Smoke followed him, saying in an exasperated tone of voice, "When are you going to leave?"

He gathered she had plans to do some more serious drinking with the remains of her last paycheck. He boiled the water and poured them both strong cups of coffee. Sitting down at the kitchen table of cracked green Formica, he signaled for her to be seated. "First, you and I are going to sell that old clunker of a car. Then I am taking you to the airport and putting you on a plane back to the reservation. I'll call your family and tell them you're coming. They can get you to a medicine person there who will dry you out in the inipi ceremonies. I will keep your Pipe safe with me.

"When you're sober and ready to pick it up, then I will give it back to you. Don't give me any guff about this, Rising Smoke. You're about to kill yourself. The alcohol is a one-way street to hell, and you and I both know it. It has poisoned our people." It was a long speech for Hawk; he reckoned she knew he meant every word of it.

Like a snake rearing its head to strike out, Rising Smoke puffed out her chest in protest, sputtering, "You've no right to tell me what to do, you two-timing son of a bitch." Her self-pitying, accusative monologue spewed venom, calling him every name in the book of shame, to no avail. He remained impassive, sipping his coffee, a determined expression on his face.

Finally, tired of her barren words, Hawk interrupted, "I'm putting you on the plane home, because I love you, Rising Smoke. Deep down, you're a good woman, but the alcohol has got you now by the throat and won't let you go. You need help."

"Good woman, you say? You don't know . . . ," she hissed at him and narrowed her eyes into an evil expression.

"I don't care to know what you've done. It's what you're going to do now that's important. You make things right by changing your life, not drowning yourself in hatred and self-pity. Go pack your bags. I'll let your landlord know you're not coming back."

"How do you know I won't be back?" she challenged him.

It was time for the hard truth. "Because," he acknowledged, "I don't want you in my life, Rising Smoke. I love you but I'm not *in love* with you. I'm sorry for your hurt, but it took me some time to figure out the difference."

Her shoulders sagged. Hope—embattled and bitter within her—collapsed in defeat. Her words had failed to provoke him.

They spent the rest of the morning in silence. She gathered together her few belongings. He sold her car to a used-car dealer and notified the landlord. He drove her to the airport, bought her ticket with the car money, and telephoned her family in South Dakota. As they sat in the coffee shop waiting for her plane, Rising Smoke looked longingly at the cocktail lounge and remarked, "You know they serve drinks on the plane."

Hawk nodded, "I've taken you as far as I can. It's your choice. You can drink yourself to death or you can help the people."

The announcer called her flight number. He walked her to the gate. She turned around, gave him a long hug, and planted a kiss on his lips. With the back of her hand, she wiped away the tears on her cheeks. "I'll always love you, Hawk."

He watched her walk away from him and out of his life.

Today he had kept her sober. Tomorrow was always another choice for her. He had done all he could do. She blew a sultry kiss at him before disappearing into the belly of the plane.

The large silver bird roared down the runway and lifted into the air, heading west toward the setting sun. The disappearance of the airplane into the darkening sky drew out a deep sigh of relief from him. Stopping off at the airport shop, Hawk purchased a baby rattle decorated with red cherries and the words "Traverse City." He tucked the bag under his arm and headed, whistling, for the parking lot. Sliding comfortably into the old pick-up, Hawk accelerated eastward toward Suttons Bay, Meggie, and his baby.

THIRTY-FIVE

GENERATION

They think it's easy to be dead. . . .
. . . They think you just lie down
into dreams you will never tell anyone.
They don't know we still have plans, a yen
for romance, and miss things like hats
and casseroles.

—TESS GALLAGHER
Tableau Vivant

Stopping off at his trailer to don fresh clothes, Hawk spied his father's cardboard box of junk in the back of his closet. Pulling it out, Hawk sorted through the rummage of medals, old coins, nail scissors, shoe polish, one torn photograph of his father, Social Security card, scraps of paper with illegible, water-stained handwriting, cloth bandannas, bone buttons, belt buckles, and odds and ends that record a man's existence. At the bottom of the box, he retrieved a dog-eared black address book, filled mainly with the names of women in various states across the country. In it, he discovered his own name with a South Dakota address—a residence occupied years ago when he was still living with Rising Smoke.

Under the address book was a leather neck-pouch, hard to the touch at the center. Hawk pried open the leather loops and fished out the contents—a round stone the size of a quarter, with a pinprick hole in its center. As he held it aloft by the window, the tiny stone aperture condensed the rapidly fading sunlight into a beam which Hawk could direct onto the room's walls by gentle shifts in the stone's position.

"This is your Stone Man, isn't it?" Hawk spoke to the memory of his father.

"This is the Stone Man you told me about in my dream. He has come to work with me." Hawk placed the stone back into its protective pouch, pulled the cords tightly, and strung it around his neck.

"I will wear it. I will honor this Stone Man who has come to me from you. *Mitakuye oyas'in.*" Hawk retrieved the photograph of his father and slid it into his pocket.

"Adam! Eva! Come here!" Lucy called out the door to her children, who were swinging on an old tire suspended from a maple tree. They came tumbling toward her, like a couple of uncoordinated puppies, out of breath and fumble-footed. She noticed that Hawk's truck had returned and wondered whether he had spent the previous night at Meggie's place.

The children headed straight for the kitchen where she had put out cookies and milk. On the kitchen table sat her new tape recorder, loaded and ready to play. "Sit down," she commanded, always surprised to see how fast her rambunctious children were growing. They scraped the chairs on the floor, bit into the cookies, and slurped their milk. "Careful. Don't spill on the tape recorder," she cautioned them.

They looked surprised that she had left the recorder sitting out in such an unprotected place. She explained, "I have a tape made by your grandmother. She wanted you both to hear it. Okay?"

The kids nodded solemnly.

Lucy pushed down the "Play" button.

"Okay," the old woman's voice squawked, "Okay, Lucy, this tape I make for you. You listen to it when you're ready. Okay? Maybe I wasn't the best mother for you, Lucy, but I always loved you. So, I make this tape for you. Just like when Davis died you made me a place in your home, your family. So, now, I make you a place in my family. You keep this tape and play it for the kids. It is for them, too, I make this tape. . . ."

I love you too, Mom. There was no bitterness left in Lucy.

I'd rather be playing outside. Eva kept her thoughts to herself.

Every day, Grandma, I think of you. Why did you go away? Adam paid close attention to the words on the tape, the sound of her voice, the clear images of her that sprung to his mind. Her words spun for him a fabric of belonging, weaving her grandchildren into the lineage of the people.

Dusk was rapidly approaching as Meggie finished up her work for the day. Thanksgiving was coming, and she needed to plan for the holiday. Her parents would arrive soon at Chrysalis. *At least,* she sighed to herself, *I won't have to explain the pregnancy.*

She imagined her dad asking her the embarrassing question: "Where's the father of the baby?"

She envisioned her mother inquiring, "Where's the husband?"

It would be better not to tell them about the baby and the miscarriage. Instead, their questions would be directed to her heaviness.

"You're getting a little soft around the middle," her father would observe.

"Meggie, darling, don't you think you need to diet a little bit?" her mother would chide her.

In such ponderous matters, Meggie knew, elderly parents and middle-aged children reinstate the old patterns of advice given and advice forgotten.

Darkness had settled over the Leelanau Peninsula by the time Hawk headed to Chrysalis. While driving the old pick-up, Hawk kept returning to the image of the Stone Man, whose hollow center channeled the light. The voice of Three Legs interrupted his thoughts:

"Greetings, Nephew."

Turning to his right, Hawk started; there lounged his Spirit teacher on the passenger side. Inadvertently, Hawk jerked the old gal across the center line, distracted by the apparition.

"Watch the road," Three Legs commanded, grinning.

Hawk corrected the straying truck but couldn't restrain himself from double-checking the reality of his teacher.

"Grandfather!" He could barely find his voice.

The man sitting next to him had a small, wiry frame. His face, bracketed by long, unbound gray hair, looked weatherbeaten, with deep-gullied wrinkles, a wide flattish nose, eyes that danced with life, and a smile of both humor and joy. His clothes were of tanned elk skin, fringed and plain of bead. He stared straight ahead as the truck snorted along M22.

It was clear to Hawk that the old man was enjoying his surprise.

"Grandfather, what brings you here?" Hawk's eyes had grown large in disbelief.

Three Legs laughed at him. He cranked open the truck window; the November breeze soon chilled the interior windshield. Hawk turned up the heater.

"I needed some fresh air," Three Legs began.

Hawk nodded, his eyes riveted to the road, his fingers clutched onto the steering wheel. Every time the truck swayed to a curve in the road, his father's pouch banged unfamiliarly against his chest.

"You live in the world of the Stone People," Three Legs commented, sweeping his hand across the window and pointing to the rolling hills carved by the retreat of ancient glaciers. "It is to Them that you must keep returning for teaching, for They form the backbone of the Grandmother. The Stone Man around your neck is round, solid, and hollow at the center. So, too, you must learn to live within the circle, to stand strong, and to be open at the core. If you live within the squares of the white people, you will keep bumping into their angles." Three Legs laughed at the image, tapping his nose as if stubbing it against a wall.

The lights of a passing car cast the shadow of Three Legs onto the seat. *How can it be that he comes from another dimension and yet casts shadows in this one?* Hawk smiled to himself, his right hand slipping off the steering wheel. No sooner did Hawk brush the fabric of the seat, than the old man's fingers briefly touched Hawk's hand.

Three Legs continued his teaching. He drew a circle in the air with both hands. "All his life, your father carried that Stone Man, but he was unable to be hollow at the center. Every time he tried to carve himself a hole, he fell into it; he wasn't strong enough to withstand the emptiness. When you ask Wakan Tanka and Unci Maka to work through you, They will use you, but you must stay balanced, grounded when that happens. That's where the Pipe will help you. The Chanunpa Wakan will protect you from the intensity of the healing powers."

Hawk nodded, both hands back on the wheel, slowing as he drew nearer to Meggie's place. He didn't want the conversation with his teacher to end. Yet, his heart urged him toward Meggie. *Was it always going to be like this? A choice between the Pipe and the woman?* he wondered.

Three Legs noticed the entrance to Chrysalis. He concluded, "When you focus your mind and energy, the light that shines through you will illuminate the questions. That is one of the teachings of the Stone Man. It can be a light of healing. It can be a light of learning. It can also be a light that will burn you to a crisp.

"Don't play with these powers or let your ego take over. A man can grow to love his own shadow and mistake the image for the source of light. Your Pipe, hollow at the center, is stronger than you. Love that Pipe, and it will keep you alive."

Hawk turned into the driveway of Chrysalis. Three Legs motioned for him to stop the truck and let him out. "I welcome the fresh air," the old man exclaimed. "You don't need me around to help you with women. Besides, I wouldn't know what to do with a white woman." He laughed, remembering randier days. Slowly he lowered himself out of the truck and slammed the door shut.

"Grandfather," said Hawk, digging into his jeans pocket, "here is some tobacco for your smoke." He handed the old man a half-used pouch of pipe tobacco.

"*Pilamaya,*" the old man acknowledged. Moving off into the shadows of night, Three Legs hooted, "Remember, Nephew, love is very tricky."

In the distance, Hawk could hear a canine yipping.

THIRTY-SIX

OF DAMS AND WILD RIVERS

The soul has many motions, body one.
An old wind-tattered butterfly flew down
And pulsed its wings upon the dusty ground—
Such stretchings of the spirit make no sound.
By lust alone we keep the mind alive,
And grieve into the certainty of love.

—THEODORE ROETHKE
The Motion

Fritzie was the first to hear the old gal rumbling up the driveway. He barked a shrill alert of warning, a second cry of inquiry, a third, uncertain yelp of welcome—before retreating to the house. The sound of the truck's motor up the last hill was familiar to him. His tail lowered to a friendly wag. The man had returned.

No sooner had Hawk opened the truck door than Fritzie jumped into the truck and into his arms, unbidden and emboldened by their acquaintance. Fritzie licked his face, taking in the old aromas: the smell of pipe tobacco, the skim of soap, a shirt hung overlong in a cramped closet, and the odor that demarcates one two-legged from another. Fritzie sniffed for cookies but found none in the man's hands. While greeting his friend, Fritzie extended the reaches of his nose to all parts of the bench seat.

Over by the far window, Fritzie picked up a faint, unidentified smell, still outlined on the warp and weave of the seat fabric, a scent most like air that has been lightning-charged—sharp and permeated with ozone. He didn't recognize the odor and wanted to investigate further, but the man scooped him up and deposited him back onto the driveway. Fritzie sniffed all around him but could catch no other drift of the stranger.

The possibility of playing ball forced Fritzie to abandon his investigation. He retrieved an old tennis ball, frayed and flapping with yellow fuzz, but Hawk strode on toward the house, disinterested in a game. Disappointed, the terrier dropped the ball and scampered after him. Long ago, Fritzie had learned about the unpredictability of the two-leggeds.

In the kitchen, Meggie was whipping up a second batch of low-fat gingerbread cookies, an unsatisfactory compromise between her sweet tooth and her need to lose weight. Not expecting visitors, she had dismissed Fritzie's barking as hyperactivity. She pulled down the oven door to extract the baked goods.

The kitchen door opened so quietly that it was the shift in temperature and not the sound that alerted her to Hawk's presence. "Oh," Meggie uttered, spooked.

Two gingerbread people slid off the cookie sheet onto the linoleum floor, fracturing upon impact. The gingerbread amputees disappeared rapidly into Fritzie's mouth. The terrier looked at her expectantly, licking his lips.

Hawk gazed at her ravenously.

Assailed by thoughts at every turn, Meggie found herself uncharacteristically mute. Her thoughts tumbled chaotically: *What to say to him?*
I love you.
Do you love me or that other woman?
I've lost the baby, Hawk. Can you forgive my body's betrayal?
Where have you been all this time?
Goddamn it, I have needed you here!
Where have you been?
In shame, in anger, she turned her eyes away from his.

Hawk stretched out his hand toward her, across the table's barrier, touching her arm, turning her toward him. "Meggie," he whispered her name, low and soft.

She bit her lip against hope. She blurted the truth to stanch the wound, "Hawk, I lost the baby."

She pulled away from him, presented her back, and stuffed a tray of gingerbread babies into the hot oven, unwilling to yield her grief to the release of tears. The choke in her throat, the desiccation of her heart, the hardness of her determination crowded in on her. Her neck muscles strained to catch and stifle the cry.

His silence rebuked and condemned her.

Hawk had expected joy upon his arrival. He was going to tell her how much he loved her and the child in her womb. He had not anticipated the eyes of pain and blame which accused him over the kitchen table, eyes that spoke of confusion and doubt, eyes that hid from him. So caught up had he been in his romantic wishes that he had dismissed the days of silence marking his absence. He felt shamed by his insensitivity.

"Meggie," he whispered. *Oh, Meggie, let me love you,* he had meant to say.

Her voice sounded harsh, pragmatic, devoid of feeling. "Hawk, I lost the baby."

She convicted the "I" with dry emphasis. She pivoted and turned away from him, shoulders slumped, her hands busy at the oven.

Stunned into silence, he witnessed his dream crack and break, a child slipping once again out of his life, a woman defeated and dragged down by the death in her womb, her back to him. Assaulted by feelings at every level—past remembered, future dismembered— Hawk could feel himself lose his bearings. In the pouch around his neck, the Stone Man began to vibrate. With his left hand, Hawk grabbed onto the pouch and silently asked for help.

"Meggie," he whispered, "I love you."

In the hollow of himself, he first felt his tears as he wept for the lost baby and the woman's pain.

Anxious, Fritzie scooted under the table, bridging the gap between Hawk and Meggie. First, he licked the spicy hand of the woman, redolent with the smell of cinnamon and dough, as she opened the hot box. Next, he pivoted, placing his nose to the knee of the man, his tail slapping against the back of her leg. The woman turned, her knees facing the man. Under the table, Fritzie wheeled in slow circles, licking, nibbling, sniffing—one end to the man, the other end to the woman, his body pulling their attention toward each other.

"Fritzie," both two-leggeds simultaneously spoke his name. Then, and only then, did he relax.

Patting the anxious terrier with her hand, Meggie looked up at Hawk, spotting tears in his eyes. Clumsily, he wiped his face with the back of his arm.

He is crying for me.

Astonished at his tears, in contrast to her own parched response, Meggie could feel a barricade burst open inside the back of her throat. Grief flooded her; unchoked and free to flow, the feelings surged chaotically through her, like a rushing river too long pent up in a narrow neck.

He is crying for me, for my pain, for the death of our baby. She spun her hand out to him to steady herself. He pulled her around the table into his arms.

"I love you, Meggie," he whispered again and again, his lips by her ear, his voice gravelly, the wetness in his eyes seeping through her hair. Again and again, his words washed over her, soothing the wild rush of feelings inside of her. Meggie buried her head into his shoulder, anchoring herself into the certainty of his presence, letting her own tears spill over the banks of her eyes.

"Good woman," Hawk said. "Tell me a story. For I have been travel-ing a long time." The look of Coyote mischief briefly crossed his face as they sat at the kitchen table, delving into each other's eyes.

"Oh, I have such a wicked story to tell," Meggie teased, remember-ing the words of Mole Woman.

His fingers traced a pattern up and down the soft inside of her left arm.

"Oh, I have such a wicked story to tell," she repeated, "but it's al-ready grown cold and old in your presence. Maybe it can be different this time. Maybe we don't have to circle round and round in life, chas-ing the ancient tales, pursuing them to the same conclusion. I'd rather warm myself in the creation of a new story."

And so, they wove the simplest words together, their arms knitting the strands of love in the keenest terms, touch upon touch. Her hand upon his cheek, his expressions of compassion and adoration, the smell of his body and clean clothes, the pungent aroma of gingerbread cookies upon her fingers, the kisses, one short, one lingering, the oth-ers long, hungry, and full of passion.

She forgot the cookies in the oven.

He didn't.

He rescued them from the oven and the heat of the moment. Lined up in rows of three abreast on the cookie sheet, the army of ginger-bread people awaited consumption.

With one hand to his midriff, Meggie fired his attention onto her; with the other hand, she led them off to a lover's feast.

They mounted the stairs to the bedroom.

∴ ⁙ ⁙ ⁘

He truly loves me. I know that now. Meggie's heart began to heal.

∴ ⁙ ⁙ ⁘

I love this woman. Home will always be wherever I can find Meggie. Hawk's mind banked into this realization, before desire obliterated any thought except making his body, soul, heart, and mind one with hers.

THIRTY-SEVEN

FIRE AND SMOKE

Love consists in this, that two solitudes
protect and touch and greet each other.

—RAINER MARIA RILKE
Letters to a Young Poet

After their lovemaking had tamed the first fire, Hawk served Meggie hot cocoa and gingerbread cookies in bed. He recounted his experiences with the Stone Man, and with his Spirit teacher, Three Legs. He told of his time with Laughing Bear, of his loneliness for her in South Dakota. He spoke nervously of Rising Smoke and dispatching her back to the reservation. Meggie seemed to take no offense. Of Coyote and the tracks, he said little, except to repeat, "I've been a fool, Meggie. I took what I had with you, and I wasted it. Loved by two women, pumped up by a spiritually hungry community, heady with medicine power—my ego took over. I lost my balance."

She shifted her position on the bed for a better view of him. Turning on his side toward her, Hawk sighed, "It took a dead baby to set me straight."

He checked her expression and saw that her grief was done for now. He felt relief. She was nibbling all around a gingerbread man; she licked her lips, gathering in the crumbs, sipped the cocoa, and smiled at him. He leaned against the headboard, angling his legs toward her while maintaining enough distance to see her clearly.

I am home now.

Holding the mug of cocoa in her hands, Meggie confessed, "I nursed my anger at you, Hawk. Pride blinded me. I was pregnant with our baby but I made it mine. I had no right to do that. I'm sorry . . ."

"Shhh," he put his fingers to her lips, "There is no Sioux word for 'sorry.' When you make mistakes, you change your behavior. The apology is in the act, not the word. I can't take back the hurt I've caused you, Meggie, but I've learned about my own ego. It will not happen again."

A mischievous grin spread onto her face. "Just what do you have in mind?" she asked, placing her empty mug onto the bedstand. Yes, indeed, actions were more interesting than words.

Below, Fritzie flopped into his own bed and began to chomp furiously at a flea.

After the second fire had banked into long repose and night had closed in on the daylight, Meggie asked the question again, "What do you have in mind?" She knew she was forcing the issue, but the time of waiting was over for her.

He pretended not to understand the question, "Again, Meggie? I'm forty-one years old."

She ignored his humor. "Where do we go from here, Hawk? If you become a medicine man, how will I fit in? What's to become of us?" Her face was intent, serious.

He nudged her with his feet and slowly pushed her out of the bed.

"What are you telling me?" She clung to the mattress, laughing, but the slipperiness of the sheet was no match for the strength of his legs. She landed on the cold floor.

"We're going outside," he announced, snatching up clothes from the floor.

"Outside? Are you crazy, Hawk? It's the middle of the night."

"With your Sacred Pipe," he added.

"Huh?" She sat there naked on the rug.

"Put on your moccasins, warm clothes. We're going outside to pray together," he commanded. Hawk pulled on his jeans and shirt.

"Brrr, it's cold out there," Meggie protested, standing by the bed, her skin pricking up in goose bumps.

Hawk threw a shirt in her direction. "It's going to be a lot colder without clothes than with them."

With a final look of longing at their bed, sheets entangled with blankets and pillows, Meggie reluctantly slipped into some sweat clothes to ward off the chill. *What a peculiar man. He disappears for weeks on end, returns for confession and passionate lovemaking, and then wants to venture outside and pray in the cold.* Meggie shook her head in disbelief.

She checked on Fritzie. In his bed and on his back, the terrier continued to sleep, all four legs extended into the air like spindly fence posts. "At least one of us has the right idea," she muttered, pulling on a pair of pants.

While Meggie retrieved her medicine bundle from the closet, Hawk fetched a large Hudson Bay blanket from the front seat of his truck. The sound of the kitchen door opening and closing finally aroused Fritzie from his nap; he jumped out of bed and traipsed after Meggie on her way out the porch door. The Lake Michigan wind blew cold to the bone. The moonlight outlined dark shadows and grotesque shapes slinking around the edges of the woods. *Where is he?* Meggie shivered.

Hawk rounded the edge of the house, carrying the large blanket and a small cedar box. Kneeling on the damp ground with Fritzie's nose poking into her hands, Meggie retrieved sage from her bundle, then rolled and lit it in the smudge bowl, wafting the smoke around the three of them. She assembled her Pipe, so that the lightning design on the stem faced her. Hawk opened the cedar box, extracting two eagle feathers. He knotted them to the leather string on Meggie's pipestem; the two feathers fluttered around the Sacred Pipe.

"*Pilamaya,*" Meggie spoke.

"It is good for a Chanunpa Wakan to have the feathers of *wanbli* on it." Hawk nodded for her to continue. As it was her Pipe, it was up to her to conduct the Pipe ceremony.

She washed the feathers through the smoke of the sage. Slowly, in the ancient ritual, she filled the Chanunpa Wakan with tobacco and prayers. Facing west, she lifted her Pipe and began praying:

"Wakan Tanka, we stand here and give thanks for our lives. We can never fully understand the sacred mysteries nor the power of the Pipe, but we ask You to help us grow aware of Your directions for us two-leggeds. We are a part of Your Creation. Help us to become human be-ings."

Hawk nodded in agreement. She added another pinch of tobacco:

"Wiyohpeyatakiya, from You comes our vision. We give thanks for our teachers, those we know and those we have yet to know. I ask that You continue to give us visions that we can follow and that will help the people. I am grateful for this Pipe that came from my teacher, Winona Pathfinder."

Meggie smudged another bit of tobacco and added it to the bowl. She rotated the Pipe toward the north.

"Waziyata, we give thanks for the healing of our hearts. What once was almost broken comes back strong in the spirit of love. I give thanks for the strength that is returning to my body after the loss of the baby. We ask You to help us walk in balance once again."

"Hau!" echoed Hawk.

Meggie turned the Pipe to the east:

"Wiyohiyanpata, with this Chanunpa Wakan I have asked You to bring me the man with whom to make a family. As You can see, Grandfather, he is here now with me. For this, I give much thanks. I ask You to help us keep warm the fires of the heart, to know from deep within the truth of things."

Hawk nodded vigorously in agreement.

Meggie held the pipe toward the south:

"Itokagata, I ask you to watch over our baby as she makes her way back home toward You. She had such a short time on this earth . . ."

Her tears choked back the words. Her body trembled in the cold. Hawk placed the blanket over her shoulders. He huddled closer to her and hunched his own shoulders against the wind as Meggie offered the Pipe up toward the sky:

"Wakan Tanka, Sky Beings, in the pitch of night, You brighten our way with the stars and the moon. You reassure us that when all seems black and empty, there is light out there. The powers of the Thunder

Beings and the Lightnings bring us the gifts of water and fire; we two-leggeds must learn to use the gifts wisely."

Low blue-black clouds scurried overhead. The blanket sheltered her. Meggie pointed the Pipe to the ground:

"Unci Maka, Grandmother, it is to You we always return in our prayers. It is You who feeds us, clothes us, and gives us a place to live. For this, we give thanks and pray that we always walk upon You with reverence. Grandmother, this is your granddaughter crying out. Take our baby home."

Once again, Meggie fought to compose herself. She could feel Hawk's body bend into hers, as if to take part of her pain into himself and return love to her.

"*Mitakuye oyas'in,*" she finally added.

Hawk burst into the Pipe-filling song, while Meggie's tears dribbled down her cheeks. It was the first time she had prayed with Hawk since the death of their baby. His powerful voice echoed through the woods:

Kola lecel ecun wo!
Kola lecel ecun wo!
Kola lecel ecun wo!
Hecanu ki, nitunkasila
waniyang u ktelo.

Friend, come do this!
Friend, come do this!
Friend, come do this!
If you do this, your Grandfather
will be watching you.

The Lakota words of the White Buffalo Calf Woman swirled around her, the compassion and the promise of the Chanunpa Wakan:

This sacred ceremony
when you sit down to begin,
remember me when you fill the Pipe!
If you do this, what you wish
will come true.

The song was telling her, White Buffalo Calf Woman was telling her, Hawk was telling her that the world sorrowed with her and that life would go on. Grandfather was right there, listening to her words, caring for her. Grandmother was right there, cradling her body, lending her strength. The Pipe was right there in her hands and would give her what she needed to live. Hawk's voice resonated strong in the night air:

> *When you sit down and begin*
> *the ceremony with the Pipe,*
> *remember me as you fill it.*
> *If you do this, what you wish*
> *will come true.*

For nineteen generations this song has been sung by the Lakota people. Nineteen generations of grandparents, fathers, mothers, and children loving, living, losing, and always the Pipe, right there, waiting to be filled with prayer and tobacco and song, easing the human beings back into balance with the Creation. Hawk was singing her back into balance:

> *Kola lecel ecun wo!*
> *Kola lecel ecun wo!*
> *Kola lecel ecun wo!*
> *Hecanu ki, nitunkasila*
> *waniyang u ktelo.*

> *Friend, come do this!*
> *Friend, come do this!*
> *Friend, come do this!*
> *If you do this, your Grandfather*
> *will be watching you.*

As the last note trailed off into the deep night's silence, and the last tear trickled down her face, Meggie held out her Pipe toward the west: "Tunkasila, Wakan Tanka, Grandfathers in All the Directions, Unci Maka, Wanbli Gleska, our Medicine Helpers. I stand before you with this lightning Pipe. I ask you to recognize this Chanunpa Wakan. Thank you for my life. Grandfathers, I ask you to watch over my elderly parents. Keep them healthy so they can have a good time in these last years of their life. When it is time for them to cross over, I ask that You take them quickly and without pain. Grandfathers, I ask You to watch over the people that come to me with sickness in their hearts and minds. Help me be sensitive to their wounds, to be a circuit in the healing energy between You and the Grandmother.

"I ask you to guide the travels of all those who have crossed over this year: Winona, Savannah and Sasha Todd, Hawk's father, our unborn baby girl. I ask you to help those who are searching the ways of the heart: Katya and Paul, Lucy and Larry. Look after the lonely ones: Bev, Karl, Rising Smoke, and Sam Waters; let them find meaning in their solitude.

"My heart sings with joy that You brought this man, Hawk, safely back to me. Help us take the time we need to sort out the feelings. Watch over him. He is a good man. Grandfathers, I also ask you to keep an eye on my four-legged. He has been a true friend. *Mitakuye oyas'in!*"

Meggie raised the Pipe and lowered it, then passed it over to Hawk.

The eagle feathers lifted in the breeze, twirling on the end of the fringe. Hawk held it a long time, the stem pointed toward the west. His voice was soft and thoughtful. He called the Grandfathers, the Grandmother, the Spotted Eagle, Three Legs, and his Medicine Helpers, and he asked the Spirits to bend low to hear his prayer:

"With Winona's Pipe, with this Pipe that has come to Meggie, I stand here before You, saying that I want to marry this woman. With the Chanunpa Wakan, I will ask Laughing Bear to perform the blanket ceremony, so that when I marry this woman, it will be forever. Not just in this dimension, but forever—in the next dimension and the one beyond that.

"Eleven months ago, my teacher, my relative, Winona, pointed me toward this woman and warned me to treat her right. I stand before You now to swear by the Pipe that this will be a good marriage. You told me to go slow with her and treat her with respect. I will wait for her answer. Hau! *Mitakuye oyas'in!*"

Meggie snatched up her breath. *Was that a proposal?*

Hawk handed her back the Pipe, not daring to look at her.

For a long time, the two of them stood there, side by side in the silence, watching the stars play hide-and-seek with dark, moonlit clouds. Hawk picked up an edge of the blanket and placed it over both of them, creating a pocket of warmth in the cold night air.

Dark and light, warm and cold, love and prayer, white and Native American.

Will my life always be like this, at the crack between two worlds? Meggie wondered.

She lit the Pipe and offered it to the Grandfathers and the Grandmother. With her hand, she washed some of the smoke back toward her face. Hawk remained silent. She handed him the Pipe, saying, "All My Relations."

Her mind ran at full debate:

I love him. But can I be the wife of a medicine teacher, always balancing between two peoples, two cultures?

I don't know.

Do I want to see his face every morning, greeting me with the sun?
Yes.

Do I want to hear his jokes and cuddle into the night with him?
Yes.

Will I marry him?
I don't know.

Hawk finished smoking the Pipe and returned it to her, saying, *"Mitakuye oyas'in."* Not another word was spoken.

Carefully, she separated the bowl and stem, packed the bowl with sage, and placed it in the pipe bag, followed by the stem, tamper, lighter, and tobacco. She angled the feathers to protect them from being crushed. Wrapping up her medicine bundle, Meggie noted the expectant look upon Hawk's face.

"Well," he asked, "what do you have to say to me?"

Meggie reminded him, "You promised the Spirits that you would give me time to make my decision."

Hawk nodded thoughtfully, "Right." He picked at a blade of grass. "I don't want you to feel hurried. It's an important decision."

He plucked a second blade of grass and twined the two together.

"Date other men if you like. Talk to your friends and family. Do whatever you have to do to make a decision. Take all the time you need. This time next week, give me your answer."

"Next week?"

Hawk grinned at her. He handed her the braid of grass, saying, "What was two is stronger together as one. I figure a week should be time enough."

THIRTY-EIGHT

THE WORLD IS ALWAYS TURNING

Oh my Joannie, don't you know
that the stars are swinging slow,
and the seas are rollin' easy
as they did so long ago.
If I had a thing to give you,
I would tell you one more time
that the world is always
turning toward the morning.

—GORDON BOK
Turning Toward the Morning

Meggie's parents arrived for Thanksgiving. Meggie informed them she had invited both Hawk and Bev for the roasted turkey dinner. Cranberry Jell-O salad, oyster stuffing, wild rice, Brussels sprouts, sourdough biscuits, and sparkling grape juice complemented the turkey. With everyone seated at the dinner table, the food steaming hot, the plates full, Meggie stood up and lifted her glass, saying, "I want to make a toast.

"Many years ago, when the Pilgrims were starving, the natives offered them food. This feast today commemorates that gift of welcome. I would like us to remember that people of different races can come together, help each other, teach each other, and celebrate their different gifts."

She paused a moment. "From across the sea, the whites, followed by the blacks and then the Asians brought diverse visions and a genius

for seeing new possibilities. Rooted in this continent, the native peoples taught and continue to teach respect for the land and *all* its inhabitants, the truth that we are *all* in this Creation together. Their gift
of food to the Pilgrims, to us, bears witness to the Giveaway energy
that marks the very essence of Life itself. This is the true meaning of
Thanksgiving."

Everybody raised their glasses and cheered the sentiment, especially in Hawk's direction. He looked slightly embarrassed and
amused.

Meggie's toast was not yet finished. She raised her glass again. "In
the esteemed company of family and friends," Meggie nodded to each
respectively, "I would like you to know that Hawk has asked me to
marry him."

Meggie's mother gasped. Her father choked on the grape juice.
Everybody's eyes riveted on Hawk. Taken off-guard by her announcement, even Hawk stared in amazement at Meggie. She grinned back
at him, enjoying the dramatic effect.

"What is your reply?" Bev asked, the only one able to recover from
the shock of the moment.

"He gave me a week to decide, and that was seven days ago." Meggie was thoroughly enjoying the suspense of the moment. Hawk
looked like he could drop through the floor.

"And?" Bev asked impatiently.

Meggie addressed her stunned parents: "Over the years, watching
the two of you, I've learned a lot about marriage. How, with patience,
you continued to support the dreams of each other. How, with humor,
you negotiated the clashes of two strong personalities. How, with respect, you remained appreciative of each other's strengths. How, with
compassion, you filled in when the other felt weak and scared."

Her mother looked at her father lovingly; he patted the back of her
hand but still looked dumbfounded by his daughter's revelation.

Hawk stared at the table, guarding his face against a premature
smile.

He knows what I am going to say. Meggie's eyes began to water.
Overwhelmed with a sense of love and gratitude, she struggled to
maintain her composure.

She took a deep breath. "I will tell what this past year has taught me. Love is a force far beyond simple human equation or psychological insight. It is the very energy that powers the universe and illuminates our brief lives on this earth. Love comes from All the Directions, bearing gifts of meaning, of balance, of connection, of identity.

"To say that Love wears only the human face is to be, indeed, ignorant. Love bears the face of the whole Creation. The offering of the Pipe. The authenticity of another human soul. The loyal companionship of a dog. And last, but not least, the awesome beauty of the dark woods, the wildflowers of the meadow, the fruit and blossom of the apple trees, the hush of a soft wind, the sunrise in the morning.

"Love is a story always waiting to be told. Again and again and again."

Meggie paused, her gaze sweeping over these people whom she cherished most dearly in her life—her parents, her friend Bev, and Hawk. She added, "I do not consider my first marriage a failure but, rather, a primer in relationships. I didn't know if I ever would get a second chance."

Hawk looked up at her with curiosity. His fingers fiddled nervously with a spoon.

Meggie arched her eyebrows toward him and extended her arms toward the windows. "Chrysalis is my home, passed down to me through the generations. It is the place where the spirits of my grandmother and great-grandmother walk the land. It is where my mother shelters her wild dreams. Where I spent my childhood summers learning that the land took possession of me, tattooed my very soul with its imprint, and called me home for its healing. The house has gotten old over time, requiring constant attention. The land needs the loving ministrations of those who will cherish its mystery and walk upon it with respect. And so, I want you to know, Mom and Dad, in the spirit of Chrysalis, I am saying 'Yes.' "

"Yes what, dear?" Her mother looked puzzled.

Meggie turned to Hawk and spoke to him. "Yes, yes, yes!" She silently mouthed, "I love you."

His face turned red. He was pleased and a little embarrassed.

Meggie's father stood up stiffly, glass in hand, awkwardly searching for the right words, "I would like to make a toast to my future son-in-law. May you both be blessed in as wonderful a union as I have enjoyed all these years." He glanced down at his wife of sixty years.

Meggie's mother rose, grasped her husband's hand, and smiled at him, then turned her attentions to both Meggie and Hawk. "I never doubted your ability to live here alone, Meggie. But to be able to chronicle your life with another human being, to find humor in the bleakest hours and laugh with each other, to celebrate the little moments of the day together, and to tell the stories of a lifetime of love— what more can one ask? Welcome to the family, Hawk." She blew him a kiss over the table.

Meggie leaned over and whispered triumphantly into Hawk's ear, "Gotcha!"

He took firm hold of her hand and laughed.

She had surprised him, that was for sure.

Coyote is no stranger to her home. It was a sobering thought. Hawk knew that all his life would be filled with surprises from this woman. She was a strong woman, quick of wit, full of vitality, and he knew he would love her forever. Not just in this life but in the next and the next, however many lives they were to live. Together, they would bridge the two cultures. Together, they would educate each other, trying to bring the best of both worlds into their life.

In the midst of his happiness, Winona marched into his mind. *Yes, you would approve this match, wouldn't you? You always thought I needed a strong woman to ground me.*

He looked up at Meggie, glowing with love for him.

"Gotcha," she whispered into his right ear.

"Gotcha," gloated Three Legs into his left ear.

"Gotcha," nuzzled Love into his heart.

Of all the holidays, Fritzie loved Thanksgiving the most. With a belly bloated from snacking all day long on turkey, rice slopped with thick gravy and drippings, the burnt edges of sourdough biscuits sporting dollops of butter, oyster bread stuffing, and bits of Brussels sprouts, which he promptly spat to the kitchen floor, he belched heavily all night long.

Soon, it came time for the old folks to depart, an event that always left a sad place in his heart. The elderly woman was an easy target for his beseeching eyes, good for nibbles of bacon under the table. The old man tended to drop crumbs regularly on himself, which made for a fast food shakedown at the end of the meal. Both of them loved to call him "Baby" for some inexplicable reason, but they were welcome to call him anything as long as they would simultaneously rub his ears or scratch that delicious spot above his tail.

"Good-bye, Fritzie. Take care of Meggie," said the old man, leaning down and rubbing his chin.

" 'Bye, Baby," said the old woman, planting a big wet kiss on his long nose.

When the woman returned that afternoon without the old people, Fritzie curled up in the living room for a nice, quiet nap, recovering from all the excitement of the family visit. But it wasn't long before he heard the rumble of an old pick-up truck, grinding up the driveway. Fritzie jumped up and dashed to the kitchen. The woman was there before him, opening the door.

Out he rushed, hurling himself upon the man who was carrying a large duffel bag packed with clothes. The woman followed, laughing. The man swooped him up in his arms, and Fritzie squiggled, delirious with excitement.

I can smell it.

The man let him down, and while Fritzie tore at the duffel bag with his claws, the two humans wrapped their arms about each other and squished their lips together.

It's there. I know it.

The woman grabbed his collar and pulled him back. The man leaned down, unzipped the bag, and reached into its dark interior.

Yes! Yes!

The excitement was almost too much to bear.

There come those special times in one's life when everything seems to come together—the sound of joy in the human laughter, the sense of security when surrounded by love, the moments when one comes close to a sense of fulfillment of one's potential, one's destiny—such was this moment for him. Fritzie hurled his body up into the air, defying gravity, defying dogdom—up, up to the falling object of his intense desire:

The yellow ball.

"Davis, you sonuva bitch. What took you so long to find me?" Winona scowled, shook her finger at her husband, and let it drop. *Handsome as ever.* "I've been waiting a long time for you. I thought being married by the Pipe meant you'd be right there for me when I crossed over! Isn't that what 'forever' means?"

He strolled over to where she was sitting. "Hush, old woman," he replied affectionately, "I'm here now. Earlier wouldn't have done you any good. Lucy, the grandkids, Hawk, that psychologist—they had to release you. Otherwise, they'd still be binding you to them."

"Them two kids got engaged," Winona's voice was proud.

Davis nodded, wandering around to her back. "You needed time to stop meddling in their lives, to let go of them, before moving on with your life here. But I see you still have one strand attached to that past life." He pointed to her back where she could feel the gentle tug of a single gossamer thread.

"What's that?" she asked.

"You have to let go of the lightning Pipe. If you keep attached to that Pipe, the psychologist woman will never be able to find her own way to Wakan Tanka."

"What if she's not strong enough to handle the Chanunpa Wakan?" Winona's hand held onto the thread.

"Winona, none of us is ever really prepared to carry the Pipe. We do the best we can and trust the Pipe will protect us from our own foolishness."

Slowly, ever so slowly, Winona let the thread slip loose through her fingers. "I'm dead to that world, aren't I? I don't belong there anymore— with Lucy and the grandkids, with Hawk and Meggie. Lucy has to learn how to be a Lakota in the modern world. That's not an easy task."

"If she pays attention to the stories, she'll find her way," Davis spoke with authority.

"Adam Stands By Dog—what a fine grandson I've got," Winona boasted. "The boy's got a good ear, pays attention, different from most people. I hope the whites don't school him into blindness. I told him, while I'll always hear his prayers, I can't continue our visits together. It's hard for him to understand."

Davis nodded sympathetically.

Winona continued, "That white psychologist, Meggie O'Connor, is just beginning the hard work of spanning two cultures. I knew that old coot, Laughing Bear, would give them two a hard time about marrying, what with her being white and Hawk being red. So, I fixed his wagon," she laughed.

"Even dead, you're a threat to the living, Winona. What did you do to my favorite student?"

"No magic. I simply nudged a beautiful and sassy Polish American gal right in front of Laughing Bear's lonely eyes. And now that man's done fall in love and is having to choke on his own words."

"That's the kind of stuff you've got to stop doing," Davis chided her.

"Well, that Meggie O'Connor is a strong woman who can take care of herself. Hell, she's even learned how to tell a story or two, like I showed her. I guess she doesn't need my help any more. She's savvy enough to pick up the Pipe when she's lost."

"That's because you taught her the ways of respect."

"Hawk's going to have to continue teaching her," Winona added, "just like you helped me, when I came to live with you. I pity that boy, Davis. He doesn't yet realize how hard it is to walk the medicine road, what the people will ask of him. But, like me, he's lucky to have found his soul mate; she'll help keep his feet on the ground. They truly love each other."

Davis stood there, waiting patiently for his woman to figure it all out.

"I'm dead to them. That's the truth, isn't it? I can't keep looking back onto them, finding out what's happening in their lives, cheering them on, prodding them with a pull here and a push there. I've got to release them, don't I?"

Davis nodded.

Winona looked up at Davis's face. "It's hard to say good-bye. It's hard to let go of my love for them and move on."

"It's time. There is the journey here." He held out his hand. Already her face had started growing younger.

One last time, Winona turned around for a long, lingering look. She could see Lucy and Larry sound asleep, Adam and Eva in their own dream-time, Hawk and Meggie wrapped up in each other's arms. Taking Davis's hand in her own, she rose from her seated position.

Free at last to move forward.

"Will I miss them?" she asked Davis.

"No," he answered.

She queried him with a puzzled look.

"They will certainly miss you," he explained, "until they realize that love doesn't die at the end of one's earth walk. Love simply changes form and moves on to what comes next."

"And what comes next for us?" she inquired.

"We have a long journey to make—to the lodges of each of the Grandfathers, beginning first with Wiyohpeyata and ending with the lodge of Itokaga. It's time to go, Winona." Once again, Davis was assuming the role of teacher for her, as in the old days.

"What happens now to Coyote?" Asleep, Meggie and Hawk, Lucy and her husband, and the grandchildren looked so vulnerable.

Davis laughed. "He won't be bothering you, for sure. He's got his hands full with the human beings Back There. He'll continue to practice his mischief, tripping up and putting the two-leggeds back into balance with the Creation, teaching them not to take themselves so seriously. Whether they learned from Coyote is up to them."

Taking one last glance backward at the old life, one first step forward into the new, Winona's voice resonated with a tone of compassion for those she was leaving behind.

"Love is very tricky," she observed, "and Coyote's tracks are all over the place."

MITAKUYE OYAS'IN.

GLOSSARY OF LAKOTA WORDS

Chanunpa Wakan: sacred Pipe
Hanbleciya: crying for a dream, vision quest
Hanhepi wi: dark sun, moon
Heyoka: person with vision of the thunder beings, contrary one, clown
Inipi: sweat lodge ceremony
Inyan: rock, stone nation
Itokaga, Itokagata: Grandfather of the South, toward the noonday sun
Lila wakan: very sacred
Mahpiyata: in the direction of the clouds
Makatakia: down toward Grandmother Earth
Mitakuye oyas'in: all my relations
Mni: water
Pilamaya: thank you
Ptesan Wi: White Buffalo Calf Woman
Tatanka: buffalo
Tiyospaye: a band of people
Tunkasila: grandfather
Unci Maka: Grandmother Earth
Wakan Tanka: Grandfather, Great Spirit
Wanbli: eagle
Wanbli Gleska: spotted eagle who takes the prayers to the grandfathers
Waziya, Waziyata: Grandfather of the North, toward the pines
Wi: sun
Wicasa Wakan: holy man
Wiyohiyanpa, Wiyohiyanpata: Grandfather of the East, toward where the sun rises
Wiyohpeyata, Wiyohpeyatakiya: Grandfather of the West, toward where the sun falls off
Wopila: thank you to the Creator, the Spirits

To honor those writers of past and present whose language scintillates throughout *Compass of the Heart,* and to encourage the reader to journey deeper into experiences of beauty and balance, I want to acknowledge the following for their words of poetry, harmony, and wisdom:

Aiken, Conrad. "At a Concert of Music," in *Collected Poems,* second edition. New York: Oxford University Press, 1970, p. 480.

Black Elk (as told through John G. Niehardt). *Black Elk Speaks.* Lincoln: University of Nebraska Press, 1961, pp. 2–3, 194.

Bok, Gordon. "Turning Toward the Morning." Sharon, Connecticut: Folk-Legacy Records, 1975.

"Coyote's Quarrel with Mole Woman," traditional. For a version, see Morning Dove, in *Coyote Stories,* ed. Heister Dean Guie. Lincoln: University of Nebraska Press, 1990, pp. 113–118.

Dickinson, Emily. "A Narrow Fellow in the Grass," in *The Complete Poems of Emily Dickinson,* ed. Thomas H. Johnson. Boston: Little, Brown and Co., 1960, p. 459.

Dickinson, Emily. "A Throe Upon the Features," in *The Complete Poems of Emily Dickinson,* ed. Thomas H. Johnson. Boston: Little, Brown and Co., 1960, p. 37.

Ecclesiastes 1:4–7. In *New Revised Standard Version Bible.* London: Collins Publishers, 1989, p. 629.

Eiseley, Loren. "Men Have Chosen the Ice," in *Notes of an Alchemist.* New York: Charles Scribner's Sons, 1972, pp. 28–30.

Eliot, Thomas Stearns. "The Rock," in *Collected Poems 1909–1962.* New York: Harcourt Brace & Co., 1963, p. 147.

Estés, Clarissa Pinkola. *Women Who Run with the Wolves.* New York: Ballantine Books, 1992, p. 15.

Frost, Robert. "Mending Wall," in *The Poetry of Robert Frost,* ed. Edward Connery Lathem. New York: Holt, Rinehart & Winston, 1969, pp. 33–34.

Frost, Robert. "The Secret Sits," in *The Poetry of Robert Frost,* ed. Edward Connery Lathem. New York: Holt, Rinehart & Winston, 1969, p. 362.

Gallagher, Tess. "Tableau Vivant," in *Amplitude: New and Selected Poems.* Saint Paul: Graywolf Press, 1987, pp. 102–103.

Harley, Bill. "Coyote," in *Coyote.* Round River Records, 1987. (For distribution: Debbie Block, 301 Jacob St., Seekonk, MA 02771.)

Hopkins, Gerard Manley. "I Wake and Feel the Fell of Dark, Not Day," in *The Harper Anthology of Poetry,* ed. John Frederick Nims. New York: HarperCollins Publishers, 1981, pp. 448–449.

Irish blessing, as heard recited by Boston storyteller Maggie Pierce at a National Storytelling Festival, Jonesborough, Tennessee.

Iroquois Invitation Song. In *Bartlett's Familiar Quotations,* ed. Emily Morrison Beck. Boston: Little, Brown & Co., 1980, p. 928.

Jung, Carl G. *Psychology and Alchemy,* translated by R. F. C. Hull, in *Collected Works of C. J. Jung,* vol. 12. New York: Pantheon Books, 1953, p. 13.

Kazantzakis, Nikos. *Zorba the Greek,* translated by Carl Wildman. New York: Simon & Schuster, Inc., 1952, p. 269.

Kern, Jerome, and Otto Harbach. "Smoke Gets in Your Eyes," PolyGram International Publishing, 1933.

Limericks, traditional. In *The Penguin Book of Limericks,* compiled and edited by E. O. Parrott. New York: Penguin Books, 1984, pp. 21, 180, 189.

MacLeish, Archibald. *JB.* Boston: Houghton Mifflin Co., 1956, p. 124.

Newton, John, 1725–1807. "Amazing Grace! How Sweet the Sound."

Niebuhr, Reinhold. "Humor and Faith," in *Discerning the Signs of the Times: Sermons for Today and Tomorrow.* New York: Charles Scribner's Sons, 1946, p. 111.

Porter, Cole. "Let's Do It (Let's Fall in Love)," in *Best of Cole Porter.* Miami: Warner Brothers Publications, 1928.

Rich, Adrienne. "XII. Sleeping, turning in turn like planets," in *The Dream of a Common Language.* New York: W. W. Norton & Company, 1978, p. 30.

Rilke, Rainer Maria. *Letters to a Young Poet,* translated by Stephen Mitchell. New York: Vintage Books, 1986, p. 78.

Roethke, Theodore. "The Motion," in *The Collected Poems of Theodore Roethke.* New York: Anchor Books, 1966, p. 235.

Seferis, George. "On Stage," in *Three Secret Poems,* translated by Walter Kaiser. Cambridge, Mass.: Harvard University Press, 1969.

Sexton, Anne. "Words," in *The Awful Rowing Toward God.* Boston: Houghton Mifflin Co., 1975, p. 71.

Shakespeare, William. *Romeo and Juliet* (II, ii, 1), in *William Shakespeare.* Boston: Houghton Mifflin Co., 1942, p. 985.

Simmerman, Jim. "Maddy's Woods," in *Moon Go Away, I Don't Love You No More.* Oxford, Ohio: Miami University Press, 1994.

Stoppard, Tom. *Rosencrantz and Guildenstern Are Dead.* New York: Grove Press Inc., 1967, p. 115.

Swedish folk song ("Who Can Sail Without the Wind"). For a version, see Sally Rogers, in *Generations.* Chicago: Flying Fish Records Inc., 1989.

Swinburne, Algernon Charles. "Atalanta in Calydon," in *The Harper Anthology of Poetry,* ed. John Frederick Nims. New York: HarperCollins Publishers, 1981, p. 434.

Twain, Mark. "Pudd'nhead Wilson's New Calendar," in *Following the Equator.* New York: Dover Publications, 1989, p. 256.

"Vision Quest Song" (Lakota). See Albert White Hat, Sr. (translator), in *Lakota Ceremonial Songs.* Rosebud, South Dakota: Sinte Gleska College, Inc., 1983, pp. 10, 18–19. The translation used in *Compass of the Heart* is by Priscilla Cogan, from the original Lakota.

Wilde, Oscar. *The Importance of Being Earnest,* in *Oscar Wilde,* ed. Isobel Murray. New York: Oxford University Press, 1989, p. 485.

Woolger, Jennifer Barker and Roger. "Persephone: Mistress of the Dead," in *The Goddess Within.* New York: Fawcett Columbine, 1987, pp. 226–268.

Yeats, William Butler. "Ephemera," in *The Collected Poems of W. B. Yeats.* London: Macmillan, 1985, pp. 16–17.